FORBIDDEN

Every Shadow Lifted Series
Book One
FORBIDDEN
Ellie Maureen

Published by
Ellie Maureen

All scripture quotations were taken from the New King James Bible

Cover illustrations © 2020 by Ellie Maureen
Map illustration © 2021 by Cora Hurst
Edited by Ellie Maureen and Pam Humphrey

ISBN 978-1-7379029-0-4

To my family,
without whom, I'd be lost to the monsters in my head.

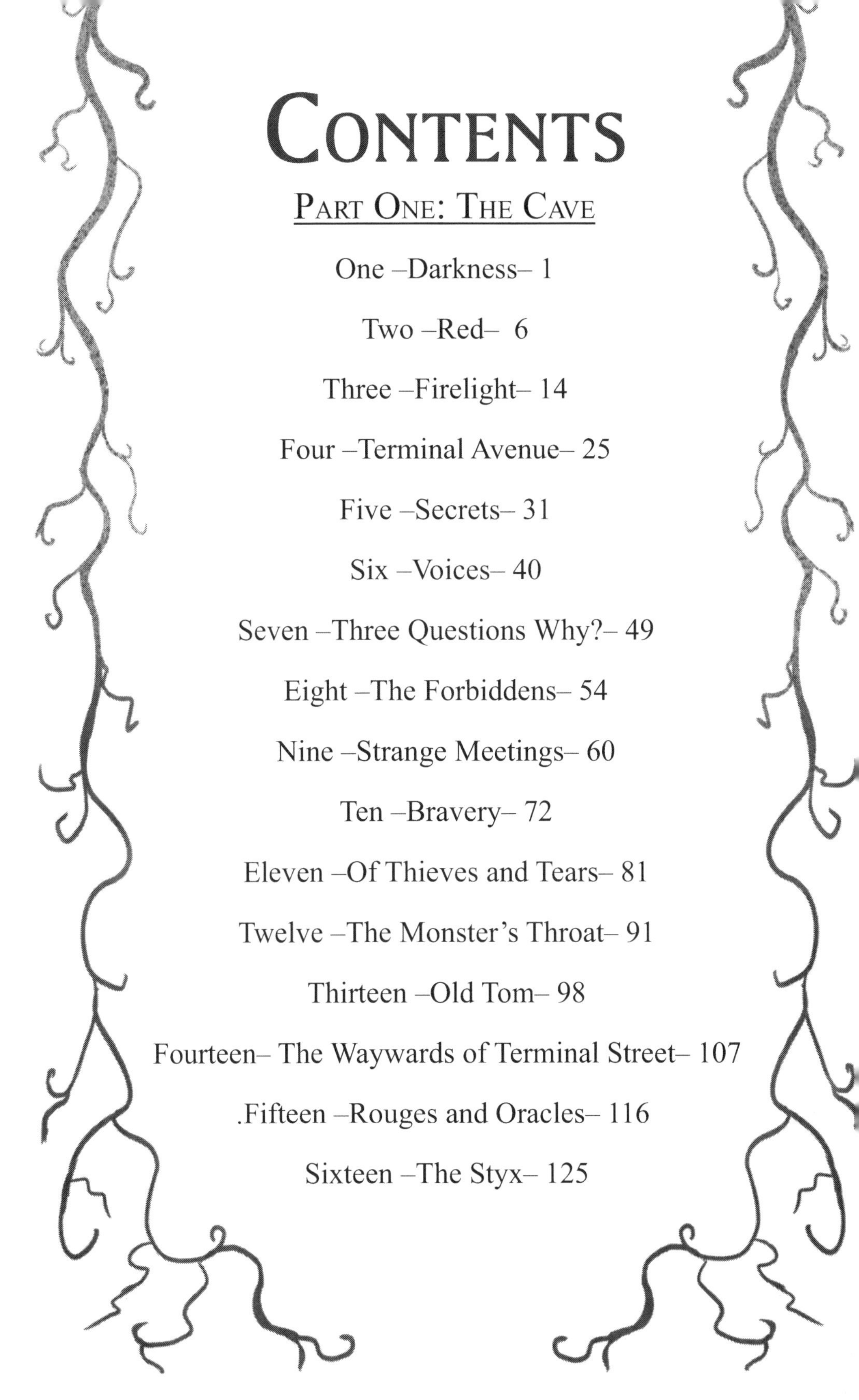

Contents

Part One: The Cave

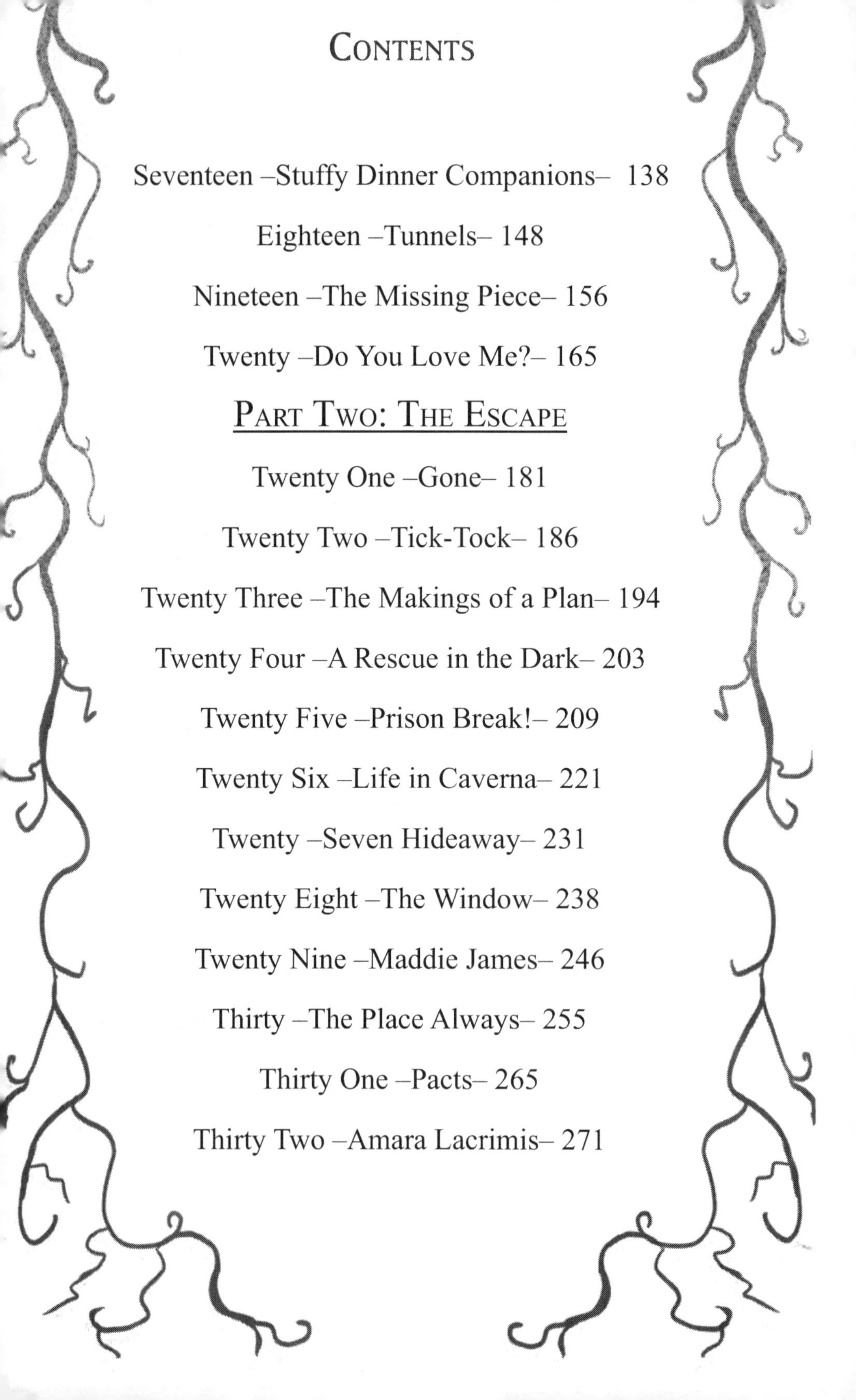

Contents

Contents

MAP OF CAVERNA

By Cora Hurst

Part One

And the light shines in the darkness, and the darkness did not comprehend it.

John 1:5

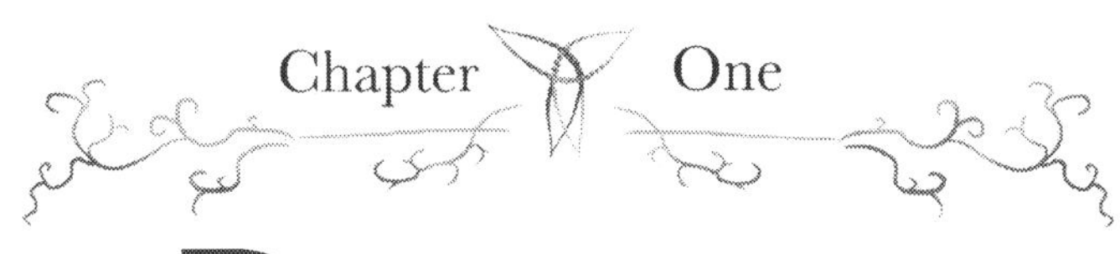

Darkness

The darkness was suffocating, blacker than pitch. Here there was no sky for the stars to dance in, nor moon for the stars to dance with. A black world, a cold world, with no morning to right this violation.

Only one minuscule light could be seen, moving fast in the interminable, dank murk. The flame of a lantern jumped and danced about in the pitch oblivion, so frantic that the flickerings suggested the image of a rabbit struggling as it hung from the vice-like jaws of a wolf; the girl who held the light, even more frantic. She stumbled and tripped as she ran through unlit streets she had trekked many times before, choking on the black air and her own fears, fleeing from nightmares she could never fully escape, not while she resided here.

Slowing ever so apprehensively, at last, she reached her destination and dropped to her knees. The same horrible dark surrounded her, but she knew she had arrived because she felt safe.

Almost . . .

She sat with her legs under her, pressed against cold stone, and her head in her trembling hands. She questioned her own sanity. For how could she dream up such horrible things, if not damaged somewhere deep in her subconscious? But this wasn't her first night flight, and she was stronger than to simply let the monsters in her head break her.

The girl forced herself to stand, taking up her lone lantern and using a spill to reveal the location of another light hanging by a metal chain that climbed up and into the dark above. She held the burning stick close to her face and ignited into existence a second lifeline, gazing quietly at the dance of the flame as if the light itself could brighten her ghastly thoughts and dreams. Then, one by one, as she wandered about in the dark, lanterns burned to life. Like magic, the area was soon filled with radiant, warm light. Stone walls crawled out of the shadows and a narrow stream running through the vault-like room awakened from what could have been an eternal slumber.

A quaint, little room when lit up, the hideaway appeared seemingly more lived in then the girl's own bedroom. The right wall housed a small and cracked metal-backed mirror, and a long shelf supporting the girl's favorite private collection of forbidden gems. The treasures shimmered in the candescent light, aiding the already shadow chasing light in its efforts to recover some form of sanity for the quiet girl making her rounds about the room. The gems were forbidden, just like every other pure thing, now made into rare oddities most didn't even know existed. But they all found a home here. The girl made sure of that, gathering them to herself like a magnet for the wonderfully bizarre. Yet, such an abundance of forbidden things could stay here solely because of the hideaway's secrecy, making it one of the only places left where beautiful things could remain safe. The girl's mother had called them gifts from the Creator, but she was gone . . . and where was the Creator then?

Under the shelf supporting the gems, resided an exquisitely engraved dark-wood chest, covered in markings of vines twisted in endless knots. The girl weaved her way through the hanging lanterns pushing them aside here and there and knelt down to the lock on the chest.

For one stagnant moment, she only stared, barely breathing, barely moving, save for her hand as she traced the markings with her finger. Tears brimmed in her eyes, but never wetted her cheeks. Lifting a delicate necklace up and over her head, she pressed the charm into the lock, a butterfly-shaped charm, wrought of both silver and black iron twisted together, its wings a tangle of the same strange knots decorating the chest. She heaved up on the creaky lid, setting free the musty smell of age and sour parchment, the chest filled to the brim with old books[1] which were, as the necklace, gifts from her mother. Holding the lid up with one hand, she gazed into the dark area inside the chest as the tears made her vision misty. A familiar ache, never fully gone, surged with a fresh wave missing, like an irritating stick poking at an ulcerated wound that refused to heal. She had always been there to comfort her when the nightm-

---

1. Naturalist journals penned by an unnamed author

ares came, but now all she had left were these old, dusty tomes. Digging in the chest, she forced herself to get her mind off memories that stung and pained her and lugged out one of the heavy books. She moved to the other wall where a few blankets and a pillow she had smuggled here long ago lay in a disheveled heap.

Though she was told that there was nothing outside of her dark, cold confinement, she believed what she read within the tattered pages of her mother's precious parting gifts. She snuggled down into her makeshift bed and cracked open the cover. This particular volume was one of her very favorites, its entirety dedicated to the fantastic creatures she had learned were called fish. All the books were bursting with information and wonders of a world wholly unknown to her, her lack of knowledge only fanning the fires of her fierce affinity.

The small stream that snaked across the length of her little room trickled out from a crack in the wall under the gemstone shelf and ended in a shallow pool at the other end of the room. There lived the girl's only friends, her very own fish, four of them, each one sightless and terribly unattractive. She read to them often and they listened, better than most people. In her loneliness, she had even given them names, calling them each after some of her favorite precious stones: Amethyst, Tourmaline, Citrine, and Emerald. She adored her little handicapped friends, unsightly visages and all.

Sitting in contemplative silence, she settled into something close enough to peace. Then as the girl read out loud to her blind friends, the book came alive and (with a little help from her imagination) so did the great arapaima. So very fascinated with this majestic creature, she longed to one day see it in all its enormity, to admire the ruby scales that fleck its pitch body. One might tell her, if they could, *be careful what you wish for.*

The fear traveled to the back of her mind and ebbed to a numbness that she could bare, her lids drooping with the adrenalin crash and sudden lack of terror. She thought she'd give herself only a moment to close her eyes and, before she knew it, drifted off, head lulling to her side.

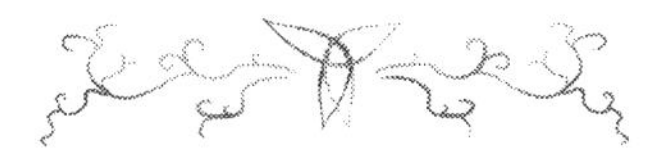

The ear-splitting banging of the town bell[1] hammered out the call of midnight and she bolted upright with a gasp as if from the dead. Heart and mind racing, she couldn't believe she let herself fall asleep here again.

In an urgent rush, she doused the lanterns and took off back home. The girl charged her way through the lonely dark, never lost, but also never knowing just where exactly she was, relying solely on a kind of certainty proven by a gut feeling rather than sight. She caught her breath when she, at last, arrived at her door and quietly slipped inside, careful not to wake her father, her small feet noiselessly padding on the cold stone floor as she snuck past his door and returned to her room.

Then, as she lay awake in her bed, exhaustion once again overcame
her fears only to send her adrift into another sea of dreams.

Black surrounded her and cobblestone tunnels stretched on before her, tunnels that carried both a familiar comfort and dread, yet she still didn't know where they led. She had been here before, she just had no clue when or why. She held a light in her hand and at times she could see herself as a cloaked and shadowy figure, even the lantern couldn't illuminate. Other times she saw only forward, knowing neither if she was girl or specter. She moved through the tunnels, an uncertain fear growing in the back of her mind. Sometimes she walked, other times she simply appeared at a closed door, and just before she could check if it was locked, in the blink of an eye, she appeared at a fork in the tunnel she hadn't seen before, all without even moving a toe.

Then things halted, and the jumping about ceased, almost as if the crossroad before her demanded she make a choice. Nothing moved, not even her. She stared at the black wall in front of her like she had gone blind. With some effort, as if her neck sat on rusty hinges, she turned her head to the right. Firelight lit up a narrow tunnel with a cheery glow that promised safety and rest. The flames had no vessel, no point of reference; they just were, burning brightly on the wall with an eternal presence. Then they did something incredible, lifting up off the walls and rushing towards her in

---

1. The universal and virtual only method of telling time in. Its tolls echo throughout all of town, but you'd be hard pressed to find anyone who is privy to its actual location.

a powerful flurry, like an autumn breeze. They danced and spun playful circles about her. The flames licked her arms, but they didn't burn, giving kisses of warmth that healed rather than scorched. Closing her eyes, a laugh escaped her throat, and when she opened them again, the flames were back on the wall, flickering quietly as if they had never left. Yet she knew, they beckoned her to follow their pathway to something, but what?

The girl turned to see what things the opposite way would hold. Before her yawned a cavernous corridor, blinking with blue lights.

Blue fire.

The corridor tingled with the whispers of mystery and new extraordinaries. The girl stepped a foot towards the miraculous wonder without a second thought, all but forgetting about the passage now to her back.

Towering stone pillars, topped in huge bonfires of blue, rose some twenty feet high, and smaller ones at chest level guided the way down the hall. She followed them into the distance, but soon realized she didn't feel any heat from the flames even when she walked close. Instead, she almost shivered from the cold. She wondered if they wouldn't burn like the last flames and reached out a hand to the nearest blue torch. The tongue nicked her finger and she recoiled with a yelp. It didn't burn; it froze with an icy bite. Her hand shook with pain and where the flame had touched, the skin had gone black. And that black grew, creeping up her finger and spreading across her hand, with no signs of stopping.

Without warning or reason, her lantern, the last warm glow untainted with blue, snuffed. Her heart pounded with fear. Then, when she thought it couldn't get any worse, six grotesque, dark figures materialized out of thin air and began advancing towards her. Smoky black as if composed of pure shadow, their eyes burned blue in their lifeless sockets like the hottest flames in a sooty furnace. They bared their hideous teeth, and she didn't need any more persuasion to run. But her legs felt heavy and weak. She couldn't gain the momentum required to flee. A clawed hand grabbed her from behind. She tried to scream, and only a choked garble escaped.

The girl squeezed her eyes shut.

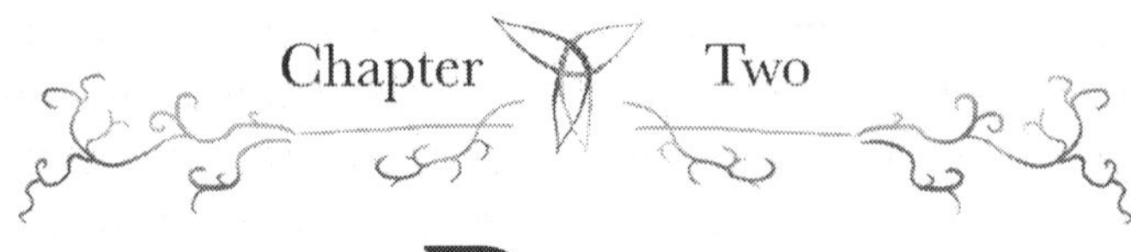

Chapter Two

Red

A threatening and (in so few words) very unhappy voice resounded off the cold walls of their tunneling home and ripped Kiara from her sleep, the shouts of a tyrant. Her father's rage-fueled shouts throbbed in her ears and though he had pulled her out of the nightmare, she wouldn't say she was grateful. In fact, the ice that filled her veins and froze her in place just then made any remembrance of her dream feel like a fairytale. To make it worse, the adrenaline still coursing through her veins coalesced with the reality of his temper in this hazy area of sleep and waking and made her feel she had yet to awake from any horrors. Tears welled in her eyes.

"Kiara!" he boomed from down the hall. "What is wrong with you? You're going to be late for class! Again!"

He didn't yell all that often, but that didn't mean he was very kind too often either. It just meant that now he was especially angry. He never hit her, and yet his thundering voice and the ferocity of his anger and disappointment, were enough to make her fear him as though he did. She stiffened with such powerful fear, it controlled her every muscle, her every thought. Constantly, she lived with an awful dread of the next time she would do something to upset him so terribly and the time had already come again. She shuddered with a violent and uncontrollable shake.

"Answer me, girl!"

Kiara wanted to, she really did, anything to pacify his rage, but her lips could only manage to quiver, the heavy falls of his feet growing louder with each stomp. Oh, how she wished she could throw her sheets over her head and disappear forever!

Kiara thought her heart would beat right out of her chest and escape, knowing its keeper wasn't about to move or hide herself, when her father burst into the room, face a raging red. Finding her just sitting there, his eyes flared with a new wave of anger.

"What is the meaning of this?" he interrogated. "Kiara, you're a princess!" He shut his mouth after that, his silence demanding an answer, his severe features sharpening further with a glare in his dark blue eyes and a scowl on his thin lips. His eyes were so dark that from afar one might question if they were black, though close, you could see they were blue, like sodalite, and could be unquestionably piercing, but for Kiara, they were only something to fear. And he always had a scowling mouth, but at the moment, it was deliberate.

"I-I couldn't sleep all night . . ." Kiara stammered under his gaze.

And yes, she was the princess of this accursed city, unavoidably making her father the dreadful king. Of course Benevolent King Nnyric was ever the collected, humble ruler to the people. Sometimes Kiara thought his greatest wish was to make her life, and hers alone, a miserable darkness, forever uncertain of his love.

"I suppose you'll blame that on your nightmare then?" Nnyric scoffed, his voice quieting to a more natural volume for him, but retaining every ounce of serrating harshness. "That may have worked on your mother when you were young, but I won't be so manipulated. You're much too old for that pretext. I mean, really? Do you expect to tell your teacher and the whole class that you were late because of nightmares? I think not. My daughter, the princess of Caverna, will grow up and tell her class that she overslept, that she's a lazy, woolgathering girl who thinks she's much too good for school."

"But–"

"No! Now get dressed and fix your hair! You look ridiculous. You have no idea how much of a grievance and an embarrassment it is to me." With that he left and slammed her door, not only her bedroom door, but the door to her heart as well. While he stormed down the hall, Kiara thought she heard him say some one word derision like, *unacceptable!* But it also wouldn't have been that hard to imagine.

Kiara fell back on her pillow, her wild, fiery curls sprawling freely like the rays of a clear dawn's sun. One, hot tear escaped her eye quicker than she could acknowledge the extent of her heartache, and she swiped it away with a fist. She grabbed a spiral curl from her flaming crown and pulled it straight. She twisted it in her fingers, crossing her eyes as she glared at it, pulling on the curl until her skin pleaded for her to relent, wishing she could just rip it all out by handfuls.

So what if he hated her hair? It wasn't as if she didn't also despise it's hideousness. But why did he treat her as if it was somehow her fault? Like she could do something to fix it?

He couldn't just be quiet about it, as if it actually pained him to have such an ugly daughter. It was the same with her grandfather Gareth's hair, her mother had told her before. Nnyric never could stop moaning and complaining about the color, an atrocious red just like hers. Gareth was her mother's father, just another person she missed. And Kiara could understand. With everyone else and their beautiful, ebony locks and pure, blue eyes, they did stick out very much like a horrible, pus-covered wound on their perfectly soft skin. But that didn't mean the words and looks didn't hurt.

Of course, when Kiara knew her grandfather, his hair had already whitened with age, but his eyes had never dimmed. They had always shown as green and bright as her own. She never knew why they were different. Whenever she asked her father, he just got angry and told her there was no reason, that she was just the odd one . . . the misfit. It was the same with her mother. It had been four years since she died, but he still never wanted to talk about it, though Kiara had never once entertained the idea that his silence was due to grief.

She tried to get past it all, she really did. She needed to, before he returned even more furious. But her face stayed red with anger. Forcing herself out of bed, she placed her feet on the ground, despising the bite of the cold stone. She stomped over to her dressing table and flopped down on the low stool. Kiara fussed with and pulled on her curls until they stood fluffed and a thousand times more wild than before. She grimaced at her unsightly reflection and gave up, slamming her head on the table top with a moan.

She would cut it just so there was less of it, but it wasn't the fashion and for a princess of all people, it would be an utter disgrace. So she was forced to pull it back or conceal it beneath ridiculous, formal headdresses whenever she had to attend any banquets, ceremonies, or high class events.

She thought to sit up, but her head felt like lead. She could actually feel the heat in her cheeks, in her chest. So much anger . . . and for who? If she was honest, most of it burned against herself. Why couldn't she just be better? Why did she seem to do everything wrong?

After a great deal of fuss, Kiara put her curly catastrophe into a disheveled bun in a haste of uncommitted forfeit. As much as she hated her unruly curls and their cringe worthy color, she couldn't stand being made to pull it back, every strand stuck tight to her scalp like she carried around the plague on top of her head and she had to keep others safe from it.

Kiara dressed herself, having long ago told her maids she didn't need nor want their help. She threw on one of the many drab dresses she owned, cursing its lack of color as she did every morning and slipped on a pair of confining shoes as fast as possible for the greater good of rescuing her feet from the frigid fate of the stone floors. Lastly, as she returned to her mirror, she attempted to practice her best princess face for the day, but her features twitched with anger and then fell in sorrow.

Contrary to her own opinion, Kiara was always an adorable child and had grown into a kind of beauty, wholly unique to her. But it was those very things, the ones that set her apart and made her so striking, that she resented the most. Kiara had a pert, round face, dotted with freckles on her soft cheeks and button nose, and a curious collection of smiles that could usually portray more emotion than most words, being at times an unabashed beacon of blinding light or diminishing to a reserved and polite turn of the lips. Her smile could be playful and disarming or very sad indeed, to the point that you wouldn't have believed there could be such a mix of emotions on a young lady's face. Her big, bright eyes twinkled as verdantly as emeralds and seemed the very embodiment of innocence and at times happiness, but of late they were filled with tears and her fine copper brows, often knit with sadness.

Her eyes shifted in the mirror from her own reflection to that of the tapestry her mother had made years ago. Just the two of them, holding hands with simple smiles on their still faces. Kiara didn't turn around. She knew exactly where it hung on the wall and how the thread had frayed where it held on to the nails. But the mirrored image held her gaze, vision growing hazy and obscure. It was moments like these, moments of such stark and aching loneliness, when she cried and no one came to wipe her tears, when she hurt and no one consoled her fears, that pained her most, that she missed her most.

A soft knock on the door did little to tear her away from her dark contemplations.

Swiping the tears off her face, she mumbled, "Come in,"

hardly caring who it was.

A young servant named Lucida walked in to see her sitting there, face still red and her hair a mess. “Oh, Miss, you poor thing. It's that father of yours again, isn’t it? I heard him yelling at you. Positively awful it was. He has no right. No right at all.”

Lucida was Kiara’s favorite servant, yet too young to be crusty like some of the others and too kind to gossip and tittle-tattle with her catty peers. A little out of place (much like herself) Lucida was about the only person that could ever cheer Kiara up. She had long, wavy, black hair that was almost always in a low bun and blue eyes like everyone, but though they were the color of ice, they were as warm as the tea rattling softly on the tray she carried in. Her voice was the sure opposite of her father’s, never harsh; always comforting and kind, with a soft lisp that could be heard most in her trailings and mumblings which she so often did.

When she finally turned to look at her, Kiara gave her a sad but brave smile. “I’m alright, Cida.”

“I'm sure you are. Tough as stone you are, Miss. But it doesn’t mean it’s right for him to treat you like that. Let me fix your hair for you. And here, I made this fresh for you.” She placed the tea in front of her.

Kiara just sat there. If it was anyone else she would have already screamed at them to go away and never touch her again (the majority of the royal staff had learned this first hand) but with Lucida she felt safe, and she could let her take care of her, at least every once in a while.

Lucida took her hair out of the bun, letting the long wild curls fall where they may, and then began putting it back up in a much tighter, neater knot.

“Did you have any more nightmares last night, Miss?” Lucida asked while she worked, her lisp coming out as she trailed off, as if she didn’t actually want to know.

Kiara fidgeted her thumbs in her lap. “A few . . . but nothing I can’t handle.” She tried to force a smile into her voice though her face begged the opposite, as she lied through her teeth.

Lucida’s hands stopped for a moment. “Right, of course.” And the conversation was over.

Finishing the coiffure with one last pin, Lucida took a step back. “There, now you look like a princess,” she said with a wry grin.

“Thank you, Cida.” She took a sip of the tea and savored the feeling of the warm liquid gliding down her throat. She didn't want to go. She wanted to sit with a blanket around her, play Backlobash[1] with Cida, and finish her tea.

"I should go. I'm already late."

"Try to have a good day, Miss."

Kiara managed to offer her a sad smile, knowing trying to and actually having a good day were two very different things.

Kiara made her way to leave, perfectly fine with not saying a goodbye to her father and allowing her temper to match her fiery hair when, like a fox
just meandering through the greenwood, she spotted an opportunity for a bit of fun without even looking for it.

As she walked past the kitchen, the clamor of the cooks and the warm smells wafting to her nose turned her head and stopped her feet. Cida would have made certain that something was already prepared for her, but she was far too late to sit down and eat a meal, and yet . . . she'd have to put up with a disruptive stomach if she didn't swipe something away now.

She rerouted for the detour into the narrow hall of rough stone, and that's when she saw him, standing close to the entrance, most likely trying to get his greedy, sausage fingers on something before breakfast was actually done. Shrike stood with his back to her, yet she could recognize his squat, little stature anywhere. King Nnyric's personal dullard, Shrike was a right excuse of a man. His scribe, message man, and virtual henchman, he did absolutely everything the king asked, obeying his every whim. He had a hooked beak for a nose, sunken-in, beady eyes, and sallow skin, stretching tightly across his plump face that never seemed free of a greasy sheen. His immaturities rivaled that of a child, all the while he slithered through life as slippery as an eel. His soul was as twisted as the most complicated knot, as nasty as the drippiest cavern, and as cold as the stone floor of their world, and yet the reason Kiara despised him the most was the blood boiling fact that her father paid more heed and attention to this imbecile than his own daughter.

Sure enough, as she approached, she could see him hunched

---

1. A strategy board game used to settle the scores of bickering politicians or just to enjoy with a friend over a cup of tea, most likely originating with the English, though I have yet to find one record of it actually being played in England. Most certainly nothing like Chess.

over something he had already snatched from the hard working cooks, shoving little bits of a pastry into his smacking jaw.

Kiara sped her pace, racing into the kitchen and skipped a step as if she had tripped, shoving all her weight into him as she stumbled. Taken off guard, his opposite shoulder slammed the wall and his most coveted pastry jumped up and out of his hands, hitting the filthy ground with an unappetizing splat.

"Ooooo!" Shrike whined, his face scrunching in anguish as he gaped at the ruined pastry. Then, raising his face to identify his clumsy assailant, he gave a growl of a sigh, puffing his round cheeks. "You wicked child!"

Kiara stared with shock-widened eyes at the flattened pastry, before her lips curled into a cruelly innocent grin. "I'm so sorry, Mr. Shrike! I didn't see you there, and I'm so late already."

Shrike straightened and though he was a short man, he could still look down on Kiara. "Oh, you stand in my line of sight for a moment longer, girl, and I'll give you a reason to be late for school."

"Oi! Is that anyway to talk to your princess?" asked a tall lady with a wooden spoon in one fist, now planted on her hip and a piece of charred toast that she waved at him in the other.

Kiara threw the head cook a smile. "Really, Shrike, I don't think that qualifies as an acceptable way to greet your princess."

Shrike tried to win with a razor glare of his beady eyes, but resigned with a growl and turned away.

Flitting into the kitchen, Kiara grabbed the burnt toast from the cook's hand before she could toss it. Turning to leave, she talked around a piece already in her mouth. "Thanks, Loretta!"

The cook just rolled her eyes.

When Kiara passed Shrike, she shook her head to see him, bent over and actually trying to pick the crumbs of the pastry off the grimy kitchen floor.

She wanted so badly to ask him if his brain was broken, but then she spotted something that would be immensely more satisfying. The shelf above him held a pale of filthy, black water meant to be dumped, the same shelf she had found out a week ago was loose and only held things when balanced perfectly. An impish grin curled on her lips as she contemplated her plan. It wouldn't be the first time Shrike was the victim of her wicked mischief. One time, before even the servants got up for the day, she snuck into his room and placed a board, spiked with hundreds of black nails, at his bedside, her only regret being she hadn't stayed to watch him sprout wings and fly.

Kiara moved to the other end of the shelf where a stack of heavy pots worked as a counterweight, hoping no one had fixed the shelf since she had seen it knocked down the first time. With a suppressed grunt, she lifted them to the ground and, to her delight, the shelf teetered, then it leaned, everything in the middle sliding to the right where Shrike scrambled on the ground below. Kiara hiked up her shoulders, bringing her hands together like a small child awaiting a surprise. She held her breath as the dirty water sloshed out of the bucket, the shelf growing ever more unstable by the seconds. Finally, tilting far just enough, it fell, soaking Shrike and his beloved pastry. The bucket swallowed his head, dazing him for a moment as the metal rattled in his ears. Kiara grinned at how beautifully her plan had worked, but she didn't laugh, the kind of joy she got from the sight, very cold indeed.

Shrike raised his hands to pull the bucket off and she made ready her escape, but the handle caught under his chin. Snickering quietly now, Kiara listened to his muffled shouts. Instead of just dropping the bucket back down and moving the handle, Shrike only grew more and more furious, yanking and pulling to no avail, legs sprawled out in the sopping mess. All the cooks began to laugh at him now too, as he had started to make quite the scene with all his bellowing and griping, and they all thought it was an accident.

Kiara did begin to feel rather bad, with so many eyes and mockery trained on him, but not enough to help him, knowing he would not look past her prank just because she offered him a hand.

At last he grabbed hold of the handle, seething hot breaths echoing off the walls of the bucket, and yanked it forward and off his head, but Kiara had already turned tail and booked it, so he only caught the fluttering sight of the hem of her dress as she zipped around the corner.

"Hrmf!" he growled, slamming a fist into the sour water.

Then he shifted his glare behind him at all the gawking cooks, sludge dripping from his hair and nose.

"What are you all lookin' at?" he roared, flying out of the puddle.

Clearing their throats and tripping over each other, the cooks resumed their duties.

Chapter Three

FIRELIGHT

Kiara felt better after that. Shoving the last bite of bitter toast in her mouth as she navigated her tunneling home, she could count on feeling good for at least a little bit, knowing she had succeeded in making her nemesis' life that much more miserable.

She arrived at the wide foyer entrance and paused before pushing open the doors. Kiara actually liked this room of the palace. Having an expansive rug (that was *almost* soft) to cover up the cold stone beneath, and wooden pillars adorned with an illuminating amount of golden sconces, it always seemed a little warmer than some of the other, more cellar-like rooms.

Leaving her home, she walked down the tunneling darkness of the King's Corridor and squeezed her eyes shut as she came out into town so she wouldn't see the stone guardians standing watch on either side of the tunnel's entrance. Horrible, demented looking things, the watchers[1] were supposed to be a symbol of protection and had been carved from the rock face of the King's Corridor to ward off evil. But, friend or foe, Kiara preferred not to look upon their bugging, glaring eyes and mouths so agape with razor teeth and long, protruding tongues. She had enough nightmares as it was without the helpful imagery of their grabbing, gnarled claws; twisted horns; or whip-like, scale plated tails.

She hastened into the midst of town, slowing to a lonely plod as soon as she traipsed into the still quiet streets. Oil lamps brightened the cobbled and stone paths well enough, but above her head lurked a darkness so deep, you could drown in it if you stared too long, one of the many reasons Kiara preferred to keep her head

---

1. Spiritual beings of sketchy origins, existing somewhere in between tangible and intangible. No one has ever had any proven sighting of them. Some claim to have talked to them...

low on her walk to school. Even the gentle waking of the day would not change this tragedy. But, if nothing else, it was normal. The people of Caverna had no knowledge of a dawn scattering darkness, or how a blooming light in the east can steadily wash each color of blue from the atmosphere one shade at a time. Darkness was simply part of this strange world Kiara lived in, like bars are to a cage. They knew no different, just as they knew no freedom. Yet, with one look at them, you'd see they felt its absence, in the heaviness, in the weightlessness . . . Without the sun, what reason did they have to get up in the morning instead of the evening? What taught them hope, if not the rising dawn ending even the darkest nights? With all the lamps ever to be found, one could never compare to pure, golden sunlight and its ability to lift the shadows. Without it, life lacked even a semblance of veracity . . . and they felt it. Every soul in Caverna felt it, even if they didn't know it.

Finally at the wide steps of her school, Kiara raised her head to the imposing, stone building, built one brick at a time by people now lost in history's devouring fog, people she never knew, people her wandering mind wondered if she would have liked.

She set her jaw with a huff and began taking the steps one at a time, dragging with her a pair of feet that just wanted to stop, and once more averting her eyes from the stone watchers placed on the roof and at the great, double doors. Already her feet ached from the type of shoes a princess was expected to endure. They pinched her toes so much, by the end of the school day, her feet would scream at her for putting them through such tortures, but anything was better than walking barefoot on stone so clammy it made her skin crawl.

Kiara crept through the halls, dark and now eerily quiet with everyone in classes. The tap of her shoes on the smooth floor echoed off the stone walls and gave the illusion that someone followed her in the dim, flickering light of the wall torches. Kiara always felt uneasy in these halls, even when they swarmed with the raven cropped heads of her fellow students. But now, in the abandoned quiet and concealing shadows, her skin crawled as if unseen eyes roved about it.

She remembered last night's terrible dream and ones passed and suddenly it wasn't just *someone* following her, but a watcher. All in that split second of black before you open your eyes from a blink, her mind conjuring up what the predator would look like with flesh instead of stone.

Kiara shivered with a familiar dread. All too quickly, her fears morphed to devouring proportions until even the irrational turned to waking reality, her legs suddenly running before her mind even condoned the action. She hated this with all her heart, but she had little control over how real it felt. It just happened, her mind creating its own kind of danger, like a rainforest and its storms, to the point where she never felt very safe at all.

Beating her feet on the ground, the echoes ricocheted off the walls even louder. She threw wild glances over her shoulder with paranoia widened eyes. Though she saw nothing each time, she couldn't stop, not after seeing the kind of monsters she had in her head.

Reaching the door of her class room, she wrested the handle with both hands, wanting nothing else than to wrench the door open and fling herself inside, but she halted.

Kiara closed her eyes, demanding herself to stay put until she calmed down. She counted the seconds of each exhale, waiting for her shuddering breaths to steady. Opening her eyes, she kept her hands on the door handle, knowing all too well just how violently they would tremble if she lifted them. Now in the silence, Kiara scanned up and down the dark hallway, only moving her eyes, but the search turned up nothing more than a whole lot of empty space.

Of course there was nothing. Why would there be anything?

Her cheeks began to burn with color, another thing she couldn't control.

"Get ahold of yourself, Princess!" she hissed to herself.

It was a great enough torture to have to walk in there, but this made it that much more unbearable. The saddest part, it was her own mind inflicting the pain. She wished she could sprout wings like the birds she read about in her journals, and skip school altogether, spending the day safe in her hideaway. But that, she knew more than anything, was a sure way to gain the wrath of her father following her inevitable return.

Resigning herself to her fate, Kiara let out a slow, heavy breath before she turned the brass knob, trying to open the door as silently as possible as she walked in.

Composed of the elitist offspring of the highest class citizens of Caverna, each member of her class had their very own chip on their shoulders and though she was princess, she wasn't very popular at all. Her body lacked even a single flirtatious bone, which the other more approachable girls seemed to have in abundance.

She kept to herself, mainly because she didn't even know how to talk to most of them, and the majority of them left her alone. Her quiet disposition more intimidated and scared away than asked for attention. Nobody really liked Kiara and, if she was honest (which she usually was) she didn't really like them.

As a sixteen-year-old princess lost in a dark world she felt she didn't belong in, life demanded a certain effort that, at times, she didn't feel inclined to give. Today was one of those times.

Countless blue eyes turned upon her in judgment, casting her in a shadow of shame that separated her further from the rest of the world, even to the point of torment. The heat in her cheeks spread to her ears as Kiara hunched her shoulders, trying to grow as small as she could. Her fiery bun bobbed up and down through the class room of black headed students like a burning ship on a moonless ocean. She dropped her gaze and dared not raise it higher than the floor, dreading to meet any of their cold eyes, and sat down at the furthest available seat to the back.

Her teacher, all the while. never skipped a beat. He droned on and on about how to survive a cave-in. You might think it a strange thing, but the unlucky Kiara Cornelian, princess of Caverna, lived in a cave and how to survive a cave-in was something you needed to know.

The whole structure of the city was quite impressive, but to live without ever seeing the sky is far greater a price than to live without seeing this city. At the center of it all was the Town Circle, a wide open area where the market, and buildings such as clinics, bakeries, schools and churches (in which Kiara didn't really care what everyone worshiped) were located. She knew the proverbial balderdash well enough; she just didn't care.

You see, Fleard was the supposed creator of their world. It was said that there were once two gods in the High Realm, Elohim and Fleard, who fought over how a world should be created. Fleard had won the battle and the chance to create a world, one where gods were to be respected; not loved. He sent Elohim and his foolish ideas of freedom and unnecessary color to Sheol, a place supposedly even darker than their world, where (in exile and punishment) he must watch Fleard's world for eternity.

Kiara had never fully believed in the stories all that much because the Creator that her mother always spoke of differed from Fleard so much.

Then, out from the center of the city, like legs on a spider, halls stretched out from the body and led to the tunneling living areas of Caverna. There were lower class halls and upper class halls. Of course Kiara lived in the most superior, the King's Corridor. Naturally, her hall was the shortest of all because there were so few worthy to share quarters with the king. Beyond town, lurked the Forbiddens where not a soul was permitted to enter. Very unlike the neat and ordered halls of Caverna, the never ending tunnels there seemed to have a mind altogether of their own, twisting and turning and crossing one another like noodles in a soup. Kiara's hideout was, in fact, located in said never ending tunnels, and on her lonely search for answers, despite the rules, she explored them quite frequently.

Beyond the Forbiddens, if anything at all, awaited the Void where, if ever accessed by man, his mind would collapse into a white, hot madness, losing all knowledge of the difference between right or wrong; light or dark; up or down; forward motion or standing still until, at last, his conscious mind abandoned him all together.

Kiara desperately wanted to disbelieve this legend, for her sanity's sake, but it was made difficult as her classmates and servants endlessly spun and passed around scarystories[1] of fools venturing too far only to never come back. Yet, the most chilling story of all was of the man who did come back, the deaf and mute beggar of Terminal Avenue. Some say he's blind too. No one knows his name and yet everyone knows who he is. Kids at school said he's a survivor of the Void and that most times he just sits around like there's nothing left in his head but cobwebs and dust. But there are times, mostly at night, after everyone's put out their lights . . .

Course it's at night! Kiara had thought. *It's always at night!*

. . . that the madness takes hold and the old beggar sets his empty mind and wicked hands to do some truly awful things.

Kiara knew most of her classmates had never even met the old beggar of Terminal Avenue, but the tales alone (no matter how full of bat guano) were enough to keep her from venturing too far into the Forbidden Caverns.

The tunnels were also said to be the dwelling place of the watchers, the very beings carved in stone all over Caverna. They supposedly made intercession for Fleard on behalf of man, as the

---

1. The youth of Caverna's term for such fabricated and thrilling tales, many revolving around the Void.

only creatures able to come and go from the Void with their sanity intact, and yet Kiara had never seen one on any of her trips to her hideout, their mysteriously unproven existence perhaps strengthening their hold of terror over her. Still, her need to escape the city somehow managed, without fail, to conquer all fears, all unknown and known consequences, long enough for her to plunge into that unmapped darkness time and time again.

As Kiara fought fatigue, class was finally dismissed. Well, most of class . . . She trudged her dragging limbs over to her teacher as he called her over and gave him a polite smile, a look she had taught herself early in life, ever since she realized back talk and sass only got her reprimanded and yelled at, a simple but protective blind over all heartfelt emotions.

Sitting at his desk, her teacher stared at her for a moment, his head level so that his eyes looked up disappointedly. Finally, when everyone left, he said, "I'm disappointed in you, Kiara."

Kiara could have rolled her eyes for how easily she predicted those words.

He laboredly removed the glasses from the end of his skinny nose and rubbed his eyes with two fingers. "You can't just stride in here whenever and however you want just because you're the princess."

Kiara thought with a little sarcastic cynicism, if she could have a drop of truth for every time she heard that, she might actually know what was so wrong with the world.

"This is a place of knowledge and we take the way we learn very seriously. Kiara, this isn't the first time and you simply can not keep doing this. Do you understand?"

"Yes," she said meekly.

The scowl he had brewed didn't budge an inch. "I don't think I can trust your word."

"I swear," Kiara insisted. "I understand." Her eyes faltered to the ground and he tilted his head to find her gaze. "I . . . I'm sorry, Mr. Forsithe. I'm . . ."

Her teacher's brow scrunched. "Yes?"

"I'm lazy . . . and a daydreamer. Sometimes I think I don't need school . . . I will try harder to be on time from now on."

He narrowed his icy eyes in skepticism. "Hhmm." Then with a slight motion of his head towards the door, her *ever so kind* teacher sent her on her way, perched his spectacles back on his nose, and gave his attention back to the mountains of paper that never seemed to leave his desk.

Kiara struggled through the rest of school, fighting her fatigue and depression with only halfhearted attempts to try. She kept her eyes on the stone floor as often as she could, but sometimes it proved too difficult a temptation to confirm her suspicions created by a burning on the back of her neck.

Her own words crawled around in her head all day, like spiders in a dark burrow, and even as school, at long length, let out and she walked out onto the stone steps, she could not forget.

What rubbish! And yet she found herself feeling guilty as though every word was truth. It was moments like these, that everything, even the moods of others, felt like her fault, that the world came caving in.

Kiara walked out the double doors of her school, while those who threw her daggers less than an hour ago, refused to look at her and avoided all means of even a simple, "See you tomorrow!" She sat on the school steps, not caring to go home yet, and certainly not to the market, despite her father's encouragements. Head in her hands, the worst parts of her day ran through her mind. All those humiliating looks from her fellow students! They might not have said as much, but the looks said it all. Not one of them didn't regard themselves as more fit for the role of princess or prince. Truthfully, she didn't even blame them for thinking she was rude or unfit for royalty. But none of it mattered. She didn't want them as her friends. They were as cold and empty as the caverns they all lived in.

The last person she could call friend, was ripped from her life five years ago and, frustratingly enough, just about as unexpectedly and mysteriously as her mother and Grandpa Gareth. Betsie was her name, and she had a spirit as gentle and sweet as a flower, of which, Kiara wondered if it truly did smell as sweet as her journals told her. Betsie's black hair and blue eyes ticked the boxes of a normal citizen of Caverna, but her similarities to everyone else stopped there, dead in their tracks. Full of life and a hope that could not be dampened by even the dankest cavern, Betsie seemed to create her own light in some ways, always looking at things in a way Kiara never thought possible. She had an innate knack to chase away the frequent bouts of sadness Kiara regularly fell into, even as a young girl.

Both quite young when they met, Kiara's mother, Eleanor found orphaned Betsie in the poverty riddled district of town, starving to death, and barely clinging to life. She took her in and looked after her until the giggling bundle of energy and joy bore hardly a hint of resemblance to the crumpled little girl dying on the streets of Terminal Avenue. Though she never did lose the limp she was either born with or had sustained from some sort of injury.

The queen gave her a job as Kiara's personal servant, but Eleanor knew from the beginning that the girls would grow to be much more than simply a young princess and her handmaid. Almost immediately the two girls became absolutely inseparable, Betsie all but joining the family as a second daughter, at least for Eleanor and Kiara. Fused at the hip, the two used to make believe that they lived in a different world, in a different time, where it wasn't so grey and dark, where dreams could come true.

But she was gone . . . and so was the color and hope from Kiara's life. If only she could find the lively place they dreamed of as kids, but the older she got, that world looked less and less real, her hope steadily dying away, like a flame that has used up all its fuel.

All these people, the only ones that cared for her, disappearing . . . And with them, little pieces of herself did too. It was that feeling of no longer mattering to anyone at all, drifting untethered through life, that made her feel like she could fall right through the floor. They all knew her name, everyone of them, but that's it. That's all she was to them, red hair and a name. Not a person; just a ghost.

Just then, exactly the person Kiara wanted to talk to hopped up on the step next to her and punched her on the arm, ripping her straight out of her drifting.

"Hey, there!"

Rubbing her arm, Kiara looked up and did her best not to sigh. Mallory Knettle, one of the only girls in her class that ever talked to her (though Kiara never knew why) beamed at her with an over exaggerated grin. She could never understand what Mallory's angle was. Possibly just because she was the princess. She knew well enough that Mallory didn't like her all that much and, quite frankly, she didn't like Mallory at all.

The only girl in her class with short hair, her dark wavy tresses playfully swayed about her shoulders while she talked. She had cut her hair recently, spinning something about a glue incident, and though she should have been laughed at as the silliest kid at school, every girl in their class agreed that Mallory's hair suited her well, even if they hated how well it suited her. She wasn't especially pretty, but her apparent self-confidence and natural buoyancy made up for it, making her popular and liked.

Kiara's honest impression of her? Bossy, at times rude, and seemingly above it all.

"What is it, Mallory?" she tried not to sound too impatient.

"Goodness, I just came to say hello."

Apparently she didn't try hard enough. "Well, hello to you too. But if you don't mind, I'd like to be alone right now." She looked straight ahead, refusing to acknowledge her any more than she already had.

Mallory scooted closer, unable to take the hint. "So what's the reason you've been coming to school so late?"

There it was.

"Look, Mallory, if you're looking for gossip you can save your breath, because I would really appreciate to save *mine.*"

"Oh, no, no, no. Nothing of the sort. This would just be between us." She paused. "As friends!"

Kiara felt uncomfortable at the sound of the word friends being used to describe the two of them. "There's no story, okay. So I would prefer . . ." Kiara looked up, confused as she felt a slight touch on the top of her head.

A stalky, pimpled faced boy with ice blue eyes that held some kind of impish joy in them at all times, extended his hand out over her head, stretching his fingers and turning them frequently. His eyes roved about the stone yard of the school as if he stood, minding his own business.

"Buford Mellard," Mallory almost spat the name. Then, arching an ebony brow, she asked, "You got a problem?"

The boy jumped like he hadn't noticed them and, bringing his eyebrows together in feigned remorse, he began, "Oh, I'm so sorry! I seemed to have mistaken you for a torch, Princess."

Kiara cocked her head and narrowed her eyes. "A torch? In the middle of the school's steps? Huh, that'd be odd, wouldn't it?"

"Very," Mallory agreed.

The corners of his mouth twisted into a devilish grin. "Well, my hands are positively frozen, and it seems to very well be working." His eyes rounded as if he had only just discovered something truly fantastic. "Maybe the horrid color is so bright that it actually gives off heat?"

Kiara's cheeks burned into a fury, but she only looked away.

She wished so badly she had something to say, something that would make him think twice or maybe even cry, but her mind abandoned her to the torment, so she tried her best to ignore him.

"Hey, I'm talking to you!" Buford bullied.

Mallory looked on in dismay, waiting for Kiara to speak up.

"You know, you should take that ugly pyre of a head to Terminal Avenue," he spat. "Maybe in their cold houses, its stinging light and eye burning heat would be welcomed. Anyway, it would be out of my sight and all those who'd be thankful to never have to see your unsightly appearance again. It'd be better for the whole town."

Kiara lifted her eyes to the aforementioned, dismal hall. Across town she could see it snaking away into the dark. The most desolate and lowliest corridor in all of Caverna, Terminal Avenue's position consequently aligned directly opposite and across town from the King's Corridor.

Buford moved to knock his knuckles on her head when she failed to acknowledge him once again, but his arm was stopped short by a firm grip equipped with unusually sharp nails which she dug into his skin.

"Hey!" Mallory said. "Leave her alone! And don't you touch her." She edged the words with a glare in her eyes. "Unless, of course, you find it appropriate to assault your Majesty, the Princess?"

Buford froze. He looked caught, unsure if her words meant nothing at all or just about everything to him. She could see the gears turning behind his eyes, their wicked sharpness giving way to an insecure boy who seemed to have forgotten his place. Since he made no indication of deciding, Mallory reinforced her question with a cock of her head and a slight raise of her brows.

At last, Buford sighed and began to relent, so Mallory let go, but a sneer had already crept back on his smug face when he retreated. "That's fine, Mallory, you want to throw your lot in with 'er? But I wouldn't get too close. You know what people will say if they start seeing you with Princess Candlehead. And I won't give your name a wink of good words."

"Oh, shove off Buford, and find someone else to make miserable, would ya'? 'Cause it's not working here."

"I will! I just wished when I left, it'd be the last time I saw either of your ugly faces."

"Die in a cramped hole, Buford!"

Kiara looked at her as she threw the words like knives at his back, but her distant eyes only partly saw her, half her mind in a different place. Mallory had just stuck up for her . . . She had a hard time believing she did it entirely for unselfish reasons, but still, she didn't have to do it at all. She didn't even think she knew what that felt like before now, and had no idea what to say.

"... Thank you." Kiara could barely manage to say.

Mallory smirked. "Don't mention it. Buford Mellard is a scourge."

Kiara cracked a grin at her unapologetic insults.

"Now what were we talking about? Oh, yeah! Why have you been coming to school late, it's not really like you and I just thought . . ."

Mallory's rambles died away as Kiara remembered all she cared about was gossip. She tuned her out, let her mind wander away.

Just like everyday, the poverty stricken district of Caverna lay quietly on the other side of town, unobtrusively minding its own business. Any other day she might have given it so much as a pitied glance, but, remembering the warnings of her father and his commands to stay away from "the slums of Caverna," as he called them, she would avert her gaze and plod off to the market instead. And yet, today, for reasons she wished she understood, it held her attention like a captive, the sight of the dark arch of the street entrance, searing itself to the back of her mind, so she saw it even on her eyelids when she blinked. It was a strange tug of her heart, like someone calling her name, and she wasn't sure if she should answer. But maybe Buford was right. Maybe there she could actually do some good, where people needed help, even wanted it. And if her dear Betsie was from there, it was utterly impossible for her to believe they were as terrible as her father said.

Suddenly her legs pushed her to her feet, and she mumbled an apology to Mallory. "I'm sorry," she really wasn't, "but I have to go." With no idea what she was getting herself into, she let her feet take her, knowing if she thought about it a moment more, she'd never go.

"W-wait!" Mallory jumped to her feet. "I thought we could laugh about Buford some more! And you never answered my question about school!"

Kiara didn't turn around, feeling less guilt about leaving her by the seconds.

"So I guess we'll just chat tomorrow then?" Mallory called. "Yeah, okay. Sounds good!"

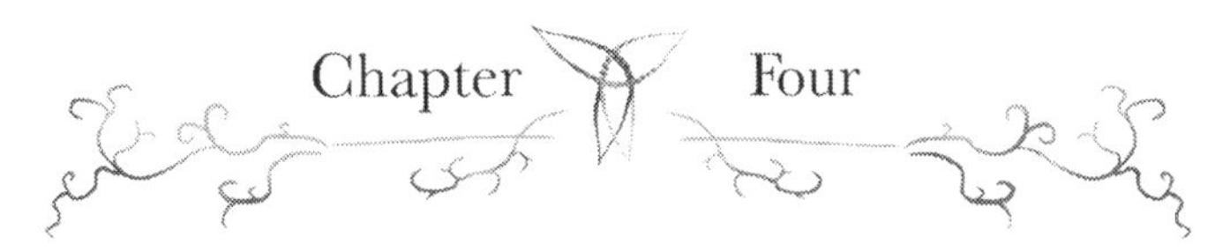

Chapter Four

Terminal Avenue

Not a soul stopped her to talk on her way across town, but she would have been honestly shocked if they did. Now, with the situation fully past its time, Kiara's mind began to fill with all the hundreds of things she could have said to Buford Mellard, her cheeks burning with a rage fueled by unavenged wrongs. She wished she could have said something to him when she had the chance, something to make him hurt as badly as he had hurt her. Maybe then he'd leave her alone for good. Maybe he'd leave everyone he bullied alone . . .

Probably not.

But it didn't matter now. All anger and hurt feelings flew out the back window of her brain as she suddenly found herself gaping into the yawning maw of Terminal Avenue.

She fought the urge to hold a handkerchief to her nose as the acrid smell of waste and rot bit her senses and made her eyes water. Walking hesitantly, she advanced into the deepening darkness, suddenly unsure of what she intended to do in the first place.

The tunnel yawned wide, its throats swallowed up in unknown distances, every inch smothered in an ever present and strengthening darkness.

The ruddy, dim lights of the lanterns did their best to illuminate the vague environment of the Avenue. Sub streets ran perpendicular to the tunnel, turning both left and right and small, crumbling buildings sat smack in the middle of the throughway, like a little town all of its own. Kiara had heard of this in some of the larger streets, but had never seen it for herself.

Thin, rotting doors (if any at all) lined the walls of the tunnel, entrances of some of the meager homes, others still resided high above on a second level where old ladders full of missing rungs and wooden staircases led to the rickety platforms and natural stone catwalks running overhead, skinny and coughing layers of rock dust whenever feet traversed across. And still, with all this ample living space, there were those without even the simplest of homes.

Shoeless, bedraggled strangers wandered about with nothing but old rags for clothes and a sad sort of desultory shuffle to their feet. Others sat against the cave walls with no more than a creaky crate for sitting and an empty cup for begging to call their own. Tear streaked and hollow faces stared mindlessly at the stone walls. Most of them seemed to have nothing to live for, no hope, no joy left to spark even the smallest of fires.

Kiara looked on in indignant disgust at people literally living on top of one another and in their own garbage, the stench that coated the air persistently attesting to the latter.

She didn't know what she had expected. She always knew it was bad over on this side of town, but . . . deep down she always wanted to believe that, yes, they had less than her, smaller houses undoubtedly, but in her mind they, at least, all had homes, at the very worst living simpler lives without nearly as many pleasures as a royal, but not wholly devoid of comfort. To her they were . . . Cozy, tucked safely away, across town. And yet here she was, eyes open wide for the first time and seeing for herself the true extent of their need.

She had never felt right about the excess amount of near to everything her family always had, knowing that there were others with less. But this . . . This was inescapably painful. And she knew, after one glance, that she would never be able to spin herself such lies again.

Kiara had just enough time to comprehend and then grow thoroughly overwhelmed by the millions of thoughts running through her head, before people began to take notice of her, shaking her out from the insides of her mind, their dim eyes lighting up with a surprised kind of light.

This wasn't supposed to happen. She came to look, to observe, but here, people looked back.

Such a turbulent mix of feelings sloshed in her mind, feelings of desperately wanting to change the tragedy her eyes beheld into something better, but also of a horrible fear that she could not overcome.

Savages . . . she could hear her father say. *Lawless scum, itching to rob any respectable person at the first chance they get . . .*

Kiara shifted her eyes from one hollow-cheeked face to the next as the people whispered amongst each other in a disbelieving hush.

"Is that the princess?"

"Princess Kiara!?"

"What is the princess doing *here*?"

One boy, who had a mop of black curls, and one sleepy eye almost dropped something (unidentifiable in the low light) that he carried for an old woman, hobbling along with him, and just stared at her, but not like the kids from school did. He, like the others surrounding her, looked shocked, yet not without a little wide-eyed awe, jaws slack like someone had knocked them all silly. It did her no good. Their looks only forced her to acknowledge the fact that she had never come *before*, had never thought to try before, their glances, so flummoxed, almost begging the question . . . Why now?

Kiara's heart beat faster with each sunken gaze she met. Her foot slid behind her and she found herself longing to follow its lead.

What could *she* do to help them?

But could she really go back to "not so blissful" ignorance after all she had seen?

Didn't she kind of have to?

Her mind continued to fight much like this for some time until her weakness finally grew strong enough to turn her face and then her back on the only people that had ever looked at her with something other than disdain.

But no sooner had she turned than her gaze swept over a little girl, looking up at her with filthy black ringlets draping in her raindrop eyes, her sooty face streaked with the evidence of past tears. The sight of her nailed Kiara's feet to the ground. She felt a smile grow inside her, but when it surfaced, it was tainted with sorrow. The young girl took a step towards her despite her father, a strong, but worn-looking man, cautioning her to come back.

"Lass, no," he said, but Kiara knelt down in front of her, and on seeing her tiny outstretched hand, she fumbled for the small pouch on her belt. She fished out two argents[1], meant for the market to buy her anything she fancied. She placed them in her hand, her only hesitation that she feared someone might take them from her. But she had an adequate protector to go back to, and he watched

---

1. Silver coins somewhere in the middle of Caverna's currency, worth less than arums, but more than aerises.

them now with a fragile smile.

The girl peered into her hand and gave a sweet gasp, her eyes twinkling with delight at the two silver coins.

The smile that spanned Kiara's face wrinkled her nose. "Hello there," she said gently.

"Your Majesty," said the girl with a curtsy, remembering her manners.

Laughing softly, Kiara asked, "What's your name?"

"Abigail," she answered.

"That's a very elegant name, fit for a princess."

Abigail giggled, a smile blossoming on her face that faded just as quickly as the flowers. Yet, seeing a rare kindness in Kiara's eyes, she found the courage to ask her something Kiara had never heard out of the mouth of anyone but her own.

"Princess," she began, her brow scrunching as if the fate of life itself depended on the way she phrased the question, "do you ever think there's anything more to this life?"

Kiara answered, "No, Miss Abigail." The girl's eyes fell to the stone ground, but Kiara hadn't finished. "I don't think; I *believe* there is. And one day, I swear to you, lass, I'll find that something and I will bring it back here. Don't lose your courage and don't give up. No matter what people tell you, no matter how much they beat you down, you can not stop dreaming. Please, don't let fear stop you from fighting for your hope."

Kiara leaned back where she crouched, realizing she was talking to herself as much as she was the precious little girl in front of her. She hadn't trusted in words such as those in a long time, but here they came, pouring out and cracking a proper tear in her heart so she was forced to feel every bit of love and pain.

Her vision blurred with a haze of tears, welling without her consent.

"Promise me?"

Abigail gave a brave nod, and Kiara's smile was very sad (but that was partly just her smile) as she gently tapped the girl's nose and rose to her feet. One look around and countless gazes of awe locked her in a net she wanted nothing more than to squirm out of, their eyes starving for more words so life giving. They didn't bow, but still, they stared in enough reverence to make her face pale with the weight.

What they needed, she couldn't give them. She was no princess.

She turned before she could no longer move, leaving them all to stare at her back as she abandoned them.

She hastened her steps only to be stopped cold once more, feet glued in place as her blood turned icy. There he was, none other than the deaf and mute old beggar. Kiara knew it was him from the red scarf he kept around his clenched left hand, they say, to cover a wound he sustained in the Void that will never heal. At first the shock of color in their otherwise dreary world delighted Kiara despite herself, but then her head swarmed with every terrible story she had ever heard all at once, and it was all she could do to keep from trembling.

Just outside the entrance[1] he sat slumped against the wall, staring numbly at the ground, left out, kept apart. Kiara could almost picture spiders crawling out of his ears, dragging cobwebs behind them.

He felt her gaze and, proving he still very much had his sight, looked right into her eyes. His face registered some confusion, very human confusion, and suddenly Kiara felt extremely rude. His mind wasn't sucked clean by the void like the kids said; he was just a very old, sad man.

Kiara opened her mouth to apologize and depart, but words bunched in her throat.

Then he smiled, an atrocious and incomplete smile, and yet so pure and real, it wiped all previous happenings clean, like some kind of wonderful forgiveness more powerful than any words. Deep lines of well cultivated joy ran from his pale eyes like the harvest of a happy heart. Kiara couldn't help but return his kindness with a smile of her own, and though timid as it was, his grin only grew bigger as if he couldn't have asked for more.

And that's what crushed her. He wasn't even begging. He just sat minding his own business, only hoping someone, anyone would find it in their heart to spare a smile and make his lonely day more bearable.

Kiara found *her* brain to be the empty one after that, but she managed to offer a small wave. He waved back to her with his good hand, almost childlike in his enthusiasm.

Kiara wished to gather up each and every child and adult alike that she had ever heard speak a word of rumor against him and

---

1, Tragically, physical impairments and deformities were treated very harshly and drastically in Caverna. Most likely the reason for is exclusion.

line them all in a row just so they could see him here so full of life and receive a smile that would force them to chew and swallow their own bitter words. Instead, she turned away, unable to endure this sadness a moment longer, and started home.

Her heart, aching as only a heart can, suddenly felt out of place like it didn't even belong in its royal host anymore. She cursed it for feeling so much, but how could she go on having more than enough when there were those who had nothing to call their own? She had to do something, even if only to stop up this hole and cure the ache. And if she could't, maybe she could prompt someone else to. She was their princess after all, even if she didn't feel like it. And there was something delightful about that, knowing that she could finally use the title she despised so greatly and felt so unworthy of to do something she could be proud of.

She knew she'd have to talk to her father about it, and though she dreaded what he'd say, she couldn't have been more eager.

Is this what purpose feels like? she wondered, her steps growing lighter with each one she took.

Something she seldom felt in this dull life tingled at the ends of every nerve like life giving electricity, fueling her soul with new vigor as she ran home. For once in her life, she felt like she could do something right.

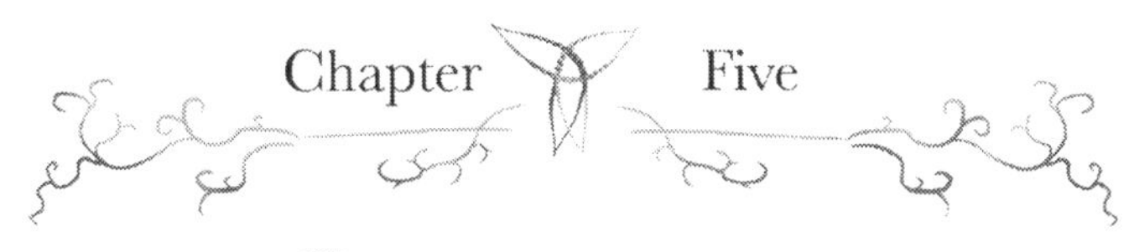

SECRETS

Kiara burst into her house. "Father! Father!" she shouted, wearing a wide smile in spite of herself. She had nearly forgotten the manner in which she departed earlier, thinking if he listened to her this once, she would forget every other time he mistreated her.

"Father, I have to tell you something!" she shouted again, but there was no answer, the palace house relatively quiet.

She wandered further into the wide foyer, cocking her head. "Father?"

She thought to search the usual rooms he could be found in just when a sour-faced servant named Leandor sidled around the corner, dustpan in hand.

"His Majesty is unavailable," he said, nasally and flat.

"Unavailable?" Kiara repeated the word as if it was impossible.

Leandor just sighed.

"You mean to say he is in his study, of course?"

"No, I believe he is out."

"Out? But where?"

Leandor pursed his lips. "Didn't say."

Kiara's eyebrows scrunched as she racked her brain for any possible place her father could be at this time. As far as she knew he was always here (or at least she thought) and she would have thought she knew his schedule rather well.

"I assume he didn't want to be disturbed," Leandor said, eyes drooping with disinterest.

In her perplexed state, Kiara forgot he still stood there. "Right, of course." Then, attempting to regain regal authority, she said, "Thank you, Leandor. You are dismissed."

The deadpan servant didn't try to hold in the heavy sigh as

he gave a lazy bow and turned to go.

Kiara stood alone in the foyer in a contemplative silence. For as long as she could remember, there had never been a day her father wasn't there when she got home. But then again, she usually didn't get home at this time *either*, at least not on Thursdays. Thursdays were her market days and she usually went to browse the stands and shops for a while after school. Her father had . . . encouraged her to go, said it would better her social skills, something outside of school where she saw other human beings.

Maybe it was nothing. After all, he *was* the king and it wasn't unimaginable for something to have changed in his important schedule. Kiara would just wait till he got home and ask where he'd been, simple as that.

She decided to wait in his study, but on her way there, she passed Shrike's room and skidded on her heels when she saw him inside. With his back to her, he didn't even notice her.

Freakish little man as he was, Shrike kept a towering structure of rectangle stones on his desk and added a new addition to its height every now and then. She watched as he tried to find the perfect placement for the newest piece, taking painstaking precautions so it wouldn't crumble the whole tower, now built to outrageous proportions. Kiara shook her head, knowing nothing he did would work. She had already scrutinized this construction top to bottom while he was out with her father on business she didn't care to ask about. It was then that she needled out the piece that would bring the destruction of the tower. After about an hour, sitting in his chair, diabolically analyzing each piece, she found the stone that, if removed, would utterly ruin the stability of the whole thing. After that, it only needed for Shrike to place the next piece and it would all come crashing down.

But that was two days ago. Kiara couldn't believe her luck! She never imagined she'd actually get to witness the fruits of her tedious labors, and now she just happened to walk by at the exact moment of the tower's demise? What luck indeed.

At length, Shrike picked a placement and (holding the new stone) hovered a stubby-fingered hand above the spot. His concentration shot like lasers from his eyes, the silence thick enough to stir in a bowl. Then there went a subtle *chink*, and there would be no completion of this Babble, the hundreds of stone pieces all cascading down each other in a crumbling cacophony and finally clattering to the ground. All because one piece escaped the confines of the foundation and didn't look back.

Kiara pulled a fist down from the air, a wide grin stretching her face, and scampered off before his shock wore away. Oh, he was going to be furious, but Kiara had bigger things to worry about. Shrike would find the missing piece mysteriously in the bottom of a goblet or some other obvious place soon enough, but right now, she could only think of her father and seeing Shrike, bumbling about the palace like he had nothing better to do, made the situation all the more perturbing.

Curling up in a chair in King Nnyric's study, she tried to read a book while she waited, but the sort of books they read in Caverna didn't often hold her attention.

Before you judge her patience and attention span, consider if a hundred page book entitled, *The Art of Stone Smoothing,* could keep you interested for more than a minute.

As Kiara scanned an entire page devoted to describing the individual textures you can achieve from smoothing different kinds of stones, her mind started to drift and concerns turned to anxiety. And after one last, valiant attempt to find something interesting in the grey, little book, she snapped it shut.

"What if he did lie to me?" she thought out loud. "What would he have to hide? What reason would I have to suspect him?" She hopped up to put the book away and pace the room. Just as her concerns mounted to almost too much to bear, she heard footsteps in the hall and she knew the gate well. The sound tightened her chest, despite having nothing to fear at the moment.

Kiara spun around just as he passed through the doorway. "Father!"

"Ah, Kiara, are you ready to apologize for your irksome behavior?" Her father greeted, pulling at his black gloves one finger at a time.

"*Wellll,* sort of, but first I was wondering where you were today, Father," she said cordially.

His face washed with a disconcerted pallor, though Kiara knew not a single reason why. "Oh, I . . . Just off on official matters." He recovered.

"I just thought I'd ask—"

"And you thought wrong!" he snapped. "It's really none of your business." Sighing, he added, "It'd probably bore you anyway . . ."

Quietly, Kiara's reply came like a plea. "I wish you wouldn't assume how much I want to hear from you."

If he had thought on it for a moment, he might have actually been touched, so naturally, Nnyric changed the subject. With another sigh he asked, "Don't you have an apology to make?"

It is never good to make someone say they're sorry, because they will almost inevitably and always fake it. Consequently, with her eyes downcast, only the irrationally guilty parts of Kiara meant it when she said, "Yes . . . I'm sorry, Father."

"Very well, that's settled."

Pouring himself a drink from a crystal stopped vessel on his desk, Nnyric spoke with baited words. "You know, I talked to Shrike before I left today."

"Oh?" Kiara asked innocently. "You did?"

Nnyric suppressed a grin behind the rim of his goblet as he took his first sip. Kiara loved when he made that face. It was playful and somehow made him more handsome in her opinion. It made her heart lighten at once to know she had actually done something to amuse him instead of vex him for a change.

"You very well must put an end to this." He wagged a finger, but not wholly without a little good natured fun. "I can't keep telling him he's clumsy as a drunk. Fleard knows, he already doesn't believe me."

Kiara swept her hands behind her back. "Whatever could you mean, Father?"

He tried not to grin again, so as not to encourage her any further. "Yes, well, I suppose Shrike does deserve it in some ways. Scummy little fellow." He chuckled. "He has this suspicion that he's made an enemy, or so he's voiced as much."

"Ah . . ." Kiara nodded, enjoying (maybe a little too much) hearing her father call Shrike a *scummy little fellow*. "Perhaps one of the servants," she said. "It's not as though he takes much care to be kind to any of them."

"That's what I told him." Nnyric rounded his desk and sat down in the high backed chair.

"So, I might have returned later than usual, but you never said why you came home *early*."

"Oh!" She remembered. "Of course. I actually skipped the market today and ran straight home, anxious to tell you something."

"Well, what is it?" he said, absentmindedly scanning unopened letters on his desk, suddenly impatient.

Kiara's heart sank, all of a sudden unsure if she was ready

for his pleasant mood to end. She wanted to eat up this time and not have to share it with a soul, or maybe just leave and actually depart on a rare good note. She knew it was selfish, but was it such a bad thing to be selfish about? He was *her* father; not theirs. Right? Then on the other side of the tug of war, Kiara knew exactly how she'd feel if she walked away now, never being able to clear her head of all their desperate faces, just barely hanging on to the most fragile of hopes. And what better time to mention it than when he sat so placidly.

"Well I . . ." Kiara began, giving a gulp of resignation. "I went to Terminal Avenue today, and—"

Nnyric shot to his feet. "You did what! Kiara, I've told you they're too dangerous!" he said, placing a firm finger on the desk. "What were you thinking?"

"I . . . wanted to help them. Isn't that what we are supposed to do as the royal family, do good by all of the city and have the best intent for *all* the people?" she cried.

"Ah, so you weren't thinking at all. I see." He sighed, raising his face to the ceiling. "Kiara, no. Not like that. How many times do I have to warn you, before you have a healthy fear of that which should be kept separate?"

"But, if you would just see them!" Kiara raised her voice in desperation now, not caring who heard. "You could not help but feel the same! You would know just how much they need us."

"Oh, do you think so?"

"Yes! Father, please—"

"No! Now, you can not change my mind on this!" He sighed and rubbed his forehead as if this was just too much for him to bear. "Just go," he said, with a flick of his hand. "Get out of my sight."

Those last words, though the most gently spoken, hit her with a jolt of pain. The entirety of Kiara's face flushed a repressed shade of red, as she tried her bravest to fight back tears. Even as the edges of her eyes burned and grew pink with the strain, his scowl did not relent. So she bolted from his sight, just as he had asked, feeling the full sting of his rejection as the salty droplets started to roll down her round cheeks. She swiped them away furiously, hating just how easily and deeply he could hurt her.

Closing herself in her room with one lonely lamp lit, she ripped pin after pin from her hair, taking fistfuls of copper strands with them, until every curl fell free and down her back.

She flung herself upon her bed, curls flying over her face,

further hiding her tears that she already smothered in her pillow to muffle her terrible sobs. Her heart ached with an empty grief (even more than usual) as she longed so desperately for something she could never have again: the comfort of a mother. She would have been grateful for even just a piece of her, she thought as she wept. Just to hear her calming voice, or maybe just her smell, *something* to know she was there and wouldn't go until the tears stopped.

The worst part of this sorry situation was, she had only just begun to forgive her father, even though she said she never would. Maybe she should just keep her word this time and save herself the heartache.

For so long she had floated by life and consequently life by her, but now she had this chance to do something, and he ripped it right from her feeble grip.

She only wanted to help the weaker, the helpless. Was that so wrong? Kiara couldn't believe her father could be opposed to such an idea, almost as if he feared them. But they weren't the animals he thought they were. They didn't even try to attack her like the savages he called them. Why couldn't he see that?

Am I wrong to want to help them?

As if cut loose from the safety of the harbor, her mind floated adrift on raging seas and the whipping wind kept telling her that she was insane and hopeless. She didn't know why, but she felt foolish and messed up. She cried so hard, her throat filled with mucus and made her sit up with sputters and hacks. Her hair stuck to her right cheek, glued with tears. As the coughs subsided she bore a listless gaze into the tapestry her mother had made her.

"I miss you, Mom . . ." she whispered, wishing she could be done with tears, but they kept leaking out. ". . . So much."

Her blurred vision warped the picture at first. Then, wiping the tears away, Kiara looked again at the knitted version of her and her mother holding hands. It had hung on that wall for so long, Kiara couldn't even remember a time when it was bare, and had cherished it as her most colorful possession for just as long, a shocking exception her father had allowed to the strict rules of Caverna.

It hurt to look at it. It hurt like nothing else hurt. Because when you live your life and no one, no one at all, comes close to the love, the light, the warmth of that one and the things you've shared in hours of nothing at all, in laughter that makes you cry, and just plain old tears . . . When nothing compares to this person that's a part of your very heart, and then they're just gone . . . you may never stop missing them, you may never want to. You might never be the same again until you find them, until you find your way back to them. And that's okay.

As much as it hurt her to look at it; it killed her not to. And so she let her eyes rest on it like a shelter away from the storms, every day since it was made and even more so after her mother was gone, but today, after years of familiarizing herself with each stitch, each perfect mistake, Kiara saw something different. She blamed it on her wishful imagination that the rays of light shining down on them from above looked like arrows pointing towards the edges of the piece, but still she found it hard to ignore. Kiara sniffed a sob back and began to turn her face from the odd sight, but a curious scratch bade her give it one last skeptical glance.

It couldn't be denied. They didn't just look like arrows, they were arrows, plain as candlelight.

Tilting her head, she mused, *Could there be . . . No, not after all this time. That precious, old rug has been there for years.*

Kiara slid off her bed. Closing her eyes, she sighed through her nose. Part of her just wanted to tell herself she was crazy, but the other part told her to shut her mouth. She bit her lip and inched ever so slowly closer. When she at last crossed the short distance, her fingers only brushed a corner of the masterpiece, before her heart hammered so hard, she could hear it in her ears. She froze, unable to move. She couldn't let herself be ripped apart by another disappointment. She feared the pain and the paralysis of that fear only grew stronger the longer she thought. Then the other part of her started to talk back, the part of her that wasn't afraid, the part that needed something to hope for so desperately, it would never give up. What if there was something her mother left for her behind it? Something like a key, a long awaited way of escape to the world, she so badly longed to see. And how could it really matter if there was nothing. Could she really let that stop her from finding out?

Kiara looked at the woven face of her mother and into the blue eyes, piercing like beacons, and with a deep breath that felt like it could last her an hour, she flung the tapestry back. There, a deep depression in the wall tunneled back a couple feet. Uneven and broken up, the alcove appeared natural and suddenly Kiara could easily imagine her mother finishing the tapestry and knowing immediately just where to hang it. Wisps of cobwebs reached out like ghostly fingers. Kiara shivered as she examined the tunnel.

Though she had no actual memory of it, some of the cracks and angles looked eerily familiar, each detail painting little, grey pictures in her mind. Stranger still, each image was like looking out from within the tunnel as if she had once sat inside for some time when she was yet small enough to fit. And then, less like remembering and more like someone whispering it in her ear, she knew there was a smaller cavity yet further in and to the side. Without discussing it with her head, her hand reached in and found the hidden hole just where she knew it would be. But then her fingers brushed something she did not expect and a creature with far more than four legs skittered across the tops of her knuckles. With a squeak, she jerked her hand back to safety. Looking about her room, she hoped no one had heard her.

It shouldn't have frightened her, the object certainly didn't feel alive, but its dark hiding place and the critters seemingly guarding it, made it into something to fear without much effort. Kiara flexed her fingers one by one and clenched them again, preparing herself for another search. Easing her hand back in, she desperately willed all spiders, centipedes, and every other leggy cave dweller to retreat back into their crevices. She reached the place of her previous retreat, thankful for every inch she made it without encountering another spider. She fumbled about, at first only finding more clammy stone, but stretching farther, her finger tips bumped against wood. She squinted as she stretched her hand around what felt like a small box and pulled it from its hiding place. She left it at the edge of the tunnel and dusted her hand off. There sat a chest identical to the one in her hideaway that held her books, but smaller. The top was caked in countless layers of mineral dust, but not so much that Kiara couldn't see each intricate engraving. It made her heart swell with such a poignant sense of missing, the sights painting her mother fresh in her mind.

How . . . was all she could think as her hands began to shake. She placed them on the chest to steady them. At once, she couldn't stand another moment not not knowing what was inside. She pulled on the lid, her fingernails gathering years old cave grime, but it didn't budge. Kiara held the chest close to her face to look for a keyhole and found a depression she knew like the back of her hand. She touched her chin to her chest to look at her necklace, unsure why she hadn't thought of it before. When she raised it over her head, the chain caught in her hair and she ripped it even though it hurt. Pressing half the pendant into the slot with her thumb, she gave it a twist of her wrist and heard a subtle click. She tried the lid again, this time it began to open with only a few, creaky complaints from the hinges. Kiara squeezed her eyes shut. She realized she had absolutely no idea what could be in this petite chest, not in the slightest, and she thought, if she closed her eyes and opened them slowly, she might bear it easier. Heart almost beating out of her chest now, she lifted the lid all the way, listening to the tiny squeak of the hinges, then eased open one eye to the unexplainably disappointing sight of . . . nothing?

Empty! her thoughts screamed. Out of all the things she couldn't expect, empty was certainly farthest from her mind.

Her heart drooped with the weight of the letdown, but refusing to give up just yet, she searched the interior again with both eyes and brought the box closer to the light. Her heart startled her with the way it fluttered back to life when the flicker of the flames illuminated something thin, lying flat on the floor of the chest, almost the same dark brown as the wood.

A letter.

Chapter Six

VOICES

Kiara's fingers moved in slow motion before her eyes as she picked the letter so delicately from the chest, fearing she would shatter the featherlight paper like glass. Gathering all she could from the front, Kiara gingerly flipped it over, sucking in a breath at what she saw. There on the back was her name, written in her mother's flourish and elegant hand. The shock stole the strength from her legs and she fell back onto the edge of her bed, a trembling hand involuntarily moving to her face.

Kiara looked about her room, suddenly not wanting to be alone in this, but who was she kidding? There was no one to show the letter to, no one to tell.

Prying open the letter, Kiara spotted a date in the upper, right hand corner, and her heart stopped for one cold, disbelieving moment, the numbers proclaiming in faded, but prominent characters, the day her mother died.

My dear Kiara,

I miss you so much even as I write this and to think, I just ate breakfast with you and sent you off to school this morning. I think my heart knows more than my head just how indefinitely this goodbye will last.

Kiara's throat choked with emotion. She had absolutely no room for the flood of feelings flooding her body, so they poured out through her eyes. She sobbed, louder than before, the pain she felt now so different from when her father sent her from his sight, and in some ways so much more difficult to endure. The tears ran like an unstoppable river straining to reach some unattainable ocean. What could she do, but force herself to read on? Grounding her gaze on the old parchment, she held her breath as if it would stop the tears.

I hope you won't have had to wait long to read this. But I don't doubt your clever mind and I know you'll find the clues in the tapestry sooner than later. Of course, I made the tapestry to cover that awful hole. I remember when you used to hide in the tunnel. Your father never could find you and I'd say he was sufficiently impressed with your hiding skills

The writing trailed off as if Eleanor had found, mid scrawl, not the heart to write of such things, then picked back up with a surer hand once again.

But, I also made the tapestry to create a secret place, just in case I ever needed to hide anything for only you to find. I never knew it would be for a letter such as this.

Kiara felt the corner of her mouth twitch with the rumor of a smile, as she thought how that was just like her mom to constantly think ahead for outrageous things they might just need one day. But how sad was it now that one of her preposterous premonitions became a need?

She read on.

My heart hurts when I think about how long you might believe your father's lies, but, Kiara,

Without even thinking, Kiara had hopped her eyes over to the next word before their time had come and before she knew it, she couldn't get air back into her lungs.

I'm alive.

Shallow breaths through her nose were all she could manage to keep herself conscious as her eyes remained riveted to the shortest, but most unexplainably shaking sentence in the whole letter. It built her into a tower, tall enough to push past the impassable darkness and broke her into shattering pieces all in one short moment. It both lifted her with the buoyancy of hope beyond words and drug her down into a whole, muddled mire of joy-leaching pain.

"You're alive?" she breathed.

Her scrunched brow squeezed out more of the tears that had almost stopped. Kiara began to frantically scan the rest of the letter, soaking up all information until there was nothing left to learn.

I wish I could tell you myself, but you must believe me, because it's true and you deserve to know. They will take me away today before you get home. If I would have known, I would have held you so much tighter this morning.

Your wicked father is sending me to a prison deep in the rainforest. If I am honest, I did it to myself. And I'm sorry, Kiara, but I could not bear to remain silent, not after I found out about

Once again, the words trailed off without reason, and Kiara wondered if she had written it in some kind of hurry

I don't know if I should tell you. All you need to know is, you have to get out of there.

I threatened to tell, and for that I feel a conflicted remorse. But if not me, it would have been someone or something else. Truth will always win, for what's done in the dark will come to light. And what solid truth it is. I gave you those books for a reason, my Dear. I desperately hope you didn't think it was all a wonderful fantasy. Because if you do, Kiara, it's real. There's a whole, wondrous world out there, beyond the confines of this darkness, and it's just waiting to be explored by you and your big, beautiful, green eyes.

I know you will find a way to escape; it's in your blood to be free. But not a day will go by that I won't worry about you. Not until I see you again. If you can find those worthy of trust, cling to them. This life is a tragic mess when we try to struggle through it alone. And I know I'd rest a little easier knowing my little girl wasn't fighting her way through a hostile jungle with death laid like traps under every tree all by herself.

There's so much to tell you, so much more that you deserve to know, but there are some things that should be saved for the tongue to say and the ears to hear, some things the heart shouldn't process alone in the solitude of written words. I promise you, I will tell you everything when you get here.

I dearly hope you haven't blamed the Creator for all this. Remember our real enemy, Kiara. He's wicked and ugly. He doesn't want you free. Make no mistake, he is prepared to do everything in his dark power to keep you imprisoned, in more ways than one. But you can trust the Creator. He loves you, and He sees you as perfect. He will keep you safe and guide you to help. You need only ask.

I wrote you a riddle on the back of this letter. And I know, the last thing you need is more mysteries, but no one else can know what I'm telling you. I hope it leads you to some truth and answers

I overheard some of the men discussing the route we will be taking to the prison. When you escape, head north until you find the river. It will lead you to the prison.

I long for the day when secrecy is no longer a necessity. When I will hold you again, weep with you, and together we will not be afraid to lift the shadows of the dark recesses of the world.

Be safe, sweet girl. I believe in you.

I will pray for you every day and miss you even more.

I love you, Ara
Mom

"You're alive . . ." Kiara couldn't stop whispering. Then came a boiling hot anger, her hands clenching into fists, so she crinkled a corner of the letter. For four, long, dreadful years she had believed a horrible lie!

How— *why* would her father do this? What else was he lying about? What else was he hiding from her?

Tears streamed down her face as she read the letter again, and when she came to it, Kiara found herself reading the sentence about hugging her tighter over and over again.

She realized she hadn't the vaguest memory of that morning, (it was, after all, just a normal morning) only recalling coming home and the nothing that filled her soul almost forthwith. Oh, she remembered that night well enough, the servant that came to her room because her father didn't even have a shred of decency to tell her himself, the fierce tremors that started in her lip and then took over her entire body after the servant had left, as she stood there alone, unsure if she would ever breath or move again. She remembered the countless lonely nights she fell apart, crying herself to sleep, and the just as innumerable mornings she struggled to put herself back together, every time losing a few more pieces to the puzzle. She could vividly recall the exact moment the black grief fell over her life like a stubborn shadow, just not that morning. The only thing she ever wanted was a proper goodbye, and she could have had it, had she only known. If she only knew, she wouldn't have hugged her tighter, she thought; she would have wrapped her arms around her and never let her go again.

Over the years she had learned to grow numb at best to these sorts of things, but this . . . This ripped the stitches afresh into a new, searing wound.

She squeezed her eyes shut, ran her hands over the top of her head, still clutching the letter. Her many lines of thought ran zigzagging, intersecting, and tangled paths in her head, until she doubted her ability to even see straight if she opened her eyes.

She had to leave the Palace, but where could she go? Her hideaway would have been her first thought, but she never went to the Forbiddens during the day, for fear of being seen. Then she remembered, she still had a watch shift at the Aperture of the Void, and couldn't believe she had almost forgotten. The small mercy the thought gave her would have to do for now.

The Aperture of the Void was said to be the place where their world ended and the interminable Void started. Years before Nnyric, kings had always set guard shifts there so that they would know if any beings of the Void were to cross over, and even after lifetimes with not so much as a ghostly cricket passing through those imposing doors, the practice remained.

Wiping the tears from her face, Kiara gave a mindless glance at the short riddle written on the back of the paper, and knew at once, her brain would be of no help at the moment. She decided to give it a try later after her nerves had gotten a chance to settle and her mind to clear.

Putting the delicate note back in its only home for its whole four years of life, she locked the chest and hid it back behind the tapestry.

"You've been hidden this long, you better stay hidden!" she threatened with a pointing finger and went to her mirror, briefly wiping her eyes and nose as best she could, but the puffy redness would not depart from her miserable face.

She shrugged half heartedly at her reflection. "It's not as though Father wouldn't have expected you to have been crying, Princess."

She didn't try to sneak up on him, padding down the hall from her room, but Kiara was naturally a quiet person, light on her small feet, and always feeling like she could physically shatter the firmly established silence if she walked or talked too loud. Her father simply didn't hear her coming.

She heard him though. By the sound of it, she placed him just around the corner, in the drawing room, breathing heavily and rambling on to himself. Something unknown, like it was hiding, prickled her skin and quickened her pulse. If not for fitting so perfectly with the rest of the strange day, Kiara might have brushed the feeling off. But because of the way the day had already gone, she took hold of the lead and only needed to follow it a short distance before she knew something was wrong.

Arching a brow, both concerned and questioning, Kiara silently slipped up against the wall just where the hall ended. She couldn't see him from this angle, so slowly and carefully, she peeked around the corner. Her chest and shoulders collapsed with an inaudible sigh of relief. He wasn't looking in her direction, and there was no one else in the room to spy her. But that relief led to a question. Who in Caverna was he talking to?

With a huff, Nnyric started to turn. Kiara wrenched her head back around the corner, bit her lip, and listened.

"She won't find out!" her father insisted. "And even if she does, you know I will silence her!"

Fear shot through Kiara like ice into her veins. *Find out what? Silence who? Oh, dear god, please don't let him be talking about me!*

Then came another voice that broke her from her thoughts and sent slippery, skin-crawling chills down her spine. *"Ssshe will find out."* It dripped, slowly, hungrily. *"And when she doesss, you will clean up the messs before it is seen."*

That was not her father's voice, it was deeper, almost inhuman. She had always thought her father had such a command to his voice, but this . . . *thing* made him sound small, weak even, in comparison. It not only commanded, it anticipated, clipping its words with such knowing as if it was always five steps ahead of everything and would never be caught falling behind.

Kiara wrung her hands. It couldn't be helped. She had to steal one more glance to make sure no one else stood in the room. Letting her eyes fall shut, she stole her nerves, believing the knowing worth the risk. Even as she saw it, she couldn't make herself believe it. The other voice came straight from her father's mouth. It took every bit of her strength to pull herself back to the safety of the hallway, her body trembling so violently. She thought she was going to be sick, all the while their gut wrenching conversation persisted.

"How could this have happened? We took precautions for this not to happen!" said her father's perplexed, angry voice.

"You let it happen," came the slimy reply, calm as stagnant water. *"And the moment she showsss any sign of knowing, you will sssend her to the same place you sssent her wretched mother. That*

was your first daft missstake, capturing that Scottish women and her irksssome father."

"It's not as if it was my idea. I wasn't even king yet. That was my father's doing."

"And where is he now?" the voice cooed. *"Dead. I really don't think you know how eeeasy you are to supplant, how disssposable you really are to usss."*

And just like that a thick silence fell, like a candle snuffed out. Kiara didn't move. She didn't breathe. She squeezed her eyes shut and hoped to wake up as if it was all another one of her horrible dreams.

Then, ripping at the silence like thin fabric, came a growl not unlike a wolf's and something shattering on the ground. Kiara stifled the scream that clawed at the insides of her throat as she nearly jumped out of her skin and began to scamper away, but then the hall looked so dark and she couldn't go back to her room, not now . . . not alone. Just the sight of the swallowing black, sent shivers through her being.

She thought if she could just pretend she was only just coming out of her room to see what the crash was, she might be able to leave the palace without further complications. If only she could shake the quivers in her voice.

Rounding the corner, she found him doubled over and picking ceramic shards from the ground. At first all she could do was stare at him, feeling, all at once, like she knew this man less than she even thought she did.

"Father?" She tested her voice. "Is everything alright?"

Fabricating some concern in a quick second, she folded her hands behind her back to hide the way they trembled. Nnyric jumped, the few ceramic pieces he had gathered clattering to the stone floor.

"Oh, Kiara." He straightened, dusting himself off. "Yes, I'm quite well. You know, I was just coming to see you when my foot caught on this blasted table," he kicked the leg of a low end table, "and I knocked over this vase," he said and lied.

Kiara's eyes shot to the shards on the floor, shards of a vase she recognized and knew had never once sat on that table, but had always decorated the one on the exact opposite side of the room, now bare.

"Oh . . . Well, alright. Is there something you wanted to say?"

"What?"

"To me?"

"Oh!" He ran a hand through his jet hair. "No, nothing of impor-tance." Then, bending back down to resume picking up the shattered pieces, he asked. "You?"

"Yes, actually," Kiara replied, as evenly as she could. "I just realized I still have a watch shift at the Aperture of the Void."

"Yes." He didn't look up. "Yes you do. You should go—Ah!"

Nnyric flicked a particularly sharp piece to the ground, a fresh, scarlet stripe stretching across his thumb. As the blood started to run, he fixed the cut with a scrutinizing look as if he had never seen himself bleed.

Kiara felt a prick in her heart. The hard anger abandoned her, dripping down inside her like melting ice. She didn't like to watch him hurt, but maybe it was more because watching him bleed like that, crumpled on the floor, felt too much like listening to the horrific conversation just moments ago, as he was all too easily bled, perhaps not of blood, but of surety and command.

She moved to kneel down and spoke without facade. "You're hurt."

He held out a swift hand to keep her at bay. "I'm fine!" he said tersely.

Kiara backed further away than she was before. Chilling her tone, she glared at him. "Why don't you get one of the servants to do that?"

"Ah!" He threw down the few pieces he had gathered. "I will. It just— I didn't think I should need to." He looked up, narrowing his eyes at her. "Didn't you say you have a watch shift?"

Something about his eyes from that angle looked so different, less intimidating, but in the same moment, they were filled with annoyance and disdain.

She puffed a breath through her nose, like a laugh or more accurately a scoff. "Yeah."

She left him, still hunched over the broken vase, and set a course for the foyer. Walking away Kiara realized what she hadn't placed before: in all her sixteen years of being his daughter, she had never once seen him look up at her. It was always a stern glance from above. Even his smiles held a lofty superiority. But today he looked up from the ground in more ways than one, making her shudder as she left the palace with the questions, who or what was that thing and why did it have so much power over the King of Caverna?

Three Questions

Why?

Kiara avoided all eye contact as she scampered along the outskirts of town to the wide chamber that held the encompassing, gate-like doors of the Void. She tried her very best to bottle up her emotions into an uncomfortable jar they didn't fit in, every step she took cracking a new, hairline fracture in the glass.

Upon arriving, she found one of the other Void watchers slumped against the wall, head drooping with sleep or (more likely) boredom, and breaths just beginning to snort.

"Hello, Gilbert!" Kiara greeted, loud enough to startle him.

Gilbert, a youngish man with feathery black hair, gasped as if she woke him from dreams of drowning, and jolted his every muscle.

Kiara never could decide on an exact age for his boyish yet nigh on wrinkled face. And she couldn't very well ask him. That would mean starting a conversation that reached beyond hellos or goodbyes, and she didn't want to force him to talk to her.

"My turn." She gave him a painted grin.

Gilbert's wave was accompanied by a perplexed look. Just like she could never figure out his age, he could not understand and would always wonder why their princess had such giddy enthusiasm to watch a gate, no matter how giant it was! It never did anything and nobody ever came in it. But he only yawned and with one tip of his head, handed the watch shift over to her.

Kiara followed him with her eyes as he walked out of sight, waiting a few extra moments to make sure she was completely alone, before the glass of the jar shattered into a million pieces, and she collapsed to her knees in the middle of the empty, echoing room, just a small crumple of clothes and wild hair in the entirety of that wide cavern. The walls took every soft sniff she made in an attempt to stop the tears from returning, amplified them, and shot them back across the room, as if playing catch with her sorrow.

Kiara held her head in one hand and gripped her metal necklace in the other, squeezing it so tight, the sharp wings stabbed through flesh. She winced as pain shot through her palm and flung her hand open wide. It had drawn blood. She removed a handkerchief from the pouch on her belt and carelessly wrapped the wound. It still hurt, but she just looked numbly on the poor bandage job. She wanted to shut off her brain, not let the pain of the day affect her, and thought numbing herself to the pain in her hand could be a start.

Kiara raised her head to the imposing, double doors. As the princess she wasn't really required, let alone supposed to have a Void watch, but by the process of erosion, she had worn her father down until, finally, he allowed it, if not only to keep her quiet. Impervious and sealed as tight as a crypt, the doors were not an entrance or an exit. No one had ever left through these doors, because no one leaves, and Kiara had no idea how anyone could come in through this way without some sort of battering ram . . . Even then. But finding a means of escape through the doors was not why she had fought her father for a reason to come here. She had come to grips with the impossibilities long ago. It was the perfection that shown above the doors that called her heart back to this place time and time again.

Light.

True. Pure. Light.

Everyone said it was a gateway to the Void like the doors, but more transparent. Some liked to think of it as a communication portal for Fleard, even though he used his watchers for that. Others, more devoutly committed to their religious learnings (like King Nnyric himself) knew it as more of a symbol, something to remind everyone that Fleard, though distant, could still look in from the Void and, in fact, see all. Finally, there were still those, most even, that had no knowledge at all of the anomalies' existence.

Of course, Kiara knew differently from all of them. Because to her a window was just that. Simply a piece of glass. And oh how superior glass was to stone, because of this magic that it did not dare try to hold back. Sometimes the light wasn't there, like now, and Kiara would wonder what could have been so awful to have taken it away, mourning its loss until it came back. And that's just what it did. Somehow the light always came back.

When it decided to grace her with its cheer, watches felt

short as she sat her whole hour in the center of that vast empty cavern and basked in the rays streaming from the one, wide window. Streaked with dirt, the round, grimy panes didn't allow for any sights from outside, but that did little to hinder her childlike affinity for this place.

Kiara gazed up at the now almost grey tinted window, the light it let through, now more ambient then anything, her eyes pleading and filling with the tears she didn't want to cry.

"Come on, light . . ." she whispered, but when whatever created the sad grey haze persisted, she hung her head.

One tear, clinging to the lashes of her half open lids, refused to drip. Then it sparkled, glinting with golden light. She felt it first, the rumor of warmth tingling her skin.

With the subtlest flutter in her heart, Kiara raised her head. A smile tickled her mouth.

The light had come.

She let it dry her eyes, let the warmth reach the deepest parts of her, even to her soul, closing her eyes to try and soak as much joy from this gift as she could.

Kiara gazed up, squinting to see something, anything, through the filthy glass, but to her continual disappointment, not the vaguest shape could be discerned.

If the letter was real and if her mother was right, the rainforest, *the world,* lay just beyond those doors . . .

But how could she be right? How would she know?

Kiara pushed herself to her feet and crossed the room to the doors that rose and just kept rising over her head. She placed a hand on the old wood as if she could feel the freedom that waited on the other side. She touched her forehead against the wood as identical tears slipped down both her cheeks.

Why? Why? ***WHY?***

Why was life so indefinitely hard?

Her thoughts twisted in loops and knots, until it actually hurt her mind to try and untangle them by herself. She wished that someone would just tell her everything, what to do, what was happening.

She had so many questions, but three in particular kept taking turns, making their cryptic rounds of unanswerable uncertainty.

Why would her father do this? Why do they insist on keeping everyone trapped in this horrible pit? And why, if He was really out there, did the Creator let it happen?

Truth is, after her mother died— was taken, her thoughts toward the "Creator" as her mother called Him, came less often everyday she spent in this prison. And her mother's letter only reminded her of how angry she had become with the whole idea. She did blame Him. If He was so real and in control, then it was His fault. Soon the question wasn't why, but even *how* could He let this happen?

In an attempt to at least sort the questions, she tried to recall back on her day, starting with the very beginning, but found even that small task a difficult feat, at least in her state of mind. Even her strange dream, once a vivid display of haunting images, was now disjointed and blurry.

Was that even this morning? she questioned. It felt so long ago already.

It was the same with the rest of the day, like a hazy sheet had been drawn over the details, or she had already left them far enough behind to have forgotten. Maybe it was better that way, at least for now.

She tried to focus on things that were certain, once identified, she spoke them out, so she could hear them said.

"Father hates me . . ." Her voice cracked. "He lied to me . . . about who knows how much. I need to get out of here . . . Mother is alive. I *need* to save her."

No longer just in her head, these things were reality, near to tangible, and with the truth of the situation growing heavier, gravity itself seemed to grow stronger, pulling on her limbs and the stings of her heart.

Kiara's hands began to shake. "Mother is alive . . ." she whispered again.

She knew what she had to do; she just needed to know how to do it. She had searched the Forbiddens for a way of escape for years now, each failed investigation, leaving her more and more discouraged. But then this happens, an unnatural suspicion begging her to listen until she couldn't ignore it a moment more, and what does she find? Not an exit, not her mother; a letter, a very vague letter with most information only hinted at, not to mention dropping the fact that her mother was still alive right on her head. But that right there, and her mother being sent away, was the very thing that proved there was a way out, a way that her father knew about. So she couldn't give up. Not now.

Hundreds more loose questions fluttered about like moths

escaped from a jar with no lid. Even if she caught one she could never keep it long enough to gather its match or, in her case, its answer.

Who, or better named, *what* was her father talking to? And what did the voice mean when it called her mother "that Scottish woman?" How did her mother know so much about the world beyond the darkness, even before she was sentenced to exile? What did she find out that she couldn't keep silent about? Simply the truth about the outside world? Why wouldn't she tell her and find an escape with her?

And there was the matter of how she would actually get to her mother. Even if she found the oh so obscure way of escape, where was she to go?

Oh, of course, Kiara thought to herself sardonically, *travel north until you reach the river. Right. Because that's extremely informative. What in Caverna even is a north!*[1]

She half wondered if her mother, in all her haste, had erred on the word and meant to write something else entirely.

To try to navigate the uncertainty right now, meant only headaches. Like running through a twisted maze with no light at all, she knew if she went in she might never get back out.

But there was something in that same sense of purpose she had felt while running home from Terminal Ave, the same one doused by her father's chastisement, that sparked in her again now. And somehow despite all her futile questioning and running in the dark, it was enough.

Tonight she would search the Forbidden Caverns.

---

1. The traditional names for directions seemed to have gotten lost some time in Caverna's history. Instead, denizens use terms like void side, king side, forbidden side, and terminal side.

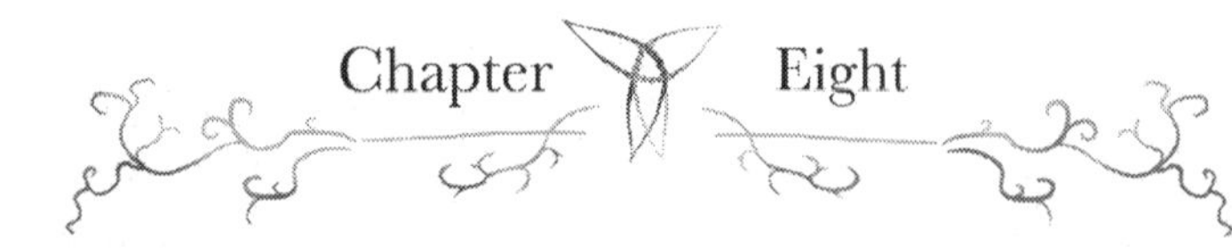

The Forbiddens

Kiara sat on her bed, waiting for her strange world to go to sleep. After her watch shift ended, she went straight home, and (without a word to her father or anyone else for that matter) she slunk straight to her room. Already, she had sat there for hours, staring up at the dark above her head and thinking until the migraine she had already acquired, reached skull splitting strengths. She didn't eat dinner. Her father didn't even try to get her to come and eat. Of course, this didn't surprise her in the slightest. But she did expect a visit from Lucida. She even pictured the knock that would come on the door, the sound of her shuffling feet, and the rattle of the tray as she brought dinner leftovers that Kiara would say she didn't want to eat even though she did, and Lucida would cheer her up and convince her she needed to.

But Cida didn't come. She must have been busy.

Kiara felt her stomach begin the uncomfortable tightening before the big rumble and thought she might sneak something from the kitchen, but it didn't matter now. Now it was almost time. She could hear the servants getting ready for bed and not long after her father would also retire.

She had dressed in what she had affectionately named her explorer attire, a thick black cloak with a dirty and tattered hem, complete with a heavy, draping hood, and knee-high, lace-up rubber boots, perfect for the drippy wet tunnels of the Forbiddens.

Every time she tied the last knot on those boots and lowered the black hood over her head, she became someone else. A giddy energy awoke inside her and she didn't have to be a lost, little princess anymore. This person could rise above the drudgeries the day consisted of, could ride the wings of the darkness and not fear them. She could pretend she had the ability locked down deep inside her to go beyond the shadows and was only searching for the very thing that would awaken that slumbering potential.

But now as she was forced to wait, she sat at her desk, resting her cheek on a fist and spinning a perfectly round, perfectly smooth stone from the Forbiddens on the desk. This gradually devolved to laying her head on the desk with an arm for a pillow and mindlessly flicking the rock about the surface of the desk, until she nearly fell asleep. But just as her patience was running out, the moment she was waiting for came. The echoing clattering of the Palace slowed until, finally, it fell.

Silence. Thick silence.

She popped her head up and listened a few more minutes just for safety. Not a sound could be heard except for the distant and pleasant chime of the city bell calling ten times. Rubbing the sleep from her eyes, she pulled the black hood over her wild hair, the skittering of her heart returning at once, picked up her lantern, and slipped out into the darkness.

She didn't light the lantern. She wasn't supposed to be out at this time, no one was. So she skulked, using her memory and sense of touch to get around, and snatched something from the kitchen to convince her stomach to stop growling.

She hated the dark so much. Somehow she felt even more confined when the shadows pressed in and her imagination, contrarily, was set loose, conjuring shapes for all sorts of fears in the secretive places of the dark. The only good that could have come from the darkness would have been the concealing of the horrifying images of the watchers, but their dark effigies stayed illuminated by torches all through the dark night.

Kiara shut her eyes as she ran past their statues, their shadow exaggerated features glaring at her to get back inside. Her cape billowed behind her, riding the musty air like a bat in flight.

Up ahead, the bloomy outer glow of a lantern shown from around the side of a building. As she approached, she heard the squeak of leather boots as the guard turned to pace the other way.

Kiara knew a path around all the night guards, but she lingered on the outskirts of their lights whenever she needed to catch her breath, regain her bearings, or just take a respite from the darkness.

She watched the guard, the warm glow of the lantern illuminating kind features. He looked like an honest man, probably had a beautiful wife and a little girl that favored him back home. She pictured the blued-eyed, little girl waiting with baited breath every day for her daddy to wake up so he could play with her before he had to go to work again. Maybe he took the job for her and not because he actually believed everyone should be held prisoner in their own houses after curfew.[1]

Yes . . . Kiara chose to believe. *He did it for her.*

Braving the dark once again, Kiara pressed on until she was only one guard away from being safely hidden in the Forbiddens. The entrance loomed like a great mouth of some terrible beast, the bumpy, wet throat steadily swallowed in darkness. But, at the moment, a guard paced much too close to sneak by. Kiara looked around. No other guards could be seen, so, kneeling down, she wrapped her hand around the first, sizable rock she felt and whipped it as far as she could away from the entrance. She watched in the shadows as the guard's ears pricked up. He stretched the lantern as far as he could and, finally, took the bait.

"Reginald?" he called softly for a fellow guard. Nothing and no one answered.

Kiara smirked. *Works every time.*

Post unguarded, Kiara slipped in through the toothy entrance, vanishing into the throat. She made her way deeper inside to where she could safely light her lantern and in that moment of fumbling blindly to get even the simplest light going, she sat in complete and total darkness. Her heart raced as she tried to light the lantern quicker than it took her head to call in the monsters. She took care not to drop her strikers like the countless times before. The familiar scrip-scrape echoed through the cavern as the sparks exploded in the air. Blooming to life, the little flame took to the wick and stilled her shivers.

She gathered up the lantern, planning for a stop at her hideaway. She counted the stalagmites when she got close and located the entrance, more accurately described as a crack, seemingly just a narrow fissure leading to more darkness. Turning herself sideways, she slipped inside.

Any remaining fears died away in the comfort of that room so completely, she didn't even bother lighting any more lamps. She walked straight to the wall where she had drawn a chalky map of her explored tunnels with pieces of limestone, far from accurate, but it did the job.

---

1. Caverna's curfew was a strict ten o'clock call for all lights out and all persons (except the night watchmen) indoors.

She studied the paths and obstacles, trying to contemplate her next move.

Next move . . . She tapped her chin. *What next move?*

Looking at her makeshift map, she had a rude realization of how many holes her plan had.

What was I thinking? she scolded herself. *Mother had never stepped foot in the Forbiddens. What am I going to find here?* Her eyes flitted over the map. *But then . . . what if these dark tunnels lead to light? What if there is a passage that no one knows about? I don't have to get out the same way Mom did. I just have to get out.*

Kiara knew if she wanted to have any success at all, she would have to search out the tunnels she'd never once explored before. Her eyes wandered to one of the chalky question marks scraped on the stone just beyond the mapped tunnels, denoting a place where there was a risk of stumbling into the Void.

"There is no Void," she told herself as her hands began to shake. "The unknown does not have to mean nothing." She gripped the handle of the lantern with a firm fist. "And I will be the one to prove it."

She left her hideaway, using the map in her mind until she ran straight off the edge and found a tunnel she had never seen before. The entrance yawned wide as if beckoning her to get lost. But Kiara refused to believe that. Somehow she had always found her way back. Tonight would be no different. Swallowing down her fear, she followed it into the dark.

Onward she marched farther and further, darker and deeper. She scoured the caverns, investigating every crawlspace. She chased the echoes of her own footfalls and the drip of the roof stalactites, wherever they led her.

Kiara splashed her rubber boots through streams and puddles, soaking the hem of her cloak and dress, but as she continued to choose which tunnel to follow with nothing more than a "feeling" to guide her and inched through compact crawlspaces she didn't know, her lantern fell lower and lower, until it just hung limply at her side. Doubt started to creep up behind her like an unknown stalker in the dark, making her question if she could even find her way back to Caverna, let alone a way out. It hadn't mattered much before. In her own naive way she didn't see the need to know the way back if she, in fact, found a way out. But now she was forced to deal with the reality that there may not be a way out . . . at least, not this way.

Kiara tried not to dwell on it, focusing all her will power on picking the right tunnels, but the passage ran straight and narrow for so long, she lost track, wondering what time it was back in Caverna, and realizing she hadn't heard the bells for some time.

I must be too far in to even hear them, she thought. *Is it the same time out here even though the chimes don't reach? What proves it's any time at all?*

That gave her a shiver and thoughts of the Void crept into her mind. She feared she had passed into it without knowing, and all at once her heartbeat far exceeded speeds once considered racing fast.

But I still have my reason. Trying to prove it to herself, she looked up, then down. T*hat's right . . . right?*

She looked left, then right, then— *SMACK!* she ran straight into a great obstruction in the middle of the tunnel, the clattering of metal resounding off the stone as her lamp fell to the ground. Kiara rubbed her shoulder. With the collision having knocked some sense into her, she felt a little more than stupid.

The fallen lantern cast her own shadow like a cloaked giant on the stone obstacle as she tried to search out a way around it, but to her horror she discovered it wasn't a mere obstruction, but a full passage, airtight cave-in.

A dead end.

"No!" She protested, throwing defiant fists on the rock face. "You can't shut me out! I will get out of here! I will . . ." Her words crumbled away like brittle stone in her throat.

Any last shreds of hope were snuffed in the face of this immovable obstacle. Always she came to an end. Always she had no power to do anything about it.

Kiara crumbled to the ground, forehead against the wall. Her lower lip trembled as her eyes welled with tears. She couldn't believe she had allowed herself such foolish hope. She really thought she could leave, but now she would die here, of starvation, or worse, some disgusting blind beast would hunt her down, relying purely on its four remaining senses, sharpened by a life in the dark.

She tried to dispel the thoughts, but she had nothing better to replace them with, so they kept finding their way back in. A violent shaking started in her hands and spread through her body, until she couldn't bear it anymore. Attempting to stand, she had to at least try to find her way back.

Fear jolted through her like a shock wave as something

grabbed her from behind. Her mind conjured up horrible things in that split second. The beast had grabbed her, its scales flaking off in decay. Blood red, sightless eyes, burning in the lamp light, glared above an open mouth, ready to eat her with razor sharp, blood stained teeth. The beast had a surprisingly soft hand over her mouth, but Kiara managed to let out a high, muffled squeal before, she could only assume, it would sink its fangs into her neck.

Chapter Nine

Strange Meetings

"You're a girl!" The monster said in a not so monstrous voice, flinging his arms wide to let her go.

A split second of freedom was all it took for Kiara to whip around, new fire in her veins. "And that's supposed to mean what exactly? What did you plan to do if I wasn't?"

"I . . . I mean—"

Kiara didn't let him finish. "How dare you! You scared me half to death!"

Clearly upset, the boy's voice raised a decimal. "I'm sorry! I really am. But when I saw you, I didn't know what to do. You see, I was gonna leave, honest! Without you even knowing I was there, but then you started to stand up and I-I panicked, okay?" he said sheepishly. "I'm really sorry. I didn't mean to scare you."

When Kiara realized he was just defending himself and thought of what she would do in the same situation, her anger fizzled and then died. She slumped to the ground with her back against the caved-in passage.

"You were just scared too?"

The boy nodded. His mop of dirty, black curls hung in a pair of honest, blue eyes, his face, hands, and patched, old clothes absolutely filthy, streaked with dirt and coal dust. With an unconscious thought, Kiara wondered if he might stink if she got too close.

"I don't often see others in the tunnels and never are the faces very kind," he explained.

"Yes . . . I guess . . . I thought I was the only one."

Standing just far enough away to prove he trusted strangers just as little as her, he shrugged. "There are a few others, like myself, but most are bumbling drunks who have no idea what they're doing here anyway. You know, the Forbiddens are not the nicest place to hang around."

"Yes, well, neither is the city," Kiara replied, and the boy, if he had any objections, didn't say them.

She let out a puff of angry air that was supposed to be a laugh. "The truth is, I'm lost. And I came here looking for something I'm not even certain exists or not." So used to floating like an apparition through life, Kiara didn't really think about the consequences of her words or how wholeheartedly she might regret them, but it'd be no use to try and keep them in either. And what did she stand to lose? . . . If she was gonna die here.

"But I just have to get out of here!" she continued. "I can't stop reaching beyond the darkness, because maybe, *just maybe,* one day my hand will find something I couldn't see before. I have to believe this is not all there is, that the world is more than shadows and pain . . . or, at least, I did. Because here I am . . . things look as bleak as ever. How can anyone escape this darkness?" Her voice lowered close to a whisper. "I feel so helpless and alone . . ."

"I know." The boy, also sitting now, spoke up when she fell silent. Kiara almost forgot all about him, by now, pretty much just talking at herself.

"What?" she asked.

"You said you feel helpless and alone. Well, I know how you feel," he replied.

Kiara had no words. *I know how you feel.* She had never heard anyone say that before, and immediately it tried to grow its grounding roots into her soul, but a wave of flames burned them first, at the thought that this stranger could just so easily assume he knew her pain.

Her next words broadcasted that mix of feelings with her uncertain tone. "No one's ever said that to me before."

"Well, I mean, does the king really expect us to believe this is it? And yet . . . there's not much reason to believe otherwise."

Maybe he did understand. And maybe it was all the thoughts of life or death and the coming to grips with her fate that gave his words such an effect on her, but a giddy sense of subtle joy rushed through her nerves hearing him say it, all the same.

"That's dangerous talk," she said, though her dry tone said she didn't care.

"So I've heard, but— Wait . . ." As he thought on her last words, the boy realized he'd heard her voice before. He inched closer, shining the light of his lantern on her face, and sweeping his sooty, black curls out of his eyes.

Kiara leaned away from him, unsure of the way he studied her face. Then realization dawned in his eyes.

"PRINCESS!" he exclaimed.

Relieved and annoyed, Kiara rolled her eyes. "Ugh! Don't call me that." But then she shot to her feet. "Oh no!" All that she had said came back to her at once. "My father's going to kill me . . ." she whispered. "Please, you can't speak this to a soul! I'll give you anything. How much do you want? Fifty Arums?[1] A hundred?" She threw the bribes out faster than she could think.

"Whoa! I don't want your money," he said.

"Then what do you want?" she asked, starting to panic.

"Nothing. I don't want anything." He put a finger to his lips. "I won't say a word."

She sighed and looked at him uncertainly. "Do you mean it?"

"Of course. Who would believe me anyway?"

Kiara gave a soft laugh. "Good point."

She searched his innocent blue eyes. A small scar on his left lid gave the eye a vaguely sleepy quality, and set a nagging feeling in her gut that their paths had crossed before. "I feel like I've seen you before. What's your name?"

"Hadyn."

"Mmhh. I can't place my finger on it. Well, Hadyn, I owe you."

"Not really," he argued and decided not to ask why in Caverna the princess was in the Forbiddens all by herself, in the first place.

Before Kiara could insist, a thought shot through her mind out of absolutely nowhere.

"The riddle . . . I didn't read the riddle!" she muttered under her breath. She wanted to kick herself for forgetting, when it could have been helping her all this time.

"What?" Hadyn asked, clearly confused.

When her roving eyes finally settled on him, she looked through him a moment, then gave her simple reply. "I have to go."

She started to run back up the tunnel, but Hadyn caught her by the arm to stop her. "Wait! I thought—"

"Unhand me!" Kiara demanded.

---

1. Gold coins valued as the greatest form of Caverna's currency

Startled and embarrassed, he quickly dropped her arm, his cheeks flaring red. “Uh, I thought . . . I thought you were lost.”

Now he wasn’t the only one feeling foolish. “Oh!” she moaned, casting her eyes to the floor. “You just had to remind me.” She felt a familiar dread start a trembling in her core when she thought again of never finding her way out of these dark tunnels, the thought never having occurred to her that Hadyn could know the way out, or that he would help her even if he did.

He saw the hopelessness etched on her face. “Actually, you are in luck, Pri— Err, if you don’t want to be called Princess, what should I call you?”

Kiara fought a smile. “Just Kiara’s fine.”

“Just Kiara,” he repeated with a smile of his own. He had a shy, sweet smile that Kiara couldn’t help but notice, she liked very much. “Well, Kiara, you’re in luck! This tunnel just so happened to be my tunnel of choice. In fact, just beyond this point–” He swept a hand toward the cave-in and gasped. He gaped at the crumbled in passage as if his grandma lived on the other side and he just realized she was now trapped under hundreds of pounds of solid rock. “No, no, no! This can’t be real! Not another.”

He ran up to the rocks, pushing on pieces here and there as if he could find a way to get it to move. Kiara walked up beside him, taking notice of his height for the first time. He was quite tall, but she was quite small, all things considered, and . . . he didn’t smell the best after all.

“I know,” Kiara observed, staring up at the rocks piled all the way to the ceiling. “Isn’t it odd how many there are now? My mother always talked about how the shakes and tremors[1] came more often every year. I never noticed the way she did, but how strange is it now that we see so many more cave-ins compared to years ago?” She looked to him for a reply, but he seemed too distraught to care.

Then, as if conjured up by her musing, the ground beneath them rumbled with a low baritone, like the groan of a sleeping beast, traveling up their spines and rattling their teeth. Rock dust fell on their heads and they exchanged uncertain looks. Then, as it passed, a smile curled on Kiara’s lips.

---

1. Occasional tremors in the caves often resulted in minor cave-ins (mostly in the Forbiddens) but a continual increase in frequency and violence has caused more and more, some even in town. Nothing to worry about, of course.

"*Whoa*." Her eyes flared with something like mischief.

Hadyn turned back to the cave-in.

"So . . . what *is* beyond this point?" Kiara asked.

"Nothing now." He glared at the blockade.

"Well, that's not true. Just because you can't get to it doesn't mean it isn't there."

Hadyn shook his head. "No. I didn't mean—" he started, but turned up unexpectedly tongue-tied.

Kiara blinked at him, eyes wandering to a small pick head jutting out the top of a pack slung on his back. The pack sagged with some weight and all at once the pieces fell together.

"I don't believe it! That's what you're doing here! You're a minor!"

"You don't know what you're talking about." He brushed her off, still looking for a weak spot in the rock pile.

"Uh-huh? And what's in the bag?" she asked, with a curious head cock as she leaned around him.

He turned so she faced him again.

"What? Scared a princess is gonna rob ya'? Please. As if I don't have more than enough already."

He sighed, dropping the straps off his shoulders. He held the pack out to her while she grabbed up her light and peered in. Aside from the pick and a few other tools the whole bag was full of crystals stuck in chunks of rock and stone, twinkling and flashing the firelight straight back into her eyes.

"Glittering magic!" she breathed. "Where did you get all those?"

Not expecting such a reaction, Hadyn couldn't help but smile. "All over. It's taken me months to get this many."

"Amazing!"

"Yeah, they'll fetch a fine price that's for certain."

"Price? But gemstones are forbidden!"

"Yes . . . they are." He pulled the drawstring on the bag and snatched it away.

"No, no! I won't tell. I collect them myself."

He side-eyed her, returning to the cave-in.

"But how do you plan to sell them . . . Unless . . ." Kiara couldn't believe her own realization. "On the Stygian Market!"[1]

---

*1. The alleged black marketplace of Caverna, also known as the Styx. A den of misfits, illegal miners, thieves and clansmen.**(see page 119)**Most certainly does not exist.*

"Exactly. Well, not me. Somcone else will do that."

"But the market, it's real?"

"Of course it's real. The Styx has been around longer than you or I have even been alive."

"Incredible! And you've been there?"

He shrugged. "I try to stay clear of that neck of the caverns as best as I can, but, yeah, I've been there a handful of times."

Kiara's eyes were as round and wide as saucers.

"Look, I wouldn't go creating the Styx into some wonderful picture in your mind. There's some dangerous people pulling the strings behind that colorful front, and they're what really matter."

"Very well."

Hadyn picked his lantern off the ground. "Come on, I'll show you the way out of here. Just follow me."

Kiara stared at him and furrowed her brow, wondering why he thought she should trust him so easily.

He stood straighter and with a silly flourish of his hand said, "I give you my word, I will guide you back to Caverna. I will not harm you or mislead you."

A smile twitched on the lips she so stubbornly tried to keep turned down in a frown. She wanted to trust him, really she did. And did she even have another choice?

"Well . . ." She swallowed. "Okay. Lead the way."

Hadyn started back up the tunnel, returning the collapsed passage to darkness. Kiara followed cautiously behind, but she noticed he always matched her pace, however slow she walked, attentive to not let her fall behind, until finally she walked next to him.

"You know," she ventured, "you should really collect, instead of sell."

"Huh?"

"The gemstones, I mean. It's loads of fun."

"Oh. I do. When I can."

"When you can?"

"I gotta reach a quota, alright?"

Kiara backed off, knowing when she had stepped too far. "I'm sorry. I didn't mean to pry."

He softened then. "It's alright. I actually enjoy it a lot. I wouldn't ever sell them, but it's . . . Well it's complicated."

Kiara wanted to ask why so badly, it could have been the death of her, but she kept her mouth shut.

"I've managed to save and collect at least one of each kind that I know of," he continued. "Except for one crystal . . . It has always eluded me."

"And which is that?"

"Alexandrite.[1] You heard of it?"

"Why, of course! A very beautiful stone and quite rare if I'm not mistaken."

"*Extremely.*" Hadyn confirmed. "I've never seen it with my own eyes, but I've heard tales that the crystal has the power to lead you out of darkness. That candlelight isn't enough, and somewhere out there, there's a light so powerful it actually draws the crystal, which is somehow tethered to it since
the day it was forged. And if you hold it in your hand, it will guide you to where it longs to go."

Kiara hung on his every word, transfixed by the legend.

He noticed. "Course, I don't believe stuff like that. I just think the thought is kind of . . . Well . . . beautiful."

She smiled. "Me too."

After that, Hadyn turned down tunnel after tunnel, lantern wagging ahead in his outstretched fist. He seemed concentrated at the most, but never hesitated, never second guessed. Either he had a profoundly great sense of direction or had been here so many times, he'd have to be struck with a sudden case of amnesia to get lost. Then Kiara remembered something he said about these tunnels that made her curious and thought it'd be a good time to ask, feeling the silence grow as uncomfortable as a wet blanket around her shoulders. Make that a sticky wet blanket. Nobody wants that.

"So . . . what made you stop coming here?" she asked. "You sure know these tunnels well enough."

"What?"

"You said this just so *happened* to be your tunnel of choice. As in, used to?"

"Oh . . . caught that, did you? Well, I didn't stop coming to the Forbiddens. I can't really. I just don't go as deep as I used to."

"Oh? So why did you stop coming here? To *these* tunnels?"

He scratched the back of his head awkwardly. "Aww, silly reasons."

That answer aided in satiating the appetite of her curiosity about as well as a cracker. "Like what?" she prodded gently.

---

1. A dramatically pleochroic, precious, and rare stone found most in Brazil.

Hadyn gave her a sideways glance, surprised by her boldness. Sighing, he said reluctantly, “Ah . . . I don’t know. Fear?”

“Fear of what?” She held his gaze then and for a moment he didn’t know what to say or how to look at those steady eyes, inquisitive, yet with the purest intentions. So green and in the firelight they seemed to sparkle like emeralds. He’d heard people talk of the Red Princess and her strange green eyes, but had never stood so close before to determine the color for himself. And now that he did and those eyes were fixed on him, he didn’t know if his tongue could call them anything at all, but certainly not strange.

Just in time, he remembered it was his turn to speak. He made a few sounds in attempt to form a sentence, though none of it could be considered words, and tried to stuff his free hand in his pocket, but when that didn’t work, scratched the back of his head again. Kiara waited patiently.

“I guess it was this entire place,” he conceded. “I don’t know why, but I let myself fall into believing the lies everyone says about it.”

Kiara liked that he said why instead of how. “Well, that’s not so silly. Wait. Do you believe in the watchers?”

“I mean, sorta. Why do you ask? Don’t you?”

“No. Have *you* ever seen one? They’re supposed to live here, aren’t they?”

Hadyn contemplated that, not that he hadn’t before, but it was different now, hearing it from the princess’ own mouth.

“But don’t think the very mention of their name won’t yet strike fear into my heart,” Kiara added, trying not to shiver the way she knew she would.

“So . . .” He squinted skeptically. “Do you not believe in Fleard?”

“Ha! No.” She shook her head. “And that one I’m certain about. Fleard is just another thing, like the watchers made up to scare us, to keep us in line.”

He paused before asking his next question. “So where do all our resources come from?”

“I haven’t exactly figured that out yet . . . But,” she held up a finger, “I do know, they are *not* miraculously supplied by Fleard.”

Hadyn fell silent. He would have never guessed Caverna’s own princess didn’t believe in the religion the city was built on.

Kiara couldn’t have cared less to take that subject any further. Dropping it, she asked, “So, what made you start coming here again?"

He laughed. A nervous laugh. Even in the dim light of their lanterns Kiara could see his cheeks turning red.

"Um . . . you," he finally said.

"Me?" Kiara stopped in her tracks, mystified.

"Well, yeah. I was there while you were talking to little Abigail on Terminal Avenue today. You said, 'don't let fear stop you from fighting for your hope.' " He shrugged. "I guess, it just got me thinking and I decided to come out here tonight for old times sake to search the caverns."

"Terminal Avenue! That's where I recognized you from!" Kiara said. "I saw you there! You were carrying something for your grandmother."

"Uh, I don't have any family," Hadyn said sadly. "She's just a friend."

Kiara felt her face grow red, wishing she could take back the words. "Oh. I'm sorry."

"It's okay," he said and sounded like he really meant it. "My parents died when I was really young."

She wrung her hands, trying to pick her next words carefully. "You know, I'd never been there before yesterday. I had no idea that—"

"That you had a living, stinking, garbage right out your back door? Hmm." He sniffed. "Why doesn't that surprise me?"

Kiara could have chomped down on her own tongue before she even said a word and still it wouldn't have hurt as bad.

"I'm sorry," Hadyn said. "I shouldn't have said that. I'm just used to it, I guess. I've lived at the old orphanage most my life. And before that, well, it wasn't like things were fine livin'. You know, the orphanage says they don't have the time or the funds to keep boys over sixteen. So tomorrow I'll be out on my own. How's that for birthday celebrations?" he remarked with sarcastic joy.

Kiara felt the hot fire of indignation stoke to life once again. Her feet stopped beneath her once more. "They'll turn you to the streets?"

Hadyn turned to her, but didn't say a word.

"But that's so cruel! How could they be so *cold*?"

"Yeah, that's life in the slums for you. I'm surprised they keep us as long as they do . . . Well, some of us," he said, detached, like he just didn't care anymore. "And you're wrong if you think I haven't been counting down the days till I get to leave that prison.

Ever since the day I got there, it's been hell. I can't say I'm sad to leave."

"Will they not place you under a mentor of sorts for an apprenticeship?"

"Mentor?" He struggled not to laugh. "You're kidding, right?"

Kiara's frown didn't budge. "Why would I do that? This is not a laughing matter."

"Oh . . . Well then, no. We're lucky if they don't sell us as slaves or something."

"Slaves?" Kiara's voice was sharp with alarm.

"It's either that or . . . I really have no clue what."

"What do you mean?"

"It's nothing really. Then again . . ."

"What!" she pressed.

"It's just sometimes the masters come to get a kid. And after he's gone . . . he's just gone. Never to be seen again."

"You mean he got adopted."

"No." he shook his head. "It's not like that. When a boy gets adopted, he has several meetings with the adults beforehand. But when this happens, they come quiet, call out a kid, and leave without a word. The boys at the orphanage call it 'snatched,' just like bread from a bakery window."

Set in a face of sheet white, Kiara's wide eyes locked him in a look of horror, her mind racing with the unexplained disappearance of her own dear friend.

"Oh, but don't worry about me, though." He waved a hand. "I'm too old now. For whatever reason, they only take the younger ones. Besides, as soon as I get my last meal and free night, I'm out of there. I'll be gone before the lamplighters are up. It's not like there's anybody who cares. I'll slip away and disappear . . . like I never even existed."

Kiara felt something inside her crack. Those words he waffled out so nonchalantly, hit her like a ton of bricks. They actually hurt.

"But," she blinked, "what will you do?"

He gave her a lopsided grin. "What won't I do? Tomorrow I'm free. I could even live here!"

"In the Forbiddens?"

He shrugged. "Why not?"

"Well they're hardly a place to live."

"Good as any home I've ever had."

Kiara didn't know what to say. He acted like he didn't care, but he didn't fool her. She could see past the act, because it felt like looking in a mirror. And he was scared, almost as if he was running from something.

"I don't believe you'll just live out here like a nobody," Kiara said. "Look at everything you've already survived. I think you could really make something of your life."

"Yeah?"

She smiled and nodded.

"Well, that's kind of you to say."

They were silent for a while, but Kiara couldn't stop thinking about how her words, spoken out of the rashness of unchecked feelings, could actually empower someone, actually affect someone.

"I really gave you courage again?" she asked.

"Well, I wouldn't say courage. But I never had much of that to begin with. Let's call it . . . hope."

Kiara's eyes wandered to the ground. "I don't have courage either . . . but, like you, I can come here almost every night. Somehow I think I feel safer here than in Caverna." Hadyn nodded in agreement. "To tell you the truth, I don't know if *I* believe what I said to that little girl . . . Life is so cold."

"I believe there is still warmth yet to be found."

She looked at him, a faint smile on her face. He smiled back and for a moment Kiara remained in a state of pleasant shock that she had met someone she wasn't irritated or disgusted with after talking with them.

"Come on," he said. "The exit is just around this bend."

When the wide open mouth of the Forbiddens shifted into view and Kiara could make out the distant specks of light from the night guards' torches, she felt a tension she didn't even know she was holding, melt from her shoulders for the first time since getting lost. Somehow they were back at the edge of town without having to crawl through a single cramped tunnel. And then there was the disappointment, crawling up from nowhere at all and pulling her spirits low.

"Huh . . . Already?"

"Yep. I told you, I know these tunnels like the back of my hand. You know, if we're counting, you double owe me now."

Kiara laughed softly. "Thank you, for getting me back."

"It was really nothing," he said, attempting to brush it off.

"No. You could have left me there, easy. You could have left me to battle the monsters in my head."

"Monsters in your head, huh? You've got those too?" He laughed and then with that sweet smile again, before he turned and went his own way, he said kindly, "I wouldn't do that."

Chapter Ten

BRAVERY

Kiara wandered back to the palace cavern, alluding the guard's with little more conscious effort than shooing a fly. She had left her mind back in the Forbiddens, pondering now with some curiosity why Hadyn had told her so much. But though he seemed to trust her, there were things he wouldn't say. Maybe because she accidentally confided in him, he knew she wouldn't say anything. She thought she might never know, but when his sweet grin found its way into her mind, she couldn't ignore a strange feeling that she had a new friend. And one who had been inside the Styx, no less. What chances! Just yesterday, she had only ever heard of them in words of myth, a legend, and now she had met someone who had seen them with his own eyes.

Here she was going to a place to disappear, to leave, and he found her, he saw her, before she was Princess Kiara or a strange red-headed girl, he really saw her, and listened. Just like a friend.

A friend . . . When was the last time she could say that?

Placing a hand on the door to the palace, she shook her head of the thoughts. Her gut twisted in embarrassment over the stupidity of it all, as if her thoughts had been proclaimed to the whole of Caverna. Really, after how many years she'd explored the Forbiddens and never come upon another soul, when was she bound to ever see him again?

All that faded to forgotten places for the moment as she stepped into her room, her mother's note and the unread riddle becoming the only thing on her mind.

She sat herself on her bed with the note in one hand and a nub of burnt down candle in the other. She kept the candle at bay, fearing that she would destroy this precious gift if she let the flame get too close. But as she sucked a breath through her teeth and flipped the note over, the darkness seemed to tighten like a noose about her sight, forcing her to bring the candle nearer. Kiara scanned the page, mostly plain aside from stains and a small area in the middle where the riddle was written, each character a simple work of art.

> *Darkness is closer than you think. In the heart of it and tragedy you will find your key and the missing piece to a dark story.*

Kiara sputtered. "What?" she cried and coughed a manic laugh. "What is that even supposed to mean! I'm *surrounded* by darkness. If it's any closer than I think . . . Oh, Mum, what's the point? This is wearing on my soul. No more darkness, please! I need light!"

She thought this would give her answers, and finally shed some light on the shadows, but all it had to say was more rubbish about darkness? What was her mother thinking?

Flopping back on her bed, she whimpered, "Oh, will I ever be free?"

Kiara stiffened at the sound of footsteps in the hall and threw the letter under her sheets. She froze, thinking in a panic of what she could do.

Lucida clopped down the hall, like the living dead, droopy lids begging for more sleep.

As well as Kiara's loyal and favorite servant, Lucida also served as the princess' "guard," though not a terribly good one, considering she was afraid of her own shadow. Kiara had no idea why Cida had been picked to be the only servant with quarters close enough to come to her aid in the night, but she also never argued it.

Kiara's own father was long since finished with checking on her whenever she cried out from her frequent nightmares. Lucida, too, had become used to Kiara's interrupted sleep patterns and usually waited for further noises before coming to check on her. But tonight didn't sound like nightmares. The Miss was just so worked up and sounded to be shouting at someone. Stranger still, now standing in the hallway, everything had fallen into an abrupt quiet.

Pausing with a yawn, Lucida gave two soft knocks on Kiara's door before warily creaking it open. Stepping in the room, she found her fast asleep, but a smoky scent hung in the air, like a recently snuffed flame. No longer drowsy, Cida's mind jolted fully awake, and suddenly she wondered if *she* had been dreaming.

"Miss?" Lucida whispered, but Kiara didn't stir. Never had she woken the princess up before, but Kiara had never remained asleep when she came in either.

She walked to the bedside and gently shook her shoulder. "Miss, wake up."

Kiara mumbled a very convincing, "What?" and groggily sat up.

Lucida's face registered deep confusion. "I-I heard yellin', Miss."

"Yelling?" Kiara scratched her head.

Lucida waited and blinked.

"Oh!" she seemed to recall. "I had another one of those horrendous dreams. Must have shouted in my sleep," Kiara tried, but Lucida didn't look quite at ease.

"It wasn't the usual nightmare screams," Lucida said. "You . . . You sounded angry. Like you were yelling at someone."

Kiara thought she would have to tell her, but then she had an idea, knowing exactly just how terribly easy of a person Lucida was to frighten.

"Hmmm . . ." she mused as if trying to recall yelling at anyone. "Nope, it was a dream. Would you mind if I told you?"

The excuses flooded out, right on cue. "Oh are you sure? I really do have to get up in a few hours. I have lots to do in the morning. I would be so obliged if I could go to my quarters."

"Very well," Kiara said. "Though it was truly thrilling!"

Kiara could taste the feigning words on her tongue like over steeped tea. She pretended because it was easier than honesty, but also because sometimes she didn't even feel like she knew who the honest parts of herself were. She hated doing it. To say she even tolerated the nightmares was like a dog licking the hand that abused it— it just wasn't right . . . But it got Lucida to leave and very swiftly.

Kiara let out a breath like her lungs had sprung a leak and flopped back down on her pillow. She stared numbly up into the darkness. Always darkness . . . Closing her eyes, she squeezed them tight enough to see sparks, little flashes of light, and desperately tried to imagine something more substantial, but she was spent and she just wanted to sleep, not that sleep was always permitted, no matter how coveted.

She opened her eyes and alas, thick blackness shrouded her sight, the kind of blackness that when she let her mind run, it seemed figures materialized out of it, hideous things like the watchers with tattered and torn wings, flying close enough to almost touch and then zooming away, taunting her, and filling her body to the brim with horrible fear. She just wanted to run, to someplace where they couldn't find her, but everywhere she went they were there, just like the darkness.

Instead of continuing to choke on the black air, (not exactly looking forward to having that nightmare twice) Kiara decided she could at least light a lantern to hold the shadows at bay. She sat up, fumbling blindly for the lantern by her bed, and grabbing up her strikers, she struck them together until the sparks took to the wick and grew into a bright, flickering flame. A soft smile played on her lips as the warmth of the glow splashed on her face. But, as she sat back again, Kiara's blood ran cold. There, beyond the light, she could just make out an inky shape. Towering over her in the dark was a dreadful wraith, awaiting to take her soul to the deepest, coldest depths of this prison! Kiara let out a piercing shriek. She shrunk from the sight, legs pushing her across the bed until there was no bed left. Tumbling, she hit the hard stone with a thud. She would have moaned if she wasn't so afraid. Her elbow felt like it could have shattered and every place of impact throbbed with continuous pain. For a moment, she just laid there, paralyzed, her panic ravaged nerves expecting the wraith at any moment, and her more reasonable mind already growing suspicious of what was really at hand. When a moment passed and nothing happened, she mustered just enough courage to take another look. Raising her trembling head an inch at a time, she peered her wide eyes over the bed, paused, and let out a huff. She could have kicked herself.

The light on the nightstand illuminated a not so dreadful, unquestionably benign cloak. Kiara remembered now, hanging it up on the hook before sitting down to read the riddle.

"I have got to stop doing that!" she chided herself.

The sound of footsteps, quicker this time, came back up the hall, and Kiara had no time or the mind to do anything about it.

The door flew open without a knock. "What is it now, Miss? Don't tell me you've already fallen back to sleep!" Lucida examined Kiara's empty bed.". . . Miss?"

"Down here," Kiara groaned, raising a limp hand.

Lucida gasped as she saw her slumped on the ground.

"Princess!" Kiara gave her a look. "I mean, Miss!"

Lucida knew Kiara's little pet peeve, but she had told her, "It just don't feel right princess, it's not respectful. But I'll settle on miss, thank you." She even called her missy when she was feeling snarky.

"What are you doing down *there*, Miss?"

"I . . ." Kiara wanted to blame it on another nightmare, but Cida was right, there was no possible way she could have fallen asleep yet. "I . . ." she mentally reached to the cavern's roof for an excuse, but she gave up, slumping further, and confessed. "After you left, I was frightened so I lit a lamp. In the shadows, I could see a dark figure, it startled me and I fell off my bed."

Lucida looked about the room, perturbed herself by the statement. "Startled is an understatement."

"Alright, so it scared the wits out of me. But when I got a hold on my imagination and looked again it was only," Kiara paused, not wanting to admit it, ". . . my cloak."

"Oh, Miss." Lucida's smile blossomed with relief and gentle amusement.

"Go ahead and laugh. I know you want to. I'm a complete fool!"

"Now, Miss, don't be so cruel to yourself. It happens to me all the time. When I was your age the slightest noise in the dark would send me cowering under my blankets. Who am I fooling? It still does."

Kiara laughed softly.

Lucida smiled too, but she had more to say. "Would you . . . Would you like to know what helps me?"

Kiara gave a small nod.

"Alright. Come with me." Lucida offered her a firm but gentle hand and helped her off the ground with surprising strength. She grabbed the lantern and led Kiara down the hall, never once letting go.

They came to a room that felt quite open and smelled of stale bread and old lard. Lucida started to light a few more candles, and as the room grew brighter, Kiara grew ever more confused, as hacked up, stained countertops appeared and ladles and spoons were revealed, hanging from hooks.

"Why are we in the kitchen?" Kiara raised a brow.

"This is where I go when I'm scared," Lucida said, simply. "I come here and I think."

Still shuffling about the room, Lucida filled a pair of cups with water and handed one to Kiara. She sat on a wobbly stool and motioned for Kiara to pull another over.

Kiara sat down and wiggled her toes. "So what do you think about?"

"Good things," Cida replied. "Very good things."

"Good things . . ." Kiara nodded with some skepticism.

"Yeah, things I'm thankful for, like blankets and comfort. A belly full of warm food. My safety. The end of a hard day's work. Clean dishes!"

Kiara snickered. "Clean dishes?"

"Oh, why not? You give it a try now."

"Oh," She looked down at her hands in her lap. "I can't think of anything."

"Sure you can. Just try."

She sighed. "Very well. How about . . . Backlobash and tea?" she asked with a cocked brow.

"There you go! That's a start!"

Kiara still thought it was silly, but she did notice her fear had already left. She tried to think of a few more and came up dry rather quickly, not because there was nothing to think of, but because all she could think of were things she couldn't have.

Her smile faded and her brow scrunched in frustration. "Mother's voice and warm hugs . . . Colors splashed without rules, unfettered hope, light . . . The truth." Her fists clenched. "Why should I think of anything good, when all of it is either kept from me or taken from me?"

Lucida ran a thumb along the rim of her cup in a show of awkward silence.

"I'm sorry, Cida. I just miss her."

"I know you do. I miss my parents too."

Kiara looked at her. She had never even wondered if Cida had parents or not. She had never cared.

"But, what a sad thing it would be if we let our great love for them become our ruin also. Hmm? And they would never want us to hurt this badly over them, if they could help it."

"You're right." Kiara took a small drink, hoping to chase down the lump in her throat. "What else do you think about, Cida?"

Lucida couldn't help but smile, a reminiscent smile like she had an old friend on her mind. "Well, if you're asking . . . Sometimes, on these long nights, when sleep seems like a distant luxury, I plod out here in the dark and there's something about the silence at this time of night, that brings such an acute sense of loneliness. I could be the only person to have ever existed and it would feel no different."

Kiara hung on every word as she managed to so perfectly put her exact feelings into words without ever having to tell Cida one of them.

"And, well, I don't know if it's in spite of that feeling or because of it? But, and I can't seem to help it, I just begin to wonder . . . what else could be out there? Not in the Forbiddens, but really out there, completely beyond the caverns. What marvelous things we're kept from! There has to be something."

Kiara stared at her, trying to hide her disbelief. Not only did she hear this from Hadyn, a boy she'd just met, but now Cida, whom she'd known nearly her whole life. She couldn't have done a sufficient job because Lucida noticed and interpreted her expression as alarm.

"I know we're not supposed to talk of such things, but they can't control what we think too."

"No. It's alright. I– Well, I can't say."

"Right . . ." Cida trailed. "Sometimes I wonder if there's someone watching over us, someone just and righteous. Someone who loves us . . . even in the dark."

Like waking up for the first time, Kiara couldn't believe all the things she never gave Cida credit for. It shamed her to think of how she never acknowledged the ability of another to have these thoughts.

She gave her a sadness tinged smile. "You really think there's a Creator?"

After a short pause, Cida's answer came, simple and confident. "Yes."

Kiara huffed through her nose. "Mother always talked of someone like you just described . . . but how? How can someone just and righteous, throw someone in a prison and let everyone believe they're dead for four years?" Kiara bit her lip. "Oh– I'm sorry. That doesn't mean anything to you."

"It's alright." Cida's eyes were soft. "It doesn't have to."

"So you understand? I mean, how can He leave us all in this dark hole and keep us from all that He's created?"

"I understand . . ." Cida sighed a tired laughed. "Life is a mess and it's so unfair. But to try and say He's not there just because bad things arc, is a different difficulty entirely. Because when you ask Him to take your fear and replace it with courage, and you feel the answer, you feel your bones strengthen," she met Kiara's gaze, eyes wide with ardor, "you'll know He's there and that He has a greater purpose for us than we can see. I might not know His name yet." She snorted. "It certainly isn't Fleard, but that doesn't change the fact that I can feel His presence."

Kiara sighed. "I wish I could see things like you do, Cida."

Knowing that was Kiara's way of being done, Lucida didn't press further.

"So why now?" Kiara asked

Lucida eyed her over her cup as she took a drink. "Hmm?"

"Why did you never tell me this before?"

"Well," Cida cocked her head, "you never seemed to need it before. You've always been so competent. You handle it all so well."

Kiara shook her head. "I just wanted to be brave or at least seem like it." Lucida didn't know what to say. "Well, now you know." Kiara shrugged. "I probably have the least bravery in this whole city."

"Now don't say that, Miss. I don't think bravery can be measured by the way you feel on the inside."

Kiara smiled. "Maybe not."

They sat in silence for a whole minute before Kiara finally spoke again. "Thank you for bringing me here, Cida. I might just sit up and," she winked, "think for a while."

"Don't stay up too late," she said with a wag of her finger.

"I won't."

"Goodnight, Miss." Lucida smiled and went to her room.

As her footsteps faded to nothing, Kiara sat in that profound silence as Cida said she did and watched the soundless dance of the flame on the table next to her. She felt that same loneliness and, for Kiara, this was a familiar thing like a trusty but unpleasant landmark one would see on a daily commute, but instead of thinking of what wonderful things could be out there, or how a loving Creator could be watching over us with His greater plans and what not, all she felt was anger. It was always anger, evinced in the fact that she had long since started to avoid any thoughts about the Creator. To believe He existed only made her sick, but to believe He didn't terrified her and drained her of hope. So why think of any of it at all?

This time though, something was different. The anger still burned with a million frustrations, but there was something else. Guilt maybe? But why? She couldn't pin it down— couldn't face it. Kiara sighed, her head sagging with sleep as her mind drifted to the night's events.

Something about meeting Hadyn seemed special. You don't just stumble upon a meeting like that, but that's exactly what happened.

Maybe Cida is right, Kiara thought. *Maybe the Creator has a plan for everyone, and we're the ones that keep messing it up . . . Maybe . . .*

"Ack!" She rubbed her face, wishing she could forget it all and go to sleep, but the thought of Hadyn wouldn't let her shut off her brain quite yet. She had come to believe very little in the kindness of a human heart, and Cida was about the last person in her life that she would ever describe as sweet.

Until now.

And tomorrow, on his birthday, he would get nothing but a goodbye and a kick out the door. They would throw him out into the wretched streets of the slums like every other sixteen year old, parentless youth.

Some sort of indignant anger flared in her again. Just another thing that she couldn't help but think, as princess, was her responsibility, and yet she wasn't even aware it was happening, all because someone didn't feel obliged to tell her. Well, she knew now, and she no longer had the excuse of ignorance.

Kiara shot to her feet, a plan already taking shape in her mind.

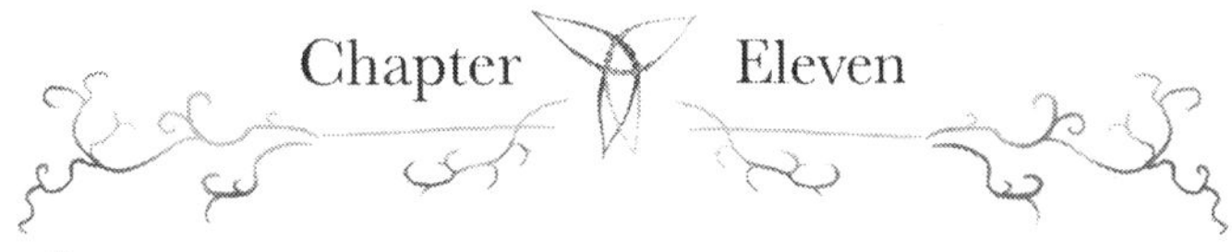

Of Thieves and Tears

Hadyn sat on the featureless floor of a cramped and abandoned storage space, one lamp flickering at his side, casting his shadow of his curly locks and boyish profile on the opposite wall. He ignored the fact that it was well past lights out and everyone else was fast asleep.

This was his secret place, a forgotten place, tucked away in a small, forgotten wing of the orphanage, where only spiders still deemed it habitable and made their own wispy homes of white, threaded silk in every corner and on every shelf ledge. No one but Hadyn used it anymore. They had moved all supplies to places easier to access from the newer wings long ago. And so he came here to be forgotten, like the old, broken broom leaning on the wall. To be alone, truly, and be able to hear himself think.

Kiara . . .

He couldn't seem to shake her green eyes from his mind. The girl he once called princess just wanted to be called by her name. He thought it strange, really, but in some ways he could actually understand. She just wanted people to treat her like everyone else, to look at her for who she was; not what she was born into . . . as did he. Still, their problems couldn't have been more different. She was the princess; he was an orphan scoundrel.

Everything about her was so different from anyone he had ever met, even the way she spoke, he recalled. She had a vague, but distinct, lilt to the beginning and end of most of her sentences he had never heard in anyone else's voice, sweetening some words with something that caught the ears off guards and begged one to listen.

He realized, as he sat in that quiet place, just how different his own impressions of the reclusive Red Princess of Caverna were from the girl named Kiara, he had stumbled upon in the Forbiddens.

Then, an unchecked thought wandered out of its cage, and something in Hadyn wanted to call her his friend, but he shoved the thought away, regarding it only as absurd and selfish. Friendships weren't supposed to cause complications, and that's just what it would do. She didn't deserve her life to be ruined by all of . . . him.

He felt his anger rise up against himself for the idea. *When have I ever needed friends anyway?* he thought, forcing himself to push her from his mind, knowing the chances of ever seeing her again . . .

A muffled crash somewhere down the corridor aided (maybe a little too much) in ripping his thoughts to something else, making him nearly jump out of his skin. It sounded close to the front entrance, and Hadyn's mind immediately jumped to a break-in, someone coming to steal, either from the food supply or the strong-box. The thief couldn't have known the orphanage had about as much food and arums as it did love for homeless boys.

Hadyn shivered. All of Terminal Avenue (because of the countless miscreants peppering it like an aggressive cancer) suffered from a severe case of questionable reputation, but the area the orphanage found itself in was particularly unsavory, the people that gravitated and stuck to the dark tunnels around there, even more so. Chances were, the person in the corridor was not just some innocent kid looking for a warm place and a meal.

He wished he could ignore it. Why risk his neck when the orphanage should handle it anyway? But, as far as he knew, he was the only one awake to hear it, which, in his mind, made it his responsibility. It was no use. He couldn't just sit there, not knowing who or what had made the noise.

Hadyn forced himself to his shaky feet and grabbed up the broken broomstick. *What kind of lowlife steals from homeless kids?*

Hadyn picked up his lantern and had to muster a bit of strength before snuffing it out and plunging himself into darkness. Heart racing now, he gingerly opened the door.

Another noise clamored down the hall, this time closer. Immediately, Hadyn wished he had risked the light, and had to keep telling himself, the stranger spotting him would be much worse than not being able to see the stranger.

Holding the sharp end of the splintered broom outwards like a pike, he drew a deep breath and took several tentative steps down the hall until yet another noise, closer again, stopped him in his tracks. He swallowed hard, though the clumsier the burglar sounded, the less afraid he felt. And even with all the things they had run into, they never made enough racket for anyone sound asleep to hear.

The person must be small, Hadyn thought, and resumed inching forward.

Then, like a bunch of mice padding across a rug, he heard the progression of advancing footsteps. Light, tiny footsteps.

Very small, he thought and suddenly he wondered if they were a kid.

Thinking as fast as he could, Hadyn crouched down and pressed himself against the wall to get out of the stranger's path.

Wrong choice.

The clumsy little thief— er, kid was using the wall to guide themself. He could hear the stranger getting closer as the hands hissed across the surface of the wall, but Hadyn didn't know what else to do. If he ran, they'd hear him. If he stayed, they'd find him. The hissing stopped and then he felt hands on his face. Hadyn froze. So did the stranger.

Kiara shook her head at herself in the darkness. She thought, if she had a parent who cared at all, she deserved a talking to for certain for acting so rashly. But here she was, stumbling around in the dark, until she found a hallway to guide her with some semblance of direction. With minimal to no guards patrolling Terminal Avenue, she was allowed a dim light and a crude, probably out of date map of the tunnels to find her way. But that light had to go out the moment she arrived.

She chided herself under her breath as she ran into yet another clattering, unidentifiable *something*. Usually she could travel so silently, moving about her own palace without a sound. But she tried to cut herself some slack, thinking she wouldn't recognize this place even lit up.

She had wanted nothing more than to bring the light inside, but with a little reason to talk back at her irrational fears of the dark, she could see how that might be a mistake. Though a day might yet come when she would wish her most egregious mistake consisted of bringing a small light to a dark building just to see where she was going.

Kiara didn't even know why she was here anymore. After

leaving the palace for the second time that night, she had stopped off at her hideaway to check for something she thought she just might have, hiding in the heaps of her forbidden treasures, but now as she tripped over her own feet, knowing little more than the floor from the ceiling, she wished she had just put her ridiculous brain to sleep and stayed in her bedroom.

What was I thinking? she questioned herself. *Oh! right! I wasn't.*

Still, she was already here, and she didn't need to find him; she just needed a place to leave the bag where she knew he would find it. So, she went on, holding a small, burlap sack in one hand and feeling the wall with the other.

Once again, she wished she could kill her wild mind, maybe then she'd stop hearing footsteps that weren't hers and stop picturing things that would never exist if the dark wasn't so blinding. But these footsteps didn't sound quiet like the other figments generated by her fears. Usually she pictured footsteps following behind her, and yet these sounded like they were coming straight towards her.

Kiara stopped, but then the other footsteps also stopped. Almost immediately she felt her hands go clammy with a cold sweat as her pulse grew louder in her ears.

Had she really heard that?

No, Kiara thought. *It was probably nothing. It should be nothing.*

Baby steps were all she could manage. The cold stone resumed sliding under her fingertips when— what was that? Hair? A face? Then as it moved just an inch, her fear was confirmed. Kiara felt a scream ripping its way up her throat. She thought she might faint. She took in a breath to fuel the scream, and then, "Don't scream!" came the quiet but pleading whisper.

Kiara jumped back, struggling to process. "Hadyn?"

No answer and then, "Kiara?"

Hearing her own name, spoken by a voice other than her father's angry tone, took her by surprise. She knew she had told him to call her that, but she had never expected him to remember. Even Cida who had known her her whole life was given to lapses.

Fuzzy outlines of words didn't want to come into view just yet, so Kiara merely said again, "Hadyn?"

"Kiara, what are you doing here!" She heard him say, but how was she supposed to reply to that?

She felt a sudden, but still gentle, grip on her hand. Hadyn cringed, thinking of the last time he did that, but whether she didn't mind or was still too shaken to mind, she didn't protest as he led her back to where he left his lantern.

Once there, he let go of her hand to light the wick. Kiara stood alone in the dark again until a little room bloomed to life. Hadyn fiddled with the lantern to get it to hang from a makeshift hook on the wall, made from a twisted piece of metal, possibly a fire poker, as she gazed into the cramped space all aglow with flickering amber light. At once, her fears melted off her tense shoulders and Kiara stepped into the tight room, eyes roving the shelves perfectly cluttered with treasures.

Forbidden treasures.

Various assortments of rocks and gemstones that caught the light by their many facets filled the room and fungus and mushrooms at various stages of drying hung from hooks on the shelves by a bit of string. The exoskeleton of some leggy insect sat here, while just over there the bones of a fish were arranged in a way that Kiara knew was not quite right.

"Is this your hideaway?"

Hadyn turned around with a bit of a start, surprised to see her so close, her expression dreamy as her eyes danced about the room.

He gave her a funny look. "I mean, I guess so."

"It's perfect."

He just stared at her, unsure what to say.

"Oh, except for . . ." Kiara reached for the skeleton on the shelf right of her. "If you just move these bones here to the tail . . ." she said, sliding the delicate pieces with a slender finger. "There!" She smiled at him. "You had it nearly right, really. I'm impressed."

Hadyn narrowed his eyes at the skeleton. "How do you know . . .?"

"Oh, never mind that. What's this?" A long, slender tube of shiny copper reflected the lamp light and caught Kiara's eye. It looked like an overly long whistle, but something had bored six holes in its body and ruined it.

She reached for the curious whistle just as Hadyn snatched it up and threw it behind his back.

"Nothing!" he said. "I mean . . . haha . . . must be one of the Head Master's whistles. I have no idea what it's doing here. Someone must've forgotten it when they cleaned out this closet." He then caught sight of the small sack Kiara carried and seemed to bristle, narrowing his eyes at it. He fixed her with a look. “What are you doing here anyway?”

Kiara felt caught, but she wasn’t just stalling. Her genuine admiration for this place had made her forget, for a moment, how much she wished she had turned around long ago. Everything about her plan looked stupid and foolish now that she actually stood in front of him.

She struggled to find the words. “Well, I thought I’d bring you this.” She held up the sack, but his hard expression remained as solid as a stone. “Because I . . .” she tried to pin down the reason. “Well, because I . . .”

“Because you what? Pity me?” he questioned, his words laced with bitterness.

Kiara’s eyes grew wide. “What? No!” Surprised by how quickly his gentle kindness disappeared and his fuse ran out, her embarrassment deepened as did the red in her cheeks.

“I don’t need your sympathy and charity, Princess.”

Now that got her miffed. “I just wanted you to have something good on your birthday, something to think about besides this dark place.”

“But can you do that for everyone, Kiara?” he asked.

Kiara blinked, confused.

“Why me? I’m not worth it. Why would you put yourself in danger for me? Do you even know what you were getting yourself into when you walked into the slums at this time of night? You could’ve gotten killed!”

Her eyes told him, she didn’t, not fully.

“Listen to me, there are plenty of other people that would deserve and welcome your kindness. Not me.”

Kiara softened. “But I don’t know why you think that. You’re good. And a fine person. It’s not everyday that I get lost in the blind black tunnels of the Forbiddens and meet someone who will lead me to safety, and then proceed to ask for nothing in return.”

He just looked at her through guilt filtered eyes, but his expression hardened all too quickly just before he turned away and busied himself with something on the back shelf. “You don’t know anything about me,” he said with a chilling bite.

Kiara stared at his back, tears welling in her eyes, but she knew better than to put herself through another minute of torture.

Gently she dropped the little sack to the floor and hurried from the room.

When he couldn't hear her footsteps anymore, Hadyn looked over his shoulder to see the little bag still there. His chest collapsed with a breath he could no longer hold in.

With shuffling feet, he moved to kneel next to the bag.

"I don't deserve this."

A piece of paper, tucked under the string that tied the bag shut, caught his attention. Pulling it free, he undid the small folds, to reveal a hastily written note.

Hadyn,

I wanted to apologize for our first meeting. It was rude and awkward.

And I wanted you to know that I long to do so much more for the starving people of Caverna, but when I brought it to my father, the benevolent king, he said no and to get out of his sight. He couldn't even look at me. So giving this to you feels something like a step to something right, however small it may be. I know it might not seem like a lot to you, but it's just the first step and it's your birthday. I know what it's like to not matter to anyone, to feel like you don't exist.

Please accept this gift. If not for yourself, then for me. May it yet guide you to a brighter future, one that outshines any darkness of your past.

You matter,
Kiara

Hadyn stared at the paper in his hand. Even the most relentlessly stubborn parts of him melted as he read those words. His eyes burned with unshed tears. He hated himself for treating her so cruelly. He hadn't even given her a *chance* to explain.

A heat of anger flared inside him when he thought of her father. What kind of man scolded his daughter for wanting to help people in need? He thought if he could, he'd make him regret ever treating her so awfully, but a quick wash of shame put the flames out in seconds. He could blame no one but himself for how he just acted. There was no one else to be mad at.

And blame aside, who was he to think that way? That man was his king, he thought, shoving his own anger down even further.

That rage . . . Just another thing that reminded him he could never escape his own father, forcing him to see he was more like him than he ever feared he'd be. Even after death, he haunted him from inside of himself.

Loosening the string around the bag, he gave it a gentle shake upside down, and out tumbled a small stone, fitting perfectly in the palm of his hand. He held it up, close to his face, and the flickering light of the lantern illuminated the deep burgundy of a sizable hunk of pure Alexandrite.

"Oh, Kiara . . . I'm so sorry."

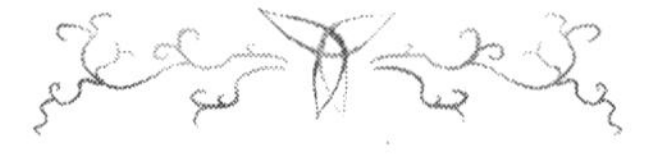

The streets whipped past her in a black, muddled tide as Kiara ran home, tears streaming down her face. She could feel herself diminishing into that nondescript little shell when every voice, no matter how quiet or false, rang like a siren and rattled around inside with nothing in between to hide behind.

She never should have gone. Part of her knew that before, but now her own thoughts berated her decision without mercy. She had her own anxieties about how he would react, but nothing could have prepared her for the severity of his offense.

He's right, she thought. *I do not know him.*

With nothing good to keep them at bay, her fears came creeping back up her spine and her embarrassment darkened to a terrible feeling that somehow convinced her that her whole world could fall apart in an instant if she wasn't careful.

Determined to hide herself under her sheets till morning, she pressed on towards home. But would there be relief in the morning? It wasn't as if she could watch the dawn's sun chase the shadows of night away. No, here they stayed and here they festered.

Finally at her door, Kiara lifted up on the handle to support the hinges and keep them from squeaking. She slipped in and closed the door without a sound, but before she turned around, a chill ran up her spine. She wasn't alone. She could almost feel the claws of the watchers that had followed her in, all the way from the entrance of the King's Corridor, tracing icy trails on her back.

A soft lisp shattered her fears. "Now where have you been, Missy?"

Kiara swiveled to see the faint, burnt glow of a candle around the corner. The light grew until Cida stepped into view. Candlelight playing under her face deepened her concerned frown. Her long hair fell about her arms a bit frazzled, and Kiara knew she hadn't slept a wink since they last talked.

Kiara's shoulders slumped in relief and she didn't even try to make anything up. Part of her wanted to tell her everything, the part of her that dreaded to be alone in this. Then she scanned Cida's deep frown and worried eyes, and suddenly she was only a disappointment, such a great disappointment, like somehow she had done something wrong simply by leaving the Palace. She didn't need anyone else berating her actions and making her feel terrible, she did enough of that herself. And why trust Cida with all her secrets, when she probably wouldn't believe them anyway?

No, she didn't owe her anything and she certainly wasn't about to stick around to receive a chiding.

Striding past her, she said, "I'm tired, Cida. I'm going to bed."

Cida wasn't about to settle for that. "Now wait just a minute. I've been worried sick since I couldn't find you in your room. I deserve to kno—"

Kiara whipped around. Now closer to the light, Cida could plainly see her puffy, red eyes and wet cheeks. "No, Lucida! You don't. You are not my mother. You're not even my sister! You're just the servant."

"Miss . . ." Cida searched her distraught face, but her own feelings were so severely hurt, she didn't know what else to say.

Kiara's heart cracked with a terrible pain when she saw the tears welling in Cida's eyes, but now was not the time for apologies. She had enough to hurt about. Why couldn't Lucida just mind her own business? "Cida, I . . ."

"No, Princess. I *should* know my place. You're right, I am your servant, but I'm not just the servant. I have loved you like my own sister ever since your mother died. I've come to your aid night after night even though I myself deal with the most horrible fears. I—"

"I never asked you to do any of that!" Kiara cried.

Cida flinched and clamped her mouth shut.

"I don't need this, Cida. I can't . . . take this. Not now. I never asked you to worry about me. And certainly won't have you telling me what to do."

Cida said nothing for one painful moment, but recovering swiftly, she sniffed, wiped her eyes, and smoothed her night dress. "Very well," she said, painting a tight smile on her lips. "Now, is there anything I can get for you before I go to my quarters, Your Majesty."

Humiliated and finished, now it was Kiara's turn to cry. She couldn't even look up, and every word she thought to say, stuck in her throat. She managed to barely shake her head, just so Cida would stop staring at her.

"Very well. Goodnight, Miss." She turned, but after two steps she stopped again. "And, Princess," she said, turning her face half way, "you may have never asked, but someone did once. And still, I hope you know, never once did I, out of obligation, do anything for you."

Kiara felt the light leave more than she saw it, and before she could even raise her head to respond, Cida had left.

She didn't even remember walking to her room and collapsing on her bed. She had watched another one of her bright ideas rot before her eyes, and felt the sting of its pain as it lashed back at her with the repercussions. All she could think about as she cried herself to sleep was the guilt in Hadyn's eyes and the pain in Lucida's.

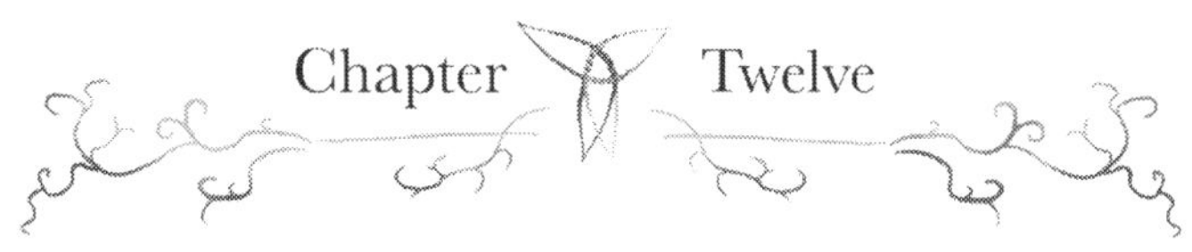

The Monster's Throat

The following days oozed by like muddy water off some dripping stalactite as Kiara shuffled through them in a perfunctory fog. She didn't smile. She didn't cry. She walked to school, came home, ate dinner— sometimes, (it's not as though the drudgeries of white[1] and/or redmeal and mash[2] appetized her normally anyway) and slunk off to bed. Skipping the market all together, she found her father mysteriously "not at home" every day that week. But she didn't feel inclined to risk his wrath by bringing it up.

Even when she happened upon Shrike, finishing off his morning tea and watched him tip back his cup only to nearly choke as the missing tower piece miraculously found its way into his mouth, she could only smirk, her amusement as fleeting as his coughing fit.

She soon became the juiciest talk the Palace could sink its teeth into. No matter how hushed the servants gabbed, sound found strange ways to travel in the palace that they apparently weren't aware of, and she'd catch them through the tunnels swapping remarks and rumors about her as she made her way from her room to school and then back again.

"She rarely says a word anymore," one would say. Then another would counter, "Well, did she ever before?" And Kiara could all but cue the cackles. Or she'd hear some secondhand information like, "Greta told me she's seen her skip dinner again," and the collective gasp that would ensue.

Gossips! Each and everyone of them.

---

1. Caverna's strangely obscure term for any kind of white meat, presumably chicken or fish... Presumably. Likewise for red meal.

2. Some sort of puréed and canned vegetable. Sometimes mixed with liver... Most times.

But Kiara hadn't seen Cida. She would have feared she'd quit but for the absence of any tittle-tattle.

After about a week, she'd had more than an adequate amount of time to stew. Her own words had begun to burn holes like acid water in her brain,
until every time she thought about it, she felt sick enough to wretch. She would do anything to apologize and make it right, but she feared she had destroyed that friendship for good.

Cida was the only person, besides Betsie, and members of her own family, that had shown her true kindness, true friendship . . . and now she had gone and messed that up too, leaving a hole gaping wide in her heart.

Kiara could only mope about for so long though, and after the week had passed, she got sick of licking her wounds and feeling sorry for herself. The pain had lessened to something more of a numbness, and after the first school day of the week came to a close, Kiara walked out onto the steps, for the first time in a long time not itching to get back home.

"Kiara!" Someone called her name. She spun her head about until she caught sight of, none other than, Mallory Knettle.

Mallory gave her a wide smile and encompassing wave, as if she might miss her, and skipped up beside her. "I just wanted to let you know, I heard there's a few new books at the library. I know you like to go there."

Kiara eyed her. ". . . Thanks."

She shrugged with a little grin. "That's all. See you tomorrow, Kiara!"

Kiara gave her a small wave and even managed to return her smile, as she watched her trot away, mystified. That was probably the nicest thing Mallory had ever done for her. She wondered if Mallory had noticed her gloomy mood lately or if she just somehow knew she needed a kind face. Whatever the case, it was sweet of her, and Kiara tried to let it mean as much as it should have.

Maybe she wouldn't go straight home after all. She decided to make a stop at the market for the first time in two weeks and started for the heart of all the shops where a stone building that had served as a library for as long as Kiara could remember resided.

Stepping in the door, she was greeted by the most arresting sound, the sudden beauty making her heart flutter with such lightness, she thought she might take flight. Looking up, she found the thing deserving of attention. Five silver tines surrounded a wooden ball all hanging from a hook at the top of thc door, like a bell to sound the arrival of customers, but each carried a different pitch and sang with delicate perfection. Kiara took a breath of wonder, much too delighted to look away, and when the tines began to still, she thought she'd open the door once more, just to hear it again. Refraining from the childlike urge, she closed her eyes instead and breathed in the musty smell of old parchment that had managed to get wet somewhere in the caves and then dry out here again, countless times over. Even though most of the books bored her to death, something about that old building gave her a sort of peace she found in few other places, making it worth coming back to, even if just to try and figure out why.

She roved her eyes about the many spines, scanning the shelves, and then, walking a few paces inside, she spotted a face that she knew, not very well, but still, she knew it. Really, she could have passed him by as a stranger, and never been the wiser; he looked that different from last they met. Gone were the patched and tatty clothes and sooty locks. He had washed his face clean of grime and even attempted to calm those wild curls. He very well looked the part of a fine young gentleman, maybe with less social skills and decorum, but could she really fault him there?

With an armload of much too many books, he struggled to place just one back on the shelf. Craning his neck to see who had walked in the door, he almost dropped them all when he caught sight of her.

Kiara half expected him to look away, and prepared herself for the slight, but instead, arms still preoccupied, he beckoned her over with a jerk of his head. She wanted to let her hurt and anger be her guide, turn away from him as he had done the other night. After all, what was she to say? Or how could she know what he'd say? Then again it wouldn't bode well for her, as the princess, to snub a citizen wishing to make amends for ill behavior. Not that she cared . . .

Kiara gave herself a mental slap on the cheek. *Just go over if you want to and leave if you don't!* she told herself, and before she knew it, her feet were carrying her across the library.

"Hello there, Miss. What can I do for you?" he asked amiably, looking up from his jumble of books.

Catching his joking, Kiara ignored it and began taking the books from his arms. "I knew you could do it, Hadyn."

He maintained his counterfeit, librarian smile. "Sorry, Miss, is that the title of a novel?"

She gave him an impatient smirk, and continued stacking the books in a neater pile in her own arms. "I knew you *would* do it," she revised. "Just look at you. No one could even imagine you were thinking about living in the Forbiddens."

"Hey!" His eyes darted about. "Don't say that so loud." But his grin sobered after that. He took the tower she had stacked and set it on the floor. Straightening again, he swept his hair from his eyes. "I read your letter," he said. "My mind hasn't changed. I don't deserve your kindness. And you shouldn't have endangered yourself for me, but," he sighed, "I'm sorry. Really. I treated you awfully, and I should have . . . walked you home." He smiled then, a real smile, the sweet one that she liked.

Kiara smiled too and even blushed a bit. "Thank you. But I still don't see why you think so poorly of yourself. You saved my life. Bringing you the alexandrite was the least I could do."

He sighed. "I can't make you understand."

Her curiosity was derailed by another dulcet tune, similar to the last, but new at the same time. It floated on paper thin wings to her ears and wrested her heart. Suddenly distracted, she turned and saw the woman stepping through the door.

"Oh, what are those charming tines?"

"The chimes?" Hadyn asked. "You like them?"

"Like them? I've never heard something so beautiful!"

"I brought them here. Thought they could replace the old, noisy bell."

"They're perfect." She smiled contentedly.

Hadyn found it hard not to smile at her.

But Kiara's attention was stolen as she caught the eye of a sallow-faced, shifty character with a hooked beak for a nose, so indiscreetly hawking at her from in between the shelves.

Of course Shrike was watching her. *Scummy, little fellow.* She heard her father's words in her head and smirked. But her smile fell as she knew, her father was undoubtedly the one who told Shrike to spy on her.

She tried to hide the shiver running through her body. Then in a louder, obvious voice she said, "Actually, sir, you *can* help me. I'm looking for quite a particular book." She placed a hand on her chin, grabbing for an adult like professionalism.

Hadyn followed her gaze across the room. Raising his eyebrows, he caught on faster than she had hoped. "I see . . . And what may this particular book contain?"

Kiara put a casual sway in her walk as she began to browse the shelves. "Oh, the very best of things! Adventure, wild experiences, and good characters who are people of true integrity and strive to put things right. They're not perfect though. They have their struggles and hard times and have to band together and learn that they can't do things by themselves."

Kiara heard the door and turned to see, she had bored Shrike enough to make him abscond.

Yes. Nothing to report here, Shriky . . .

"Sounds like a very good book," Hadyn was saying. "And *adventure*, I don't think I'm familiar with that word."

Kiara turned back to him, blushing. "Neither am I . . .but I do think it sounds most wonderful."

"I'm afraid we don't have anything so wonderful," Hadyn said as he searched over the shelves one last time for good measure. "But," he held up a finger, "since we can't find such a book, might I interest you in another?"

He didn't ask her to follow, but, curiosity intrigued, Kiara weaved through the labyrinth bookshelves after him anyway.

Finally out of the thick of the bookcases, Hadyn hopped over the library's main desk and disappeared behind it in a flash. Kiara cocked her head and shuffled toward the desk, unsure of what he could be retrieving. She flinched as he popped back up and slammed a heavy book on the desk's surface.

"Take a look at this."

Kiara walked around the desk to stand beside him, and Hadyn tried to swipe away the dust with his sleeve, but like all his previous attempts, some of it was just too caked to budge.

Kiara ran a hand over the cover. "It looks ancient."

He stood back to let her examine it. "It is."

She picked up the old book. Markedly plain, Kiara searched the cover for any kind of inscription or symbol, for a clue of where it came from. Small letters in the upper left corner appeared almost carved straight into the leather binding.

"Life in Caverna?" Kiara read the dusty thing with disgust.

"Hey, don't judge the cover. I think it's a journal. It was written by a girl named Madressilva."

"No last name?" Kiara asked.

"Not that I could find. But I did find a date." His words carried a certain suspense. "See, look." He turned the book over in her hands and pointed the numbers out.

Kiara gasped. “This book almost dates back to the beginning of Caverna!” she cried, and fumbled to wrench it open. Her shoulders slumped. “It’s locked.”

“Strange, isn’t it? And look at that keyhole.”

Kiara squinted at the strange shape, almost heart-shaped from a mere glance, but odd angles and lines turned it into something totally asymmetric. She’d never seen a thing like it.

She raised a brow. “Know any locksmiths?”

“Ah . . . my dad actually. Knew a thing or two.”

“Oh.” Once again, Kiara had no idea what to say next, but she wouldn’t just give up on the journal. Somehow, somewhere inside was something about how all this got started. She just knew it.

“Alright, well, I’ll take it home.” She hugged it closer. “Maybe I can find a way to open it.”

“Actually . . .” Hadyn’s eyes trailed to the floor, “this isn’t exactly a library book. It’s mine. I got it from the orphanage when I aged-out. I guess I’m related to her or something.” He shrugged.

“What? Why is it here?”

“Wellll, I don’t exactly have a home right now, so I wanted it to be safe. I thought, what better place for a book than a library! . . . Right?” He laughed nervously.

Her face fell and the book drooped in her arms. “You don’t have a place to stay? Where do you sleep?”

“Well, Mr. Craggs has been letting me stay in his warehouse where he keeps extra books.”

“But that’s ridiculous!” Kiara was indignant, and Hadyn noted with mild amusement how her strange lilt, he had noticed the other night, became more pronounced when she shouted or got upset.

He raised his hands. “There’s no need to get so fired up about it. It’s not all that bad. And it’s just until I can earn enough to get out of the slums and have a nice place someday.”

But Kiara wanted to get fired up. “My father’s hopeless . . .” she muttered to herself and stomped her foot. She looked down. Her foot had hit wood, a small trap door of sorts.

“What's this?” she asked with a curious cock of her head.

Hadyn looked just as confused. “You know, I thought it was where Mr. Craggs keeps his extra books, but those are at the warehouse. He told me as much and to ask, ‘No more questions about the door.’ ” He wagged a finger, mimicking Mr. Craggs’ low and gravelly voice and Kiara covered her mouth to stifle a giggle. “Anyway, this door is always locked. See.” He bent down and pulled on the handle to demonstrate its stubborn tendencies, but to both their surprise, it opened to a gaping, black hole.

Chapter Thirteen

Old Tom

Now, to say Kiara wasn't frightened, would be a blatant lie that I'm almost certain you wouldn't believe. But to say she was only frightened would also be an untruth. Because when she saw the supposedly locked tight trap door fling open to such unending darkness, she was indefinitely, unmitigatedly *terrified.* The unsearchable dread that seemed to pour up from its depths like a rank cloud of stench stole the breath from her lungs. She didn't fully understand it, but she didn't need to. Deep inside she could feel some vile presence as if evil had made a home in the bottom of this hole, where it lurked in its rotting bed of bones and lost souls, but remained cloaked like a shadow so it could not be identified.

And to say I was telling you this wholly for reasons other than stalling for suspense would also be an untruth, and I'll get back to the story now.

Kiara gasped to regain some semblance of breathing. Jumping back from the hole, the sudden fear stole the strength from her arms, and the heavy book flung from her grasp. Hadyn lunged to catch it, but he didn't get a decent grip and the weight of it slipped through his hand, into the abysmal darkness. The deepening tunnel, like the throat of some great beast, didn't flinch as it swallowed the book as a meager offering.

Kiara stumbled and fell backward, unprepared for the shock of her jump. Without hesitation, Hadyn reached for the trap door and slammed it shut. Like a lid on a box of curses, immediately the whispering fears stopped and the cold chill of dread receded.

Mouth dry and wordless, Kiara looked from the trapdoor up to Hadyn. "Oh, Hadyn, I'm so sorry!" she cried. "I don't know what got into me."

Hadyn looked at her, saw the way she trembled, and held his breath, trying to think of some way to comfort her. He didn't want to just lie and say the book wasn't important to him.

"It's okay," he said. "It startled me too."

"But your book! I threw it to the monster!" she protested. "—I mean, I dropped it!"

"Don't worry about it. We'll just say you triple owe me." He said with a lopsided smile, pulling her to her feet.

Kiara didn't think it was funny. "No. I have to get it back. It's down there somewhere. It's not as if it was really swallowed."

Just then, a nosy woman, sifting the titles on the shelves nearby, started browsing things other than books. Hadyn gave her a polite wave to let her know she had been spotted. Kiara offered a smile too, knowing how curious the sight might seem. The eaves-dropper took her leave most hastily then, finding a sudden interest in books much further away.

Hadyn rolled his eyes and Kiara shook her head with a sniff, but with heads preoccupied with matters more pressing than a wayward busybody, both their eyes wandered back to the trapdoor and just kind of stayed there for a moment.

"That wasn't real . . . right?" Kiara ventured.

Hadyn gave her a sideways glance. He may not have fallen over, but he had felt something all the same, like an icy dread creeping up from somewhere he could not see. He scrunched his face. "No. It just surprised us, is all."

"Right . . . " she agreed, but their eyes couldn't fight the pull, drawing them back to the wooden hatch.

"We have to get that journal back," she said, decided.

She might not have dared to admit it, but in the recent absence of fear, curiosity had already begun its mischievous work, tangling itself up in places where it couldn't be undone until its hungry questions were thoroughly sought out. She had to know what was down there that seemed to leap up and inflict terror on whoever came across its path.

Meanwhile, Hadyn fought his own mind. How could he deliberately bring himself and another into possible danger? Exhaling noisily, he said, "I did want to know what was in that journal . . ."

"So did I."

He eyed her undecidedly, but she could see him swaying. "Ah! Fine! But I'll retrieve it. *Alone*."

"Not a chance! I won't let you go by yourself. It's my fault it's down there at all. It will be fine. We'll go down the tunnel, get your book, and come straight back up. Nothing to it."

"Straight back up?" He questioned.

"Of course. And who knows, maybe there is nowhere to go down there."

"A tunnel leading straight down to nothing?" he said, dully.

"Okay, so there's something down there. But we don't have to investigate that something . . ."

"Right," he nodded.

". . . unless we want to."

"No!"

"Alright, alright!" She raised both her hands.

"Good. So we'll meet back here after curfew tonight."

"Sounds like a plan." Kiara felt a giddy shiver run down her spine as she thought of sneaking out for something other than escaping nightmares and running to her lonely hideaway, but her smile melted fast. "I guess I should get back to the Palace then."

"You don't sound like that's a good thing."

"It isn't. I mean— Maybe . . . I just can't make you understand," she said with a smirk, using his own words against him.

He waved a finger at her. "Sly." Then, absentmindedly straightening some things on the desk, he asked, "Do you *have* to get back? I mean, is it . . . required of you?"

Kiara laughed. "No. I guess not, but what else am I going to do?"

"Well, my shift here ends soon, and . . ."

Kiara cocked her head. "Yes?"

"I read what you said about wanting to help the people of Terminal Avenue . . ." He stumbled over his words here like obstacles in his path, fiddling with objects on the desk and never looking at her directly. "And I have this package I need to deliver . . . I guess, well– I thought maybe– Ah, it's stupid really."

"Oh, tell me." She blinked patiently.

He finally looked at her. "I guess I wondered if you'd want to . . ." he cringed, "come with me?"

She brightened. "Do you mean it?"

Hadyn scratched his head. "Well, you could. You don't have—"

"Of course!"

He looked dizzy. "Really?"

"I'd love to! When can we go?"

"As soon as the bell chimes the hour and Mr. Craggs gets here."

"But that can't be over a half hour away!"

"Right. But while you wait you might want to do something to hide . . ." His cheeks reddened with embarrassment and he couldn't finish.

Kiara's face fell. "My hair."

"No. Well, I was going to say, hide that you're the princess. I suppose that is the most obvious thing."

"But, why? My father seems to think they're so dangerous, but they're not. You saw it. You were there."

"I hate to say this, but I'm near certain you got lucky that first time. Everyone was too shocked to do anything. I wouldn't expect such hospitality the second time."

"What do you mean?"

"Trust me, Kiara. I grew up there. I live it and see it all the time. Things are not good, and some days, it's every man for himself."

Already having had her own misgivings about how calmly they received her, Kiara thought it'd be outright foolish of her to refuse to believe he knew better.

"Alright," she said solemnly. "I'll walk to the Palace and retrieve a cloak."

Hadyn hated to see how that one thing crushed her spirits. "I'm sorry, Princess— Kiara."

Kiara shrugged a shoulder and gave him a soft, sad smile. "It's not your fault. Meet outside on the hour?"

". . . I'm counting on it."

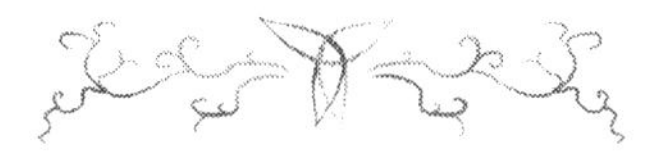

When Kiara returned home, she stopped only long enough to change. But, one look in the mirror, and she realized with her hair properly hidden or not, her fine dress alone would be a proclamation to the whole city that she was not a mere local to the avenue. So she rummaged about in the servant's quarters until she found a dress in need of a thorough washing that would fit her. Her hair, already pulled back in a low bun, hid easily under the hood of her cloak. Lighter than her black one and of a slate color, the cloak tied plainly at the neck and draped off her shoulders nearly to the floor.

When Kiara wandered back into the heart of town, she rounded one last building and there he stood outside the library, hands in his pockets and watching everyone that walked by. For a moment, Kiara just soaked up the sight. She couldn't think of a time when someone waited for her like that. She felt a grin on her face and wiped it away.

When she walked close to him, he barely glanced at her before continuing to search for her. "Excuse me, miss," he asked, "but have you seen–"

Kiara giggled, giving herself away.

"Kiara? I hardly recognized you!"

"Well, isn't that the point *exactly*?"

"I suppose. Where did you get that dress? It's filthy."

"One of the servants," Kiara said simply. "Shall we go?"

Hadyn forced himself to stop staring. "Right. Of course," he said, sweeping up a bag sitting on the library's steps, and moved to go, but Kiara had a thought.

"Oh! I have to hear those chimes one more time before we go." She took the stairs two at a time.

"They're gone," came Hadyn's tragic statement.

Kiara froze, one foot hovering over the last step. "What?"

"Mr. Craggs took 'em down as soon as he got here. In a proper fury too."

"He can't just do that!"

Well passed anger, Hadyn shrugged. "But he can."

"But—"

"Kiara, we're not supposed to have them anyway. I just didn't think it would be any harm."

Kiara didn't see how that could be true. They were forbidden too? An hour ago she didn't even know what chimes were.

"Do you still want to go?"

Shaking out of it, Kiara smiled. "Of course."

So, without another word, Hadyn took the lead through town.

They received no more strange glances after that. To onlookers, they appeared as two young people from a squalid district, perhaps even a brother and sister, returning to their hovel from a trip to the market.

They made their way across town where they reached the entrance to Terminal Avenue. Without the countless citizens gawking at her and stealing her attention, Kiara could actually take every bit of the imposing street in, as if for the first time. It still smelt and was cluttered with all sorts of strange and boring junk, but something about it captured her awe in that moment and wouldn't let her go.

To you or me, it might look just like a great alleyway, but with a covering, rock roof and tunneling turns. Old mats and clothes hung out above their heads on lines running back and forth from top story windows in the tunnel walls, like a giant spider's web. Bits of color popped out from the otherwise brown mess in this place where rules prohibiting forbidden things just weren't as enforced. With so many turns and tunneling ways, Kiara imagined one could spend years here and still have not explored it all. It reminded her of the Forbiddens and if anything at all, it proved an interesting change in her perfectly banal life.

She took it all in through wide eyes, feeling like she had left Caverna behind in some ways. Still dark and drippy cold, and yet it seemed less regulated and more wild.

"Watch out!" she heard Hadyn warn just as three children came barreling by in a game of chase, turning on a hairpin just inches in front of them. The last in line, a young girl, failed to turn sharp enough, collided with Kiara, and fell to the ground.

"Oh! I'm so sorry, ma'am!" she said.

"No. It's alright. I didn't see you either." Kiara knelt to help her up. The way her dress rumpled up when she fell, revealed a fresh scuff, adding to a proper collection on her knees.

"Are you alright?"

"Yes, ma'am, I'm okay." The girl stood, brushing her dirty curls out from her sight.

Kiara recognized her inquisitive blue eyes at once. "Well, hello, Miss Abigail!"

The girl looked at her, no doubt wondering how she knew her name. Her face fell dumb and then she gasped. "Your Majesty!"

Kiara held a finger to her grinning lips. Abigail looked at her poor clothes and seemed to understand, at least well enough. Kiara gave her a wink and sent her to run along after her waiting friends.

They spun loops around piles of waste and danced through the junk as their very own playground, tearing through the street and giggling the whole time. Just before they zoomed out of sight, they ran straight past an old, grizzly man, half unconscious on a rickety wooden crate with a bright red scarf tied around his left fist.

Kiara gasped, despising the fear that squeezed her throat and stomach without reason. "There he is again!"

"Who?" Hadyn followed her locked gaze. "Old Man Thomas? What about him?"

"Thomas . . .?" Kiara tested the handsome name.

As if the name itself possessed some kind of power, she could no longer look at him the same way. If any far fetched fears remained, they scattered the moment his wrinkled face was given a name.

"Some of the kids at my school like to spin stories about him," Kiara started to explain, more than a little embarrassed.

"About Old Tom? Are you joking?"

"No. They say he's been to the Void and back, that it cleaned out his brain so there's nothing left but madness."

Hadyn's face registered amused shock. "I've never heard anything so ridiculous! Don't tell me you believed all that."

"Well, it's easy to believe stupid stuff when the rumors are all you hear. I never even knew his name. The kids at school call him the deaf, mute beggar of Terminal Avenue."

"Well, he is that." Hadyn nodded. "Can't hear a squeak, so he doesn't know how to speak right."

"That's so sad." Kiara's heart broke as she watched him.

"I know. So you shouldn't stare," he said, resuming their trek. "What kind of kids make up scarystories about a deaf old man? Didn't their parents raise them better? I mean, what's the point of the upper class, if they aren't held to some sort of standard?"

Kiara was silent and Hadyn feared he had offended her. "Sorry . . . I—"

He turned and found nothing but empty space at his side. He whipped his head to the right— still nothing.

Did you just lose the Princess of Caverna? his thoughts screamed.

He would be charged with kidnapping or high treason against the crown if she wasn't found, but strangely that didn't even cross his mind, much too worried about her and if she was in trouble.

He began calling her name, but he could never raise his voice above mild concern, fearing to draw more attention to the situation. His eyes darted about. Everyone near minded their own business and nothing at all looked suspicious. If she was drug away, she would have struggled. But maybe someone hit her on the head. She didn't just leave, did she?

He knew he should have never brought her here, but (like an idiot) he did, and now the princess was lost and it was all his fault.

Hadyn spun around and around, frantically scanning the area they had just been.

Where was the last place I knew she was with me . . .?

There was Old Man Tom, sitting in the same place they saw him and . . . *There!* Crouched before him was a petite figure in a grey hooded cloak.

Hadyn's shoulders slumped as relief loosened every muscle. She must have walked up to him when he kept going. He marched over to them, hands clenched and jaw set, but what he saw next surprised and amazed him so much, frustration had no place, and all he could do was stare.

With some quick hand gestures and no lack of animated expressions, the two of them had already waded deep into a lively conversation. Hadyn had never seen a bigger smile on Old Tom's face. When he walked up, the two of them were so engrossed in their conversation, they hardly noticed his presence, though he didn't mind in the slightest, rather enjoying watching them communicate.

Then Kiara pointed to Hadyn, her brows raised questioningly. Thomas nodded and continued to sign. Hadyn felt his ears begin to burn and he shifted his weight from one foot to the other. Suddenly it wasn't so easy, not knowing what they were saying.

Thankfully they said their goodbyes fast enough after that. Gently, Kiara took up his crippled hand in both of hers and gave him a smile so warm, it could melt the most frozen of hearts. It played at the corners of her eyes with sweet innocence and banished all hints of sorrow or fear with incorruptible disregard.

In that moment, Hadyn saw a nobility in her that he had scarcely noticed before, and realized she had more princess in her than her avoidance and careless mask tried to hide.

Old Tom offered him his good hand and Hadyn shook it with a smile before they left.

Kiara smiled softly as they walked, but Hadyn could only fret.

"So . . . what did you two talk about?"

"Lots of things." Kiara beamed.

"Did he say something about me? I saw you pointing."

"He said that you're trouble and that I should be more careful about who I hang around."

Hadyn scrunched his brow in genuine surprise. "He said that?"

"No." Kiara chuckled. "He said you're the sweetest young man that he's ever had the privilege to know." Hadyn's cheeks flushed with color. "That you've never been anything but good to him and everyone else he has seen with you."

"Well, that's not many people."

"No?"

"No. Now, come on. It's still a ways up."

"Where are we going, may I ask?"

He gave her half a smirk. "You'll have to wait and see." But his face melted to a look of anxiety. "And, Kiara . . . I don't think we should go down the hatch tonight."

"Why ever not?"

"It's just too dangerous. I can't believe I even brought you here."

"Nonsense. If this is about me wandering off, I won't do it again. I swear."

"It's not just that . . ."

"Hadyn, possible danger doesn't change the fact that there's a lost journal that needs finding. And what do you mean? We're here and things are going better than I could have ever imagined. Not one gawking glance. It's like I'm finally normal!" She gave a giddy laugh.

Hadyn didn't have the heart to argue with her or dampen her spirits, so he led on in silence.

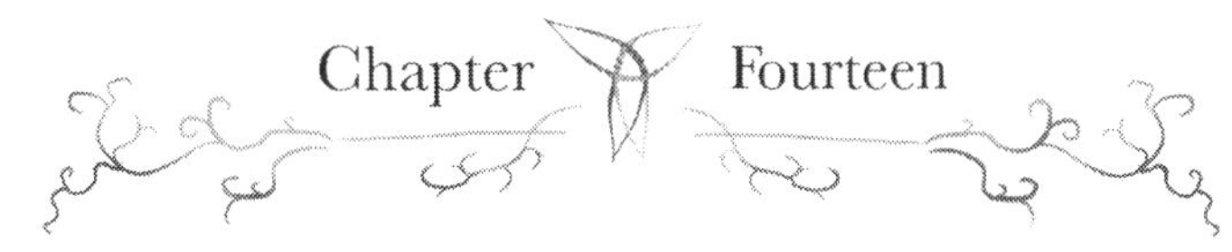

The Waywards of Terminal Street

Kiara had only been this far down the street after curfew and now, seeing all its twists and mazy turns lit up with torches and lanterns, she couldn't believe she had even found her way at all.

The further they traveled in, Kiara's awestruck wonder slowly died away to uneasy trepidation, turning her blood icy. The hubbub of town grew more and more muffled until the silence seemed to develop a sentient body of its own, one with watching eyes and a creeping way about its walk. Things skittered in and out of secret places and skulking characters stepped out of shadows to glare at them with hungry eyes, while reclusive spooks drew their curtains and dissolved into the dark.

Kiara walked closer to Hadyn as she caught an ever increasing amount of staring eyes. Not the kind of dumbstruck awe she got as the princess; more a predatory stalk of a helpless, young girl who might just be an easy catch. Kiara was almost certain they would've already made their move if Hadyn wasn't there.

"Don't worry about them," Hadyn spoke softly. "We're almost there. Just try not to look them in the eyes."

Oh yes, Kiara thought, *I shall try, while their gazes burn holes into my skin.*

"This way." Hadyn led her down a turn into a narrow way, only for the tunnel to debouch moments later into the wide stoneyard of a looming, cobbled building. The dark windows glared like many sinister eyes with severe gothic arches as brows above every one. The building itself, at least the exterior was only about a few feet deep, built straight into the rock face, a toothed parapet on the roof giving it a cold, fortress-like appearance. The rest stayed hidden, deep within the hollowed stone.

Kiara looked at Hadyn questioningly. "The orphanage?"

"That's right."

"But I thought you hated this place."

"I did. Still do. The fact that I still have to see this ugly, stone monster is not what I'd call a blessing, but I couldn't just forget about the Waywards of Terminal Street *altogether*."

"Who?"

Hadyn didn't answer. He just walked up closer to the stone building front, dropped the bag down, and cupping both hands to his mouth aimed a suppressed shout up at an open top window. "Waywards! Waywards of Terminal Street!"

Kiara joined him where he stood, growing more curious with each passing second, but nothing moved in the top window. Hadyn scratched his head awkwardly.

"They usually come right away . . ."

"Maybe try again?"

Hadyn raised his hands to his mouth again, and said with a little less patience, "Waywards!"

Just then a curly mess of black hair pushed above the window sill and two blue eyes peered down at them. There was a gasp and the boy was gone, but they could still hear him shouting throughout the rooms. "Hadyn's back! Hadyn's back! Everybody, Hadyn's back!"

Kiara smiled and Hadyn said with a grin, "That would be little Ben."

Before Kiara could fully comprehend what was happening, a group of about twelve boys, aging anywhere from six to eleven, came pouring down the orphanage's steps. They rushed around Hadyn and coincidentally Kiara, shouting his name and asking what he had brought them this time. Hadyn set the bag down to let them rummage through what would mostly be food, just something extra to fill their constantly half empty bellies for once.

"It's nice to see you all too," he said, watching them tear into the bag like a bunch of starved puppies. After sometime he began to intervene, making sure they all got something and handing out a few specific items to individual kids.

"Here, Achan." He handed a small box to a quiet, lanky kid. "New drawing pencils. Try not to let the masters find these ones."

Achan's eyes lit up when the box was laid in his hands, too happy for words. "Thanks, Hadyn!"

"And . . ." Hadyn waved a finger across the boys. "Ben! You said Daniel broke your glasses?"

The little one named Ben nodded. "Did anyone get you new

ones yet?" He shook his head. "Didn't think so. Here, try these." Hadyn fished out a pair of wire rimmed spectacles, a little scratched and dinged, but whole all the same. Ben perched them on his nose and hooked them around the back of his ears. They dwarfed his boyish features, not fitting quite right, but the biggest smile stretched across his face once he put them on.

"I can see! I can see!"

Kiara watched boy after boy light up over the little treasures, and some of them only the simplest needs. In that moment, she didn't mind being invisible. In that moment, she couldn't have asked for anything more than to just sit and eavesdrop on this rare joy. Kiara watched Hadyn with a soft smile, as he attempted to manage the incorrigible group. Though, she did start to wonder where he had gotten all this . . .

The boys gibbered and talked over each other, mouths never closed for too long at any one time. Hadyn let this go on until, at length, he decided they needed some help remembering their manners.

"Gentlemen!" he said, turning his mouth down in a play of authority. As if prompted by the word, they each straightened up, falling silent, one after the other, until the only sound heard was the smacking of their mouths as they munched.

Once he was sure that he had all of their attention, he started again. "Gentlemen, this is Kiara." He swept a hand to her.

Kiara had watched the boys come to attention with an amused grin, but it evaporated the moment Hadyn directed their attention to her.

The boys gaped at her like she glowed with the essence of some lofty realm she had just stepped out of.

Hadyn cleared his throat."*Princess* Kiara . . ." Raising his eyebrows, he spun his hand to elicit some respect.

An awkward round of nudging and elbowing began in the group, starting with the oldest, trickling all the way down to little Ben until each one of them bent deeply at the waist, and none of them seemed to have plans of straightening again.

"Oh get up!" she said, laughter and a smile clearly heard in her voice. "All of you! There is no need to bow."

"But, Princess." A boy who had just recently lost both his front teeth looked up at her. "It is too great of an honor not to bow."

"And I say, to meet you all is far too great an honor to *have* you bow. So rise— oh, what is it you call yourselves?"

"Waywards, your Majesty."

"Right. Rise, Waywards of Terminal Street!"

The boys stood straight, all except one.

Kiara giggled. "You too, Ben. There, that's better. And, please, call me Kiara." Then, roving her eyes over them all, making no exception for Hadyn, she asked. "While on the subject of names, however did you all come up with a name like that?"

"Like what?" one of the boys asked.

"Waywards. What gave you the idea to call yourselves that? From my experience, it is not a very pleasant thing."

"Well, Your Majes— Kiara," the one with the missing incisors stumbled, "we strays, and ain't no adult can control us, least not for long. Nobody cares too much about what the Waywards do." He said *nobody* so indefinitely and with such pride. It made her sad that he thought of it as a good thing.

"And street . . .? You say street even though this is Terminal *Avenue*."

Achan looked up from admiring his new drawing pencils and shrugged. "Sounds better that way."

"I see."

"But what about you?" one boy asked. "I mean no disrespect, but . . . what are you doing here?"

"Eh . . . Well . . ." Something about the question made her freeze, like something got stuck in the gears of her mind.

"I asked her to come," Hadyn said simply.

The boys' eyes grew wide and they traded impish grins. One of the older ones spoke up. "Hadyn, why didn't you tell us you were courtin' the princess? You've been holding out on us!"

Kiara's cheeks burned like fire, but a quick glance told her Hadyn's did too, and she didn't feel so bad.

"No! It's nothing like that, you little mite!"

"It's not? Then why are you blushing?" He took a step towards him.

Hadyn locked him in a head hold and messed up his hair, before pushing him playfully away. "No. Now that's enough from you if you want the *princess* to think any good of you at all."

Seeming to realize how important his reputation was to him, his eyes grew wide. "Oh! I'm sorry. I didn't mean anything by it. Really!"

Kiara laughed. "It's quite alright."

Hadyn smiled at them all, but after a hasty headcount, his

face fell. "Where's Sam?"

The boys all looked down, toeing the ground.

Hadyn's face washed of all color. "Boys?"

One finally spoke up. "He . . . He got adopted."

"You're sure? He didn't . . ."

"No, no, no!" The boys waved their hands. "He didn't get snatched. A good lookin' couple—"

"Much too good lookin'," another said.

"Came and picked him up not two days ago," the other finished.

Closing his eyes, Hadyn sighed with relief, and Kiara realized she was holding her breath. "Well, what are you all moping for?" he asked. "I thought I told you to always be glad for a fellow Wayward."

"But they'll turn him awful proper!" they whined. "They'll ruin poor old Sam!"

Hadyn sliced them all a look and they silenced. "I won't hear it. That's not the Wayward way. I'm glad Sam's got a family. That's one less of you I've got to worry about."

They slumped. "You're right."

"Good."

Just then, a mangy looking creature crawled out from under a turned over crate and hopped straight into Ben's arms as he bent down for it. Its black, greasy fur was matted and patchy, straight down to the skin in some places. A proper bag of bones, its ribs showed through its saggy skin and what should have been a long slender tail was clipped to a numb.

Kiara couldn't believe her eyes. "What is that?"

"Marbles?" Hadyn asked. "We call his kind devils."

"Marbles isn't a devil!" Ben held him closer, stroking his scabby head.

Kiara laughed. "They're not devils; they're ca—" She stopped herself, clearing her throat. "I mean, I agree with Ben. He doesn't look like a devil at all."

She of course knew what a cat was from the journals. But here? In Caverna?

"How have I never seen one before?" she asked.

"They tend to stick terminal side[1] for whatever reason," Ben explained.

---

1. *Caverna's term for the south side of town.*

"And they weren't seen at all until about twenty years ago," one of the older boys said.

Kiara scrunched her brows. "That's not possible."

He shrugged. "People say it wasn't long after King Nnyric took a wife, that they started seeing them. Some say they're rejects of the watchers. Too small to be scary, you know? That's why we call them devils."

Still held in Ben's arms, Kiara came close and scratched behind the cat's tatty ears. His close set eyes seemed permanently cross-eyed above his crooked nose, and one of his back paws was clubbed and deformed.

"What's wrong with him?" Kiara asked.

Hadyn came to her side, giving marbles a pet. "They all look like that." He shrugged sadly. "Some say, it's because there's only so many of them, messes with their genes."

Marbles closed his eyes in bliss as she scratched under his chin, stoking to life a roar of a purr. Deformed or not, he wasn't a watcher reject, he wasn't a devil; he was just a cat.

Then, for whatever reason, Marbles decided he was done being held, struggled free, and scampered off. She watched him limp away, wondering how long it was before something like that happened to the people of Caverna too . . .

One of the boys, maybe eight years old, turned to Hadyn. "Sorry it took us so long to come down."

"That's alright, Dylan. It wasn't all that long."

"Jack was teaching us a new game," Dylan continued and the one who was teasing Hadyn grinned proudly. "We use all our collected scabs and trade them and stuff when we roll the right dice!"

Hadyn gave Kiara a glance out of the corner of his eye and could visibly see the shades of green deepening in her face.

"And when we get enough scabs—"

Hadyn pulled him close and put a tight hand over his mouth. "Ah . . . Ha ha, I think that's a game you should keep between the boys."

Dylan talked behind his hand in muffled gibberish.

"Why?" A younger boy cocked his head. "It's just a . . ."

Hadyn shook his head, eyes wide with warning, and jerked his head towards Kiara. Dylan's eyes went wide and he gasped through his nose. Struggling free he said, "Oh! I mean . . . what? We don't actually do that. That's ridiculous! Disgusting actually." He forced a laugh. “I was just, uh . . . joking!”

“Uh-huh,” Hadyn nodded. “I’m sure you were.”

“Honest! Why would we do that?” All the boys nodded their heads.

Hadyn didn’t feel inclined to stifle the laugh that bubbled up at the sight of them all nodding in unison, which only made Dylan more upset. “I’m telling you—”

A nerve-shattering bell cut him off, rattling all their spines and a shrill voice from inside screamed, “All boys in the yard, get inside at once!”

The boys cringed. “Warden calls!” one said, but then they just stood there.

“Well, you best be off then!” Hadyn reminded them, and still they waited. “Go!” He shooed them with flaps of his hands.

Like stubborn cattle, the boys finally started to get moving.

“It was very nice to meet you, Princess— eh Kiara!” the boys all tried to say at once and some of them bowed while backing away despite Kiara’s protests.

“Get outta here.” Hadyn laughed at them. “All of you!”

The boys scampered away, pushing and shoving each other. Some acted as though they wore manacles joined at the ankles or dragged a ball and chain behind them.

Hadyn shook his head. “Stay outta trouble, Waywards! Especially you, Jack!”

Jack touched a hand to his forehead and gave him a nod as though with a hat, before they all filed in the door where the “Warden” waited with a deep scowl and a tapping foot. She made sure to give Hadyn an icy glare before slamming the heavy door shut.

Hadyn’s shoulders slumped when the door finally closed. He turned away and screwed up his face. “. . . Sorry.”

“Sorry for what? I haven’t seen a more lively bunch in well . . . forever!”

“They’re just a rough lot.They can be so . . . so . . .”

“So very much like boys?” Kiara raised her brows. “Hadyn, it’s alright. I may have never had a brother, but I do go to school with a whole lot of boys.”

“Yes, but they’re different. The refined and mannered type.”

Kiara laughed. “They just might surprise you.”

“Thanks for coming with me. The look on their faces when they realized who was standing in front of them was priceless. You really had them beaming."

"Me? I didn't do a thing. You're the one who put the smiles on their faces . . . You brought them so much joy. It was amazing to watch."

"It's really nothing. More like the least I could do."

"No. No, it's not. People should wish they could say they've done half as much good in their entire lives. I should wish . . ."

"Well, I don't really see it as an option."

"And that's why it's real."

He looked at her and flashed a sudden, soft smile.

They walked in a contemplative silence for a time, until Kiara's ever wandering brain woke back up for the day.

"There is one thing I've been wondering, though. How is it that you can give to them? I mean, where did all that stuff come from?"

"Oh." He laughed nervously. "About that. It's funny really that you should ask."

Kiara jerked to a stop and stared at nothing. "*Impossible* . . . It's the gems! You trade the gems you mine on the Stygian market for food and things for the boys!"

"Shhhh! Would you please lower your voice!" he hissed. "It's more complicated than you think."

"What could be so complicated about that?"

Honestly shocked she wasn't upset, he only looked at her, his expression pained, but wouldn't open his mouth.

Kiara's mouth twisted into a grin and her eyes nearly glowed with the mischief kindled within. "You have to take me there."

"What! No! Take you to the Styx? You're insane! Mad!" Then, remembering himself, he blurted a hasty, "Sorry," but Kiara hadn't taken offense. She simply had entertained one of her abominably curious thoughts and would be hard pressed not to follow it to the end.

"Look, I'm in disguise already."

Perhaps it would have been easier for Hadyn to oppose her, if she didn't so often seem to make so much sense. "Gah! Why do you do this? Don't you want to live?"

"Not here." She followed her terse reply with a question. "Do you?"

Hadyn didn't feel like giving her an answer.

"Fine then. I'll go by myself," she said, turning on her heels.

"And just how do you think you're going to find it?"

She didn't look back. "I'm going to look."

Hadyn rolled his eyes. If only she had spent more than an hour or so in this hostile cesspit. Maybe then she'd think twice before stomping off into Terminal Avenue alone. Part of him wanted to wave a hand and turn away from the situation entirely. It was her decision. But too much of it felt like his responsibility. He was the one who asked her to come with him. She probably would have never even imagined heading into the depths of Terminal Avenue if he wouldn't have brought her here and told her to disguise herself so she wouldn't get caught. Watching her disappear around a corner, he huffed.

As Kiara walked deeper into Terminal Avenue, she was determined not to let herself, for even a second, think that she needed anyone's help. With her new disguise what could go wrong? But she wouldn't say she was unhappy when she heard footsteps trotting up beside her.

Kiara smirked. "Change of heart?"

"Not exactly what I would call it," Hadyn said through clenched teeth.

Kiara stopped and turned to him, her eyes caught in a strange state somewhere between surrender and fighting. "Look, I know you think this is just another whim of a girl who's grown up getting every little thing she wants. But it's not. For as long as I can remember, my life has been filled with nothing but half-baked truths and deceptions too numerous to count. This *whole* city was built brick by brick upon thousands of lies . . . but the worst part is, I don't even know what those lies are. Then you told me that the Styx is a real place, not just a story, and suddenly one of those lies had a shape. Because everyone around me wants to say they don't exist. Why? Don't you ever wonder? Yes, I've been fascinated with the place since I was little, but it's the mystery I loved, and maybe some of that will lift if I go there."

Hadyn listened the whole time, but finally he took his turn to speak. "I just don't want you to be crushed when you find out it's not everything you dreamed it would be."

It took her a moment, but Kiara finally smirked. "I guess I'll just have to see, won't I?"

Chapter Fifteen

Rouges and Oracles

Kiara faced the solid stone wall. Not even the door to a residence marked the dead end of Terminal. It just stopped with nowhere to go but back.

"Is this some kind of joke? Something you conjured to make me look stupid."

Hadyn grinned innocently. "Now, why would I do that when you've gone and done such a good job all on your own?"

She drew a breath to retaliate, but then just fixed him with a glare and returned to searching the wall and surrounding area.

"I just really wanted to see how you were going to find the Styx by yourself."

"And you mean it when you say, the market is at the very end of Terminal Avenue?" She searched his face when she questioned so she might detect any hint of a lie.

"Yes, the *very* end," he said obviously. "What would I gain from lying to you?"

Kiara narrowed her eyes. "I'm not sure."

Resuming her searching and musing, she paced with an elbow propped in her opposite palm and a hand on her chin. "It doesn't make any sense. Unless . . . the Stygian Market is a pop-up market and it's not here today because it's not open!"

"How did you know?"

"Really?" she beamed.

He laughed, shaking his head. "No. I assure you, the Styx is always there."

Kiara dropped her arms. "What! But where is *there*?"

"Giving up?"

Kiara arched a brow and put her hands on her hips. "*Giving up*? What in Caverna would give you that idea? If you think I would give up that easily, you best think again. 'Cause I—"

Hadyn stood straight, ears trained on something up the street, and eyes narrowed with concentration.

"Are you listening to me?"

"Shhh!" he hushed her and then Kiara could hear it too—voices, a few of them, and footsteps coming their way.

"Is it trouble?"

Hadyn didn't turn his face from the direction of the voices. "Could be."

"What do we do?"

His eyes darted about the dead end area. "This way."

They ducked under the tattered, tent-like awning of one of the houses and in through the crooked doorway just before three filthy men walked up the way. Everything about them, the roguish posture, the boisterous cussing and cackling, even the way they took each step, never once looking behind their backs, told Kiara they owned this street, especially the one refusing to engage in the raucous the two behind him were making. He walked several paces in front of his companions, aloof and looming, and stood at least a foot taller. A thick beard the color of pitch and a wide brimmed, ripped hat concealed a face, replete with secrets. The more Kiara watched him, the more the other two looked like a couple of sniveling rats next to him, one a turkey necked goon with floppy hands and skinny limbs, the other a bleary-eyed, copper-nosed thug who seemed to have not been fully awake when he put his shoes on that morning.

The man with the wide brimmed hat searched the area with deep set, wicked eyes, sampling the air as if he could smell something off.

"Silence!" he barked at the two, who immediately swallowed down their tongues with their fear. "On both your irritating lives, I could have sworn I heard something up this way."

"I didn't hear nothin'," the skinny rat said.

"Yeah, Boss, me neither," added the other.

The man in the dark hat growled. "That's because the two of you were too busy flapping your own loose jaws! I ought to have them stitched shut!" Then he got quiet. "I know I heard something." He spun his shadowed face around the area, scrutinizing every hiding place.

Kiara and Hadyn held their breath as he squinted straight into the windowed door they hid behind. He cocked his head, but they couldn't move now. Hadyn primed his muscles to grab Kiara's hand and run.

"Begging your pardon," one rat attempted an apology. "We didn't meant to be so loud."

"Yeah, sorry, Boss."

He turned on them. "Oh, would you two shut up! And get moving," he said, giving up his search. Then added darkly, "We have work to do."

Hadyn released the contents of his lungs and Kiara realized she could relax.

"Now do you see why I didn't want to bring you here?" Hadyn whisper-yelled.

Kiara looked from him to the backs of the men. Through the grimy, cracked panes she saw them walking away. "Who are they?"

"Someone you should never have to meet."

"Look!" Kiara watched them file one by one into a door across the street. "They went inside. I think it's safe to leave."

"Don't have to." Hadyn's voice was suddenly distant and Kiara turned around to find him nowhere in sight.

Broken glass crunched beneath her feet as she stepped into the empty, little, rough-walled room. She wanted to look away as soon as she turned, but the sight demanded her attention and wouldn't let go. Only scanty light actually found its way through the limited and unwashed windows, yet Kiara could tell with what sight she had (and smell) that the room housed little else but garbage and waste. A thin mat in the corner could have served for a bed if you didn't mind the risk of disease and parasites.

Hadyn came around a corner with a lit lantern, but Kiara couldn't rip her eyes away from the room. He could see the pain in her face. She was trying to come to grips with what she saw, but part of her wouldn't let herself believe.

"Come on. It's this way."

She blinked at him. "Does someone live here?"

Hadyn shrugged. "Sometimes . . . I'm sure."

Kiara's eyes roved the room. ". . . How?" She shuffled through the rubbish and stooped to pick up the remains of a fabric doll, one arm dangling dangerously by a single thread.

"You really knew nothing . . ."

Kiara raised her head and it pained her that he could look so sorry for *her*.

Being so used to it, Hadyn hadn't let himself feel sad about things like this in a long time, but her fresh eyes forced him to acknowledge every inch of the tragedy laid out over the whole room, like a mite infested blanket, full of so many holes and tears sown over and ripped back open countless times. It forced him to see all over again how wrong it really was. She shouldn't have had to see it, he thought, but neither should the rest of the innocent kids growing up in it.

"Come on." He jerked his head away from the mess. "We haven't made it to the Styx yet."

"We're still going?"

"Well, I've come to terms with the fact that you won't go home until you find it, so I thought I might as well save you the time and me the headache by getting you in and back home safely myself."

Kiara smirked. "You know you don't have to. I understand it's dangerous."

"Nah, we should be fine. Besides, we're almost there and you shouldn't have had to come here for nothing."

Hadyn turned back down the narrow hallway he had just come out of a minute ago, which got her mind working on a level much past perplexed. The farther he walked the less Kiara could consider following into that ever darkening, spiderweb festooned hallway with who knows what at the end of it.

She fidgeted where she stood. "Um . . . the door is that way, remember?"

"Remember?" Hadyn called back. "I said we didn't have to go back out. Are you coming?"

"Working on that at the moment."

Hadyn walked down the dark hallway without incident . . . she told herself. *So can you. It is just a dark hallway.*

When Kiara finally bolstered the necessary will and trudged up the hall, she fixed her neck with imaginary bolts. She could feel the gaping rooms yawn open to hollow darkness at her sides whenever she passed a room, but she could never look inside or wouldn't.

She found Hadyn at the very end of the hall, waiting for her at a narrow, wooden door. It looked like a pantry door, but a creepy pantry door, at the end of a long, dark, creepy hallway. She could tell by his smirk, he'd tossed around the idea of teasing her, but thought better of it when he saw the pallor of her face and proceeded to open the door without a word.

If a spider could speak, I'd imagine it'd sound a lot like the whiny creek of that door, and the odor that wafted out of the dark space inside hit them like a wall built of dead cats, collected and embalmed by dog sized-spiders.

Kiara fought the urge to retch. "Ah! It smells like something died in there!"

Hadyn wrinkled his nose. "Probably vermin[1]. After you."

She gave a nasally laugh, two fingers pinched firmly on her nose. "You just agreed that something died in there, and now you want me to go first?"

"Do you want to see the Styx or not?"

Kiara frowned at him lamely for a good moment and then wrenched the lantern from his hand, plunging into, what was indeed, a pantry. Opposed to the rest of the house this room was actually filled with something. Yet, that something was not food, but coats, oddly enough, dirty, ripped coats, but coats all the same, all hanging from bars running along the ceiling.

"It's at the back," Hadyn instructed.

"Course it is . . ." she grumbled. "Whatever *it* is."

Kiara pushed her way in. The light didn't provide all that much illumination, clogged by countless, smelly coats, and the stench of death only grew worse the further she went. Shoving through, trying to avoid the entanglement of sleeves and belts, she at length, reached an end. Hadyn, being right behind her, stepped out, knelt down, and wrenched open a round hatch on the ground which reminded her a fair degree too much of the trapdoor in the library, except when she shined the lantern, she could see the bottom of this one only some six feet down.

"I'll go down first and check if it's safe."

Kiara's eyes grew wide. "You're going to leave me up here?"

"Trust me. You're much safer here."

He tried to take the lantern back, but her fingers wouldn't let go.

"Oh! Right. Sorry." She pried her own white fingers off the handle.

"I'll be right back," he assured.

When she heard him jump to the ground and the lantern went out of sight, Kiara thought she might faint, sitting in the stark

---

1. Caverna's term for any kind of rodent or small, furred or not quite furred creature.

darkness with a stench so thick she could choke on it. Once again she was way over her head, following what? A capricious fancy? No, it was more than that. She'd said it herself and she knew it to be true. But was it really worth it? The way had only gotten darker the further she delved, and she was really taking a risk, trusting a boy she had only just met for the third time. Her breaths came quicker, and she thought of turning back while she still could, but Hadyn didn't keep her waiting and returned before she could make any solid decisions.

"It's clear!" Hadyn called up. "It's safe for you to come down now."

When she didn't respond, he called up again. "Kiara?"

She could hear it in his voice, the tremor of disappointment. He didn't fear she had run into trouble; he feared she had left.

Kiara snapped out of it and quit hugging her knees, fairly certain she wouldn't even be able to find her way back on her own. And anyway, could she really leave him after what she'd driven him to do?

"Coming!" she called.

Turning herself around, she began to work down the ladder. The moment her hands touched the rungs, she realized just how wet her palms had become, the clammy metal encouraging her stomach to twist sickeningly. Skipping the last three rungs, she hopped to the ground where an explosion of dust puffed out from beneath her feet.

Hadyn turned to her from his scanning of the tunnel. "You alright?"

She gave a tight, little nod. "Mhmm."

"Don't worry. We're nearly there now."

Kiara looked around the cobbled tunnel. "What is this place?"

"An entrance to the Styx. Or the Stygian Market, as you call it."

"*An* entrance? As in, there's more than one?"

"Countless." His simple reply echoed off the tunnel walls.

Hadyn swung his lantern in front of him as if to suggest they continue moving. "Fortunately for us, because this one's so close to the actual market, it doesn't need to connect to any of the others."

"Where are the other entrances?"

"In homes and shops like this one. Where else? Some people know about them, others have no clue they're even there." He caught the wide-eyed look on her face. "Homes on Terminal Avenue, that is. You don't have to worry about a bunch of thugs coming up through a secret hole in your pantry, or anywhere else in the Palace."

Kiara relaxed. Then, eyeing him cautiously, she noticed, for the first time, he had put on one of the high collared coats from the smelly pantry.

She arched a brow. "A little cold?"

"Hmm? What?"

She nodded to his heavy jacket.

"Oh. That." He dusted off a chalky residue on the lapel. "No, but . . . there are some who would prefer not to see my face in the Styx."

"Some? Like the men we saw in the street?"

He gave her a sideways glance, but didn't speak again until they slowed at the end of the tunnel.

"We're here," he said, stopping at another rusty ladder.

Kiara tensed. This was it, and a dreadful mix of excitement and fear was all she could comprehend.

"Look. If we don't talk to anyone, or buy anything, we should be fine."

Kiara nodded. "Got it."

"I'll go first, like before, and tell you if it's safe."

Hadyn clenched the lantern in between his teeth and began ascending the ladder. She heard the creek of the trapdoor, but Kiara was busy looking over her shoulder, hoping against hope, nothing would materialize out of the darkness.

"All clear!" Hadyn whispered.

Quick as she could, Kiara climbed the ladder and took Hadyn's hand when she reached the top, allowing him to pull her the rest of the way into a dimly lit room. Immediately Kiara was choking on a cloying smell that seemed to line the insides of her throat, the air so thickly laced with incense, they could see it in blue, wispy strands of smoke. Scarlet sheets draped from the low roof to the walls, encompassing the place, and strings of beads hung in walkways to separate rooms.

"Oracle's place," Hadyn explained. "Best we leave before she knows we're here."

Kiara didn't argue. She didn't need anybody telling her how her future was going to go, especially not someone allegedly influenced by watchers. Oracles in Caverna were all the same, a bunch of lying cheats, and she'd give anything to get out of this acrid smell.

She followed close behind Hadyn as he pushed aside the hanging beads and stepped into the main room where they found a woman (dressed much like the room, in draping clothes and adorned in beads) passed out on a long embroidered couch, drool dripping from the corner of her discolored mouth. Her wrinkles ran deep like trenches across a pale desert landscape and she had little elegance left in her smoke dried skin, but to Kiara, she seemed like some kind of ancient and sacred beauty, never having seen even royalty so exquisitely dressed.

Hadyn puffed out a breath. "Thank goodness. She's asleep."

Just then, the second cat Kiara had seen that day strutted into view. A little better kept than the last, it yet had its whole tail, but its nose was still crooked and it favored a front twisted paw.

Hadyn silently pleaded with the feline, eyes urgent that it not make a sound. But with an innocent mew, it leapt up straight onto the woman's lap.

The oracle jolted to life like a body from the grave. "What? Where?" she squawked. "Who has come to learn their fate?" But all she saw was the gentle swaying of the hanging beads, before she fell back on the couch in a content stupor.

Kiara muffled her snickers behind her hands just around the corner as Hadyn looked over his shoulder.

"That was close!"

"Yeah." Kiara smirked. "What's the deal there? You got a problem with her or something?"

"Just the fact that she won't let you go if she gets a hold of you. That woman's mouth doesn't know how to stop running. And I don't need a stranger trying to tell me things they know about me or predicting what's going to happen to me."

Kiara surprised herself when she understood him more than she expected. She smiled, but then she saw a glimpse past him and suddenly forgot what they were talking about.

She walked past him without a word, her feet sweeping her along, and didn't stop walking until she met a short cobbled wall. High up on a loft-like balcony, Kiara gazed down on the Stygian Market, smaller than she expected, but no less incredible, or busy. Countless people milled about as if on a mission. And the noise! The noise filled her ears with chaos unparalleled. Color flooded her eyes. Everyone of the many tented shops, boasted its own unique design, each one trying to outdo the last in artistic bedlam. And if the tents were so colorful, Kiara couldn't help but marvel at what could be inside. The high, open roof itself was draped in a mismatch of capricious fabrics and patterns, none of which went together, like a patchwork carnival tent.

Kiara breathed deep, the air wild with a mingle of spices. "You never said it was so beautiful!"

Hadyn didn't look at the market. He'd seen it plenty of times before. But he couldn't help himself when it came to admiring Kiara's utter rapture.

"Didn't have to," he said. "You already thought highly enough of it."

Kiara's gaze roved over the strange new place. "Not like this . . ."

Hadyn just smiled and finally turned to the market. "Welcome to the Styx."

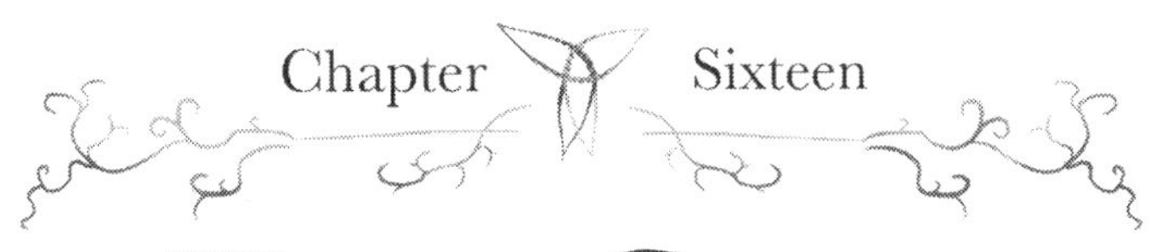

Chapter Sixteen

THE STYX

Faster than if a cloud of bats came and spirited it away, Kiara's fear disintegrated like crumbling stone when faced with such incomprehensible wonder. She searched for a way down and it was all she could do to keep from running when she spotted the top of a narrow spiraling stair.

Hadyn caught her eyes for just a moment, her blazing green irises flashing with some sort of wonderful mischief that both intrigued and terrified him, before she zoomed to the stairway, cloak fluttering behind her. Hadyn ran to catch up with her, taking the turns of the staircase at a breakneck speed, lucky he didn't fall flat on his face. Then without much warning at all, he was forced to a sudden halt. Taking care to watch his feet, he barely looked up in time to see Kiara at a dead still at the bottom of the steps. By a mere inch, he managed to miss her and prevent the collision. He paused to catch his breath and find out why she had stopped.

She stood in spellbound awe, barely managing to take in all the sights, sounds, and colors. Hadyn smiled, not simply because her joy and wonder was beautiful, but because it was contagious. It took a hold of him and insisted he open his eyes and see just what she saw. And when he did, it did not disappoint. Before he knew it though, Kiara giggled girlishly and took off again, all too eager to get lost in the color.

He followed her around as her voracious appetite for the new, the strange, and the incredible flitted from one shop to the next, her eyes devouring every little wonder faster than he could keep up. She kept an eye on him well enough, beckoning with a nod of her head to *catch up*, or *come see this!* every now and again.

And despite all his misgivings, Hadyn actually began to enjoy himself. While still well aware of the many dangers this place harbored underneath its ever shifting scales, Kiara's childlike joy in every new exploration had him wishing this could all be as good as she saw it, and for a moment, she helped him forget . . . that is, until he did the inevitable and peered inside the wrong shop at the wrong time, catching sight of a brute of a man interrogating a member of a rival clan with little to no care for those around him. He saw the smaller man shake his trembling head. He didn't know anything, he'd most likely say. Then he saw the hulking one grab up his hand and could all too easily imagine the sickening sound of crunching bones, just before he ran to catch up with Kiara again. The man's screams were lost in the din of the crowds, but it wasn't the only crime in the Styx that people would rather just turn a blind eye to. Kiara just didn't see it. She didn't know what to look for. But a small mark of a skull or some sort of ragged beast on a coat or hat, chalked in white limestone, gave them away easily enough. And if not that, then their posture alone undoubtedly proclaimed who they were. Clansmen[1]. . . kings in their own right, men of power, men of greed . . . They weren't exactly hiding.

Hadyn's chest tightened and he found himself pulling his collar higher to hide his face, and searching every man's jacket for any sign of a white beast's head, mouth agape with rows of fangs. The mark of the Whitefangs, the deadliest, most ruthless cutthroats of all the clansmen. Fortunately his search came up fruitless, but he knew they were here somewhere. Because in a place with no rules, colors weren't the only thing running rampant.

"Hey, Kiara? I don't know about you, but I think we should go soon. You know, before we run into any trouble." When she didn't answer, he spun around, scanning the crowd for her. "Kiara?" but she was nowhere to be seen.

A hand went to the back of his head as he spun once more for good measure. "Not again." He huffed. "Not here. Of all places, not here."

His heart raced with the dangers. If he had been terrified the last time, this was something entirely different, a devouring panic, filling his brain with images he knew, first hand, as stark realities. If she was taken *here*, he knew he'd never forgive himself. But he tried not to jump to such crazed fear, and scanned his surroundings, heart pounding in his ears.

There! Finally, he spotted her across the way, but the sick

---

1. A group of scoundrels and criminals. They owned the Styx and ruled it with and ruthless fist.

ness in his gut wouldn't leave him alone.

Kiara had wandered up to an extensively wrinkled woman, laden with chunky, heavy-looking jewelry. She peered down into a glass display box, filled with necklaces and such made of old pieces of twisted and bent metal.

"Ah, does the lass spy a trinket that catches her fancy?"

Kiara glanced at the woman's round, hungry eyes, but she didn't say a word.

"She sure would make all the other young'uns mad with envy," she enticed.

"No, no." Hadyn rushed up and placed his hands on Kiara's shoulders. "Sorry, Ma'am, but we won't be needing any of . . ." he looked at what she was selling, "those . . . today."

The wrinkled old woman frowned, but Kiara had spotted something boundlessly more beautiful than any piece of jewelry could ever be to her. Her squealing gasp startled them both. "Chimes!" She exclaimed and again she was gone.

Hadyn sighed and bolted after her.

"So you see most of everything's on sale today, but that don't mean I'm up for haggling," a plump woman with a large mole besmirching her round, porcelain cheeks informed her.

Hadyn stumbled to her side. "Kiara, we really should, before—"

"Well, look here," the plump woman began and Hadyn cringed. "If it isn't the little Blackcoal of Mereaze's clan. He'll have your head if he catches a whiff of you here. You know that, right?"

Hadyn held a finger to his lips. "Of course I do. Have you seen him?"

"Have I seen him," she chortled. "When don't I?"

"Alice," Hadyn pressed in desperation.

She put her hands on her hips. "Now mind your tone, Boy. Yes I saw 'em. Strode past here with Vermin One and Two clinging to his coat tails like dried mud, not five minutes ago. But what's this?" She eyed Kiara incredulously. "Since when did you get the rubbish idea that the Styx would be a good place to bring a girl?" She clicked her tongue disapprovingly. "Didn't the orphanage learn you better manners on courtin', Hadyn?"

"Of course not and— What?" He shook his head. "This is not . . . I didn't bring her here."

"Yes you did," Kiara said.

Hadyn looked at her and puffed a breath through his nose, at a complete loss.

Finally, Kiara understood the awkward insinuation. "Oh . . . but it's not like that. I asked him to take me. We're . . . cousins after all!"

"Cousins?" Alice grunted. "Well, bless me. I didn't know you had a cousin."

"Neither did we!" Kiara said, a little too loud.

Hadyn took up the baton. "Y-yeah!" He grinned. "It wasn't until I got out of the orphanage that we knew we were even related. Distantly, mind you."

Hadyn didn't think shrewd Alice would believe him, but she broke into the biggest grin.

"Well, bless me! Cousins . . . I'm just glad you found that you have some family after all."

Hadyn smiled and felt himself relax a bit. "Thanks, Alice."

He turned to Kiara. She had that wonder in her eyes again, lost in her own awe as she gently tapped the chimes to hear them sing.

"You want one, don't you?"

Kiara whipped her head around. "What? Oh, but you said—"

"Yeah, but it's Alice." He gestured to the woman's pleasant, round face.

Kiara raised her brows. "Do you mean it?"

He shrugged. "Why not?"

Delighted, Kiara spun on her heels to scan the many hanging chimes, but she didn't have to look long. She already knew which one she wanted, because it sang just like the one Hadyn had hung in the library.

"How much is this one?"

"Em . . . let me see . . ."

Kiara was already pulling out her pouch to see if she had enough on her.

"Oh, lassie," Alice said. "Arums and Agents won't do you any good here. Stones are all I'll take."

Her face fell and she looked to Hadyn for an explanation.

"Gems," he said.

Crestfallen, Kiara frowned at the pouch in her hand and fought herself to tie it closed and give up.

To Hadyn it was all wrong. All that wonder and with one statement it was snuffed out like a light. She had all the money in Caverna and yet she couldn't have one of the simplest things she could ever have want for.

"How much, Alice?" he asked.

"For this old thing?" She turned down her mouth in contemplation. "I'd say an amethyst druzy or two should cover the cost."

Hadyn frowned, knowing full well how outrageous that was, then reached in his pocket and fished out a small bag of his own. "I only have one amethyst left, but I could substitute the other for a class C opal?"

Kiara pushed his hand down. "Hadyn, no. I couldn't let you do that."

"It's not like it's anything you haven't already done for me." He turned away from her. "So what will it be, Alice?"

She shook her head. "I told you, I won't be haggling."

"And I thought you said everything's on sale. Two druzy doesn't seem like much of a deal."

She narrowed her eyes and steamed, but conceded in the end. "Fine," she grumbled. "I'll settle for the one amethyst."

Hadyn grinned and dropped the gem into her chubby hand. "Glad to see—"

"*And* the opal." Alice waved her fingers, an all too sugary grin on her face.

Hadyn coughed up the opal, and Alice examined it like it was on trial for murder. At length, a satisfied grin curled her lips. "Pleasure doing business with you, Blackcoal."

Hadyn bristled at the name calling, but didn't say a word.

"Here you are, my dear." Alice plucked the chime off its hook and handed it to Kiara, who in turn held it like a sacred artifact.

"Now, what did you say your name was?" Alice asked, shattering her revere. I feel like I've seen your face a'fore . . . plenty of times, actually. Just never really met you."

Heart suddenly racing, Kiara turned to Haydn for help and to better hide her face.

"Your name, lass?"

"Uh, Betsie, ma'am."

"Betsie? But that ain't what Blackcoal called you. I could have sworn, on my ma's urn, it started with a K."

Hadyn did his best not to look guilty. "Oh! K-Kara. Her name is Kara Elisabeth. But she prefers to go by her middle name."

Alice squinted at him. "No . . . Kiara!" she exclaimed.

"*That's* what you said; not Kara. Funny that. That's the princess' name."

Kiara kept her head down and to the side, all but trembling beneath her cloak.

"Come now. There's no need to be shy." Alice leaned to better see her face, but Kiara turned further away. "Unless . . ."

Silence reigned between the three while chaos ensued around them. Neither Kiara nor Hadyn moved. Would Alice shout if they did?

Kiara's stomach fluttered uncomfortably. Suddenly all the sound and excitement that beckoned her before, entrapped and confined her. Unexpectedly the room grew darker and the crowds began to quiet or maybe that was just her own vision and hearing. She felt her hands lather with sweat and inch by inch the chimes began to slip from her weakening grip, until, almost slowly, they fell. Each chime clattered with its own deafening racket in her ears, somehow as the only sound she heard.

"Princess . . ." Alice breathed in wide-eyed realization. "Hadyn, what have you done?"

"Nothing," Hadyn hissed. "Just don't say anything, and everything will be fine."

"Don't say anything? If Mereaze or any of the others find out about this, I'll be lumped in with the blame." The fear in Alice's eyes reminded him of how scared he should be. "Hadyn . . . how could you?"

Hot breath on the back of Hadyn's neck, drained his blood of warmth. "If Mereaze finds out about what?" came a gravely baritone, as two meaty hands clamped down on his shoulders till it hurt. "I thought I smelt a stench around here. I just didn't know it was the smell of a coward."

The clobbering hands spun him about so he faced him. But there at eye level, Hadyn stared at the head of a fanged, white beast chalked on the lapel of a soiled, brown jacket. It wasn't till he raised his eyes did he meet the wicked, nigh on toothless grin and unnaturally hideous face of Hamish Clungston. His pale bug-eyes, it seemed, still had not come to an agreement on which one should decide where to look, the whites muddy and discolored. Just under seven feet tall, the unsightly man easily dwarfed him. And Kiara had thought *Hadyn* was tall.

Hamish raised his wildly unkempt brow (he only had the one) and fixed Hadyn with the one eye he could get to go places.

"What are you doin' here, Blackcoal?" His breath reeked like a sewer drain.

"Just passing through, big guy. I—"

Hamish squeezed him tighter and Hadyn felt his feet leave the ground. "No one just passes through the Styx."

Hadyn swallowed down a lump in his throat. "You know, funny thing is, we were just leaving. No harm," Hamish squeezed his shoulders tighter, all but crushing his bones. "done," Hadyn finished with a squeak.

"We?" Growled the siege tower.

Hadyn closed his eyes, scrunching his face in anguish from both pain and regret of his words. He craned his neck to look at her, pleading with his eyes for her to run, yet she just stood there, terrified, but not about to leave him.

"And who do we have here? Blackcoal found hisself a lady friend?"

"It's the princess." Alice, who had watched in silence until now, deliberately doomed them both to save her own hide.

Hadyn shot her a glare and she grinned smugly back. Hamish seemed to look at both Alice and Kiara at the same time, one eye trained dangerously on both. Then he burst into roaring laughter.

"It's true!" Alice shouted above his outburst.

"Alice!" Hadyn couldn't believe her betrayal.

"Shut your trap, Blackcoal! You brought this on yourself."

Hamish's laughter died and he looked at them each in turn. When he came to Kiara once again he seemed to finally understand.

"What have you done?" He spat at Hadyn. "You've doomed us all!"

"Doomed us?" came a wickedly amused voice as calm as darkness itself, and suddenly Hadyn and Kiara weren't the only ones scared spitless.

Alice retreated to the corner of her booth and Hadyn looked into Hamish round eyes. The big man knew to fear that voice just as well as him. He could see it in the pallor of his face and feel it in the way his grip weakened ever so slightly around his shoulders. Hadyn's own pulse quickened as the clomp of boots approached.

The man with the rugged, wide brimmed hat stalked into view, and Kiara cowered under the glare of his cold eyes.

"My, my, my. What do we have here?"

Hamish shook Hadyn around. "This un's brought all hell on

us, Mereaze. Brought the bloody Red Princess to our doors, he has!"

The dark man called Mereaze didn't smile, but his eyes did seem to flash with some sort of horrible pleasure, beneath the brim of his hat. "The Red Princess, indeed. But you're wrong, big fellow. This is not a sentence, but a grand opportunity, laid right in our lap." He crossed to Kiara and grabbed up her face in one hand. "Yes. She'll fetch a fine ransom from her father, the king."

Kiara wrenched her face free. "He won't give you a single aeris!" she spat. "He'd rather see me dead!"

"My dear, you've got some fire." Mereaze didn't flinch. "And we'll just see about that, won't we?" Then, giving her one more appraising look that made her skin want to crawl right off, he turned to Hadyn, still clenched in Hamish Clungston's crushing grasp. "Well done, Blackcoal. I don't know how you managed it, but I really should let you in here more often." He started to walk away. "Put him down, Clungston. He's not the one you should be carrying."

"You what?" Hamish looked like he couldn't decide whether to listen or snap his captive in two right there. Hadyn decided not to wait for his decision

Pushing back against his stoney arms and hands, Hadyn used the leverage and brought his knee up hard into his gut. Hamish's eyes bugged out of his head as he fell back and dropped Hadyn straight to the ground.

Forcing the wind back into his lungs, Hadyn shouted with all he had, "Run!" but Kiara had come to help him up. He pushed her away. "No! You have to get out of here!"

"Just get up and I will!" she screamed.

Hadyn shot to his feet faster than the more lumbering Clungston could even figure out what hit him. In the distance Mereaze sent him a calculated glare across the gap between them. He didn't move, but it was that look of complete certainty he wouldn't have to move a muscle, that nailed Hadyn's feet to the ground.

He felt a tugging on his arm.

"Come on! What are you waiting for!"

He had lingered so long Kiara had already picked up the chimes she dropped and stood at his side, urging him to move. When he looked back at Mereaze, a curling grin had crawled into the clansman's lips as he raised a silver whistle to his mouth.

If Kiara wasn't there to get to safety, Hadyn didn't know if he would have ever moved, but her incessant tugging helped his feet to remember their ability of flight. Hadyn clasped her hand, refusing to lose her again (despite possible consequences of her offense) and took off away from both Hamish and Mereaze just as a piercing note screamed a bleeding cry. The whole of the market would hear that alarm and clansmen from all around would come to its call in seconds, especially those bearing the mark of the white beast.

Hadyn threw a look over his shoulder and saw Hamish already giving chase. He beat his legs so fast, he feared he'd have to drag Kiara, but she kept pace step for step, adrenaline and terror all but giving her wings.

Kiara ran in a fury. Not wholly unaided by the burning rage she had kindled toward herself for being so stupid.

Men poured out of tents and shops like roaches from a crack in the wall, mean, unsavory looking men. All the while, Hamish bellowed orders at each of them to give chase.

It seemed like every direction they turned, there to greet them was a new face that looked ready to flay them alive, and then she'd feel another wrench on her arm as Hadyn pulled her in another direction. Grubby hands reached and grabbed at them from all sides. One absurdly hairy man with a gruesome knife even nicked her on the shoulder before she could get out of reach. Kiara yelped and Hadyn spun around and kicked him in the shin before bolting again.

Kiara began to tire rather quickly, she could feel the tension building in her arm as Hadyn got further ahead of her. It wouldn't be long before she couldn't keep up with him, she thought, just when they burst into the more open area of the outer ring, encircling the whole market.

Hadyn turned to go right, but stopped short when he saw Mereaze standing stone faced and behind him approached a whole army of ruffians, carrying any means of weaponry they could find. Kiara whipped her head the other way, but there was Clungston and the two rat-like men bringing up the other half of the clansmen.

"Hadyn . . ." her voice quivered, and he followed her gaze. "What do we do?"

Hadyn searched the surroundings like a trapped animal, for any form of safety or escape, until finally he looked up. High in the balcony area, people still milled about unaware for the most part.

He spotted the narrow doorway for one of the spiral staircases and bolted for it. If nothing else, at least only a few would be able to follow them at a time.

At the top, Kiara scanned the crowds and shops. "We need to get out. Where's another exit?"

"I don't know!" Hadyn nearly shouted. "I don't know all that many."

Footsteps and shouts echoed up the stairs. Kiara bounced on her toes and chewed on her lip, eyes ever searching.

"Look!" she exclaimed. "It's the oracle's place! We're back where we came in!"

Hadyn thought about it. It seemed like a gamble, but their pursuers didn't give them much of a choice. Into the crowd they went just as the first clansman reared his ugly head around the last bend in the stairs. Every time Hadyn turned around, he caught site of at least one man with murder in his eyes, but ever so steadily they began to put more people between them and the clansmen. And when it came time to duck inside the oracle's shop, they might have actually lost them.

Pressing themselves against the wall, Hadyn and Kiara both breathed a sigh of relief to see the wrinkled woman yet dreaming in oblivion on her embroidered couch.

They waited for the sounds of malintent to pass by, hoping with every second that none would get the itch to check inside the shop of a zonked-out fortune teller. A cold sweat dripped to the end of Kiara's nose and her hands grew slippery. They measured their breathing well enough, but the quiet almost begged for something to destroy it, and something obliged.

Slick with sweat, Kiara's fingers grew slothful in their vigilance, and one after the other two chimes slipped from her grasp, swinging by their strings.

Clink, chink!

Kiara's heart stopped in her chest.

"Wha?" The pile of wrinkles and drapery burst to life. "Who wakes Madam Grizella!"

"Oi? What's that racket?" came a voice from outside.

Kiara felt another yank on her arm that nearly pulled it out of socket and dearly hoped it was the last. They rushed to the back room and held their breath as heavy footfalls thumped into the shop. Immediately, the ancient oracle accosted the men she thought had disturbed her slumber.

"Ah! So nice to have visitors! Would one of you like me to read your fortune?"

"No. Step aside, old bag," a baritone voice said. "Have you seen the princess?"

"Oh, take no offense, but I don't have to read your palm to see there isn't no princess in *your* future . . . Oh, but I can tell you what is in your future, among . . . other things."

"I said, no. What don't you get about that, hag? Did any suspicious characters walk in here just a moment ago?"

"Its the Styx, darling, who isn't suspicious?"

"Test my patience one moment longer, hag!"

A pause. Then Grizella's croaky voice again, "No."

"But you were yappin' at someone." A third voice said.

"Yes. You."

"No, you started blabbering before we ever set foot in here."

She ran an appraising hand under her chin. "Fortune teller . . .?"

They heard a sigh. "Come on, Clungston. We're wasting our time."

Kiara's eyes grew even wider than they already were. That brute lurked on the other side of the wall they hid behind!

They heard a growl of reluctant resignation and the same heavy footfalls departed from the shop. Then as they waited in stunned silence, shocked they still had heads attached to their necks, they heard another thud as Madam Grizella fell back into another unconscious stupor.

After all that running and heart-pounding fear, the sound of her narcolepsy had laughter tearing at the seams of their fear. Kiara was the first to snort, but soon they were both snickering under their breath, choking on their own suppressed giggles.

"That was so close!" Kiara whispered.

Her hood had fallen in the mad chase through the market and the candlelight of the incense burners illuminated wayward tendrils around her ears and forehead that had escaped her efforts to pin them back. She caught Hadyn staring rather intently at the loose curls, and bristled, shoving them behind her ears, and stepping away from him.

"What?" she accused.

"I'm sorry. I didn't—" His eyes fluttered. "You're bleeding."

"Hmm?" Kiara looked at her shoulder to see a cut in her sleeve and a crimson gash still wet with blood where one of the clansmen had knifed her. "It's nothing." But when she moved her hand to cover it, she couldn't help but wince. "I'll clean it up when I get home."

"Right . . . home," Hadyn said. "Let's get out of here."

Walking back up the hidden tunnel, lantern in hand, Hadyn seemed oddly reticent, and in the silence Kiara couldn't help but feel the guilt building up on her.

"Something on your mind?"

When he answered, it was barely a whisper. "*I just snuck the princess into the Styx . . .*"

So hushed, Kiara couldn't be sure he was even talking to her. "Yeah, I know. I'm right here."

"I just snuck the Princess of Caverna into the Styx," he said, louder.

"Yes. Now are you finished or shall we repeat that until we get back?"

"Don't you get it?"

"Yes, it was amazing and . . . atrociously dangerous."

"Exactly."

Kiara shrugged. "What do you want me to say?"

"Nothing. I messed up."

"No. I won't let you take the blame for this. This is my fault. I wheedled you into it."

"But I never should have told you about the Styx in the first place. And even after, I should have told you no."

"You did . . ." Kiara looked at him sadly. "Hadyn, I'm sorry."

He fixed her with a ruminative glance. "Yeah, well, I guess we're both to blame," he said, yet refusing to let her take all the responsibility.

"Those men . . ." Kiara faltered. "Mereaze . . . Will you—"

"I'll be fine." He forced a grin. "This isn't the first time I've been the catalyst and brunt of Mereaze's rage . . . and it probably won't be the last."

Kiara scrunched her brow. "But why?"

"Look. I've put you in enough danger already. Please don't ask me anything more."

"But—"

"Please!"

It took everything in her to shut her mouth. She didn't have it in her to just turn her face from the situation, but the intense look in his eyes told her, she must very well try.

"... Okay."

They walked in a pained silence the rest of the way. Despite Kiara's attempts at refusal, Hadyn insisted on walking her at least to the Library in the middle of town.

"Are you sure, you'll be alright?" Kiara asked as they prepared to part ways.

"Yes. I'm just glad you're safe."

"Oh, I never got to properly thank you with . . . what happened back there. For the chimes, I mean."

"The way I see it, neither did I," he said, fishing a burgundy gem out of his pocket.

Kiara recognized the alexandrite right away and gave him a soft smile. Then an awkward silence followed and neither knew how to fill it.

"So," she swung her arms, "I'll see you tonight then?"

"Uh . . . Oh yeah!"

She frowned. "You didn't forget, did you? We have to get your journal back."

He squinted at her. "Haven't you had enough danger for one day?"

She shrugged up her shoulders, her smile scrunching her nose, and without another word she turned and trotted home.

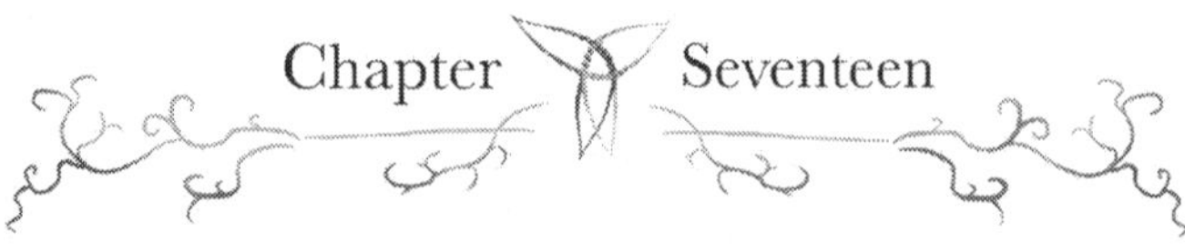

Chapter Seventeen

Stuffy Dinner Companions

Before Kiara went home, she stopped at her hideaway to drop off her chimes and find a place of honor to hang her new treasure. When she finally got home, she walked into the palace, trying to look as much like a servant coming back from a market errand as possible, not that any of that would help if she actually had to talk to someone. She had an idea to prank Shrike while she was in disguise, knowing he'd be baffled that it wasn't her, but thought better of it, and miraculously made it to her door without a single incident.

Kiara looked up and down the hallway before stealing inside and locking the door behind her. She breathed a sigh of relief. Finally she was safe from snoops, thieves, clansmen, and whatever else. She tossed off her cloak and strode to her bed to try and nap before she left again that night, but a certain reflection stopped her in her tracks. There in the mirror of her vanity, stood a girl, filthy from head to toe, hair a frazzled mess of fuzz, and bleeding from a gash on her shoulder. She had half the mind to think it wasn't a mirror at all, but a picture of someone else if not for the fact that there was but one redhead in all of Caverna. She cringed at the sight. She hadn't thought she could get any uglier and yet . . . there was this. The dust on her face contrasted her hair and somehow made it flair even brighter. Her bloody sleeve and ragged dress suggested she was nothing more than a vagabond trespassing in the princess' royal chamber.

Striking a pose, she gave herself a silly grin, not because she found any sort of fondness for this new look, but because it proved all that had just happened, even if her mind wanted to play games with her.

Then her arms dropped and her shoulders slumped under a sudden heaviness. It wasn't all a fantastic escapade. The events and mistakes of the day crumbled on her with the weight of a collapsing cavern. What did she expect from a clandestine den of criminals? Peace and hospitality? What's worse, she had charged straight into it, danger and all, with a boy she hardly knew. She could just see her mother shaking her head. And now, because of her, that same boy was in trouble . . . all because of her.

Kiara knew she wouldn't get a wink of sleep until she removed the dirt, so stripping down to her linens, she called for clean water to be brought to her room. She scrubbed at the dirt until her face and hands were raw, as if she could also clean away her shortcomings if she only washed vigorously enough.

Cleaning the cut took a little more care. She pressed a warm, wet cloth to it and winced at the sting burning like a fire stoking to life in the wound.

A knock on the door distracted her from the pain.

"Kiara?" she heard her father call and her heart jumped in her chest. The handle jangled, but thankfully she had locked it. "Kiara, would you open this door? I'd like to speak with you." He didn't sound happy.

Kiara's eyes flicked from the bedraggled servant's dress draped across her bed to the murky, blood-tainted water bowls on her vanity.

"Just a minute, Father!" she called, still pressing a hand to her cut. "May I meet you in your study, perhaps?"

A muffled sigh came through the door. "Very well."

Kiara blew out a sigh as his footsteps faded down the hall. Hastily she wrapped her cut, slipped on a crisp, new dress and made her hair presentable for her father.

Rounding the turn, she stepped into his study. "You wanted to speak to me?"

"Ah, yes . . ." He looked at his feet. "Well, this is quite silly now, isn't it?" He chuckled.

"What is?"

"Kiara . . ." he eyed her carefully, "I have to ask. Where were you today?"

"Why, at school, Father."

"Yes, of course, but after school. The servants say you were gone for hours."

Kiara hesitated a moment. "Oh! The Market. I decided to go today, since I haven't been in some time."

"I see. Anywhere else?"

"I suppose I walked around town a bit, but then I came back."

"Of course. I told them you never leave the house, especially not lately, but they were so sure."

"And you'd believe them over me?"

Nnyric looked at her, undecided. "Of course not. That's why I checked your room. I was sure I'd find you there."

"I've been in my room for some time now. The servants must have never seen me return. Too busy minding business that isn't theirs to mind."

"Yes . . . insufferable lot . . . Hmmm." He turned around leaning on his desk with his hands. He ran his fingers through his rarely, but already, messed hair. He looked tired, very tired, and the way his eyes shifted about, suggested something more like paranoia than ease.

Kiara cocked her head. "Is there something wrong?"

"No," he said quickly, but he seemed unsatisfied. "It's just that someone said they saw a young lady meeting your description today. And I trust you understand why that's a hard statement to ignore," he said, gesturing to her.

Kiara repressed her offense. "Where? I went a lot of places."

Nnyric fixed her with a sharp, unsure look. "The Stygian Market."

After a moment of frozen horror, Kiara snorted then she laughed. "But that's preposterous. It doesn't even exist! . . . Right?" Her eyes widened. "The Styx aren't actually real . . . are they?"

"No, of course not. You know how I deplore those rumors."

Her face fell as if disappointed. "Then why the questions?"

"Well, because . . . he seemed so sure. But you're right." He shook his head. "It's ridiculous. He must have had one too many drinks at the tavern and didn't know where he was or what he saw."

They stood in silence for a moment. Kiara bounced on her heels. "Anything else you wanted to talk to me about?"

"Actually, Kiara—" he stopped mid sentence, eyes locked on her left shoulder. "You're bleeding!"

Kiara followed his gaze slowly as if this was news to her. There blossoming from the seam of her sleeve was a dark splotch of blood. She whipped her hand up to cover it. "Oh! That." His gaze demanded an explanation. "Well, you see, my dress had a tear and in an attempt to mend it, I pricked myself quite deep. Rushing to see you must have caused it to bleed again."

"You tried to mend your own dress? Kiara, we have servants for that sort of thing."

"It was a small tear. I didn't think to trouble them."

"Small or not, why bother fixing it when you can have a new dress made up?"

"Of course. I best go bandage this up. So if you have no further need of me . . ."

"Yes, go ahead. But, Kiara?"

She stopped.

"I'd like you to eat dinner tonight."

Kiara searched his eyes for the catch, wondering at his sudden concern in her eating habits. "Very well. I'm feeling better and suppose I could work up the appe—"

"In the dining hall," he demanded. "With me."

Kiara shut her mouth.

Her father took a breath before he continued. "Lady Cunningtin is coming to dine with us, and I'd like you to attend as well." Kiara made a face. "Before you start." He held up a hand. "I know your feelings full well. I want you to come."

Kiara wasn't so sure he knew her feelings well enough . . . but how could she say no when he actually wanted her for something?

Setting her jaw, she blew a breath through her nose. "Yes, Father. I'll see you at dinner?"

"Yes. See you at dinner."

Kiara walked from the room with a heavy plod because the many thoughts weighing her down, when from out of the quiet she heard a hushed, "What?"

"I didn't—" Kiara started to say, but another voice cut her off, a voice that froze her blood in her veins, a voice she hoped, more than anything in her life, she wouldn't have to hear again.

"*Don't what me,*" it wheezed, slipping ice cold shivers down her spine. "*You know precisely why I'm here. What do you think you're doing?*"

"I think I'm doing my best," her father said.

The wheeze, the thing, the villain scoffed, "*Your best! Ha! What preposssterous premonition would ever give you reason to believe that was your bessst?*"

Nnyric sputtered.

"*Mmhh?*" the phantom pressed.

"I didn't know what else to do. If she finds out—"

"*It's over!" the other voice finished for him. "All of it! Done! If she finds out about the stones . . .?*" The sentence ended in a guttural growl.

The stones? Kiara mouthed.

"Oh, would you leave me alone? I'll fix this."

"*Leave you alone?*" The voice held such an amused smirk, carrying into dark laughter with low and wicked pleasure. It infiltrated Kiara's head and consumed her mind. A terrible heat radiated like a consuming fire in between her shoulder blades and up her neck. Her legs wobbled and didn't regain their strength again until the laughter subsided.

"*You passed by any chance of us leaving you alone long ago.*"

"Now you listen to me!" Nnyric tried to sound bold. "You don't own me— Ahh!" he yelled in pain and fell silent.

"*Think again, slave,*" it spat, "*and you'll find we do. We own every soul in this prison. What makes you any different?*"

Nnyric panted with some strain, ". . . I thought—"

"*YOU THOUGHT WRONG!*" it roared.

Kiara cupped a hand to her mouth to stifle the scream.

"Please," Nnyric begged. "Just give me another chance."

"*Shhh!*" It seemed to sniff the air with suspicion. "*Someone's here.*"

Footsteps tapped in her ears, but Kiara couldn't move. She hyperventilated with the need for wings.

Nnyric stumbled, his head still dizzy from the pain, and rounded the corner to find a dark empty corridor.

"You were wrong . . ." he said. "There's no one here." But his head was just as empty as the hallway. The voice was gone.

Kiara locked her bedroom door, and slammed her back against it. She stared into a void with wide-eyed fear, her chest spasming with rapid, shaky breaths.

Once was bad enough. Denial, however irrational, could help her forget or ignore it once. But again? This stranger, this demon was back to haunt her, forcing her to acknowledge its existence.

Sliding to the floor, she hugged her knees. Who was this being to call her father, a king, its slave? How long? How long had the master not been the master at all? Was it a part of him? Another personality? Separate but the same?

All at once, her breaths coalesced into one violently trembling heave, and she held it like she couldn't get it out. But after a jittering exhale, she forced herself to stand.

"Get it together . . . Get it together . . ." She rapidly patted her cheeks.

In some ways, it explained a lot, ripping open all the questions of unexplainable cruelty and all but giving them a name. Because if something had taken over, how much of Nnyric was even left? How much of her father was left? Was there any at all? There had to be. She saw him from time to time. And that's what made it so painful. Letting him in time and time again when he seemed better, when he was better, but then getting crushed, every time worse than the last. She felt sorry for him and hated him at the same time, because deep down, she knew he wanted this. He chose it, and he let it happen.

A rap on the door made her jump off the ground, but it wasn't her father's pounding knock.

". . . Yes?" she tried not to squeak.

"Dinner in an hour, Your Majesty."

She relaxed. "Thank you."

In all the horror she had rightly forgotten about her father's dinner plans, and suddenly she didn't know if she could face him. But she supposed this was him speaking, not the . . . She swallowed hard . . . *Voice*. It reeked far too much of his regular political schemes.

With another deep breath, she did her best to make herself ready for dinner, properly binding her cut and changing for the umpteenth time that day. She didn't understand or care to learn the ways of politics or why it was so important for her father to keep a good image with a woman he liked about as much as the next person in power. Apparently she was the wealthy widow of some politician her father used to work with closely, which by some ridiculous turn of fate dubbed her a lady of renown, but that's about all Kiara knew. That and if ever there was a family of louder blowhards, she had yet to know they existed.

Getting ready was painless enough until it came time to do her hair. Her father would prefer if she hid it, and she preferred not to vex him, but then she could only glare at the headscarf she had laid out on her bed, missing Cida, knowing she'd do the painful job of making her presentable, so she wouldn't have to.

She thought she should be grateful that he even wanted her there, that it was important to him for her to look good in front of his guests, but why. . . Why couldn't the request come purely because he wanted to eat with her, ugliness and all? Just her . . . his only daughter.

She couldn't let it get to her. She had wasted too much time fretting already. Swallowing down the throbbing in her throat, she concealed her hair in the headscarf, wrapping it properly and strode with as much dignity as she could muster to the dining hall.

Near the table she found her father talking to a tall, slender, well-dressed man. The man had his back to her, but her father looked unreasonably happy to be talking with him. She stepped into the room hesitantly, taking no care to hide the confusion on her face.

"Ah, Kiara!" her father finally noticed her presence. He looked normal now that he had cleaned up, so fraudulently pleasant, but normal. "Lady Cunningtin couldn't join us tonight," he continued. "Unfortunately she has taken ill quite suddenly."

Kiara tried not to show her relief so blatantly. "I'm sorry to hear that. I hope she's alright."

"Yes. It seems nothing too serious. But," Nnyric continued all too brightly, "her eldest son has graciously come in her stead! Kiara, you know George?" he said and the "unknown guest" finally turned around and tilted his head to her, flashing her a pleasant but stiff smile.

Kiara's spirits rose only to sink deeper than before. The dread she had brewed for this dinner grew to a dark power, looming over her and twisting her gut. If Lady Cunningtin, George's mother, was arrogant, he was so full of his own rubbish it was coming out of his ears.

She smiled politely. "Of course," she said and tried not to be appalled when he took her hand and planted a kiss on the back of it. There was nothing impolite in it, but Kiara had always found the custom barbaric. She also reluctantly refrained from wiping that same hand on the skirt of her dress when she caught her father smiling at her, not because of the smile, but because of the prodding look behind his eyes, begging her to behave for once in her life.

George displayed the very image of an eligible (not to mention wealthy) gentleman, perfect for marriage, and even more perfect for politics, something her father would call a proper suitor, but George was eighteen, practically a man, much too concerned with himself to really even see the world around him, which had soured him and made him stuffier than a boring book, and Kiara didn't want anything to do with him.

As they prepared to seat themselves, Kiara fixed her father with a glare, stuck her hand up into her head scarf, and wrenched out a handful of curls so they hung in her eyes, fairly certain he got the message.

Without a word, Nnyric took his place at the head of the table and George held a seat out at his side for her, but Kiara pretended she didn't notice and strode to her usual place at the entire opposite end of the stretching table and flopped into her seat. Hesitating only a moment, George took the seat he would have given Kiara.

From then on, Kiara counted the seconds until she would be able to leave. While the servants served them their meals, she twisted her curls in her fingers and snuck looks at George, who most evidently was trying to concoct an interesting question.

Drumming his fingers on his chair, his eyes lit up with an idea. "Kiara," he began with a tight smile, but he looked pained, as if he'd rather be somewhere else or with someone else, "have you ever given the Forbiddens much thought?"

"No," she lied, trying her best to keep her jaw from slacking open.

"My mother thinks I should acquire some work ethic before I climb the ladder of social standing and politics." He waited for admiration, but she said nothing. "She thinks the city's night watch would suit me well. Personally, I wouldn't have thought anything less for myself, but it is always such an encouragement to know one's own parent has the same high hopes and valid expectations."

"Hm," she huffed dryly, stirring her mash absentmindedly.

"Oh, yes!" Nnyric joined in. "I nearly forgot! George is well on his way to becoming one of Caverna's very own night watchmen, his only wish, to be placed out by the Forbiddens. Isn't that exciting?"

"No."

"Personally," George sniffed, "I believe it takes a great deal of courage and discipline to carry out a job of such . . . caliber with," he blinked, trying to find the word, "decorum."

Kiara squinted as she tried to determine if he even understood his own speech.

"Of course, though as I said before, I expect it of myself, I still wouldn't know if I was up for it, but mother thinks I'm more than adequate."

Kiara stifled a laugh with a cough. "Excuse me."

Nnyric sent her a warning smile around a bite of the finest cut redmeal.

George just fluttered his eyes, and took in a breath for another self eulogy. "Personally—"

"Oi . . ." Kiara said under her breath and spoke up. "Personally." She simpered. "May I?"

He blinked.

"Personally, I don't think there should be a night watch. And if you allow me to explain, it's as simple as this. We already cannot go in the Forbiddens even during day hours, a place so dangerous we apparently must be kept safe from. But I say, an individual's safety should be left up to the individual. So long as they are not causing others harm, why care where one man or woman steps foot, except for the reason of gaining greater power and control. So goes for the curfew, demanding every citizen stay inside after the lamps are doused, further encroaching on their freedom and consequently degrading their self-worth." She ended with a tight lipped, polite smile.

George's eyes fluttered like they'd never fluttered before, while Nnyric looked at her in stark horror. But when their dinner guest whipped his flabbergasted gaze from Kiara to Nnyric, her father slapped on a disarming smile, waving a hand with a chuckle as if her words were inconsequential trifles to be laughed off in all good humor. George joined with a nervous snicker and Kiara slid further down in her chair, face a glowing red.

"Are you not hungry, dear?" Nnyric asked.

"No," she replied, and adopted those yes and no answers (mostly no) as her strategy of survival for the rest of the meal, until she finally broke down and asked to be excused. The meager appetite she had forced herself to work up all but gone, Kiara had barely picked at her food.

"Father? I have a headache. May I be excused."

Nnyric looked like he might argue, but remembering himself, gave George an apologetic smile. Turning back to Kiara, he said, "Of course."

"Thank you." She rose and they followed suit.

George gave a shallow bow. "As always, it was a pleasure

to see you," he smattered, his tone doing very little to convince her of his sincerity.

Kiara gave him a polite smile. "Likewise," she forced herself to say. "Good night."

Back in her room, Kiara did begin to feel rather poorly about the way she acted. She feared she'd never be suited for courting fine gentlemen (not that she wanted to be) or forbid it all, marrying one. Wrenching of her headdress, she asked herself why she even cared, when she didn't want it anyway. But she knew why. Because even if she did want it, no one would want *her*, and she couldn't escape the pain that brought her.

To get her mind off things, she pulled her mother's letter from a drawer and began to read the riddle over and over again.

"The heart of darkness . . . Heart of darkness? What does that *mean*?" She gave an exasperated sigh. "Will I ever know?"

Kiara laid down on her bed, exhausted from the day and emotionally drained from the night. Her headache excuse wasn't a lie, and she just wanted to rest a little before she had to leave again. Holding the letter close to her chest, she rolled onto her side and curled into a ball as a few tears leaked from her eyes, wishing her father would come in and apologize for the way things went, and knowing he wouldn't. Before she knew it, sleep pulled her into oblivion.

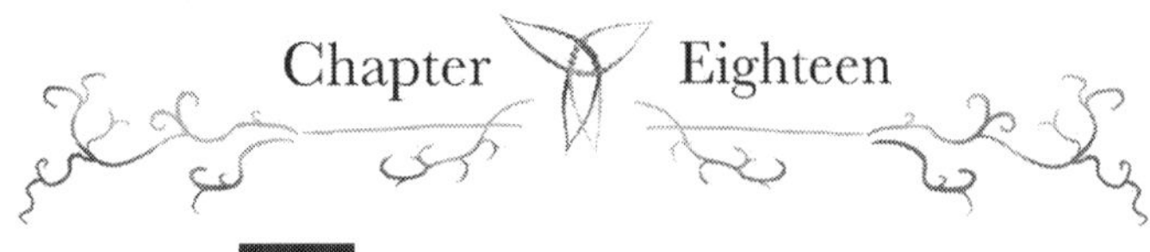

Chapter Eighteen

Tunnels

Something jolted her awake, something like a nightmare, but she couldn't remember a single detail. She only felt the heart racing fear, and the adrenaline primed limbs ready to take her away, because for some reason she needed to leave . . .

Catching her breath, she took note of the silence in the palace. Not a single creek came through the walls.

What time is it? she wondered.

Then she realized she *did* need to leave, but not to get away from something, to get to something.

Hadyn! her thoughts screamed at her, and she couldn't believe she let herself fall asleep.

Rushing to leave, she didn't even have time to question if she should go or not. She just swirled up like a silent cyclone and took off for their meeting place. But when she arrived at the steps of the library and peered into the dark building, she had half the mind to believe she beat him there.

She opened the door and the creak of the hinges welcomed her into the dark. The musty smell coupled with the near to unbroken blackness, surrounded her like an old, smothering blanket. Suddenly the place that always made her feel so safe, didn't seem so harmless and comforting anymore.

"Hadyn?" she worked up the courage to whisper.

"Over here," came the muffled reply and she followed his voice to the place where they had found the trap door.

Relief flooded her chest to hear him shuffling around, but his apparent immunity to the dark perturbed her.

"Why didn't you light a lamp? I can't see anything."

"Are you insane? There are guards nearby." Then he thought about it. "I don't like it either, but we *will* get caught if we risk a light."

"Hmph. Very well."

"What took you so long? I thought you forgot."

"Sorry. Tonight took a turn for the worst and when I lied down, I sort of . . . dozed off."

"Oh . . . What happened?"

Still standing rather far away, Kiara continued their hushed conversation. "Well, nothing really. My father just had George Cunningtin over for dinner, and let's just say we're not friends."

Silence and she could just picture him thoughtfully nodding his head. "Who's George?" he finally asked.

"He's the eldest son of one of my father's . . . acquaintances. But I'm sure you couldn't care less about all that."

Hadyn only reverted back to silence.

"Is it still unlocked?" she asked.

"Yeah. It's so strange, it's been locked since I started working here, and now it's open all day? It just doesn't feel right. Kiara, I don't know what we'll find down there."

Kiara edged a bit closer now and blew out a breath. All her gusto seemed to have gone out with the lights in the place. "But we have to try, right? We have to get your book back."

After a long pause, Hadyn said, "I just think we need to be careful."

Kiara swallowed hard. "Agreed."

He sucked in a slow breath and held it as he cautiously lifted the trap door, trying not to make a sound. But with one minuscule whine of the hinges, a dark mass awakened and burst out of the hole with an eruption of fluttering flaps and agitated chirping. Kiara swallowed down a screech, but as quick as the cloud exploded, it dispersed, up into the rafters of the library.

"It's okay!" Hadyn reassured. "I think it was just those winged vermin from the Forbiddens."

"Oh," Kiara snorted, "bats." Then her eyes widened. "Er—that's what I call them," she recovered.

". . . Right." Hadyn reached down into the now gaping hole. "I think . . ." he shuffled about, " there's some stairs here. I'll go down first." Kiara didn't respond, heart still racing over the bats.

Hadyn started to crawl in, but stopped again. "You alright?" he asked.

"Hmm? Oh, yeah." She paused. "No . . . I'm not. I'm terrified."

"Me too, but, Kiara, whatever we meet down there, just

know, I won't leave you."

"Thanks. We can watch each other's backs. We'll be alright," she said to herself just as much as him.

"Right." He sounded like he was smiling. "You ready?"

She nodded, but quickly realized he probably couldn't see that. "Yes," she said.

"When you come down, close the hatch door behind you." And with that he began the descent into the beast's throat.

Kiara waited a moment, repeatedly telling herself she could do this, then followed him in.

The "stairs" were little more than indents carved from the rock face itself. More suitably called a ladder, they ran straight down, smooth and grip-less.

She closed the door with a silent thud and the darkness apexed to opaque, thick blackness. Her mouth went dry. She couldn't speak, all words blocked by the colossal ball of fear in her throat.

"Kiara?"

"Yes?" she managed to squeak.

"Just making sure you were there."

They descended for what felt like five minutes, pitch black minutes that stole from them their sense of direction. It didn't take long for them to start to wonder whether they traveled up, down, sideways, or anywhere at all. Kiara felt the pressure building in her ears and she feared if they didn't reach the end soon, her head might explode. But why were they so sure the tunnel even had an end?

Thoughts of the Void crept up her spine and into her mind and for the first time, she wondered why they hadn't heard any sound when the journal fell. Her hands trembled, sabotaging her already uncertain grip. She nearly shouted out to warn Hadyn to stop when she heard a soft *thud.*

Hadyn called up to her. "I made it to the bottom. I think . . . I think I can see a faint light."

Collecting her ridiculous thoughts, Kiara climbed down the remaining steps. She could hear Hadyn already shuffling around on his hands, searching for the journal in the pitch darkness, and it wasn't long before he exclaimed in a whisper, "I found it!"

"Excellent!" Kiara said and took to what she presumed to be scanning the area, but not a thing changed. If not for the ground beneath her, she wouldn't have even known she was spinning. Then she stopped as something caught her eye. Faint and so very distant, she thought her eyes were playing tricks, but then she recalled what Hadyn had said. It *did* look like there was a light in the distance or at least around a bend, because it had no shape or point of reference. Suddenly Kiara wondered if she was looking back up the tunnel and someone had opened the trap door. She took a step and grew dizzy with nausea.

Finding a wall to steady herself, she asked, "What is this place?"

"No idea. But I don't think it was meant to be found."

"Yeah . . ." Kiara wondered about her father and his strange actions of late. She wondered if this had something to do with him, if it was the place he'd been going to that he didn't want her to know about.

"What are you thinking?" Hadyn asked.

"Um," Kiara wasn't sure she wanted to tell him. "Don't you want to know what's down there?"

He didn't answer, but she could imagine him rolling his eyes.

"Kiara—"

"Look, I know what I said. I don't know how to make you understand and I would never expect you to come with me, but I have to know what's down here. I can't just leave without answers."

Hadyn thought for a long moment before he said, "How can we watch each other's backs if I don't come with you?"

Kiara beamed at him, though he couldn't see it in the dark.

They started for the light, walking as straight as they could manage. They crept along, preferring not to trip over or bump into anything if they didn't have to. Kiara tried to keep her mind off monsters and ghouls, but the ample darkness seemed to beg her to conjure such thoughts. A drip from the tunnel roof plopped on her head and she just about jumped out of her skin.

"You alright?" Hadyn asked.

"I'm fine," she quickly replied.

The light's intensity steadily grew, forming vague rock walls out of the darkness and for the first time they could dimly see the enormity of the tunnel. The roof disappeared into the dark well above their heads and six could walk down the wide lane with their arms stretched out and still never touch, the rough walls seemingly carved out by the teeth of some giant worm, a stone eater of ancient time . . .

Soon they could see that the light came from a perpendicular turn to the right while the main tunnel kept on going straight into abysmal darkness.

Hadyn looked down the disturbingly black tunnel. "No use going that way."

Kiara turned to look directly down the lit tunnel and found the source of the faint glow, a lone lamp stand, still several paces away. Companionless as it was, something about it almost seemed . . . abandoned. It really wasn't all that bright either, but the horrid darkness contrasted it enough to lead the two light-starved scavengers to its solitary station.

"No," Kiara agreed. "But I wonder, if this tunnel keeps taking turns like the one here, is there any use in going this way either. We might not find our way back."

Hadyn contemplated that for a moment. "We could give ourselves three more turns. If it takes a fourth one, we can turn back. We'll keep track and flip the lefts and rights on the way back."

"That . . . sounds reasonable," Kiara mused and looked down at her right hand, a strange feeling drawing her eyes down. There in her own hand was Hadyn's, when or how it got there, she had no idea. She raised the hand slowly. Hadyn's eyes flashed with surprise and he let go immediately.

"Sorry," they both said at the same time, and without another glance at each other began taking their first steps towards the lamp stand.

An irregular and unusual design, the bizarre fixture had six candles held by six arms, outstretching from the top of the stand, set in a circle. Each arm was taller than the last, giving it the look of a winding staircase leading to nowhere at all, each step set ablaze. The bottom of the stand had been formed to look like the clawed feet of some great beast and the six arms clutched the candles with sharp, black talons.

Kiara couldn't be sure, but tickles on her spine told her it was an omen of what they were to meet at the end of the tunnel. Then again, at least they could see again.

They took slow, contemplative steps, the silence so intense they could hear the whispering of the flames as they danced over the wicks.

"What in Caverna . . .?" The light splashed on Hadyn's face as he drew closer and illuminated a discolored patch of blues and purples around his right eye, making *both* lids rather sleepy. His lip was busted up pretty bad too, and more bruising painted his left cheek.

Kiara leaned closer. "Oh, Hadyn! What happened?"

He stiffened and turned away from her. "I tripped."

"Mereaze did this to you, didn't he?" Hadyn didn't answer. "This is all my fault," she whispered. "Hadyn . . ." she tried to place a hand on his shoulder, but he flinched so bad, she stepped back. "Why did he do this? You have to tell me. Why do you let them treat you like this?"

"Because!" He spun around. "Because he wants me to bring you to him!" Kiara stared at him in stunned silence and he blew out a ragged breath. "He wants me to find a way to bring you back to the Styx, so he can capture you. When I told Mereaze I wouldn't, he . . . well, he wasn't too pleased."

Kiara's brow scrunched and her eyes pooled with moisture. "You took his anger . . . for me?" More than gratitude, Kiara felt a crushing guilt. "Why?"

"You think I could just hand you over to Mereaze? He won't just hold you for ransom and grab his money. He won't just kill you if he doesn't get it. No, you will have wished he merely just ended your life."

"It's nothing he's not already doing to you."

Hadyn turned back toward the lamp stand and stared into the flames, but Kiara shoved her way into his vision. "That still leaves my other question— why do you let him treat you like that? Why do you stay working for him?"

"Don't you get it? Mereaze will *kill* me if I turn my back on him. Caverna is big, but not so big that he wouldn't find me eventually."

"But how did he find you in the first place?"

Hadyn sighed. "My father . . . was a gambler and a cheat. He got caught up in some shady business in the Styx years ago and somehow wound up owing Mereaze a hefty sum of money . . ." He fixed her with a look. "He died before he ever paid back a single aeris."

Kiara's chest deflated. "And he came after you, his son, for the money."

"Course, I didn't have anything, neither did my father. But Mereaze said, if I worked off my father's debt, he'd let me live. He never said he'd leave me alone. Mereaze knows I know how to find the gems, and it's easier to threaten me into service than to train someone new, let alone find anyone who will dare step into the

Forbiddens."

Kiara tried to form words, something of sympathy or consolation, but her mouth had run dry. She stared into the flames of the bizarre lamp stand.

"And here I was complaining about stuffy dinner companions . . ." she mumbled.

"Now you know why I didn't want to tell you. This isn't your problem to worry about or be burdened by, and you shouldn't let it be."

Kiara fought for the words to say.

"You don't have to say anything." He shrugged. "We should get going anyway. This isn't the end of the tunnel and if you ask me, this . . . thing," he gestured to the many flickering lights, "only raises more questions."

Resignedly, Kiara followed behind him, preparing to memorize turns and forks, but to her surprise, the tunnel didn't turn again. It just kept on going and going, until they came to yet another strange candelabrum, exactly like the last.

"I know I shouldn't complain," Kiara began, "because this tunnel is straight and easy, but these candles burn with an eerie presence and I don't know which thought is more unnerving, getting lost down here or not knowing what these are leading to."

"I know what you mean," Hadyn confessed. "I haven't been able to shake a chilling feeling ever since we passed the first one."

She leaned close to examine it. "The design is like nothing I've ever seen. So intricate . . . it's incredible."

"Hey, look." Hadyn pointed down the tunnel. "It looks brighter up ahead."

Kiara squinted into the distance. "You're right."

Doggedly, they pressed on, curiosity's roots already dug much too deep in their bones. And when they came to yet another candelabrum of the same make as the previous two, they hardly gave it a glance, because just beyond, the tunnel debouched into a vast room, lit aglow with an extensive chandelier and candelabrums placed all about. The walls wrapped around the circular room with a gentle curve, and huge bookcases littered in thousands of books covered three fourths of the stone in the room, towering all the way to the ceiling. In between every book case tunnels bore into unknown darkness and enormous scarlet curtains draped heavily down on each side of them as if drenched in blood. The empty, wide open floor, beckoned them in with a sinister wag of a finger and directed their eyes across the room. Everything seemed to point ominously to a raised platform, against the one wall space devoid of bookcases. Stairs on both sides of the platform curved up to the top.

Kiara and Hadyn's eyes followed the stairs up to the stage where a marble pedestal and rough stone altar stood proudly. With their presence and uses unknown, the very platform had a certain foreboding and nefarious nature that made them shiver in unison.

"I'd really hate to be the person who left that trapped door unlocked when whoever is hiding this finds out about it," were all the words Hadyn could manage to get out.

Chapter Nineteen

The Missing Piece

This was a secret alright, but Kiara was almost certain it wasn't a secret to her father. Once her mind began asking questions, she found it hard to make it stop. She didn't waste much time and, after standing in shock for one timeless moment, strode into the open expanse.

"What are you doing!" Hadyn whisper-yelled, his words strained as he fought to remain quiet even through his stupefaction.

She whipped around without near as much care for her volume. "Taking a look around," she snapped. "I've known that there was something wrong with Caverna ever since people started dying on me without a cause. . . Even before that, I always felt it. And I've had to keep agonizingly quiet about it for years because my father's the king. But now I could know the reason for all this darkness and tragedy. The answers may be right at my finger tips. I don't know about you, but I'm not going to pass this by."

Her hood lay about her shoulders and her long, wild hair flung about in any direction the strands pleased, backlit by the candlelight like a blazing mane. Hadyn stared at her, seeing clearly the dangerous anger in her eyes. He felt stuck. Part of him felt like it was his responsibility to protect her. After all, they were only down here because of his book. But what could he do when that protection was unappreciated?

When he didn't answer, Kiara huffed and resumed her exploration of the enigmatic room. She stomped over to the nearest book case and gazed up at the many shelves. Giant, heavy books lined the shelves, ancient books, books bearing the weight of secrets. With nothing to do but start somewhere and eyes wide with wonder, she climbed a few steps up the elephant ladder where a shelf proclaimed the title of *Law*.

She stole a glance down at Hadyn who had followed her in

and now stood at the base of the ladder, fidgeting and continually tossing his gaze about the room. Rolling her eyes, she slid her finger by titles like, The *Imperium Act*, and *Total Sovereignty*. She pulled the first book she thought she could lift off the shelf and opened it to the middle. She gasped. The writing looked so ancient, the pages yellowed and nicked with age.

"What is it?" Hadyn called up.

"Nothing. It's just . . . this book . . . it looks so old. It makes me wonder how long . . . You know?"

"Yeah."

Kiara began to read the first passage that stood out to her.

For The Protection Of Citizens Never Having Control

From this day forward, citizens born into a class will stay in that class. However hard the citizens work or do not work they will never move from their class, whether it be higher or lower. With the one exception that the ruler at the time can move specific citizens as he sees fit.

"Hadyn!" she gasped. "You have to see this!"

Kiara hurried down the ladder as fast as she could with the unwieldy book in her arm and shoved the pages in his face, pointing at the same perturbing paragraph that she had read.

He didn't smile as he laughed. It was a cold and manic laugh that sent a chill up her spine.

"Hadyn, don't you see? It's not your fault. No matter how hard you try, you can never get out of Terminal Avenue. It's not about having enough gumption or even getting the job done, it's just a sick game of false hope and control!"

He stared down at the book in his limp hands. "Gumption?"

"It's something my mother used to say." When he still didn't look up, Kiara took the book from him. "Hadyn, don't let this destroy you. My father is a monster! Don't give them that satisfaction."

Finally, he lifted his head and his blue eyes reflected his heart. Years of pain and shame tugged at every feature in his bruised face. "I just wish I could have known this."

"Me too. But it doesn't work that way. My father wants us in the dark. Literally!" Kiara climbed back up the ladder and put the book back. When she came back down she said, "Come on. Let's keep looking around."

She took a few steps, pulling the elephant ladder along behind her. Scanning the shelves, she randomly selected a book she could reach from ground level. Coal black and embossed with scarlet lettering, the title read, *The Accounts of the Nameless.* With a shiver, Kiara scanned the first page and Hadyn read over her shoulder.

The Nameless have been assembled for one purpose, to carry out the deeds of which one needs to be invisible to do. They are to be nonexistent and always ready for anything.

Sworn into secrecy and irrevocable fealty, the Nameless are bound to carry out their master's every bidding. Their lives are now owned by their masters and all have chosen this out of free will.

The origin of the idea for the Nameless was put forth by an unknown source and was put into action by the High Master immediately after contemplation.

Kiara flipped the page and started reading in the middle. Like a journal entry, a date marked the text.

"My father was king when this started . . . *Six has shown great potential,*" she read out loud, "*and has been predicted to exceed the rest. Two, however, has led us to questions and will constantly be watched. Time will tell if he needs to be taken out. Culminating to eighteen altogether, the flaws and strengths of the others are yet to be seen.*

"What is this, an assassin's log?" Kiara asked, disturbed, and hastily put the book back on the shelf.

Hadyn shook his head. "I think it's more than that. Whoever they are, the book said that they're bound to carry out their master's every bidding. I think that means more than just taking out targets."

Kiara felt an unwelcome twist in her stomach, and attempting to shake the thoughts away, walked over to the stairs. She paused at the bottom, growing ever more queasy, unsure of what she would meet at the top. She felt Hadyn waiting patiently behind her. Maybe he felt the same reluctance to brave those stairs.

With slow deliberate steps she summited the stage. A stone altar stood in the middle, quiet, but dangerously present, like a slumbering beast. Stained in red, scarlet streaks ran down its sides like tears of blood, and behind it stood the pedestal which displayed a cumbersome book, the pages splayed and ready to read. Kiara's heart kicked up a notch and she could hear her own breaths as they rushed to come and go. She had heard horrible tales of people who sacrificed other human beings for Fleard, but always she refused to believe her ears. Yet, with the red altar before her, all she could think of were those so called "tales."

She didn't want to believe her eyes either and she did exactly that. She told herself that a crimson stained altar didn't mean people had been . . . killed here. She convinced herself it wasn't enough proof. Kiara turned and saw the way Hadyn stared at it. The same mortification twisted his face. The same disbelief misshaped his eyes. His gaze wandered to her and she swallowed the lump of horror.

"That doesn't mean . . ." She couldn't finish.

"I don't know . . . I really hope not."

Kiara shook her head, still unwilling to believe, and turned her face from the sight. They walked to the pedestal and around to the front of the book. To their dismay, the book was written in a language neither of them could read. Kiara wanted to kick herself for never learning Latin in school. Though, she didn't need to know what the words said to feel the hate and malice in every scratched out letter.

A twinge in her gut told her to stop, to walk away and leave this horrible place, but her hunger for truth had grown dangerously ravenous, and like a starving lion in a pit, she'd devour anything, maybe even something harmful, just to know more.

Kiara grabbed a huge armful of pages and with a grunt shoved them to the left. There, on one of the last pages, was a list of many names and by the names sat dates. Kiara scanned the list, wondering who it was compiled of and what it meant. While she searched, her eyes kept flicking back up at the altar beyond the edge of the book.

"Hey, hey!" Hadyn said. "I recognize some of those names. James Ganger . . . Edmond Slate . . . Those boys used to live at the orphanage." He turned to her ever so slowly, a dangerous anger kindling in his eyes. "Before they disappeared. What is this?"

Kiara felt her mouth go bone dry as she continued to scan the list. Her eyes landed on one name, close to the end. Heart skipping a beat, all at once she couldn't breath. Her eyes remained riveted on a name she held almost as dear as her own– Betsie Clair and beside it the day she had disappeared.

"What is it?" Hadyn looked at her, concerned.

Kiara shook her head, biting her lip to hold back tears. "Bets . . ." She whispered.

All the life and happiness her dear friend had lived out flashed before her eyes. "My Betsie."

She didn't want to, but still, as if pulled by an unseen force, her gaze wandered back to the altar. A single tear ran down her cheek. "Father . . . how could you?"

"You keep saying stuff like that," Hadyn said. "But do you really think your father is behind all this? I know he hasn't been a good father, but you don't really think he could be hiding all this from you . . . Do you? I mean, what if he's just a pawn?"

As another hot tear escaped her eye, Kiara's face morphed from anguish to anger and she turned her head just enough to glare at him sideways. "You don't know anything." Her words were clipped, sharp as a new dagger.

She slammed a hand down on the page to grab another armful. She couldn't bear to look at her friend's name for another second, penned in the ledger as if in blood. She grabbed a chunk large enough to put it back to somewhere in the middle. Again, she felt like she should just walk away and this time the section felt heavier, like evil had its own poundage on each page. She wanted to listen. She wanted nothing more than to be rid of this book, but in her anger she acted too hastily.

No one in Caverna could ever convince her that this was merely an elaborate library after she had looked upon the images in the book, so proudly displayed on that tall pedestal. The diagrams that leapt off the pages, would be forever carved and engraved into the young explorer's memories. So grotesque, so vile, they couldn't imagine someone even thinking of doing that to another human being. And because I myself do not have the heart to tell you, I will spare you the rest of the details.

Kiara felt like she could throw up. She smashed the cover down on the book. Her eyes found Hadyn's.

Horror etched his face. He tried to speak. "Who would . . .? Why. . . ?"

Kiara felt her lungs contract and she couldn't get air back in them. She ran down from the dais with nowhere to go and limbs set on failing her, crashing to the polished floor and skittering to a stop in front of one of the giant bookcases. She could feel the panic ripping senses from her one by one. First hearing, then touch itself, so she just felt numb. Squeezing her eyes shut, she couldn't get control of her sobbing.

Hadyn, never far behind, collapsed to his knees beside her, battling his own demons. In between sobs she asked, "Who could do something like that? To innocent people! Oh Bets . . . She was my best friend. My only friend. I never knew what happened to her. I'll never forgive him."

He listened to her cry and his own eyes brimmed with tears. But as time passed and her sobs quieted to soft weeping, he surprised himself with words. "You know, I asked myself those same questions night after night as my father came home drunk and *so* angry over some bust gambling match. It wasn't long before he started hitting us. My mother tried to protect my little sister, Viviana, and I, but he really didn't care who he hurt when he got like that."

Kiara lifted her head a bit, saw the tears welling in his eyes, begging to be released. "I didn't know you had a sister."

"Yeah well, she and my mom died long before my dad ever did."

"I never understood," he continued. "What makes a man hurt his own family? But you know what, Kiara? There's nothing *to* understand and the answer is simple. Evil is out there, it's in here," He pointed to his own chest. "It's everywhere and it twists everything. So the answer is, anyone would do that. Anyone who just doesn't care."

She looked up at him, surprised by his words. His hair hung in his eyes, but they pierced through the bruises and the pain with the same intensity as his words. He turned away from her, feeling like she could see into his heart.

Kiara dropped her gaze. Even though she never asked him to say those things, she felt somehow like she was intruding in a place she wasn't allowed to be. Another tear slipped down her nose. The darkness of their broken world weighed down on her like a crushing rock and felt closer than her own skin.

Kiara looked around at her crash landing site. An empty slot on the bookcase near her head caught her attention, having noted that there didn't seem to be many empty spaces anywhere on the shelves. She tilted her head and looked at Hadyn who held a book in his arms that just might fit in the slot. He didn't see her strange glance, so she looked back at the black rectangle where a book should have been. Something caught the light and glinted at the back of the slot. Without another thought, Kiara reached her hand in and pulled out a very odd looking little key, almost heart shaped, but lopsided and uneven. The small handle was jagged and seemed broken off from another piece. She scrutinized it unintelligently and then, one by one, lights started to ignite in her head.

"Hadyn, I think—"

"Shh! . . . Someone's coming."

"What!"

Like rain, the footsteps steadily became louder, but the pitter-patter sound echoed off of every wall, so they couldn't decipher which entrance the sound originated from. Their eyes darted to each exit, knowing if they picked the wrong one, they'd be caught in seconds.

Hadyn exploded to his feet, grabbed Kiara's hand, and pulled her up off the ground. He bolted straight for the closest of those giant curtains. Behind it, they held their breath and pleaded with the scarlet fabric to stop swaying.

Kiara squeezed her eyes shut, mouthing silent prayers to whoever would listen. She felt the curtain still just before the clopping footsteps ceased and silence fell. She couldn't open her eyes. Dreadful moments passed as her heartbeat hammered in her ears so loud, she feared it would echo off the walls.

The footsteps clopped once, then twice, and finally started roaming the room at a steady pace again. Kiara opened her eyes, though she didn't see much with the dark curtain just past her nose. Every inch of her body shook with violent tremors, but she had to see, she had to know. Inching out of hiding, she peaked one eye out from behind the curtain. In the distance and dim amount of light provided by the candles, she saw a figure pacing the room like a wolf, but she couldn't be sure, so she waited till he came closer.

"Impossible . . ." he muttered with a seething growl. "How could this happen? Who would dare?"

He moved to the left now, scrutinizing the room for anything out of place. Then he turned and the fire of the nearest lantern splashed on his sharp features with a condemning light.

Kiara swallowed a gasp, unable to move back to safety. His eyes burned with an anger she knew all too well, his scowl saying more than words could of how greatly someone would pay the price of this incompetent mistake. His gaze swept the room, ever nearing her hiding spot, and still Kiara remained frozen.

A hand on her arm pulled her back to safety. Kiara turned to Hadyn, eyes as round as marbles.

"It's him!" she barely whispered.

Hadyn calmly lifted a finger to his lips, holding her gaze through every nightmarish second.

"Well, there's no one here. Satisfied?" they listened to him ask no one at all and, finally, they heard the footsteps departing down one of the many tunnels.

They waited a few more moments just to be safe. Hadyn motioned for her to sit sight and snuck a tentative glance, peering out from behind the curtain. Once he made sure the room was completely empty, he gave her the signal to come out.

Kiara stepped out from behind the curtain, staring at absolutely nothing. The betrayal, the secrets, the barefaced lies stabbed her like knives to her back.

Hadyn spun around, feeling the need to watch every tunnel at once. "Who in Caverna, was he talking to?"

"He does that."

Hadyn just raised his eyebrows.

She turned away. "Look, maybe I would have told you, if I had any reason to think you'd believe me."

His face fell. "Kiara . . . I'm sorry," he said, standing behind her. "I should have believed you. How would I know better—"

Kiara lifted a hand. She looked down. She didn't want to cry again. "I just . . . think I just need to be alone. Can we go?"

Hadyn thought the last thing she needed was to be alone, but he didn't know what he could do for her.

Sweeping his curls out of his eyes, he tilted his head toward the tunnel they came in through. "Yeah. Come on."

They made their way out of the secret tunnels and walked back to the King's Corridor in a mutual silence, both knowing no amount of words could mend the night's trials.

After sending the guards on an inevitably fruitless goose chase, they arrived outside the King's Corridor, where Hadyn stopped. Kiara walked past him, ready to continue without even a good-bye.

"Kiara, wait!" Hadyn whispered. ". . . This was all my fault and—"

"No. We could have retrieved your book and left. I wanted to see, and as much as it hurt . . . I needed to." She forced a sad smile. "I'll be alright."

He shrugged. "What will you do?"

"I just need some time to think. To figure out some things."

Still she didn't say goodbye, and when she disappeared into

the dark of the hall, Hadyn had an awful feeling, he'd never see her again.

Kiara slipped her hands in her pockets as she walked, and a shock of cold metal made her immediately recoil. Though, quickly enough, she remembered the strange key she had found in the library. Fishing it out, she thought to maybe catch Hadyn before he was gone and show it to him, but she shoved it deep into her pocket instead, satisfied to save it for another day's problem.

Sitting on her bed, Kiara knew she wouldn't be able to simply stop thinking, not after the things they had seen, the things, the horrors they had learned. It wasn't just some bad dream or scarystory she could shove off to keep sane, this was reality, her reality . . . Her Betsie.

Kiara's breaths started to come faster and faster. She thought she would be fine. On the walk back, the adrenalin crash had hit her hard and she felt sick to her stomach, numb all over, and just weak, but nothing could've prepared her for the rushing wave of nausea that crashed over her entire body just now. A heat rushed up her back, though her hands and feet felt icy cold. She knew what came next. With a heave, she shot to her feet, rushed to the nearest bucket left from cleaning her cut that evening, and spewed every bit of her meager dinner. Gasping, she wiped her mouth and sat back with a violent shiver. She crawled on her hands and knees across the clammy ground and pulled herself up on her bed, the sweet acid of her own bile coating her mouth. But not even for a glass of water would she leave her room. Curling up on her side, all she wanted to do was hide under her covers and weep, before the morning came and forced her to do the very thing she dreaded having to do.

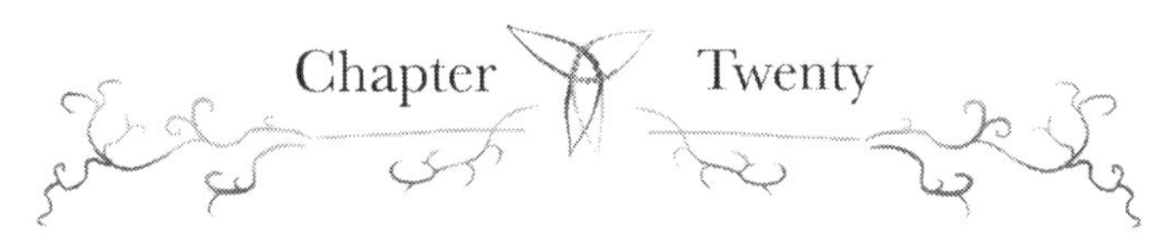

Chapter Twenty

Do You Love Me?

Kiara woke with a pinch in her neck and an ache in her back. Sometime in the midst of her sleepless nightmares, roaming her room for some place of peace, she had curled up in a cold corner of her room with nothing but a blanket and one pillow to separate her from the stone floor. How this finally achieved her needed sleep, or if she had just become exhausted enough to pass out, she had no idea. All she knew was pain (not only from her stiff muscles) pain and what she needed to do.

Kiara unfolded her crumpled limbs, easing herself into a sit and then tried standing up.

An apology was well overdue and answers needed to be had.

One thing at a time . . .

The quiet of the palace told her the day had yet to start properly. She walked to her desk and began to at last pen a letter she had already written in her head a thousand times over.

My dear Cida,

I wanted to say this to you in person, but I can never seem to find you these days. So here goes my attempt to convey the same amount of wretched shame I feel through pen and paper.

I am so sorry. I wish I could take back the words I said to you that night, even though I know I can't.

I hate myself for it. I see now that I have a lot of hate and I'm trying to deal with it. But that is not an excuse for how I treated you. I said awful things, things I didn't mean. I love you, Cida. You are the closest thing I have to family. I hurt you and I am truly sorry.

I miss you.

Kiara continued the letter by telling her about everything,

her mother, the Forbiddens, Hadyn . . . She refused to hide any of it from her any longer.

When she finished, she folded it neatly and walked it to Cida's room where she placed it on her pillow.

A sigh escaped her chest and left her shoulders to collapse in towards each other, lacking the proper strength to stay back themselves. She wished she could just leave now and escape it all, but her father had already left for the day, leaving her questions ripping at her tongue to be released. So she would endure another grueling day of school, even in her fragile state of mind. For the need of answers, she thought, or what? Some kind of twisted closure?

She sat through her classes, though she didn't listen much and she didn't learn anything.

When at length the school day had run its course, Kiara walked home and forced herself to go straight to her father's study.

As expected, he wasn't home yet, but she would wait. She had to. So much had happened . . . Her anger and hurt had festered into something ugly. Like a gangrenous wound, if something like that isn't cut off right where it begins, it can overcome the whole person, poisoning mind, body, and soul.

All her desires had pooled to amplify this one need, and though she dreaded it, she needed truth, she needed certainty. And only he could give her that.

Her hands shook and sent tremors up her arms, like an unstable cavern, but she told herself, she wouldn't cry. She would not feel anything. Feelings hurt and she was tired, so tired of hurting.

She ran what she wanted to say over and over again in her mind and tried to predict what he might say in return. Would he scream at her? Would he try to lie?

A low voice echoed through the Palace and Kiara could hear him talking to Shrike. He had returned, but she didn't get up to greet him. He would come soon enough.

When he walked through the doorway, he barely gave her a glance of a nod, before he sat down in his chair and began picking through letters and documents on his desk. He found one in need of a bit more thought, and she lost him behind it as he scanned the paper.

It raked her skin to have to be cordial to him, but she supposed he had no idea what she knew, and she had to start somewhere . . .

"Father?" she asked pleasantly.

He took a good moment before reluctantly parting with some of his attention. "Yes, Daughter?"

Kiara wrestled down a fierce panic. Even with only part of his face visible, all she could see was that thing, that monster he carried around with him.

"I was wondering," she began, "do you happen to remember Betsie?"

"Who?"

The question felt like a knife, but Kiara remained calm. "You know, my friend."

"Yes, yes . . . The name does sound familiar, now that you mention it. But, I can't remember who in the blazes it belongs to." Rather invested now, he put his papers down.

Kiara played her part. "Betsie. You would remember, Mother took her in when she was quite young. She was a servant here for some time, but . . . we were close, you know?"

He listened to her, concentration darkening his face, and finally his brows raised in realization. "Oh, yes! Betsie. The little lass with the limp."

"That's right," Kiara said coldly.

"You know I never approved of that decision. What with her infirmity and all . . . Whatever happened to her?"

Kiara couldn't believe her ears. She narrowed her eyes, but he had already returned to scanning the documents. "She died."

Her words fell flat on his ears and his eyes wandered from the words on the page. "Ah . . . that is tragic." He remembered now, she could read it like a proclamation on his face, but still he remained seemingly naive. "Tell me again why you wanted to talk about this little friend of yours?"

Her rage burned cold like dry ice as she shrugged. "No reason really. I've just been thinking about her a lot of late. And I guess I miss her . . . *My little friend.*"

He blinked at her a moment then, sniffing in a breath, he said, "Yes, very sorry, my dear."

"Are you, though?" came her quiet mumble.

"What?"

"Oh, nothing. Just thinking out loud."

"Look, Kiara, if you can not already see, I'm very busy. So if there is nothing else you need . . ." he said, obviously suggesting she leave him.

Kiara contemplated this, then, giving him a sugar sweet smile, she settled back in her chair, prepared to sit in content silence. Nnyric watched her as if he might protest, but sighing quietly, he returned to his work.

Kiara didn't know why she stayed. To vex him? To get one last little gab? He had already confirmed all that she needed to know. He had killed her best and only friend, hid colossal-sized secrets from his own daughter, and done who knows what else.

She got up to leave, part of her not caring if she ever saw his indifferent face again. But as she prepared to pass his desk, something in her made her stop, the part of her that had been begging in unshed tears, and the secret ones she cried all alone, in skipped meals, and in lonely walks home, begging, crying for a father, for the kind of hugs only one can give, the ones that are never too tight as to not be gentle, but always tight enough to show the kind of love that no amount or combination of words ever could.

"Just one more question." Kiara took a deep breath in as he sighed one out. "Father, do you . . . love me?"

Without putting his papers down, he waved a hand out at her. "Kiara, that's a ridiculous question. You know the answer to that."

"Is it?"

He flicked one corner of the page down and considered her with a noncommittal stare. "Yes."

"Then why can't you just say it?" She held her anger at bay, but it rode furtively on her words, like a secret storm on the backs of benign rainclouds.

"Because you should know it without me having to say it," he said, his answer clipped with impatience.

"I should?" She heard her own voice degrade from strong and defiant, to tremulous, all too quickly. The very thing she was trying to prevent was happening. But she couldn't stop now. Like jumping, or more accurately, falling off an edge into a bottomless abyss, Kiara knew there was no coming back from her next question, and yet she had to do it, somehow seeing the abyss as comforting compared to the fire she stood in now.

"Does it mean anything to you that I exist?"

Nnyric slammed his papers down on his desk. "Kiara, where is this coming from? I want you to stop this nonsense right this instant!"

"No!" She stuck out her chin. "If I was gone tomorrow . . .

would you even grieve?" He shut his mouth and stared at her. "Would your heart know nothing more than to rend right down the middle if you couldn't say I was your daughter *ever again?*"

He only gave her a listless gaze.

"Tell me!" she cried.

The legs of his chair grated against the stone floor as he shot to his feet. "I refuse to play this ridiculous game with you any longer. I am done with this conversation!"

Kiara flinched, but she knew he would say that; she just needed to hear it. The tears refused to stay put any longer, and as they dripped off her cheeks and his face didn't soften or change, she knew she should leave . . . yet she hesitated.

Call her a glutton for pain and punishment if you want, but this battle was long overdue and she didn't have it in her to end it half heartedly.

She forced herself to look into those dark, loveless eyes and she spoke quietly, maybe hoping he wouldn't hear. "I thought I loved you. But if you can't even say it . . ." She sharpened her gaze. "Though I know there is not a drop of love in your hollow soul, can you honestly look into my eyes and tell me that you would feel nothing . . . if I were to die. I need to hear you say it."

His face twisted. "Why?" he almost cried.

She blinked slowly to retain her composure. "I just need to."

He looked her in the eye and for a moment she thought she could see just a glimmer of something that could have once been good, a hint of a man struggling behind something like chains or pounds of rushing water. "I . . ." he tried, but all turned to a fire of contempt, consuming anything else daring to reside there. Something horrible and inhuman took over and in that gaze Kiara herself felt lifeless, inanimate even.

"I can," he said, at last. "I would feel nothing. You are nothing."

Every harsh word, every let down, and rejection she ever felt, rushed to her senses in one broken heartbeat. And every beat after throbbed like she was being ripped apart by voracious, nitpicking hands, every piece of her somehow so vilely unacceptable to even be difficult to look at. Finally she knew he would never, could never love her. Maybe no one could.

A trembling hand found its way to her mouth. Her head swam with a dizziness that threatened to take her under. Kiara ran from the study as fast as she could, but when she turned the corner, she froze.

Cida stood in the middle of the hall, tears streaming down her face. She held a neatly folded piece of paper at her side. Her wet eyes held no self pity, but rather seemed to tell of the pain in her heart for the broken, young girl standing before her.

Kiara could feel the tears soaking her own face, with one choking sob she turned and ran. She ran so fast, she risked tying her legs together in knots. She heard her father's words echo through her mind, bouncing off the walls of her skull, slamming her head with hammering pain.

I refuse to play this ridiculous game. You are nothing.

That's just what her feelings were to him, never serious; just a petty game.

Nothing.

Having felt this pain so many times before, she began to question if she should believe it.

What if I am nothing? What if I'm the pathetic girl I feel like right now? What if that's all I am and I have no right to these feelings at all?

One thing was certain— whatever she was (nothing more than rotting, unwanted refuse or not) she was free of him now and what she did next was up to her. If he would not care for and love her as his daughter, though he may still be her king, he would never again be her father.

In the end though, the sorry truth is, life's not always as black and white as we think it should be, and even though we don't like it, grey is a more prominent color in this world than we care to admit. And what Kiara did not know, is that if she would have but glanced back when she left his study, with just one look, she would have seen him fall to his knees, knowing he did feel something. It was like nothing he'd ever felt before and he hated it. But it wasn't enough. He was too weak and selfish, too proud to do anything about it.

Cida found Kiara in her room, sitting on her bed staring at the wall, and approached her with the care of one stepping towards an abused and frightened child.

Her tears had gone and dried, replaced now with a hollow gaze. She was cold. She thought she felt nothing, but for the ache in her heart. Anger nor sadness went deep enough to describe the ache, not much could. But you might not need it described if you've ever been left behind before and felt the cold shiver of abandonment brush your skin, like the chill of a marching winter, forewarned to be twice as long as the last. You would know, if someone ever left you without a care of what happened to you next, if you ever questioned why, if you felt guilty or responsible for the reason they rejected you. Because in the thick of it, the details of if they really left you or not, are the last things that matter. Because they still won't love you, and you're left to wonder why.

Cida sank into the bed at her side and rested a hand on her shoulder. Kiara looked at the hand and slowly lifted her head to meet Cida's eyes. Then, squeezing her own eyes shut, a single tear rolled down her face. When she opened them once more, Cida could see a decision already made deep within them. Kiara would tell her soon and there would be no way to change her mind.

"I'm going to leave, Lucida," she said with a quiet resolve.

Cida grabbed her hands. "But you cannot leave!" she cried. "Where will you go?"

"Please, don't try to stop me. From this moment on I am fatherless, and the king doesn't have a daughter anymore." She looked down, resigned. "The princess is no more. I'll go to the Forbiddens, where I already live half my life."

Cida sniffed, lip trembling as she began to cry. "But I will worry about you. The Forbiddens are no place for *anyone* to live."

"You mustn't worry. I'm glad I could see you again before I left, but please, think of me as dead, for that is what I will have everyone believe, and will most likely be my fate. But I have died already, so why cry for me?"

Kiara stood to start taking things out of her drawers and putting them on her bed to pack.

Cida shot to her feet, grabbed Kiara by the shoulders and made her look her in the eyes. "No. I won't let you say that," she said with authority. "And I certainly won't let you die in the Forbiddens. I know I can't change your mind, so leave if you must. Leave now. But you will starve in the Forbiddens and I will only let you go reluctantly, but less reluctantly, if you would come back." She softened, a smile playing on her lips. "Back to a place where we could meet. I could bring you meals and we could talk . . . It's not good to be alone, Miss. I don't want to lose you to your mind."

"Cida, why do you care so much? Didn't you hear my father? I'm nothing."

"Only if you choose to believe that! Your father is a liar. What you said in your letter proves that. You can't let a word he says have a place in your mind. And since when do you have a problem with not listening to him?" She smiled. "All of you is boundlessly more than any name he could ever call you. I speak these words in love, not in hate. Don't you know the difference?" Cida said, pain choking her words.

Kiara just looked down.

"I care so much because you're worth caring for, Miss." Cida lifted Kiara's head with a gentle fist under her chin. "Just promise me you'll come back. Promise me you won't give up."

Kiara blew out a breath. "I promise. But, Cida, you can not make me come back to Caverna. You'll have to come to the entrance of the Forbiddens."

"I feared you would say that. But for you," She nodded bravely. "I will face my fears."

Kiara considered her with a doleful gaze. "Thank you."

"Of course." Cida smiled. "We can meet every night that we can at midnight."

"Yes. I will write the king a letter and be known as dead to all but you."

Cida hugged her. "Please don't let your father's words destroy you. I'll see you soon."

"He's not my father." Her voice, once again, became hollow. "You should go, before anyone starts looking for you."

Kiara packed light, taking only what she could not bear to leave behind. If she was going to kill herself, she really wouldn't be taking anything at all. The last thing she packed was her mother's note. She gently put it back in the envelope and found it a safe place where it wouldn't get crushed in her bag.

Laying the tapestry back in place, she stroked the edge with a thumb and let her eyes rove across the masterpiece for the last time. She ached to take it with her, but that would expose the hidden shelf and surely raise the king's suspicions, so she resigned to committing the details to memory. She looked at her mother's smooth, black hair, falling about her straight shoulders and slender arms with regal grace. If anyone had ever looked like a queen, she did. Then she turned to her young self, the wild hair a literal mane of fire around her head and neck. Kiara smiled, eyes pooling with tears. She would have thought it a ridiculous exaggeration, if she had not in fact known her five-year-old self first hand.

The green eyes held pent up giggles and mischief, while Eleanor's blue ones remained stoic and polished, yet still kind.

A chill rushed over Kiara with a sense she was looking right at her. She thought of her, somewhere out there, waiting for her. For the first time since she disappeared, she felt close and yet . . . with no way to get to her, more distant than ever.

Fortunately, the tapestry was about the only thing she wanted to take and couldn't, everything she loved already living safely hidden in her Forbidden home. Satisfied with her scrutinizing, she filed the memory away in a quaint, little drawer of her mind, lined with peeling velvet, and smelling like rose perfume (her mother's favorite scent) only to be taken out on those really sad days, when nothing else helped and the walls were all but caving in.

Finished packing, she sat herself down at her desk to write the letter for the king. She sat there a moment, fingering the paper and quill. Strangely she felt nothing. The anger had abandoned her, the fear ran away, and the sadness dried up. She was empty like the blank page before her. Not that it was any comfort. More like waking up one morning and finding out you can't feel one of your limbs, she felt something in her die and she didn't know if she'd ever be fully alive again.

Dipping the quill in the ink she began addressing the letter, wrote an F, crossed it out, and started over.

King Nnyric,

I have become fatherless today by your choice. I am nothing and nothing does not breathe, so I have decided that I do not deserve to live. I know you will tell some lie to Caverna of how I died. I can't do anything about that. But I wanted you to know the truth so you would have to live with the thought for all of your days. I know you wouldn't want to have to have a proper funeral and bury my body so I will do this in the Forbiddens, where the watchers can devour my remains. I hope this hurts you, I hope this kills you. If it does, maybe there is some demented version of hope for you.

When she didn't hesitate to sign it as "Nobody's Nothing," the tears came unbidden once more and left their soggy marks of pain on the page.

Can I really say those things? She fought with herself, but she couldn't crumple it and throw it away. Folding it, she shoved it in an envelope and sealed it with red wax, already hot and ready.

Kiara placed it on her own pillow with a lingering hand. Pulling herself away and grabbing her bag, she ran to their grand foyer and as she put a hand on the door, she turned around and knew it would be her grand foyer no longer.

"Farewell," she whispered. "Though I don't believe this parting is fair at all."

She pulled her hood over her curly mess and left her house for the last time. Lantern in hand, she made for her hideaway in the Forbiddens.

PART TWO
THE ESCAPE

And the people who walked in darkness have seen a great light; those who dwelt in the land of the shadow of death, upon them a light has shined.

Isaiah 9:2

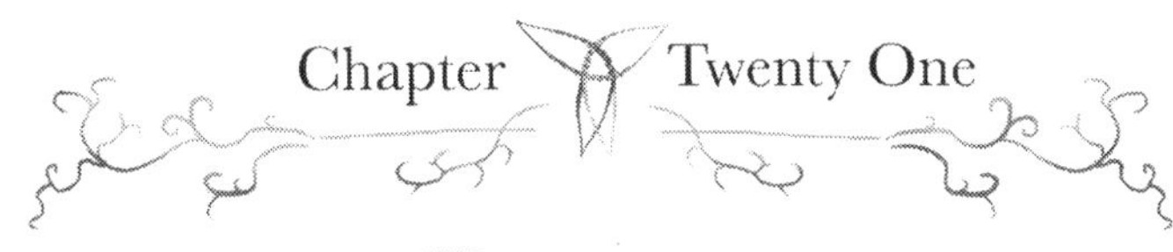

GONE

Kiara arrived at her hideaway, not even bothering to light the other candles. She knelt on the ground in the meager light, weeping into her hands, catching her own tears, tears that had no end, no matter how hard she tried to stop them.The bars lowered in her mind, sealing the exits to the maze, and she had no way to escape. Her muddled head swam with dark thoughts like hungry beasts in black water. Whenever she thought she was used to one, the game would change, shifting on herself and she'd have a fresh accusation of guilt within herself, calling out to her, taunting her.

Liar . . .

Insane . . .

Selfish . . .

How could you do this?

What is wrong with you?

Not one hurt more than another.

It all started as fear. What was she going to do now? Would she be safe here? But the fear soon burned up in her hatred, and hatred for no one person in particular. She just wanted to hate the world. It helped her to hold onto it. The burning in her chest kept out the chill of the pain. But that sword had two edges, the other perhaps more dangerous, and all alone with no one around but herself to hate, it turned on her with mountains of shame.

How could she do this to him? To anyone? But she couldn't go back now, could she? She felt so wrong like she had failed somehow. She was just a pitiful, pathetic, nothing.

How can I even think that? Kiara asked herself. She truly began to wonder that there was something wrong with her, desperately. And perhaps there was.

Kiara's head throbbed and her face felt so hot. The journals she read spoke of a sun that rises every day and lights up the whole entire world. She had a hard time believing that could be true, but even if it was so, she feared shadows like these were much too heavy to be lifted . . . especially with one single light.

She had no idea how long she sat there before she crawled to her little bed. Laying back, her eyes caught sight of the chimes she had hung over her rumpled pile of blankets.

The chimes Hadyn had given her.

He'd hear the news soon enough. She wondered if it would make him sad to know she was dead, if he would cry . . . She shivered at the black comfort it gave her when she made up her mind that he would.

Then she grew sadder still as she realized that though being dead freed her in ways, it also made her just as alone as she was before she knew anything. The one person, besides Cida, that she even cared to ever see again and she hadn't even said goodbye. She pushed the thoughts away, well aware that for him to know, would be to put his life in danger. And he had enough troubles to deal with before she had ever barged into his life.

She wanted to reach up and stroke the chimes, send them swaying, knowing that if she just heard one note, her heart would feel lighter. But she couldn't lift her hand, afraid that if she touched them, she might destroy their goodness with all her mess.

She rolled over on her side, but she wouldn't put the light out, much too scared that if she completed the darkness, she may never come back out. She closed her eyes and saw the watchers dancing on the back of her lids. She opened them and saw them just beyond the circle of light. She pulled her blanket over her head as if it could protect her and shook with sobs and fear until, finally, she cried herself to sleep.

She did not dream, but when she awoke in the darkness, she knew her sleep was not restful, she just didn't remember the dark thoughts that plagued her even in unconsciousness. She could feel it though, in the hollow drips of her leaky soul. She lay on her back and stared at the black before her eyes until it became too disconcerting to bear. She moved to find the lantern that had gone out. A dull pain shocked her muscles and a hammer started pounding on the walls of her skull.

Kiara eased herself up to a sit and held her head. She felt like she hadn't slept a wink, and with the speed her mind was still running, she couldn't be sure if it could be considered sleep at all. Just about to make her next attempt to light the lantern, a faint glow flickered in the hiding place of her peripheral. She turned, thinking it was just a trick of the eye, but it wasn't.

"What in Caverna . . .?"

There, through a crack in the stone across the room, streamed a weak, golden light. She knew of a passage that ran just on the other side of the wall and wondered if someone could be back there, maybe Hadyn, but the light was steadier than one carried in hand and brighter than just one lantern, almost as if . . . an entire, lit up room lay on the other side.

No . . . Kiara shook her head. *Why haven't I ever seen it before?*

Then again, she had never come here and sat in total darkness before. Maybe it had always been there and she simply had never noticed it with other lights in the room.

To test her theory, she coaxed a flame to life. Sure enough, one look around the room proved no sign of even the faintest of glows. Still, she had been in that passage countless times and had never seen any lights.

Kiara wondered what time it was and if Cida was waiting at their meeting spot. But with a tightening in her chest, she found she didn't even want to go, paralyzed and unable to face anyone. Even Cida. She only hoped she'd understand and not wait for her too long.

"What have I done?" She whispered to the black about her, hugging her knees and staring into the darkness.

She thought to maybe check out the passage, despite her better judgment, but that also terrified her, leaving her in the same ridged state. Then *BANG!* the choice to move or not was made. Kiara's legs flew under her and she shot to her feet. She slammed her hands over her ears as the clang ricocheted off the walls of the cavern, vibrating her spine and clattering her teeth. Her heart hammered in her chest, but before the second clang could sound, she had figured it out. The bell of Caverna, and the rumbling and falling dust that accompanied it more often than not these days, really shouldn't surprise her at all anymore, but here in the Forbiddens, it was just so loud. Especially midnight and noon. She didn't have to count the chimes to know what time it was now.

Hands clamped over her ears, Kiara waited for the ear-throbbing clangs to subside and the dust to cease falling from the ceiling.

Ever since she first started coming to the Forbiddens, it had always perplexed her that the bell chimes were so much louder here than in Caverna. Then, as she thought about the light in the crack, the gears in her mind started turning and she couldn't help but make a connection, curiosity waking with a yawn and a stretch.

But, how can something just be there, when there was nothing there before?

It was no use, she had to check it out.

When Kiara came to the passage and was greeted by only blackness she sighed in both disappointment and relief.

"Wonderful. So I'm not crazy," she whispered to herself.

But somehow the darkness made the strange light all the more intriguing. Did it just flick on and off at will whenever a stranger came near? Was it even lit by a human being?

Kiara held up her lantern, squinting to see beyond its faint and uncertain glow. She scrutinized every crack and crevice, carefully searching the walls for any kind of oddity she might have missed before. Then, shuffling along the tunnel wall, her fingers slid off the rough stone and onto rigid bumps of old, unplaned wood, worn soft by time. She jumped back and shined her light on a narrow door she had never seen in her life, yet had to have passed a thousand times before.

"Amazing!" she marveled, frozen in disbelief.

She lightly touched her ear against the wood, unable to hear a peep, and yet she knew the source of the light had to be in there.

If she was any bit afraid, her curious bones won the battle quickly enough. Holding her breath, she turned the handle and slowly creaked open the door. Peering in, her eyes beheld a quaint, well lit room. But besides size and lighting, Kiara didn't know if she had ever seen anything stranger. Motionless cogs and wheels lined the walls, and gave it the appearance of one big, sleeping machine, and where there was no machinery, gaping back holes of all different sizes bore straight into the stone walls and disappeared into the shadows of unknown places. Kiara stepped to the other side of the door. A long table stood just off from the center of the room, supporting but one object, a strange glass contraption, running with white sand.

She cocked her head, unsure what she was seeing, and took a step towards it, only to freeze at the sound of voices, distant but somehow close. Her heart beat in a flurry and she darted her eyes about the room, but no one was there. Kiara didn't know what was more frightening, people actually being there, or people she could hear but never find.

She didn't have much time to choose, because just then, from around a bend she hadn't even noticed, strode a tall man as lanky as a stalagnate, with wild, black hair that seemed to defy gravity. He walked to the table without a glance in her direction and stared at the glass contraption, leaning forward with his palms on the table top.

Kiara's insides tightened. She couldn't believe she was foolish enough to think she was alone. If he saw her, he could tell the king, and she'd have to go home. Her fear rose like bile in her throat as she thought of the consequences of being caught. She couldn't go home, not after the way she left.

She began backing herself through the room until she felt the handle of the door. Carefully wrapping each finger around the nob, she pulled it open a fraction of an inch. The door gave a quiet creek that, to her, sounded like a scream. She froze, heart pounding, but the man didn't flinch, too deep in thought to notice such a discreet noise. Kiara relaxed and continued to inch open the door, when suddenly, the wiry man finished with whatever he was thinking about. And straightening, he began to turn.

Chapter Twenty Two

Tick-Tock

When he saw her, the man got such a fright, he made Kiara jump and squeak with a start.

"I'm sorry!" she blurted. "I didn't mean to sneak up on you, honest! I didn't even know anyone was in here."

His wide, grey-blue eyes blinked at her under huge, crafty-looking goggles.

"*My*!" he breathed, his voice breathless with great surprise. "You are a strange creature!"

Kiara scrunched her nose in offense.

"Are you a spirit?"

"Excuse me?" she bristled. "No, no I'm not a spirit; I'm a girl, a normal person just like you." Then she thought of her hair and how strange it could look to someone who had never seen her, and that's just what started the slowing of her pounding heart— he seemed to have no knowledge of the little, red-headed princess of Caverna.

"I'm normal?" He pondered the thought. "That's a first . . . or at least I think it is." Shaking his head to forget the subject, he stuck out his hand. "My name is Tick." Then pulling it back immediately, before Kiara could shake it, he scratched his head. "Or is it Tock? Oh well, Tick, Tock, call me whatever you'd like. The king gave me that name, I don't like it very much. The *King* gave me a different name, though I can't seem to think of it at the moment."

Kiara was hearing nonsense. "Wait, King Nnyric?"

"He didn't tell me his name. If he did, I wouldn't remember it anyway." He sighed.

Kiara stared at him uncertainly, but didn't know what she expected to learn. "I'm K-Betsie." She stuck out her hand, using the alias for reasons she hadn't fully contemplated. Finally he shook it with a funny smile, but his eyes could never stay in one place for long. He had cold, bony, and calloused hands that, she realized, felt just like how they looked.

"Betsie," he tested the sound on his tongue. "That is a nice name. Though, I have to apologize, I will forget you almost instantly when you leave."

Kiara wanted to laugh, but the coldness in his voice and the way his eyes shifted, prevented her from feeling fully at ease.

"Now, I don't get many visitors, but I didn't think a girl could have hair the color of fire. Where do you come from?"

Kiara sighed. "Nowhere."

"Ah! So you are a spirit! A specter from the dark land that I dream about."

"No. I just come from nowhere of importance."

"Strange words you use for yourself, normal, not important . . . Seems to me you think very low of yourself indeed. Pain and deep sorrow lines your face, but there is a light in your bright eyes that I have never seen before. But I could have and just don't remember."

The giggle that couldn't find its way out a second ago, bounced from her throat out of nowhere, her heart strangely lightening at the angle at which he looked at things.

"Whatever it is though," Tick continued, "it is not unimportant."

Kiara couldn't pinpoint the origin of the warmth she felt in her heart and almost immediately found a way to change the subject. "Whatever do you wear those goggles for?"

"These?" He pointed to the things on his face. "Do you like them? I made them myself. They are my spectacles. Without them I couldn't see, and if I couldn't see, I could not work."

Kiara frowned so she wouldn't smile too big. These were not spectacles. Her grandfather wore spectacles and if anything, these were some sort of ridiculous version of them. But she couldn't deny, they suited his eccentric disposition quite fantastically.

"What do you do here anyway?"

"Haven't you heard the chimes of time that come every hour?"

"Well, yes."

"That's what I do. I keep the bells working."

"With all this?" Kiara gestured to the cogs and gears.

"Why, of course! Would you like to see?"

She nodded and stepped further into the room, where she

could then see around the corner to a cramped living space, boasting little more than a lumpy bed, scarce cabinetry and a sad little table with only one chair.

Tick hopped back to the table in the front room with two strides of his spindly legs and pointed to the glass mechanism. “This is the main chamber that holds all the sand, and it pours into each of these twelve smaller chambers. When the first one is full, it will be one O’ clock.” Kiara noted how it had only just begun to fill. “The sand will then overflow from this chamber and start pouring into the lower one and once that one is full, it will be two O’ clock! And so on . . . So, you see, each time a jar fills up, I ring this bell over here, as many times as jars are full.”

“Incredible . . . And these holes and tunnels?” She looked about the room. “Where do they go?”

“I don’t know.”

Kiara felt foolish for having expected any other answer.

“But I’m almost certain they carry the bell chimes to . . . well, wherever they need to go.”

“Right, of course.”

“But they not only take sound, they deliver it too!”

“What do you mean?”

“Wherever they lead, they bring sounds back here too, from those on the other side.”

Then Kiara remembered the disembodied voices she heard when she first walked in.

“When I forget,” Tick continued, “which I so often do, I think I’ve gone right crazy and begun to hear voices in my head, but then I remember the talkative tunnels and how they enjoy to speak.”

“What do they say?”

Tick scrunched his brow. “I . . . I don’t know.”

Kiara could have smacked her face for how many times she had forgotten the incompetence of his brain.

“But . . .” he began to recall solemnly. “Not more than a few hours ago, I heard a girl weeping . . .”

Kiara gave him a strange look.

“No one spoke to her. No one comforted her. For hours she cried, completely . . . *Alone*.” He stared at her intently, and she feared he’d put the pieces together, connecting her puffy, red eyes, to the weeping he heard. But his eyes trailed sadly away and he stared at nothing. “I don’t know if I’ll ever forget that.”

Kiara released her breath. “Have you ever heard that girl

before? Through the tunnels?" Kiara knew he wouldn't remember, but she had to ask.

"Tunnels?"

"Yes, the talking tunnels." She felt his attention slipping through her fingers, as sure as the sand through the glass invention.

His eyes grew foggy with confusion and he put a hand to his head. "Talking tunnels . . ." he mumbled. "Oh! Right. Um . . . no, I don't think so. When I try to think of the reason for the things I hear and don't hear, my head begins to spin. The tunnels might as well have a mind of their own, carrying along and letting pass whatever suits their capricious desires."

"I see," Kiara said, though she didn't in the slightest.

Then Tick scrunched his face. "Ooooh, but what was I just doing before all this?"

"Um, I believe you were telling me how you ring the bell whenever a sand jar fills up."

"Right! Oh, right. Ah! It feels so good to remember things! So I ring the bell for eleven of the jars, but," he gave a quick raise of his brows, "when all twelve are full, something different entirely happens. The weight of the sand in the twelfth jar presses on a weight sensitive plate, starting a delightful chain of reactions that allow the pulley systems to work again. They can then turn wheels which pull the cord that makes the big bell," he pointed up, "ring exactly twelve times!"

Kiara raised her head to see how the ceiling itself was, in fact, one giant bell, encompassing the entire room!

"However do you not go deaf?" she wondered, still craning her neck at its enormity.

"Ah!" He held up a finger. "That is what these are for." He walked over to the scanty living area, dug in a cramped little drawer, and retrieved a piece of ridiculous looking headwear.

Held together by a copper spring, were two oversized squares of fluff and padding that Kiara could only imagine were meant to protect his ears. Tick stretched the spring so he could fit them to his ears, and then froze as if striking a pose.

"While the main bell rings, I reset the sand!" he shouted, unaware of his unnecessary volume, "taking each individual chamber off and dumping them back into the top one!"

"Wow! that's amazing!"

He blinked at her. "What!"

Kiara grinned and tapped her ear.

"Oh!" Laughing nervously he removed the muffs.

Stifling her giggles, she repeated herself, "I said, it's all very amazing. How do you remember it all?"

He sighed. "It's the only thing I can remember. Day after day, hour after hour. It is a never ending cycle." He sounded very tired. "But I couldn't leave if I tried!" he said, his eyes growing round. "What if, all because of me, time was off a minute or worse an hour! I hate to think of it . . . Also, what would I do with myself? I can't remember a time before I was doing this."

Kiara suddenly realized something. "Wait, if you're the only one here and you have to ring that bell every hour, when do you sleep?"

"Anytime that I can, usually in half hour dozes. I can't sleep longer, there's nothing for it, an overwhelming feeling of a mental hourglass draining in my brain wakes me up before I can even begin to relax or oversleep."

At that, her heart filled with a horrible pain, but also a burning anger. "Why are you the only one here?"

"I don't know. The king never gives reasons for the things he does, or least I don't think he does."

"No." She scowled. "I'm sure he doesn't. How often does the king come here?"

"I don't know."

Kiara felt her frustration rising with all the uncertainty.

"But if he came here often I'm almost certain I would have remembered him. Though, sure as sunlight, all I can remember are his eyes. And I know that those dark eyes terrify me. There is a man in Nowhere who has eyes like that."

Kiara got a shiver when he put her own fears into words. Then as she thought through his words more carefully, her mind hit a roadblock. Kiara held up a hand. "I beg your pardon, but did you just say . . . sunlight?"

Tick's eyes wandered as if trying to recall. "Why, yes . . . though I can't seem to remember what it is."

Kiara could feel her pulse quickening. "But you've heard the word before?"

He squinted. "Maybe?"

She sighed, again thinking she should have assumed as much. "And Nowhere," she began just to make conversation, "where exactly is that?" She realized the paradox after the words left her mouth. Tick didn't.

"In my dreams, of course!" he exclaimed. "But . . ." His expression darkened. "It is a place where I never want to go. There are spirits there, with horns and rotting flesh, but some are most fair. They have shiny eyes and long hair, coming to deceive and then to devour. The very air is heavy and sour with brimstone. The ground is a cracked and parched wasteland, blistering and scarred. And it's so dark all the time, all light choked out by a horrible red dust in the air. The land is filled with every horror you can imagine, and doesn't stop at the ones you can't."

Kiara might have been horrified, if she was not herself plagued with such chronic nightmares. Instead, she felt even more instantly connected with him than before.

Tick shivered away the horrors. "But my dreams are not always of Nowhere." He smiled. "There is the Place Always, where those who don't belong will belong." He sighed the words and went on to describe the supposed, wonderful land.

Kiara thought it very strange, how he believed that what he dreamed about were real places. But she couldn't find it in her heart to fault him, he knew no more than this room, and if he had half the imagination she did, he was so hopeless. The longer she listened the more intrigued she became, and she too began to find it difficult to separate dream from reality, the lines blurring as the place began to sound more and more like the world she read about within her journals. Then she heard a detail that made her heart skip a beat.

"Wait!" she interrupted. "A sky? The Place Always has a sky?"

Tick blinked his sparkly, goggled eyes at her. "Yes . . . What is a sky?"

"But that's it!" She grinned, though he remained nonplussed. "That's how you know about the sun. The sun shines in the sky! If the Place Always has a sky, it must also have a sun, you see?"

His eyes diverted to one side. "I don't know . . ."

"No, it's true! How often do you go— er, dream of there?" Kiara asked, not even sure if she should expect a direct answer.

He looked down with slanted lids. "Sadly, not very often."

Her smile fell to see his deep sorrow. "Oh. I'm sorry."

He lifted his head, for once looking her in the eyes. "Don't be sorry for me. For at least I dream. Now, to not dream at all, that would be the tragedy."

Kiara pondered on this, never having thought of it that way.

"You know of what I speak?"

"I think so."

"I thought as much." He smiled then, and Kiara thought she liked its silly crookedness very much. She also noticed how steadily he held her gaze just now, the stranger she had met upon walking in diminishing to a mere shadow of the person she talked to now.

"You have that special light in your eyes. You—" he started to continue, when suddenly his train of thought came to a screeching halt, mid-sentence.

Kiara cocked her head as she watched him walk to the table, every movement stiff and perfunctory as if rehearsed. He followed the last grains of sand with his eyes as they entered the first glass chamber and started pouring into the second one. Then, quickly, but yet mechanically, he skipped over to the bell and rang two perfectly spaced, even chimes.

Kiara waited patiently, unsure how nearly a whole hour had already passed since she arrived. But Tick knew exactly what time it was without having to even glance at the glass contraption.

When he turned around again, his eyes widened in horror, and as if he had never seen her before. He gasped and jumped back. "My! You are a strange creature. Are you a spirit?"

Kiara jumped too, but soon enough she was only confused. "What?" She scrunched her brow. "Haven't we already addressed this?"

He stared at her blankly.

"I'm Betsie. You're Tick. I'm not a spirit; I'm a girl."

"Oh, I'm sorry," he said, completely embarrassed.

Kiara felt badly for him and suddenly only wanted to lessen his humiliation. "No, it's alright. You were just about to show me how that contraption works."

"Oh, of course!" He started pointing out things and explaining what they did again with just as much alacrity as before.

Extremely perturbed and completely uncertain of what to do in such a situation, Kiara decided she needed to leave and thought it would be easiest to do so while he was distracted. She could've stayed and talked to him for hours about his dreams. She admired the way he loved and clung to the good dreams, as though they made every dark horror worth enduring. The sane stability that had fallen over him like a steadily brightening room, told her, demanded her to believe he was not always so broken. That he could yet be made whole. He was a victim of horrible neglect and captivity. All she wanted to do was set him free, and yet she was leaving him.

Even as she silently slipped behind the door, half of her heart ripped itself from her to stay. She left the door cracked and peered back in the room. She saw him turn around with a light in his round eyes, but it quickly dimmed and soon he only looked very confused, like he didn't know what he had just been doing. A pallor of paranoia drained his face of all color and he spun around to look at the sand draining into the second hour chamber. When he was satisfied that all was as it should be, his shoulders slumped and he sighed a very exhausted and lonely sigh. It sent Kiara over the edge, shattering her heart to pieces.

She closed the door, unable to watch a moment longer, and sped back to her cavern, a dreadfully sick cold, churning a riot in her stomach. Tears streamed down her face as she broke down weeping. She felt awful inside, as wretched as the dirtiest soul, and yet it wasn't even her who had done this to him. But she knew who had and she hated him for it.

His madness has no end, Kiara thought of her father. *Is there anything too dark, too evil, for him, too base to break any form of moral standard?*

She sought refuge under the tatty blankets of her little bed and stared at the crack of light in the wall.

"No, he is the dark. King Nnyric, Lord of Darkness."

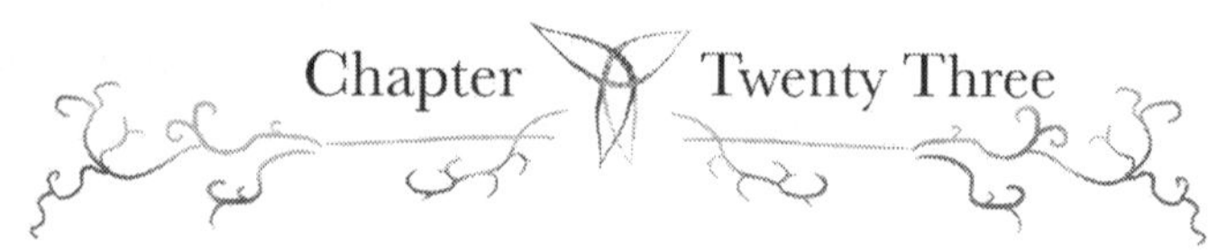

Chapter Twenty Three

The Makings of a Plan

The next day muddled into an abysmal blur Kiara didn't care to remember. She wandered through it in a depressed fog, wishing at every moment it would just end. She thought of going to see Tick, but then decided to wallow. She thought of reading, but her own mind just pulled her deeper into the dark.

She had far too much time to think about everything. But what occupied her thoughts most was the one thing she wished she could never think about again— her own father. The man who wouldn't love her. He'd find the letter soon, most likely stomping into her room after he found out she didn't show up at school. Over and over, she played the scenarios out in her mind. She cried every time, her eyes never finding the time or strength to ever fully dry.

Sometime, after noon, she began to notice her need for something to eat, not that she was hungry. Her stomach never grumbled, but she felt rather sick and lethargic, her hands developing a constant shake.

When the bell struck ten chimes for the second time that day, she shuffled her way to her and Cida's meeting point two hours early, not because she was eager to get there, but because she feared, in another hour she wouldn't be able to stand to her feet. She settled into her new spot with nothing to do but stare into the flame of her lantern. After no more than two minutes of that, time stopped moving the same way as before. Her mind wandered and part of her couldn't have cared less if it ever came back to her. In a lazy world between dreaming and waking, she saw herself going home. A man somewhat like her father stood at the door, but his eyes were a lighter, kinder blue and a strong smile softened his face. He held his arms wide to welcome her, to embrace her. Kiara's heart leapt within her chest and she ran to him without hesitation. She was nearly there, nearly held.

The bell chimed, marking the hour, and Kiara jumped as she was ripped from her stupor. The dream dimmed like a suffocated flame, shoving Kiara back into cold reality. That's when she noticed her lamp oil was running dangerously low. She thought to go get some more, but at the pace she had been moving, the light could go out on her way there and she could be lost, maybe forever! Kiara felt her heart begin to race at the entrapping feeling. Every minute that passed and the flame continued to burn, was another moment she sat there for no reason. And yet the longer she waited, the more dire her situation became as the risk of it going out on her way to her hideaway rose.

Kiara drew her knees up to her chest, hoping Cida would come soon.

Midnight struck like a death toll, and Kiara was next. Her lantern had dimmed to a feeble flicker. She was fairly certain it had devoured all the fuel and had begun feasting greedily on the wick itself, but she didn't dare check. Instead she waited for the black of her fate, leaving it's time unknown.

Maybe Cida wouldn't come at all. She couldn't blame her, because it wasn't something she hadn't already done. So what if she died here alone in the dark? She couldn't think of a reason she deserved any better.

A whispering fluttered through the caverns like a voice in her head, and she dared not hope it was anything more. But then it came again. And a third time even more clear.

"Miss Kiara?"

"Over here," she creaked out a weak reply.

Cida rounded a corner and found Kiara sitting with a dim lantern by her side.

"Oh, Miss! I was worried sick!"

"I thought you weren't going to come." With lethargic increments Kiara lifted her head.

"Oh, Miss . . ."

"I was so afraid, Cida. My fuel is running out, but I didn't know until it was too late. And then I was so weak and I knew, I just knew, I would be lost in darkness if you didn't come." A tear trickled from her eye, and her next words barely reached a whisper. "Thank you for never giving up on me."

Just then Kiara's light went out and all they had was Cida's to light the space. Cida settled down next to her and wrapped an arm around her shoulders.

"I'm sorry I didn't come last night. I was too ashamed . . . Cida, what have I done?"

"Don't be sorry, you've done nothing wrong. I'm alright and I'm just glad that you're here now."

Kiara wasn't quite sure if she felt the same joy.

"Though I won't lie." Cida smirked. "I can't very well say I wasn't the slightest bit miffed with you, Missy, when you didn't show up the first time. I'm not the kind for all this sneaking around stuff. Do you know how dreadfully terrifying this place is in the dark? Oh! And I could just hear me mum, bless her heart, and the earful she would have had for me. 'Lucida, you ninny!' " she said in a ridiculous, nasal tone. " 'Didn't you listen to a word I said about wandering about after lights out? Oh, you'll never learn!' And with a whack to my rear, she'd send me on my way."

Kiara snickered, the corners of her mouth quivering with a persistent grin. It felt so good, highlighting her desperate lack of joy. She just wished it would stay.

Lucida smiled at the hint of cheer, considering her mission accomplished. "Oh, but it wasn't all that bad. Who would have even dreamed I, *ME*, the one who flees her own shadow, would travel the unlit streets of Caverna without screeching, wetting myself, or turning back? Not me!"

Kiara grabbed her hand. "I would have. You're braver than you think."

Cida smiled. "And so are you. I prayed for you lots when you didn't show up last night."

"Thanks," Kiara said tersely.

Cida looked down at a bag on her lap. "Here, I brought this for you. You have to eat even if you say you're not hungry, for I would not believe you." She handed her the bag.

"Thank you, Cida. You're always so kind when I do nothing to deserve it."

"Now, enough of that. You have done nothing to deserve the man that is your father either."

"He is not my father."

Cida didn't dare comment back. She gestured to the bag again to encourage her to eat. "That food should last you till our next meeting, tomorrow night."

Kiara rummaged through the contents, breathing in the savory scents. Her stomach let out a roar of a growl like an animal long caged. She dug in and started devouring a piece of dried out red meal leftover from dinner and stuffing her face with a cold biscuit. Her own raging hunger took her off guard, and in a minor lapse in priorities, she forsook her manners for the greater good of calming the beast in her stomach.

Having satisfied the monster, Kiara continued to munch in a much more lady-like fashion, and returned to the situation at hand. "So what has happened? Has he seen it? Has he seen the letter?"

Cida patted her hands in her lap, looking down on them. "He has . . . This morning when you didn't get up for school."

Kiara didn't appreciate her careful tone and refused to act as concerned. She raised a copper brow. "And?"

"And he cried, Kiara! You should have seen him."

Kiara felt her anger rise from her toes to her throat, heat radiating up her back, until finally it came out as steam through her ears. She wanted to scream. How could Cida sympathize with him? She wanted to *scream* at him. She wanted to lock him up in a dark place where he could never deceive another soul. She wanted to burn him, like a useless piece of paper. And worst of all, she wanted to go to him, to touch his face, to weep with him, which made her all the more angry.

"I was standing outside the room," Lucida continued. "He didn't know I was there, and—"

"I don't want to hear it, Cida!" Kiara exploded, her eyes red with rage and held back tears. "The only pain he feels is for himself." She turned her face away.

"I'm sorry. I didn't mean . . . I just thought you would want to know."

"I don't."

Cida hesitated to lay a hand on her shoulder. "Kiara, I *am* sorry. I've got your back no matter what. You know that, right? I didn't think my words through."

Kiara turned to her again. "I know." Smoothing her dress, she said, "So, what did he do? You know . . . about it?"

"I'm afraid nothing yet. But I'm sure he will tomorrow."

"Yes, I'm sure of it." Kiara's voice had gone cold as if the very warmth of her soul had been stolen from her. Part of her wanted to believe it was that thing, whatever it was, living inside him, that made him hurt people, that controlled him, and made him unable to love. But he allowed it, it was still his fault. What could it really do to him? It didn't even have a form.

A paralyzing thought froze her solid as she contemplated, for the first time, the possibility of him not believing the letter. Between his own twisted mind and the help of that thing, what if he second-guessed?

"Cida," she turned to her friend, urgency in her eyes, "he will ask you. He is much too shrewd to not indulge his own suspicions, and much too paranoid not to have suspicions. He will ask you about me and you must be dead inside like everybody else, like him. You must tell him that you have not seen me for some time, that you're not my keeper. That is the only way you can protect yourself and me. I can be brave and live here alone, but you have to be dead to all hurt and all emotion or he will see through you and he will find me. You can't let him find me."

"I won't."

"Promise me."

Cida looked her in the eyes. "I promise," she insisted. "You don't have to worry. There will be no secrets that he can pry out of me. You will be safe from him here."

Kiara laid her head back against the stone. "I'll never be safe, not in the darkness."

They sat in silence for sometime, offering their company, but having no words strong enough to break the catatonic quiet.

Finally Cida's yawn did it for them. "I wish I didn't have to," she said, "but I should get back."

"But you *cannot* go!" Kiara cried. "I won't find my way back in the dark." Then she had an idea. "You should come see my hideaway!"

"I can't!" Cida blurted and sighed. "I'm sorry, but I won't venture any further into the place that too often plagues my dreams and torments my sleep." She smiled. "But here, take some of my fuel to get you back."

"Thank you, Cida. Don't feel badly. I shouldn't have asked." Kiara slowly stood and picked up the bag Cida had brought her. "I'll see you tomorrow night?"

"Yes, you will, most likely with news that will be difficult to speak of," she said. "Goodnight, Miss."

"Goodnight, Cida."

Kiara watched her go without another word and made her prompt return to her hideaway, fearing that at any moment her light might go out. But safely slipped back inside, she realized Lucida had spared just enough oil. Her light had just begun to weaken again, as had her resolve, when exhaustion and the weight of simply everything took the strength from her legs and she sunk to her knees. Tears filled her eyes. She wanted to go back and apologize for all she had done, and at the same time she hated herself for being so weak. But was staying here worth all this pain?

Here she wept alone and waited for the darkness to take her once again.

Cida prayed for her, or so she had said . . . She probably was now.

"Are You out there?" Kiara whispered. "Because You feel just as far as every other thing promised to be out there . . . Twice as far."

The light made its last wavering attempt at life and the smoke-choked darkness made its move.

But all was *not* dark and she wasn't alone as she had thought. A crack in the wall shown with a gentle glow. Tick was only just on the other side of the wall, also in solitude, but maybe not feeling so alone anymore. She had forgotten, but there it was, a sliver of light in the encompassing darkness. It was that small contradiction, that simple constant when she had thought all was lost, that splashed her like cold water on her face and told her to yet hope.

She found her way to her pile of blankets by touch and memory, crawling along the floor. She lay on her back and reached her hand above her. She couldn't see them, but she didn't need to. The chimes rang out, that same song as before, but once again subtly different.

She wished she knew what to call such sounds, yet no name she could form on her tongue could translate such beauty. It was like they were talking to each other, but with voices so ethereal, they didn't seem meant for this world. And when she closed her eyes, she knew they longed to take her somewhere else, somewhere she could only wonder about.

Before she knew it, she heard herself trying to speak that wonderfully strange language, driven by a need deep in her soul to be as close as she could get to the sounds that so stubbornly, yet gently defied the darkness. She clumsily reached for the notes like a small child, standing on tiptoes to grasp the next branch in a tree, hitting every note in between before matching the right pitch. And when she did, she felt it like every color, the ones she knew and the ones she had yet to find names for, shot through her veins. She didn't know it, but her heart was singing along with the chimes in time and in tune. She could see that much more of the world they talked about in their clinking, reverent whispers to each other, the same world trapped in the pages of her journals, waiting out there with greens and blues and every other color the sun wakes up to paint.

Kiara settled into her blankets, sleep just on the edges of her mind, and with the magic of dreams, she stepped that much closer to that world, far beyond all the darkness and fear.

The next day Kiara tried to keep herself busy, which proved to be a more difficult task than she ever would have thought. She loved her hideaway, more than any other place in Caverna, but never had she spent more than a few hours at time there, and two days alone were already taking their toll.

She read as long as she dared to. It wasn't like she hadn't already read each journal cover to cover countless times before. When she knocked on Tick's door, she was surprised to learn that after a brief dispatching of ideas of spirits and such, he did vaguely remember her. Kiara was grateful for the sound of another human voice, but even their chat didn't last long as Tick became too tired for company and needed to rest. She could've gone back later, but thought it past the time and though she enjoyed their chats very much, it proved too onerous a task to pull herself out of her crevice of self pity for a second time.

She ate little of what Cida had brought her, never feeling the slightest twinge of hunger. She played her chimes often and talked to her fish just as much as she talked to herself simply to drown out the voices in her head.

By the time Cida arrived that night, she found Kiara already sitting at their meeting spot, her face in her hands.

"Miss?" Cida whispered.

Kiara lifted her head. "Cida!" she said with delight. "What took you so long?"

"I can not leave until all have gone to bed and there were some still awake."

"Some?" Kiara asked.

Cida sighed. "The king was up rather late with his scribe."

"*Shrike*," Kiara said the name in disgust. "What were they up to?" Kiara more mused than directly questioned, so Cida decided not to give an answer.

Lucida stretched a smile across her lips. "How have you been?"

"Cida," Kiara narrowed her eyes. "What happened? Why were Nnyric and Shrike talking after lights out?" Cida's eyes wandered. "Don't tiptoe, Cida, I can handle it. Just give it to me straight. If there's a sting, there's no way around it."

Cida sighed. "He finally conducted a town meeting today . . ." Cida's voice had lost its strength.

"Yes?" Kiara leaned closer.

"And once everyone had gathered he . . . He announced your murder."

"I knew it!" She threw her head back in laughter. "I knew he would never tell the truth! His pride could not allow it."

Cida did not find it as amusing as her young friend. "Well, it isn't rightly the truth either."

"Yes, but he does not know that." She shook her head. "How did he explain it to everyone? What reason does he have for these claims?"

"The ruse goes, he saw the criminal just before he got away and they drug the alleged killer to the dungeon right there at the meeting."

"What!" Kiara flew to her feet, arms waving in her fury. "But I'm here! I'm fine! Nobody has killed me!"

"*I* know that."

"He can't do this! Who is it? How did he even pick someone?"

"I couldn't tell you. I'm sure he just picked the first person who caught his attention. All I know is he's the last member of the Stone family. They didn't even tell us his name. I assume that's what he and Shrike were talking about tonight."

"Stone . . ." Kiara repeated. "As in Alister Stone?"

"I would assume so." Cida shrugged her shoulders.

Kiara shuttered to think of anyone related to that man. He had worked for her father before he died and something in his eyes had always made her so afraid.

"I wonder then, if Nnyric did know what he was doing. This man has no living family, no one who will even care to prove his innocence. He'll hang without even a word of a trial." Kiara hung her head. "This is all my fault. I have to go back and show everyone that I'm alive."

"Absolutely not! You can't! Kiara, he will never forgive you and you will live your life in misery."

"But, I can't let someone who is innocent go to prison for a crime that was never even committed!"

"We don't know if he's innocent."

"Maybe so, but he did not do what he is being accused of. They'll hang him, Cida! I have to do *something*!"

"I know . . . I know you do. And I would never ask you to ignore the voice inside you urging you to do right."

"So you agree that it is right?"

Cida sighed. "Yes. But what can you do?"

"I think . . ." Kiara paused. "I have a plan." She raised an eyebrow. "But I can't do it alone. Cida, I need your help."

It took that night and the next, plotting and scheming, to ready the plan. Cida would often fret and stress over the smallest details and Kiara would have to reassure her and tell her they had no other choice, reminding her again and again the stakes at hand. They took very little precaution, partly because they had no time to, but also because there weren't many precautions they could take when they had no idea what they were getting themselves into.

When the time for planning ran out and the time to act fell upon them, Cida sat with Kiara in the Forbiddens, verbally running her through the plan until both of them had bled themselves dry of possible worst case scenarios.

At last, Cida fixed her with a serious glance. "Are you ready?"

Kiara lowered her hood. "As ready as I can be."

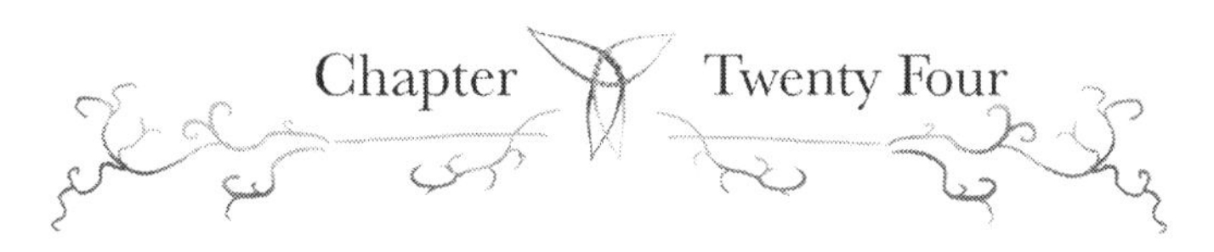

Chapter Twenty Four

A Rescue in the Dark

The plan was in motion, foolhardy and full of holes, yet better than nothing at all. If all went over well enough, the identity of the hooded figure that roamed the streets that night would never come to light.

Two men stood guard outside the entrance to the prison, a narrow staircase with a steep descent into the dungeon. They carried on a quiet conversation, unaware of the movements of the figure in the street before them. The stranger glided closer, and while one of the guards continued to prattle on with no mind, the other suddenly beheld the hooded figure who seemed to have just materialized out of the darkness. He couldn't look away, but he couldn't say a word either, some kind of shadowed power squeezing his throat closed. He just pawed at his companions shoulder, his lips moving incomprehensibly like a fish out of water.

The other guard looked at him strangely. "What's got you in such a fright, Newton?"

He followed his comrade's fear stricken gaze. His breath caught, but recovering quickly enough, he cleared his throat. "Who goes there?" he interrogated.

The figure didn't say a word, but slowly raised their right hand to the light, displaying on the index finger a silver ring inlaid with gold in the shape of three, strange, six-pointed stars, each inside of the last.

"The king's signet . . ."

The guards looked at each other as if trying to come to a decision without having to talk and then moved aside, allowing the hooded one passage.

The figure stood rigid still for a moment, staring at them from underneath the black hood and then floated by and down into the dark, feet never making a sound.

The guards were much too shaken themselves to notice, but as the figure made her way past, she trembled violently beneath her cloak, and after the first couple of steps, she abandoned her floating pace for panicked haste.

She chided herself silently, descending the uneven steps, for once again wading into a situation too dangerous, too big for her to handle. Fears she had locked at the back of her mind of what she would meet down there, pushed their ugly heads out of their cages and into the forefront of her thought. She never slowed and yet the stairs just kept going, seemingly without end, a foul smell growing steadily worse.

At length, she came to a landing. Kiara tiptoed off the steps and crept around the corner into a dimly lit room, where a hulking brute of a man sat hunched over a table, slurping up some unidentifiable slop. He noticed her the moment she entered the room and cast an alarmingly ugly scowl her way. A grating scrape cried out from the legs of his chair as he pushed his large frame away from the table. Kiara swallowed a lump in her throat as he rose to his full menacing height, not only because he was unreasonably tall, but because in all her life she had only met one person that tall and that ugly, and that was on her recent escapades to the Stygian Market. A smudge of chalk on his grimy jacket, still served as evidence of the white beast that decorated it before and the clan it belonged to.

Kiara's heart pounded in her ears and a tremor ran through her core as she stared at the unsightly mug that could belong to none other than Hamish Clungston.

He lumbered toward her and trained his cooperative eye on her. "State your business," he grumbled unintelligently, his breath reeking like rotting flesh.

Kiara did not speak, but keeping her hood low, she handed him a folded note.

His unkempt brow came low over his eyes as he glared at the paper a moment. She tried to hold the note as steady as she could, sweat dripping down the sides of her face. His eye shifted from the note to her hooded head for so long, Kiara thought she might quit breathing. Then he smiled, a wicked, yellowed smile, full of black holes where teeth should be.

"Hey, yo're quite a little feller, aren't ya'?"

Kiara couldn't have responded if she wanted to.

Clungston's smile fell lame. Finally, he swiped the note from her and walked to his table, grabbing up a jagged piece of glass that he used to magnify the contents of the page.

"Hmmm . . ." he grumbled.

Kiara watched him painfully as he took a painstaking amount of time to read the note. If she and Cida had taken enough care, he should find what looked exactly like a letter from the king, giving clear orders to let her speak with the new prisoner in private, to prepare him properly for his journey beyond the gallows and hear the last confessions of a dead man.

With nothing better to do, Kiara counted the beats of her heart as the seconds ticked by.

Hamish suddenly straightened. "Welp. All seems to be in order."

Kiara blew out a breath she only just realized she was holding.

"Right," he grunted. "This way then."

With a flourish of his hand, he seemed to mock her ranking with all her high orders straight from the king. He then walked to a door to his left and banged on it with a fist the size of a ham hock.

"Open up, boys!" He boomed.

"Password!" An antagonizing voice demanded, and somehow Kiara could just tell it belonged to a much smaller man.

Hamish growled in exasperation. "Stegler, if you don't open this door right now, I'll bash your head in next we meet."

There was a jangling noise and the door swung wide rather promptly after that, the man on the other side not challenging Kiara's assumptions in the slightest.

"You know I was only messing with you, right, Smash?" He laughed painfully, blinking up at him. "Have I told you that your arms look especially massive today?"

"Shut your trap!" Hamish snapped. "This feller has got orders from his majesty hisself."

"Oh, my apologies," Stegler snickered and bowed in mock respect.

Kiara couldn't believe the kind of treatment that those closely associated with the king received here.

Clungston kneed him in the stomach mid-bow. "Yes, orders to speak to the new prisoner alone, so get the guards cleared out."

Stegler, still coughing and recovering from the blow, didn't notice when Kiara pick-pocketed the keys right off him.

"Yes . . . " he managed, "right away," and hobbled off.

Soon enough he returned from the dark hall, several more

guards in tow.

"Go straight and you'll find him at the end." Hamish pointed down a long hallway.

Kiara turned and stared into the swallowing dark of the corridor.

"Here," Stegler handed her a lantern, "take this."

Kiara fought to take control of her rigid limbs, grabbed it from him, and forced her legs to take her down the hallway.

"Watch out for the vermin!" Hamish called. "Nasty teeth those beasties got."

Cruel laughter drifted up the hall and through the countless chambers.

Her eyes grew wide, trying to see in the dim light, but then she thought she probably didn't want to see anything, lest the sight of the horrors down here send her back before she had accomplished what she came to do. Gaps of darkness opened up to her left and right sometimes and she dared not shine her lantern inside.

Then, when they thought she couldn't hear them anymore, the stone walls carried their disembodied voices of the jailers to her ears.

"Funny that! The king's feller's going to prepare him for the other side and all," she could hear Hamish say. "But we'll have 'em broke out before they can get the gallows properly 'pared."

Kiara stopped in her tracks to listen.

"What?" another voice hissed. "Why? You'll just be caught and swing with him!"

"Mereaze has got it in his head that the lout is of more use to him. And if not, he'd much rather have the pleasure of killing him himself than merely watch him dangle from the rope."

Kiara's mind raced with the prisoner's possible identity, and suddenly began to rethink her decision to see him released.

"This ain't right."

"Yeah? Well I'd keep my mouth shut about it if I were you. Unless you want me to tell Mereaze where old Stegler's been hiding out all these years."

"No! I left that life behind for a reason. I'm not going back."

"Right . . ." Kiara could hear the twisted smile lacing his voice. "So just don't you worry your little head about it, Stegs."

Kiara heard no answer (if there was any) aside from Hamish's deep satisfied chuckles and then silence. She shook away a shiver that crept up on her shoulders, ready to make itself at home.

How many more clansmen had made this their den? Kiara couldn't believe the irony of Hamish's— or should she say Smash's side life, so close to where he should really be, yet on the wrong side of the bars.

Her extended tarry in the middle of the hall had begun to attract some unsolicited attention from the nearby prisoners. Before now, Kiara had been too distracted to even notice the bars lining either wall, but vague movement on her left and right brought her attention rushing back.

They mumbled and moaned, crawling out of their corners for a better look. She shined her light closer and her legs turned to noodles. Gaunt figures shivered in their cells and stared out at her with sunken-in eyes and hollow cheeks, some having been here so long they had changed into something horrible, unrecognizable hunched creatures, neither man nor beast. And the stench! What she smelt yet on the steps diminished to a mere fraction of the horrible odor hanging thick in the air around their cells.

Her lip quivered in fear and disgust as she fought her own reasoning to make sense of their poor conditions, kept here in the dark, barely clinging to life. But if they were to never be released, why not sentence them to the gallows like so many others? Why keep them here like this? She couldn't justify it. Even if they had done something deserving of punishment once, most of them were too old or frail now to do any harm at all. All the while, the real monsters roamed uncaged, free to hurt and carry out their wicked plans, and even watch over these locked up.

Some moved closer. They didn't say a word, at least not an intelligible one, but they didn't have to. Their desperate, pleading eyes cried out what their tongues had forgotten how to say. Kiara thought she could actually feel her heart bleed as she wracked her mind to think of what kind of person could do this. Yet she had the keys in her hand, and would *she* set them free?

Though she imagined the crimes that brought them here to have looked as benign as a mouse compared to the things Hamish and Mereaze had done, something about them frightened her, and she questioned if there was even anything left of the people they used to be underneath the bestial appearances.

A few gnarled, bony hands slipped through the bars and reached out for her. Kiara backed away, but something grabbed her cloak from behind. She stifled a scream and wrenched herself from the grasp. Like some feral animal had been let loose in each of them, the prison bars exploded with grabbing hands. Kiara stayed as close as she could to the middle, wishing she could shrink even smaller as she ran. Countless, bony arms stretched out for her like dead men reaching up out of a graveyard.

At last, the bars gave way to stone walls and Kiara could stop. She took her breaths in uncontrollable gulps, her skin crawling so badly, she longed to tear off her clothes as if spiders skittered over every inch.

Kiara no longer wanted to reach the end of this hall or the prisoner kept there, but she didn't want to go back quite yet either and what could he do to her from the inside of a prison cell?

She decided to catch her breath as she walked to get this over with sooner and it wasn't long before a cell began to come into view there at the very end of the hall. Kiara swallowed down her ragged breaths and held her light far before her. As she inched closer, she asked herself over and over if she really wanted to meet someone so important to Mereaze's clan. Then, her light illuminated the outline of a man lying on a thin cot.

He shielded his eyes from the bright glow and sat up. "Who's there?"

Kiara didn't say a word. She could only stare, because there, sitting on a maggoty cot in a dark, rotting prison cell, was Hadyn.

Chapter Twenty Five
PRISON BREAK!

Kiara wanted to shout for joy, she wanted to speak his name, or at the very least sputter out her surprise. But all she could do was stare. Here was someone she thought she'd never see again, and yet by some kind of wild twist of fate, they met in the dark once more and in even worse circumstances than before.

"Hello? Who's there?" he asked again.

She thought of answering him, but the plan was to keep her identity hidden from the prisoner for both of their safety, so she would stick to it for now.

Getting a grip on her buckling emotions, she fumbled with the keys to find the right one. Finally one of the keys fit and turned smoothly enough. The cell door swung open on its own, whining the whole way and picking up a violent amount of speed. Kiara lunged and caught it just before it could bang into the stone wall, puffed out a breath, and let it go gently. The metal clanked against the stone with a soft echo.

Still sitting on the cot, Hadyn watched this all in silent astonishment. Kiara walked in the cell, wondering why he didn't even try to run, and handed him a cloak that she had folded under her arm.

"Here, put this on," she whispered.

He brushed his black curls out of his eyes. "Wait—"

"And don't ask questions." She hesitated to sit down on the smelly cot. "The guards' shifts will change over in just a few minutes. After that, we have to move."

Hadyn scooted an inch or two away from her. "Who are you?"

"I said don't ask any questions," came her terse, whispered reply, and her echoes guided them into an uncomfortable silence. Too uncomfortable for Hadyn.

He shot to his feet. “Look, I don’t know what you’re planning or who you even think I am, but I’m not going anywhere.”

It boggled her mind to the point of vexation that there could even be another choice besides coming with her in his mind.

“Would you keep your voice down!” Kiara hissed. “You can come with me or with your ‘friends’ down the hall, either way you’ll be out of this cell within the hour, whether you like it or not.”

“Friends down the . . . What are you talking about?”

“Hamish Clungston is prepared to break you out and drag you back to the Clansmen. Mereaze is determined to make you pay one way or another.”

Like his mind switched onto a different channel all at once, he scrunched his brow and cocked his head at her.

“What?” Kiara asked. “What is it?”

“Sorry. You just sound like someone I used to know. But that’s stupid.” He shook his head. “That’s impossible, because she’s . . . well she’s gone.”

“I’m sorry.”

Hadyn brushed off her condolences. “Wait, so how do you know—” He stopped himself, nodding. “Right, no questions.”

Kiara let her silence be her reply. But as he continued to just stand there, she picked up the cloak he had left on the cot and shoved it out to him again.

“If you want to live to see tomorrow . . .”

She could tell he was contemplating her words and just about everything else, so she waited patiently, still unsure why it should be such a hard decision. Finally, he took the cloak, slipped his arms into the sleeves, and pulled the hood over his head, but he didn’t sit back down. Instead he leaned against the wall and not another word passed between them until they heard a quiet chime coming from up the hall. Kiara noticed Hadyn watching her, but she remained still and silent a few moments more. Then, when she guessed enough time had passed for the guards to change over, she stood up.

“Follow me.”

Kiara led the way, leaving the cell door wide open. Checking one last time over her shoulder to make sure he followed her, she hastened her pace, loath to relive the previous nightmare of the prison hallway.

“What in the Caverna . . .” Hadyn’s voice drifted up behind her.

She knew he had stopped. She knew what he was seeing. But she didn't want to see. She couldn't look at those horrors again. Why did he have to look?

Clenching her jaw, she forced herself to turn on her heels. There he stood, hands gripped to the bars and squinting into one of the dark cells, face a tormented twist of agony. She knew exactly what he was feeling.

Averting her eyes from the prisoners, she placed a hand on his arm and gave it a tug. "We have to keep moving. We can't stay here."

His eyes stayed fixed on the prisoners in the cell, his knuckles growing white from how tightly he gripped the bars. She could feel the tense strength in the arm she held onto and let go, frightened by the anger stirring in his eyes.

"There's nothing we can do for them," she tried again.

"Sure there is." His voice betrayed the stony look in his eyes, cracking with weakness, like a small boy asking *why?* "You have the keys don't you?"

Kiara looked into the hungry eyes of the prisoners, something she told herself she wouldn't do again. She turned back to Hadyn, making sure to keep her face hidden, and shook her head. "No. I won't."

"How can you say that?"

"We don't even know what they've done to get themselves here."

"This is exactly why I hesitated to come with you. Why should I go free while they remain in this torture? You don't know what *I've* done."

"I know you didn't kill the princess!" Kiara blurted.

"What? . . . How?"

Kiara sighed. The plan became rather hazy after this, and (honestly surprised they had even made it this far) she didn't know a better time to start improvising. Raising a hand she pulled her hood off her head.

Hadyn jumped back. "Kiara!" he whispered in astonishment, and he couldn't have hid the elation in his voice even if he had the time to think. "I knew it!" His brow scrunched. "But they said you were killed!"

"I know, and that's what I would have everyone believe."

"But why?"

"In time. But, please, right now we have to go," Kiara said, looking around warily.

Once again the prisoners were becoming too curious for her liking. Hadyn gave one last pain stricken glance at the men in the cells and turned to follow her at last.

They came to a space lit with lanterns and Kiara walked up to the door where the small man named Stegler had let her in. She puffed out a long, even breath.

"How does the plan go after this?" she heard Hadyn ask.

Without turning, she replied, "It doesn't," and knocked on the door before she could become any more paralyzed.

"Yeah, Yeah . . . just a sec," came a voice from the other side and after a short moment the door swung wide.

One look at the guard's unfamiliar face, and inside, Kiara sighed with relief.

"Oi! Smash, you didn't say there was two hooded fellers?"

Her heart skittered at the words and then went loping with absolutely nowhere to go as she peered into the room to see Hamish and Stegler still there!

"That's because there wasn't," Hamish rumbled.

Kiara watched horror drain the color from Stegler's face as he felt his sides for the keys and Hamish barreled his bulk up to the taller cloaked figure. He grabbed him by the back of the head and ripped the hood down.

Hamish grinned a rotting, brown grin at him. "Hello, Blackcoal. Running again, are we?" Hadyn didn't look at him, his jaw clenched and his gaze burning a hole in the far wall. "Haven't you learned by now what the boss thinks of running? What he does to a *coward*?" At the word coward he jabbed Hadyn in the back, where only he knew it would hurt.

Several things happened in the next blink of time.

Hadyn jerked violently, partly from pain, partly from rage, but Hamish held him fast and sent a fist to his gut. Hadyn doubled over with sputtering coughs, while Kiara took advantage of the guards' diverted attention and slid the dungeon keys across the floor to Stegler. She nodded her hooded head at him as he just stared in utter bewilderment.

The details of the next moment lost their individuality in a swirling vortex of bedlam. Quick to recover, Hadyn struggled and fought like a wild animal to break free from the vice-like grip of Hamish, but his attempts proved futile. Kiara's time of invisibility was up and the rest of the five other guards in the room came at her all at once, lunging at her with arms outstretched. She tumbled with as much poise as a dead fish and fell to the ground to dodge their grasp, leaving them to collide with each other. She grimaced and arched her back in pain, but her floor level view could be used to her advantage. Pulling a hidden dagger from her belt, she took a swipe at Hamish's leg.

Whether by surprise or pain, he flung Hadyn aside. Immediately, Hadyn bent down and pulled Kiara to her feet. Together they bolted for the stairs, almost able to taste freedom on the tips of their tongues. But one last obstacle blocked their way. Stegler stood silently between them and the stairs. It didn't mean much to Hadyn. He was prepared to push him aside if he had to, but Stegler wasn't looking at them. He stared at a ring of rusty keys in the palm of his hand. He raised his head to Kiara, though the shadow of her hood prevented him from ever knowing her face. Without wasting another moment he took one step to the right.

They were free! But Kiara didn't move. Her feet had simply forgotten how to, and she was too shocked to remember. Yes, she had given the keys back to him, not knowing if he deserved it or not, it was true, but to let them go and with the resolve that no consequence could shake? It defied every exception she would have ever placed on any stranger.

Shouts behind her vied for her attention in her brain. The guards were just beginning to rally again and Hamish was with them.

"What are you waiting for?" Hadyn said, and grabbing her by the wrist, he pulled her into the stairwell. They took the stairs two at a time, as Hamish's bellows threatened to crack the walls, carrying all the way up the stairs to alert the guards waiting there of the escapee approaching.

Before long, echoes of shouts and footsteps rushed down the steps to meet his barking. They were cornered prey, unable to move forward or go back. Kiara couldn't believe her nerve, striding into a dungeon to break out a prisoner with such a patchy plan, but now was not the time to deride her own incompetence. Frayed and wrapped up as the last bit may have been, she refused to believe the plan had no end. Her brain rushed about in every direction inside her head, as she tried to unravel the last pieces in the very midst of the chaos.

Hadyn, still holding onto her wrist, was suddenly jerked to a stop.

"Wait!" Kiara whispered and tried to think. "Get against the wall."

"What?"

"Just do it!" she hissed.

Here in a dark gap where the light of the wall torches didn't reach, they pressed themselves as flat as they could against the wall. Kiara held her breath as the footsteps thundered closer. She closed her eyes, unable to watch, but the footsteps hurried right on past and away.

Prying open her eyes, she peered down the steps and then up the other way. Their gazes found each other and they exchanged astonished grins. But Kiara didn't let it last long.

"Come on, we have to get out of here."

When they emerged into the street at last, they could hear the wrath of Hamish thundering so loud, he sounded like he would break a thousand blood vessels, berating the men that they had somehow walked straight through.

Kiara and Hadyn didn't stop for a moment. They ran like fey deer, fleeing from a ravenous wolf pack through the dark streets, trying their best not to pick up the attention of any more guards on night watch. But if they didn't raise any suspicions, the sounds of desperate pursuit starting up behind them certainly would.

A loud crash sounded to their distant right, and Hadyn whipped his head toward the noise.

"Don't worry." Kiara said. "That noise was not one to fear."

With the prison on the void side of the city and the Forbiddens directly opposite, Kiara found herself slowing before they had even reached the middle of town. She never expected it to be so hard, but she had also never run the length of Caverna for fun or survival before. If it was up to her legs, she wholly believed they could take her there and back again, crazed with adrenalin, but her lungs burned like fire and she feared she might faint if she took another step.

She pulled on Hadyn's arm to slow him and in between huffs, she said, "Wait. I have to take a break. I can't go any further."

Hadyn nodded. Rest was far from his mind, much more used to running than her, but since most of the shouts had conveniently traveled off in pursuit of the same strange crash they had heard, he could allow himself to appreciate a little break.

For some time, they just tried to catch their breath, neither speaking a word, but once Hadyn had recovered, he grew anxious to keep moving.

"Where are we going?" he asked.

Kiara straightened, pushing herself off her knees. "The only place left to go." A shout from a guard called out much too close for her liking. "Come on, we have to keep moving."

They traveled at a trot after that and at length they came to the looming entrance of the Forbiddens, its wide mouth open to unending throats and guarded with ten foot fangs. A steady lantern sat at the entrance, burning bravely and waiting patiently for them.

"The *Forbiddens*?" Hadyn asked.

"Yes," she said soberly. "You're an outlaw to Caverna now. Better yet a dead man. From this day forward, you're not safe anywhere but here."

She didn't want to believe it, but the glow of the lantern faintly illuminated the slightest hint of a grin on his lips. Positively certain she could not find even a single thing amusing at the moment, she looked at him incredulously. "What?"

"Oh nothing . . ." he laughed softly.

"Doesn't sound like nothing."

"It's just that, I do believe I recall it being you who was so passionately adamant that no one could or should make the Forbiddens their home."

Her lids drooped dully, aggravated that he could actually find this funny. Kiara picked up the lantern. "Just follow me. Lucida will be waiting for us," she said as she started walking in.

"Wait. Who's Lucida?" he called in after her.

Cida had her own sanctuary of light already prepared where she waited for them. When she caught sight of them, she rushed out after them, arms and nerves a fluttering of spasms. "What is this? Kiara, I've been worried sick, and then you just waltz in here with no hood on your head and no way to hide yourself! I thought we agreed! We would keep your identity a secret."

Kiara placed her hands on her shoulders. "Cida. Relax." Lucida bit her lip, but she looked far from relaxed. "It's Hadyn," Kiara finished.

"Hadyn?" Cida's eyes asked more than her mouth.

"Yes. The Hadyn I told you about."

Cida's eyes wandered over to him and he fidgeted nervously under her wide-eyed gaze. "Goodness me . . . What a chance." Then she turned back to Kiara. "But Hadyn . . . *Stone*?" Cida asked.

Kiara nodded her head.

"So the plan worked? It really worked? And you're okay?"

A suspicion of a smile tugged at the corner of Kiara's mouth. "Just. And yes, we're okay. Thanks to you." She gave the good news, but her face remained somber. "The ring and the seal worked brilliantly. And your little diversion did exactly what we wanted it to."

"Alright, is someone going to tell me what is going on?"

Kiara and Cida turned to Hadyn and then they looked at each other.

"We knew this would happen," Cida said. "You should be thankful he is someone you already know."

Kiara tilted her head and drew in a deep breath. "Well, I suppose a proper introduction would do some good. Hadyn, this Lucida."

"I'm Kiara's . . ." Cida's phrase ended short.

"Friend," Kiara finished. "Cida is my dear friend."

"It's nice to finally meet you."

Hadyn just smiled.

Kiara then began to explain. "We made a plan to break you— er we didn't know it was you at first . . . The plan was to break whoever it was out of the prison as soon as we heard the king had taken someone prisoner for my murder. Hastily hatched and ill thought out, the plan was patchy to say the least but," Kiara forced a smile, "here we all are."

Hadyn closed his eyes. In his mind, things had yet to add up. "Yes, but why did the king arrest someone for your murder in the first place?"

Kiara looked down, unable to meet his eyes. "I . . . ran away."

Silence fell over the three of them and none of them knew what to say. Kiara felt like it was her duty to break the silence, but they didn't make her.

The seconds ticked by with no words to fill them until, finally, Kiara drew in a shaky breath.

"The night we found the library . . ." She raised her eyes to Hadyn for a brief moment. "And you walked with me to the King's Corridor, I went home with questions in need of answers, answers that could be given by only one." Kiara faltered, realizing at that moment the extent of the pain talking about these things caused her. Cida placed a reassuring hand on her shoulder. "I knew the answers. I knew exactly what he'd say. I just . . . needed to hear it from his mouth. And I don't know why. To further punish myself for failing so miserably at everything?"

"Hey . . ." Cida tightened her grip on her shoulder and spoke softly. "I won't have any more of that."

She went on to tell him everything, though it was lengthy and at times disjointed when it came to things especially hard to say. Hadyn listened in silence the whole time and Cida helped fill in Kiara's pauses with the things she could.

The more she talked, the more her sadness slipped away and anger came creeping in. She balled her hands into fists in her lap.

"If I would have just stayed and pretended I didn't know, I might have found out so much more. If I would have just been brave for once in my life!"

"Is it bravery to sit and take that kind of treatment over and over again?" Hadyn broke his long silence. "To live in misery because you have nothing else?" He let his questions do their own work for a moment. "Or is it standing up for yourself and finally saying, no more. Rescuing yourself, knowing the lonely, difficult path ahead of you . . . Now that looks a lot like bravery to me."

Kiara searched his face, fearing he spoke rubbish, but wishing his words could be true.

"But it's selfish! It was so selfish."

"Sometimes we have to take care of ourselves before we can do any good for others. No one can be completely selfless."

"Not even a princess," Cida added with a smile.

A tear trickled down Kiara's cheek and she didn't bother to swipe it away. "I just don't know what to do. My actions have already caused others harm."

"But you got me out."

"I know, but what if I hadn't or what if I would have gotten you killed?"

"But you did and were fine. And if I may say, that plan of yours was pretty foolproof."

Kiara fought a smile. "Foolhardy."

"Kiara, no one here would've wanted you, let alone expected you, to stay."

"The whole lot of you?" she said sarcastically.

"I'm serious. You've done nothing wrong."

"And you already know how I feel, Miss," Cida said.

Kiara looked down, not able to shake the shame she felt. "But, it's all so messed up. What am I supposed to do now? I just want to find my mother . . . She'll come back and set everything straight around here."

Hadyn set his jaw and a fire ignited in his eyes when he didn't hesitate to respond. "And that's just what we'll do. We'll find her, Kiara. We'll search for light and never stop searching till we find it, or till our very last breath is spent trying."

Kiara bravely met his gaze, and what she found there surprised her, not because it was in him, but because of what it stirred in her. The raging hope blazing there, caught fire in her own heart, still not chasing out the fear, but equipping her with the courage to fight it.

"You mean . . . you want to help me?"

"Yes, I will help you."

"But why?"

He thought a moment and Kiara thought he'd answer, but he gave up on trying to find the words.

"Because it's right," Cida said. "And it's not just the three of us that long to be rid of this darkness."

Hadyn gave Cida a look of thanks, but Kiara remained quiet.

"Don't lose heart, Kiara, there's nothing in it." Hadyn smiled. "I do recall the words of a brave and hopeful girl recently saying, 'Don't let fear stop you from fighting for your hope.' "

Kiara tried to smile, but it looked painful. "I fear that girl is gone."

"No, she isn't; she's just scared right now. Don't let shame and guilt stop you from fighting against the darkness . . . Please don't give up."

Kiara sighed. "You're right. If I give up, the darkness wins. We all stay stuck in this living hell. I won't . . . I won't let it win. I won't give up."

"You better not." Cida nudged her. "You promised."

"Yes, I did, didn't I?"

"And I'll hold you to it."

"Thanks."

Cida yawned and it must have been contagious because of the chain reaction it caused in the three of them. She covered her mouth and sighed on the tail end. "Look at us." Cida grinned. "It must be nearly time to light the lamps out in town. You best be getting some rest, Miss. You must be exhausted. And I should be getting back too, before anyone notices that I'm gone. Will you be alright?"

"Yes, I think so."

"Just tell that mind of yours to stop running so much, get some real sleep, and we'll talk more tomorrow. Hmm?"

"Alright. Goodnight, Cida. See you tomorrow."

"Goodnight, Miss."

Kiara wanted to tell her, she didn't have to call her Miss anymore, but figured she would come around soon enough. She turned to Hadyn and, pointing to a bundle against the cave wall, she said, "Cida brought those blankets for you."

"Oh, that was kind of her."

The silence that followed could have been the end of that, but Kiara couldn't stop thinking about him sleeping on the cold stone out here.

"Hadyn . . . you can't tell anyone you're here, or even that you're alive. It would only put them in danger."

"I get it."

"I'm sorry . . . that this is your life now."

"Are you kidding? If it wasn't for you, I would either be rotting in a dark prison cell or getting led to the gallows, sentenced to hang for a crime I didn't commit."

"What do you mean? If it wasn't for me, you'd be a free man, earning an honest wage at the library with Mr. Crags."

"You mean a wanted man, lucky enough his crimes on the Stygian Market have stayed hidden this long, but also constantly running from the very people he does the crimes for. Think about that. As far as Mereaze knows, I'm a dead man. What more could I ask for but freedom from that lunatic?"

"So thank you. Even though I couldn't begin to deserve it, you came."

When Kiara didn't reply, the silence grew steadily more painful. Hadyn swung his arms. Kiara stretched, forcing out another yawn.

"Well, Cida was right," she said. "I am truly exhausted. Are you going to be alright out here?"

"Yeah, I'll be fine. I'll keep watch for anyone who dares to enter the Forbiddens to look for us."

"Good idea." Kiara turned to go.

"Kiara, wait. About what I said in the prison, in the barred hallway . . ."

Kiara cocked her head.

"I shouldn't have asked you to let them out. No one deserves to be put in that kind of position. It wasn't your fault they were in there. Maybe it was no one's but their own. I don't know what got into me. I guess I couldn't help but think they didn't deserve that either."

Kiara could do little else than agree, so she just nodded her head sadly.

"Hey, can I ask you a question?" Hadyn said.

"Sure."

"When we were caught by Clungston, you threw the keys back to that skinny, Stegler guy. Why?"

She shrugged "I don't know."

"I think you do."

Kiara sighed. "I guess . . . I guess I couldn't bear to think what they would have done to him if they found out it was his fault that you escaped. I don't know. I guess it would have felt like I did it to him."

Hadyn stared very thoughtfully at nothing at all.

"Well, good night," she said.

"Good night, Kiara."

Kiara felt a sense of warmth at the sound of that. She hadn't heard those words put with her name since her mother disappeared.

"And Hadyn . . . thanks for helping me fight off the monsters in my head."

"Any time."

When Kiara got to her hideaway, she lit one lantern, nestled into her blankets and fell fast asleep.

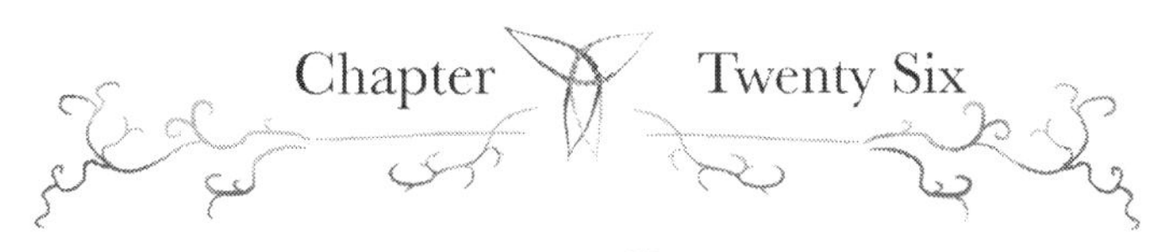

Life in Caverna

By the next morning, Kiara woke up with her mind and body minorly improved from the rest, but her heart beat so fast she hardly noticed. A nightmare ripped her from her sleep, the sort she wouldn't be able to stop thinking about. Consequently, falling back asleep was not an option, not if she didn't get up and walk around. But when she sat up, something tumbled out of the fold of her blankets and clanked to the stone floor.

Grabbing the dim lamp off its hook, she shined it closer and immediately recognized the strange key she had snatched from the secret library.

"Hello?" she said, picking it up. "I nearly forgot about you."

Before long, she remembered why she took it in the first place, and began to wonder if it really was the key to Hadyn's locked journal. Tapping it on her other hand thoughtfully, she knew just where she wanted her walk to take her now.

Coming to her and Cida's meeting spot, where Hadyn had stayed, she found him awake, looking about, busy with his own thoughts. He had made a makeshift bunk out of a ledge in the tight cavern and all the blankets Cida had given him.

Not wanting to startle him, Kiara cleared her throat and knocked on the wall next to her.

"Kiara?"

"Yeah, it's me." She stepped into the light.

"Oh." He sounded relieved and hopped off the ledge. "You're up early."

"What time is it?"

"Just after six. Like I said, early."

Kiara smirked. “So why are you awake then?”

“Couldn’t sleep.” He sat down with his back against the wall.

Kiara followed suit. “Me neither,” she said, wondering if he had nightmares too.

They were quiet for an awkward moment. “Hadyn, I found something the day we stumbled upon the um . . .”

“The library?”

She nodded her head. “It was hidden in an empty slot on one of the book shelves and I couldn’t help but notice that there didn’t seem to be many empty spaces. I took it and when you said that someone was coming, I forgot about it until it was too late.”

Hadyn looked confused.

“I guess what I’m trying to say is, I’m sorry for keeping it because I think it belongs to you.” Kiara pulled the key out of her pocket and handed it to him. He recognized the shape instantly.

“Oh, no . . .”

“Are you angry with me?”

“No, no, of course not. It’s just that the journal, it’s still at Mr. Craggs’ warehouse.” He shot up. “I have to go get it.”

“I’ll come with you.”

“No. You can’t.”

“Whyever not?”

“It’s just that . . . Your hair,” he blurted. “It would draw too much attention.”

Kiara made a face, but she knew well enough it was true.

“And no hoods, not after last night. They’d be too suspicious. No, I’ll go alone.”

“What if you get caught?”

Hadyn began to back away, palms out to her. “And if you came, we both would. Don’t worry. It’s early. Not a lot of people are even up yet and I’ll be careful.” Then without another word, he was gone.

Kiara huffed, piqued at the way he left, miffed that he was right and she couldn’t do anything about it. She grumbled where she sat, mumbling how she wouldn’t feel an ounce of guilt if he got caught. But as the minutes ticked by, past the time she expected him to return, her grumbling and griping came less often until she fell altogether silent, her anxious thoughts becoming the loudest sound to be heard. The warehouse was either quite the distance from the Forbiddens or . . . No. She wouldn’t go there. Maybe he was just taking it extra careful and extra slow.

Kiara mindlessly picked at the fraying end of her sleeve, when she nearly jumped out of her skin as the bells struck and she counted seven chimes.

"Nearly an hour? That's it!" Kiara stood, fed up, and marched to the exit tunnel.

She straightened her shoulders and curled her fingers into determined fists, fully prepared to stomp out into town to find him. But she stopped short right on the cusp, where the Forbiddens ended and Caverna began. Lantern light twinkled in the distance as the lamp lighters finished their job. Her face twisted up and she wrestled within herself, but she knew she would be caught in seconds.

"Oh, curse this hideous hair and all its troubles!"

Finally away from the people who mocked her, and it still controlled her life. She resented it for how helpless and useless it deemed her, making her no freer than a prisoner in a cell.

Footsteps pulled her from her self-deprecation and she dove for cover behind a thick stalagmite. Peeking her head out of hiding, she squinted into the dark. A vague figure began to take shape, speed walking her way. He came closer and she was relieved to realize it was Hadyn, clutching the journal close to his chest and watching over his shoulder.

Kiara stepped out of hiding, but he kept speeding ahead without looking where he was going.

"Hadyn!" she shouted before he could run into her.

He jumped back. "Ah! Oh, it's just you." Then his relief wore away to alarm. "What are you doing out here?" he hissed. "I thought I told you to wait."

Kiara shrugged. "I got sick of waiting."

He sighed. "Well, I got it," he said, holding out the book.

She just raised a dubious brow. "And nobody saw you?"

"Well, there was this one man and when he looked at me, I couldn't shake the feeling that he recognized me. It did seem like he was following me for a while, but I managed to shake him somewhere in the market, before I passed Tilda's Tavern."

"Thank goodness," Kiara said.

Hadyn didn't look as grateful. "The strange thing is, I think he was the same one watching you that day in the library."

"Shrike," Kiara spat the name like an oath.

"I'm sorry?"

"His name is Shrike. Curse his slithery hide. He's my fath—the king's personal dullard."

Hadyn looked confused.

"He's his right hand man," Kiara explained. "But he's so dense. He'd do anything the king asked. He follows him around like a slave." She laughed. "That explains why he didn't challenge you. He's far too cowardly to take on a prisoner, freshly escaped from the dungeons all by himself. He most likely planned to follow you to a hideout and then get others to do the job. Are you sure he wasn't behind you when you got here?"

Hadyn squinted. "I'm fairly certain. Stealth wasn't exactly a skill he had in abundance. When I couldn't hear him anymore, I assumed I'd lost him."

Kiara smirked. "Sounds like Shrike. After a long walk home, I can hear his breaths across the palace! Or . . . I could."

Hadyn watched her smile fall. "I don't get it. If Shrike is so stupid and cowardly, how is he the king's right hand man?"

"I don't know. Because he's unexplainably loyal to someone who deserves no loyalty. He's easily compensated by both money and food. And like I said, the king can get him to do whatever he bids. Need I go on? Or please, can we just stop talking about him?"

"Of course. I'm sorry."

"No, it's alright. It's just that . . . we have a journal to read, don't we?"

"Right." Hadyn slung a pack off his shoulder as they started back to the cavern where they met with Cida.

"What's this?" Kiara asked.

"Well, I thought I'd get the rest of my stuff too, since this is my home now."

". . . Right . . . Home."

He stopped as she walked on, considering her gloom. "Yeah, I found a few spare gems while I gathered my stuff . . . Made me think of the Waywards. I don't know who I thought I was fooling, but in my mind, before all this, I could have dropped off the face of existence and not missed a soul . . . I'm sure gonna miss them, though."

Kiara turned to him, eyes slanted in acute sadness. "I'm sure we could work out something. A way for you to sneak them small things like you used to."

He shrugged. "I'm sure we could. But you said it yourself, it would only put their lives in danger too."

Her shoulders slumped and her eyes wandered. “What a mess I’ve made . . .”

“Maybe. But once we find a way out, it will all be worth it.”

“Sure will,” she said, but her mood wouldn’t lift.

“Come on,” Hadyn prompted. “Let’s go crack open these secrets.”

Once they had procured a sufficient amount of light, coaxing the lanterns to glow and setting them about the cavern to push the shadows away, they sat on the floor together with the heavy book sleeping quietly before them like a slumbering beast, so peaceful, yet capable of great destruction.

Kiara read the cover once again and still couldn’t get past how colorless it sounded. Hadyn held the key in his hand, his eyes flicking to the book and then back to the key. Finally, He took a deep breath and tried the lock. It fit. And with the gentlest pressure it turned. There was a *click* and then, *pop*! the lock came apart.

They looked at each other, wide-eyed. Hadyn swallowed and placed a hand just beginning to tremble on the cover. Kiara reached out and grabbed his wrist to stop him.

“Hadyn, a key found in a secret library where horrible things have been done to innocent people for generations, matches the lock on a journal written by your ancestor.” He stared at her, riveted by her every word. “Whatever is in this journal . . . Nnyric does not want a soul to bring to light.”

Hadyn’s eyes wandered back to the journal, his mouth suddenly dry. Kiara let go, satisfied that what needed to be said was said. She watched until, at last, Hadyn lifted the cover. They both leaned in closer and neither even dared to breathe.

The mismatched pages, in various stages of age, and all different sizes and degrees of yellow and brown, weren’t even bound to the spine, but rather kept in place only by the closed and locked cover. Awestricken, they had yet to read a single word and still they knew it contained the truth they so desperately had longed for. They could smell it in the potent sour of each page, they could feel it in the rich texture of both the parchment and paper pieces.

They smiled at each other like children discovering a map to buried treasure. Hadyn drew a reverent breath and read the first page out loud.

This Journal Belongs To:
Madressilva James

To whom it may concern,

I feel like I have died and descended into the lowest parts of hell. Or maybe I'm dreaming and if I am, I wish to awake from this horribly dark nightmare and feel the sun on my face again.

Our leader, Salin, set us free from our cult in England, took us over seas, through storms, and trials for a fresh chance, a gift I could put no price to. I thought I would have followed him anywhere . . . I suppose I did. But now with this regret . . . I think I would have rather died.

Salin says he led us into the caves to protect us. That something terrible was coming, something that would destroy the surface of the earth as we know it. He said the caves are the only place we can be safe, but never once did he tell us how he knows all this.

Days after we settled down here, a terrible tremor rocked the caverns. It shook the walls and the ground beneath our feet. With such violent quakes, I couldn't understand how we could possibly be safer underground. Rock dust fell from the ceiling in alarming sheets as we all huddled together and waited it out with pounding hearts and numb prayers on our lips.

Then, with the end of the awful tremor, all activity ceased. The earth went quiet. I know it sounds crazy, but for as long as I can remember, I have always heard its voice, in the roar of the ocean, in the whisper of the forest, in the symphonic silence, but that day . . . That day the earth stopped speaking.

Salin says it is done. That what's left above, if anything at all, is unstable and unsafe, and we would be horrified of what our world has become. He advises everyone to accept that they may never see the sun again because there is no way of telling how long this will last.

Accept that we will never see the sun again . . . I don't believe it possible, not while retaining any shred of joy. They will not exist together. We live in nothing but makeshift homes, with hung up sheets for walls. We lie on the cold stone and go to sleep in darkness, only to wake up to the same.

But, there you have it, we're not even supposed to talk about the "old world" anymore. He says it's for the best, so that we don't grieve too heavily. I shouldn't even be writing this. But I choose to believe this defiance I cling to is too noble to put to rest. My sister thinks so too. I can't bring myself to forget the lovely world we once walked upon, and if it is to pass out of all other records, I want there to be at least one written account of the strangeness that has come to pass.

When Hadyn finished the entry, Kiara leaned back from reading over his shoulder, feeling like someone had punched her in the gut and stolen all the air from her lungs. Hadyn stared so long at the blank space between the last and next entry, he could have bore a hole in the page.

In one short moment, everything they had equally hoped for and feared became reality.

"So it's true . . ." Kiara finally spoke, but it was barely a whisper. "It wasn't always this way. The people who built Caverna knew it to be different once." She looked to Hadyn, but he could only stare back. "This was just a cave to them. One cave in the vast expanse of a whole world. Don't you see? This is the answer to the riddle."

"What riddle?"

"The one my mother gave me! This is the key," she said, grabbing up the misshapen key, and then shoved a finger down on the journal, "and the missing piece of the dark story. We found it in the heart of darkness, in the bowels of this horrible city! And now we know . . . I just can't believe the lies. How did they get a whole city to leave behind an entire world?"

"The game's been the same since the start," Hadyn said. "It's always been lies. And it won't stop until somebody does something about it. They paint on a new coat whenever the walls start chipping, but it's all the same color of grey."

The gravity of it fell on them and shut their mouths as neatly as if they were tied with string. A gift nearly as priceless as freedom had fallen into their laps, and it was all they could do to accept it. Yet in its youth, they could follow the threads to no end, each clue and premonition beckoning them to discover. But now the conspiracies had flesh and names, had morphed to brutal reality, and it made them sick to their stomachs.

But like kids lost in a maze, they had gotten themselves here by choice and they couldn't stop searching until they found the end, thrust on by an unseen force, seemingly inside, an innate longing for discovery and to map the question marks, to make the unknown known.

"We have to keep reading." Kiara said and Hadyn nodded.

Drawing another breath, he began again.

Day Ten of our confinement

Salin has given this accursed prison a name: Caverna, and though he tries to make this a happy thing, I can't help but feel a sense of condemnation. I refuse to believe that I will never again take a walk under the stars or bask in the light of an afternoon sun.

We have a store room of plants and Salin has great hopes for them to grow by the firelight. The livestock also will receive great care to be kept healthy. These should sustain us.

There is not an idle soul in this cave. Almost forthwith everyone's skills were evaluated to determine which sector we would be most useful to. I have been assigned as a baker, which was the first run of good luck in a long time. Though, with the rationing, there's not all that much room for artistic flare or experimental cooking. My sister, Cecilia, is to watch over the health of the livestock. I am already dreading how often we will be apart. Father's gone to the smithy and it doesn't surprise me that mother's fine skills as a seamstress caught the eye of the tailors.

All we have now is temporary, but Salin has not wasted any time and has started the excavation of what is to be Caverna. It's hard to ignore how he seemed prepared for this, though there were no other signs of the destruction of our world. Some say he is a prophet. I, for one, don't believe in those kinds of things, but I did always like Salin. His father was the leader of our town and cult, but Salin had a kindness and humanity in him that his father lacked. I felt sorry for him. The youngest brother of seven sons, he received the brunt of every disappointment, every fiery temper.

I just hope he knows what he's doing . . .

"That's the end of the entry," Hadyn said.

Kiara grew thoughtful. "According to the history records, Salin was the first king of Caverna, but what I don't get is, Madressilva doesn't address him as such."

"Maybe he wasn't king right away."

"Maybe . . ."

Then Hadyn asked, "What are . . ." he looked down at the journal for reference, "the stars, the sun, plants, and livestock? I've never heard those words before."

Kiara blinked at him. She didn't know why she hadn't thought to tell him before. How could he have known?

"My mother used to call them the Five Forbidden Gifts."

"Gifts . . .? Gifts from who?"

"Well, my mother would say the Creator."

"Your mother believed in a Creator? Other than Fleard?"

"Yeah, ridiculous, I know."

Hadyn shook the wonder from his face and mumbled, "Yeah, ridiculous . . ."

"So the gifts are: sunlight, plants, animals, colors and music.

I've managed to find all but one."

"Ah huh . . ."

Kiara could see the strain it caused him to try to wrap his mind around it all. "Hhmm." She put a hand over her mouth and tapped her face, trying to think.

She decided to take a break from Madressilva's journal and tell Hadyn about the naturalist journals her mother had given her.

"So, the sun is this giant light that sits in the expanse of the sky that brings warmth and . . . Sunlight!" she was trying to explain.

"Wait. But what's the sky?"

"What's the sky . . .?" Kiara repeated and huffed. She shrugged. "I don't really know. It's like, outside the caves, away from the stone, there's no roof at all; just endless blue."

Hadyn's expression read a mix between awe and the beginnings of a headache.

"I can only try to imagine what it's like up there, with nothing to confine you. No limits or walls. Think of how free the air would taste!" Kiara noticed herself getting away from her, when she caught the way Hadyn smiled at her.

"Anyway," she continued, cheeks reddening. "When night comes, the sun goes to sleep and the sky changes color, it gets darker and countless white lights fill that same sky."

"Stars," Hadyn said, looking in wonder on the journal entry again.

"Yeah . . ." She laughed. "That's right. I know it's hard to believe. I doubt it sometimes too. It just sounds so fantastic to even be real."

"But what a wonderful thing to hope exists," Hadyn finished.

Kiara couldn't believe her ears. She had known these things for years and still she doubted. And here unfathomable information of incompre-hensible wonders were just dropped on his head with the thinnest expectations that he'd even stay conscious, and his first reaction was to hope?

Why couldn't she hope?

"But what else?" Hadyn asked. "What are the other Forbidden Gifts?"

"Hmmm . . ." she mused. "Plants are green um . . . This is difficult. Well, they grow, mostly with the help of the sun and have the most wonderful and colorful things called flowers. And livestock are a kind of animal, like the ones people keep and take care of."

"What?" he shook his head. "What are animals?"

Kiara stared at him again, utterly nonplussed. It really put into perspective how much more she knew than others, despite how little she felt she knew.

"Well, even you've seen some animals."

"What do you mean?"

"Um, let's see. Oh! Like the things that I called bats, the winged creatures? Those are a kind of animal. And the little scurrying ones with the tails that everyone calls vermin. Those are rats and mice. Even Ben's little friend, that you all call a devil. Those are cats."

"Amazing!" Hadyn marveled. "You learned all that from a pile of old journals?"

"That's not even the half of it."

Then Kiara looked sad. "But I just can't seem to figure out music. Mother never would tell me much, and as hard as I tried, I just couldn't understand it."

Hadyn didn't comment; only fidgeted. Then, counting on his fingers he remembered the last gift. "And what about colors? How are those forbidden?"

"I don't know. I guess it's the *way* they're restricted. I mean, honestly, I wouldn't call Caverna a very colorful place. The most vibrant thing we have is fire."

"And gemstones."

"Right. But they're forbidden too."

"Okay, but how could it be any other way? You mean like the Styx?"

"Yes, but . . ." Kiara thought for a moment, and a childlike smile grew on her lips. "Let me show you. Come on, follow me."

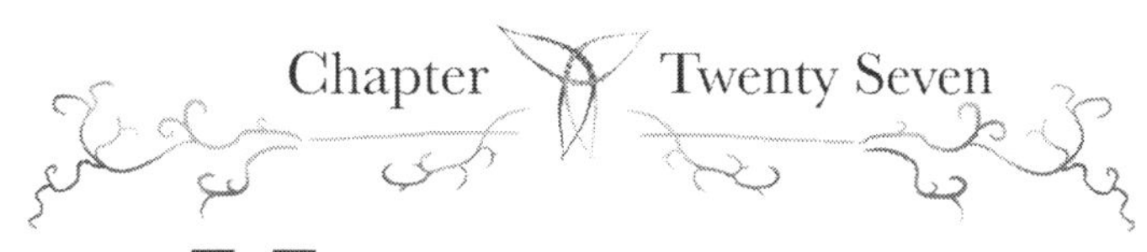

HIDEAWAY

Kiara led Hadyn back through the winding ways of the Forbiddens. But when they closed in on the entrance of her hideaway, her feet glued themselves to the stone beneath them. Once she would have given anything for a chance to share this place and all her secret treasures with someone else. But for so long now, it had been hers and hers alone. Her only safe place. *Her* hideaway. And she wasn't so sure if she wanted to share it anymore.

"What is it?" Hadyn asked, glancing at the dark fissure. "Did you take a wrong turn?"

"No. It's nothing. I just . . . well, for the longest time it's just been me and it's difficult to . . . It's just difficult to even say." She faltered.

"Like you've been alone so long, you don't even know what it means to not be?"

She looked him in the eye for the first time since stopping.

"I understand."

"You do?" she asked, then dropped her head. "Cause I don't know what's wrong with me."

"Wrong with you? Kiara, there's nothing wrong with you. Listen, you don't have to do anything you don't want to do."

Kiara huffed. "A lot of good that's done me."

"What's that mean?"

"I'm sick of being afraid, of letting my fears dictate what I do and don't do. You and Cida . . . Well, I'm not alone anymore, am I?"

Hadyn just stood there as she finished arguing with herself. Little did he know, it was only because of his gentle patience that she even thought to reconsider.

"Now, come on," she said, "before I change my mind again."

Turning sideways, Kiara shuffled through the crack and used her lantern flame to light a spill and then the rest of the hanging lights about the room. Hadyn struggled through behind her and stood just inside, absolutely silenced as the room grew brighter. The stream appeared, flowing from the crack in the wall, and its laughter filled the room with a settling peace. A pale carpet of greenery he'd never seen before grew along its stony banks, and twisted shoots sprung up in between cracks, the lampenfauna's ghostly roots exposed on the ground. He noticed the chimes from the Styx hanging from a hook next to a pile of blankets. Just like his abandoned closet in the orphanage, forbidden treasures peppered the cavern like a museum for the strange and wonderful. Stacks of books sat here and there with a wayward one or two cluttering the floor along with other items like the cloak draped over one of the chests or the pair of shoes tossed aside like they had no home at all. It was rightly a little home in its own whimsical way.

Kiara had finished lighting the hanging lanterns and for the first time Hadyn noticed her staring at him inquisitively, scrutinizing his every expression, wondering what he thought. When he looked, she didn't look away, putting him on the spot in a way that made him want to bolt.

He cleared his throat. "So this is *your* hideaway," he said with a smirk, recalling back to when she had given the title to his little room at the orphanage.

Kiara smiled and nodded. "Sorry about the mess."

Hadyn walked over to the shelf that held her favorite precious stones. "May I?" he asked.

She nodded once more. "Please."

Hadyn picked up an emerald the size of his fist. "Incredible!"

Kiara relaxed a notch. "If you think that's incredible, take a look at this." She skipped over to a chest and, opening it, revealed a whole trunk full of translucent gems of all different shapes, sizes, and colors.

Hadyn didn't have words for the sight. It was all he could do to keep his jaw from dropping to the floor. Likewise, Kiara found it hard not to laugh at him.

"Is this what you meant about the colors?"

"Sort of . . ." A glint of excitement twinkled in Kiara's eyes. "You haven't seen anything yet."

She grabbed up armfuls of carefully selected jewels and

carried them to the lanterns. Kiara walked about in a patient dance as she placed the gems on all four sides of the lanterns which, Hadyn could now see, were modified with small arms for this purpose.

Not knowing what to make of it, Hadyn turned and dug in the chest to examine the unused jewels, while she continued her work.

"I've always thought it such a fitting name for them . . ." He held up a rich garnet. "*Jewel*," he sighed, and when he said it, it did sound like they were infinitely more precious than just a colored stone. He set aside a bright aquamarine and picked out a small cluster of yellow citrine crystals. "Did you know that it was derived from words that meant, that which brings joy? I mean, how could they be named anymore perfectly?"

There was only silence behind him and then Kiara finally said, "There."

Hadyn pushed himself up from the edge of the chest and turned around, but what he saw defied belief. With all the crystals in place, the room brimmed with color, splashed on the walls and floor with just enough uniformity to hint at a pattern, but flickering and blending at the edges so that it was impossible to seek out where one color ended and the next started. Not an inch in sight wasn't saturated with greens, blues, reds, amber, or aquamarine.

Kiara stood off to the side so he could better see all its beauty and Hadyn spun around trying to take it all in.

He smiled wide. "How did you . . .? I've never seen anything like it!"

Mind crackling with wonder, joy found its mark and he felt a strange pang in his heart, something like homesickness, but not for any place he'd ever been. He stood there blinking in the filtered and refracted fire light, until Kiara laughed at him.

He turned to her. "It is most beautiful. It's as if . . . all of Caverna's life has been concentrated and hidden in one masterpiece. I don't understand how your father can be opposed to such beauty."

Kiara's smile dropped. "Please, do not call him that. You know he is opposed, so why say it? He," she fought for the words. "Well, he hates it. Every piece of him burns with disdain for good things like this. And there's no reasoning with him. His temper is unmatched by anyone I've met. That's why I have to get out of here. I can't live in a world where every good thing, every pure thing is forbidden."

"I'm sorry. I shouldn't have said anything."

Kiara softened. "It's alright. I only would have you banish any illusions of reason you have of him from your mind."

The statement plunged them into silence before Hadyn worked up a change of subject. "So, is this what it's like outside of the darkness?" he asked.

"Not exactly. The color would be much more uniform and even better than this." She gazed at the flowing colors. "For example, the sky. Like I said, it's blue, completely blue, as far as the eye can see. It seems so incredible to me. I mean, could you imagine looking up," she raised her head to the stone ceiling "and seeing blue instead of grey? And there's a jungle out there filled with the plants I told you about and they're covered with gloriously green leaves. Could you even fathom to be enveloped in a vibrantly verdant forest? Ever since I first read those words I've wondered what vibrantly verdant leaves look like."

"Maybe something like your eyes," Hadyn suggested.

Kiara gave him a funny look. "You think so?"

A red color grew on his face. "I mean . . . yeah."

Kiara skipped across the room to her mirror and gazed at her distorted, dark reflection. Her eyes flashed out from the mirror's shadowy world like green embers glowing. "I guess I've never thought about it that way. To me, my eyes are just one more tally on the list of things that make me so terribly different from everyone else. If it wasn't for my eyes being green, I'm sure it would be my most favorite color."

"Different isn't always a terrible thing."

Kiara looked at him, a soft smile on her face. "No, I guess it's not."

There was a moment of silence and then Kiara remembered. "Oh! Would you like to meet my blind fish?"

"Um . . ."

"Here. Come over here." She pulled him over to the pool and began pointing her fish out by name. "That's Amethyst and Tourmaline. There's Citrine and . . . Now, where is she? Oh! And Emerald." She looked at Hadyn. "She likes to hide."

Hadyn knelt down and leaned over the crystal pool. "Amazing! What are they?"

"They're called fish in the books that my mother gave me."

"How long can they stay under the water?"

"Forever! They breathe water instead of air."

"Fish . . ." he tested the word. "What a simple name for such incredible creatures." Then, as Hadyn observed them a moment longer, his brow furrowed in confusion. "Where . . . Where are their eyes?"

"I told you, they're blind."

"Right, but even someone who is born blind has eyes."

"I guess . . ." She scrunched brow, grinning. "I don't know. That's the way I found them. Maybe— I mean, if there even is a Creator. Maybe he never gave them eyes, because he knew they'd never need them."

Hadyn nodded, like she was onto something. "Yeah, maybe . . . How much more does that prove we were never meant to be here?"

Kiara blinked as if she had never considered her eyes in such a way, unaware of the smile splitting her face.

"What?" Hadyn grinned.

She shook her head. "I mean, yeah. Or whatever . . . Nevertheless, despite the absence of their eyes and the fact that they can go unmeasured amounts of time without any food, they are surprisingly effective hunters. Whenever something enters their pool through that crack, they are on it in seconds. I don't know how, but they sense the arrival of anything unfamiliar. It's fascinating."

Hadyn gazed at them in wonder.

"I feed them scraps every once in a while too." Kiara's stomach gave a subtle rumble, reminding her they hadn't eaten anything yet today. "Speaking of food, Cida has been bringing me leftovers from the Palace, and she brought extra for you last night. You hungry?"

At the mention of food, Hadyn's stomach spoke for him with a growl of its own, not nearly as polite as Kiara's.

Kiara chuckled. "I'll take that as a yes."

After they had scrounged up a sufficient meal and finished it off, Kiara asked, "Are you sure you don't want anymore? I thought boys ate more than that."

"Are you kidding? That was the most I've had at any one time in my life! I'm stuffed. And anyway, *I thought* princesses had better manners than that."

Kiara's eyes flared in offense and she looked properly prepared to not speak to him for some time.

"Oh! I didn't— I shouldn't have—"

Kiara watched his cheeks burn red and then began to laugh.

"I shall have to make sure Cida remembers to bring the silver and dish-ware next time," she said good-naturedly.

Hadyn frowned. "Very funny."

Then Kiara had a thought. "Hey, should we read more of the journal?"

"Sure," Hadyn said, and they trotted back to where they had left the book.

Hadyn sat with the journal in his lap, twirling and fidgeting one hand around a burgundy stone in the vague shape of a clunky, six-pointed star.

"Is that . . .?" Kiara asked.

Hadyn looked down at his hand and smiled. "Yeah. The alexandrite? I got it back when I retrieved the journal."

Kiara's smile faded as she stared at it. "So much for that legend . . ."

Hadyn's eyes wandered. Maybe because of Kiara's depressing comment, maybe because of the words open in front of them that they planned to read again, but a heavy cloud settled on their shoulders after that, and neither of them wanted to be the one to read or even say so.

"You know. Maybe we should wait for Cida before we read any more. She deserves to know too," Kiara suggested.

Hadyn nodded and shrugged. "Yeah. Sounds good to me."

He closed the cover and returned to fiddling with the alexandrite.

Kiara drummed her fingers and looked about. "Sooo . . ." she said, but never finished.

Hadyn blew out a breath. "At the orphanage, I would have my hands full with chores right now. And even after I left, Mr. Craggs kept me busy enough at the library. This feels wrong."

"I know. I feel like I should be at school or something."

The conversation abandoned them prematurely and Kiara hummed a sigh. Maybe she should have paid better heed when being taught how to hold a polite conversation as a princess.

"Oh, I was wondering," Hadyn began, "you said you found all but one of the five gifts."

"Yes, music."

"Right." He waved a hand as if he could shoo the word away. "But only three of the other four are in your hideaway."

"That's because—" She paused. "Well, the fifth gift isn't in the Forbiddens; it's in town."

"What! But that's impossible. How have you not found a way out?"

"I'm not sure I can make you understand with just words. But, I'll show you."

"Go into Caverna?" He shook his head. "No way. Didn't we just do this this morning?"

"Come on. It's on the other side of town, but we can stay along the outskirts the whole time. We might not see anyone at all."

Hadyn crossed his arms just as the town bell gave one prompt clang.

Kiara put her hands palms up. "Oh, and look who has one of his watch shifts at this very moment." She got to her feet. "What luck!"

"Wait. Who?" he asked. "Watch shift for what?"

Tucking her hair into a hood as she walked, Kiara started out of the Forbiddens.

Chapter Twenty Eight

The Window

For Hadyn's sake, Kiara gave a cautious peer around the corner into the cavernous room of the Aperture of the Void, even though the sawing and snorts echoing off the walls had already proved her suspicions yet twenty feet away. And just as she thought, there Gilbert sat, slumped against the wall, sleep drooping on his ageless face.

"I told you he'd be out," Kiara whispered.

She pulled her hood down and led the way into the room. Hadyn gave Gilbert a wary glance and then turned that same glance on the exit.

"Come on." Kiara had found a place in the middle of the vast room and directed Hadyn to stand beside her.

He gazed up at the towering doors craning his neck to see their tops.

"Kinda intimidating, isn't it?" she asked.

"What is this place? How does nobody know about it?"

Kiara laced her answer with sarcasm and raised a hand to the dirty pane of glass, washed in grey above the doors. "*The void.*" She frowned. "And people do know about it. Just not everyone."

"So what's that?" he asked, pointing to the window. "*Really*."

"*That* is what we're waiting for." Kiara raised her face to the window and closed her eyes.

Hadyn narrowed his eyes and fidgeted. "What are you doing?"

"Waiting. If it's going to come today, all we have to do is wait."

With a huff Hadyn pulled the alexandrite from his pocket and traced its edges with his finger, constantly looking over his shoulder to make sure Gilbert the watchmen remained unconscious in snore city. If he so much as stirred, Hadyn swore he'd drag Kiara out of there over his shoulder, if he had to.

"There!" Kiara gasped.

Still watching Gilbert, Hadyn felt it on his cheek first. It radiated across his skin like the heat of a flame, but warmed deeper and more evenly without even beginning to burn. When he turned, the grey little window had transformed. It glowed, shimmering with a golden brilliance. Because of the dirt and grime, he didn't have to shield his eyes, and yet it was powerful enough to fight through and spill out, bathing them in a pool of glowing warmth.

Hadyn realized he was smiling, the light somehow igniting in him a joy he didn't know he could feel. It was like hope had found a way to manifest into a visible form. It pulled at the strings of his heart and filled a hole he had never known existed, but had always felt empty. All he could think about was how he could find a way to keep it with him always.

"I told you," Kiara said. "It wasn't something I could tell you."

"I see that now," he said, turning his eyes back up to the round window.

Then Kiara gasped. "Hadyn, look!"

Hadyn followed her gaze to his hand. The window wasn't the only thing that had changed. He held up the alexandrite, now a deep, slightly blue tinged, green, as if the sunlight had actually pulled the scarlet hues straight out of it until there wasn't a trace of red left.

They gawked at the green stone like they had never seen it before.

"Hadyn, this is the legend! This is what it meant."

Speechless, Hadyn pulled it from the light and shadowed it with his hand. As quick as a flash, the stone returned to a deep red.

"Incredible!" Kiara squealed.

Then there was a snort and a rustle.

She froze. "Oh no."

Kiara and Hadyn swivelled their heads in slow motion to Gilbert stirring awake. They looked at each other and their feet might as well have grown wings for how fast they carried them out of there.

They jetted back around the outskirts of the city, and when they had made it safely back to Kiara's hideaway, still lit colorfully with all the gem covered lanterns, she couldn't hold in her laughter anymore. She doubled over from both exhaustion and cramping abs.

Hadyn didn't find it quite as funny. "I don't know why you're laughing. We could have been caught."

"By Gilbert? Don't make me laugh any harder! I bet you we were halfway to the Forbiddens before he even pried open his eyes. I know him. Even if he would have spotted us, he probably would have thought we were ghosts in his half-conscious delirium. And look at what we saw!"

Hadyn cradled the burgundy stone in his palm.

"Well, even if it was just for a moment . . ."

Kiara watched him as he gazed at the stone, utterly crestfallen. The gaping hole the sunlight had searched out and proclaimed straight to his face, felt emptier than ever.

She nudged him, shoving a grin on her own face. "Hey! I want to show you something."

"Does it involve sneaking, skulking, hoods, leaving the Forbiddens, or any secrecy of any kind?"

She frowned. "No. Happy?"

"Very."

Kiara took her necklace off to unlock one of her chests and propped the lid open with an arm.

"Wait. Your necklace is the key to that chest."

"Yeah."

"So they were made together?"

"Yes." She blinked. "And your point is?"

"Well, I've never seen markings like those before. What are these?"

"These," Kiara heaved one of the books out, "are *my* ancient journals. Though, I don't know who wrote them or drew the pictures. They're about the animals I was telling you about. Here. Go ahead and take a look at all the sketches. I'm going to put the gems away."

Kiara weaved about, back and forth from lantern to chest, while Hadyn paged his way through the journals.

"These are incredible! No one could just make this up, could they?"

Kiara began gathering a new armful of gems. "I wouldn't

think so. But my mother never would tell me where or how she got them."

"Do all royal families keep so many secrets or is it just yours?"

Kiara didn't give him the satisfaction of laughing and, dropping the last gems into the chest, she came and sat by him.

"I read these whenever I feel especially trapped . . . which is a lot." Her eyes wandered. "Except that one. It's just awful!"

Hadyn picked it up, too curious not to know what was inside that made her squirm so bad. "Snakes?" he read.

"Ah!" She shivered. "Don't even say their name. They're horrible, disgusting creatures! They don't even have legs!"

He looked confused. "Fish don't have legs."

"Yes, but fish swim. Snakes," she shivered again, "slither . . . o*n land*."

"I see," he said, while hiding a grin.

"Here, I'll show you my favorite one." She found the book and handed it to him.

Opening the cover he read, "Birds . . . Hmmm, short name."

"Yes, but there's all different sorts like eagles, macaws, jacamars, owls, and toucans."

Hadyn began turning through the pages.

"Birds are the freest creatures in the world because they," her eyes sparked with delight and she finished her sentence in whispered reverence, "can fly." She let her words hang in the air for a moment before continuing. "As high as they want and as long as they want. They can fly above everything! They're beautiful too, covered in satin colors. They talk in what's called a song, which I think sounds very lovely. And apparently their voices are pleasing to listen to."

"If I was any animal, I'd hope to be a bird. Oh, to soar above absolutely all things and take to the sky!"

Hadyn smiled at her. "Why would you ever be an animal?"

"It's just something to say. Go ahead and try."

"Try what?"

"What animal would you be."

"Okay, um . . . what about this guy? He looks tough," he said, pointing to a journal he'd left open at his side.

"That's a beetle. They're about," she made a little o with her thumb and index finger, "this big. They get snacked on by birds."

"Oh . . ." He blinked, and began leafing through the

sketches.

Kiara smiled and watched him skim the journals and soon enough her mind wasn't on animals anymore. His dark, floppy curls fell in a way that made her want to brush them aside, but with a strange urge to reprimand herself, of course she refrained. A few of the locks fell in his eyes, but not in a way that obscured them fully and with him looking down, searching through the sketches, the scar on his left lid begged her curiosity for an explanation more than ever.

"How'd you get the scar?"

Without looking up from his book, he gave an impish grin. "Which one?"

Kiara did not find the humor in the question and he realized this with some embarrassment when he looked up and saw her pained expression.

"You mean this one?" He rubbed his eye and Kiara nodded. "You really want to know?" The question did give her pause, but again she nodded anyway.

Hadyn sighed. "It was glass. He missed . . . that time, but one of the shards cut my lid. I can still hear the way those bottles used to shatter. Just another vessel for one of the many alcohols my father poisoned himself with everyday."

Kiara stared painfully at the ground.

"Not as mysterious and interesting as you thought it'd be?"

Kiara didn't answer.

"Do you regret asking?"

"Of course not. I asked because I wanted to know. Why would your answer change that?"

"It's just that, for most people it would."

"Well then, I guess you're just lucky I'm not most people."

He gave a small laugh and when he held her gaze, it was a thoughtful look. But his cheeks grew red when she looked away first.

"Um . . ." he looked back down at the journal in his lap to save himself, thinking for a good moment. "I guess . . . if I could be an animal, why not a bird too."

Remembering the conversation she so rudely derailed, Kiara asked, "You guess?"

"Yeah." His eyes wandered. "Is that all right?"

"Not really, no. You should have a reason."

"Maybe I'll think of one."

"Oh, very well. What shall we do now?"

Hadyn contemplated her question quietly, but came up with nothing.

Kiara looked about the room and drummed her fingers. "Oh! I know. Do you play Backlobash?"

"Yes. Er— I used to when I was younger, with my mom. I was actually the one to teach the boys at the orphanage. But I haven't played in such a long time. I'd love to pick it up again."

"Really?" Kiara brightened. "Oh . . . but my set is back in the Palace."

They sat back against the cavern wall disappointed. But sometimes boredom, in its most extreme cases, can and will give birth to ingenuity. "Wait," she said, sitting straight again. "I have an idea."

When Kiara had first cleaned up her hideaway, she had piled up all the loose rocks and rubble in a corner to make the ground clear and smooth. Presently, she took a sharp piece of stone from the pile and began to draw. She scraped the basic circle shape of the Backlobash board on the floor near the stream, scratching in every detail from memory.

"There." She scooted back to look at it.

Then carefully picking some small rocks, she placed them on the board, the pieces that were supposed to be the same, all being around the same size. She marked them each with an X on one side and a line on the other. She placed half on the board near Hadyn, X side up and the other half line side up on her side. Finally, she took a look at it to make sure she hadn't missed anything.

Hadyn laughed.

"What's so funny?"

"It's just . . . that was sort of incredible."

Kiara scrunched her nose. "If you say so."

"Alright, you want to go ahead and go first?"

"Again, if you say so." Kiara scanned the board for a total of two seconds, making her first move a swift one.

Hadyn stared at the board for a good moment and then made a hesitant move.

"Uh, you can't do that."

Hadyn looked at her. "Why not?"

Kiara laughed. "Because it's against the rules."

"It never used to be."

"I don't know who taught you how to play, but that move

breaks so many rules, you should go to jail."

Hadyn raised his eyebrows. "Jail?"

"Yeah." She giggled. "Backlobash jail, my knights will take you where you stand." She swept her hand over the rocks symbolizing her first row of defense.

"Okay . . ." Hadyn took the rock back and then slowly, while eyeing Kiara, started to place it down again.

Kiara smiled and nodded her head in approval.

The game began to pick up pace, they played their turns back and forth a few times, then Hadyn hesitated again.

"Wait. Can I do this?"

He moved one of the bigger rocks a few spaces toward Kiara's side.

"Mmhm."

He pulled his hand away and Kiara made her strike fast, moving her king out of what could have been shadows for all Hadyn was aware of, and taking his commander captive. She flipped his commander over so it now displayed her line.

"How . . .?"

"I said you could do it; I never said it was smart." She giggled "You're really not very good at this."

"I never said I was," Hadyn mumbled as he tried to assess how this had happened. "And you never mentioned that you were some kind of obsessed master."

"Why, thank you."

The game resumed. Scanning the battle ground with tactical precision, Kiara steadily grew her army at Hadyn's expense. But with his army now a skeleton, she did begin to feel rather badly.

"Okay. Let me try to help you out," she said, on his next turn. "Hhmm, Let's see. Why don't you turn this one unto your side? You're close enough."

"Your princess?"

"Yeah."

"Well she's done nothing wrong, you've hardly moved her this whole game. I couldn't when she's just been sitting there innocently."

"Hadyn, it's just a game."

He thought for a moment, his gaze intense. "No, there's another way. I can feel it."

"Suit yourself."

Hadyn took his turn and made a move that did no visible

damage to either of them. But it was there, the time for victory. Kiara had played the game too many times to not know the feeling of the end at hand. It tingled in her fingers and churned in her gut. She couldn't remember a time when that feeling wasn't in her favor. This particular game would be no different.

And there, she spotted it, her move to win the game. She gave Hadyn a pained face.

"What?"

She answered with an action; her last move, then said meekly, ". . . *Backlobash*."

Hadyn stared at the board with wide eyes. He knew better than to fool himself into thinking he could own the victory, but to lose this soon?

All he could say was, "What!"

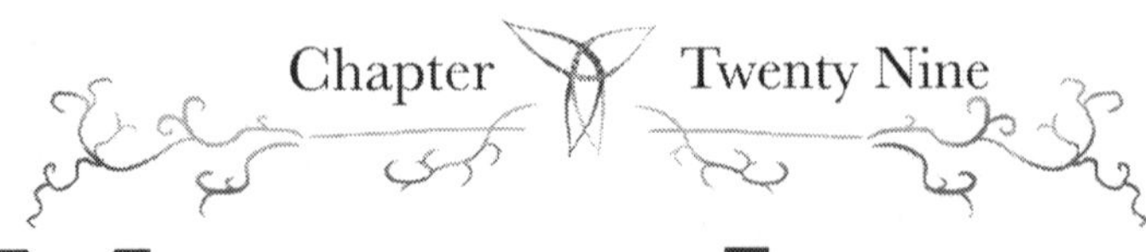

Maddie James

They played a few more rounds until Hadyn got fed up with losing and waited around until Cida arrived, soon after curfew. Sitting down with her, Kiara filled her in on everything she'd missed.

"So Caverna was started merely because of one man's lust for power . . ." Cida said.

"That's what it seems like. But, Cida, listen. My mother wanted me to find this book. She knew about it. Look!" Kiara pulled the letter from her pocket and handed it to Cida.

Hadyn and Cida both read the riddle and then Cida flipped it over. "May I?" she asked.

Kiara shrugged and nodded.

They all fell silent as Hadyn and Cida read the letter and Kiara read it from memory in her head.

"Ara. That's sweet," Hadyn remarked as he finished. "And I don't even like nicknames."

Kiara snatched the note back and tucked it safely away in her pocket once more. "Yes, I liked it too." Just hearing the name sent a pang through her heart. She feared she'd never hear it again. Her mother was the only person who ever called her that and hearing it now from another voice, just wasn't right. But she tucked those thoughts away with the letter.

"So do you see, Cida? This is it and though I dare not even allow myself to think it, this may be the first step to our escape! We'll go find my mom and bring her back here to expose all the lies!"

Cida smiled, but it didn't stay. "Your escape," she said plainly.

"What?"

"Believe me, I will help you all I can, but I can not go with you."

"But you can."

"No, Miss."

Kiara looked at her in a mix of anger and sorrow. She didn't, she *couldn't* understand.

"I was not made for a great journey into the unknown. You and I both know I would never make it far." Her face turned sympathetic and she clicked her tongue. "Oh, and besides, you need someone here to come back to, so you don't forget about everyone here."

"Oh, Cida, I would never forget. I want to free everyone. Not a soul will be left enchained if my mother, the queen, has anything to say about it. She'll set things right here."

"I believe you, but my decision is made. You have that special fire, Kiara. You were made for this."

Tears welling in her eyes, Kiara felt her heart crushing in on itself.

"Miss, please, I—"

"I understand, Cida. I do." Then she wrapped her arms around her. "I just know I'm going to miss you so much."

"And I'll miss you."

Kiara, at length, pulled away and looked at her straight. "Though, I might just have to change my mind, if you don't stop calling me Miss."

Cida laughed.

"You're not my servant anymore; you are my friend, and my friends call me Kiara."

"Very well. Sounds fair enough." Suddenly feeling like she could cry, Cida changed the subject. "So, why don't we grab this journal you've told me so much about?"

"Already got it." Hadyn picked it up from where it sat beside him and started where they left off.

Day Fifteen

The jarring events of today have left me struggling to wrap my mind around them and without words to describe them.

Salin called everyone together for a meeting tonight. Cecilia couldn't make it at first. The livestock sector needed her after hours, as they often do. I fear they ask too much of her. So I waited in the uncertain crowd with our parents, hoping she could get there soon. When Salin finally came out to address the crowd, he seemed altered. The man I once admired, now lords over us with a presence as terrible as the darkness of these caverns. I assumed the power would get to him eventually; I just wasn't prepared for it to happen so soon. Standing before us he explained that beings called watchers came to him in the middle of the night and told him of what has happened. He says they've been speaking to him all along; he just didn't know it yet.

I do not believe it for a second, I know very well what these "beings" are. They are a creation, the very figment of Salin's own, self-inflated mind. And if not, if specters did really speak with him, I doubt they're something one should engage in conversation with.

Salin said that the watchers told him how the world was created. That before creation there existed two gods, Elohim and Fleard, in the High Realm. They fought over how the earth should be made. Fleard being the stronger in both mind and body won, but being not wholly ungracious, gave Elohim the chance to create the world he wanted. Fleard let it go on for longer than he even deemed wise and seeing the depravity of Elohim's world, decided to destroy it and make a dark world, the one we know now. Here he would protect man simply by taking back their freedom. Soon, restrictions and rules would befall them.

Salin informed us that the great gate they had built up on the east side of town, seemingly overnight, now leads to the underworld and a null void of eternal emptiness hovers above us, replacing the world we once called home.

I will not believe this and I don't know why Salin does. If the Brotherhood back in England taught me anything, it is that gods are made up lies wicked men spin to control others. And if I'm wrong, if somehow these celestial beings do exist, I swear today, I hate them with all my heart. I will not waste another moment, believing my life is subject to these cold rulers. The moment we left the Brotherhood, I chose for myself to worship the natural world, as it rightly deserves, and nothing else. We came here to get away from the Brotherhood. Salin led us here, promising freedom to love and worship whatever we want. I wish I had known more about the happenings around here, but Salin is an obscure and subtle man and when I finally opened my eyes, it was too late.

At the end of his announcement, he declared that from henceforth he will be addressed as King Salin, for Fleard himself has set him in this position.

Hadyn finished the entry and looked up. "King Salin . . ." he whispered.

"So that's how he became king." Kiara flicked her eyes between Hadyn and Cida. "And what rubbish! When did they change their subterfuge? Since when did Elohim ever get a chance to create a world? And when did they just decide to say Fleard's world was the only one ever created? How did they get everyone to believe that, to forget?" She stared at them, her expression twisted, but they looked just as dismayed.

Kiara sighed. "It's just like you said. Whenever the walls need a fresh coat . . . It chills my blood to think of how deep the deception actually is." She placed her hands on her lap to fight the trembling they had begun.

"But we're going to uncover this deception. We are," Hadyn reassured. "We won't allow this to go on. It will be alright."

"But, how?" she cried. "We can't even find a way out. Look at the way they control everything." She threw a hand at the open journal. "Even what people think and believe. What can we do? How can we uncover something that has been cloaked for generations?"

"We will. You'll see. We'll find our way out and find your mom."

"How can you be so sure?"

"Because I have hope."

"He's right," Cida chimed. "We have to keep hoping."

"Hope," she scoffed. "I haven't had something as substantial as real hope for four years."

"Well, maybe it's time that it's found its way back into your heart," Hadyn replied.

She wanted to argue, lash back with something better, but knew in spite of herself there was nothing to argue. ". . .Maybe."

It was her way of dropping it; not giving in. Still quietly fuming, she maintained a stubborn scowl, but Hadyn smiled at her; not a big toothy smile, just a small grin, full of kindness, and she couldn't figure out why he would do such a thing.

"I feel badly for Madressilva," Hadyn said, turning back to the journal. "She sounds so angry."

"I like her," Kiara retorted. "She seems smart."

Cida looked disappointedly at her and sighed. "Well, I agree with Hadyn. She seems terribly frustrated and not just with the immediate predicament she's in. She takes it out on that, yes, but her scribbled venting seems to communicate more than that. She actually reminds me a lot of someone I know."

Kiara smiled and narrowed her eyes. "Oh does she? Shall we read on, or shall we waste all our time with you gibbering your own thoughts?"

Cida smirked and nodded for Hadyn to continue. Having nothing to add, he drew in a breath and resumed reading.

Day Twenty

Everyone I know has died, yet they still walk. No one asks questions; they just do whatever Salin says. They are afraid. I can see it in their eyes. They don't know what to believe anymore.

A strange cloud has settled over my brain. I fall deeper into a fog of depression and confusion each day. I can almost feel my soul slipping away, as if it has detached from my body like a ghostly apparition that just keeps falling through my fingers whenever I try to put it back in. I was once such a happy person, everyone I know would attest. I think it has something to do with the sun, as if with its disappearance so goes the light inside of me.

I know everyone feels it in some way, but I fear most for Celia. I'm losing my sister, and I can do nothing about it. She's always so tired. I can't remember the last time I saw her smile, and with the work she has to do, she hardly has a moment to rest.

I can't take it much longer. I have to talk to someone, but not just anyone . . .

"I know what she means," Kiara said, "about the sun."

"Yeah . . . I guess I do too," Hadyn agreed. "And I only saw it the once."

"You mean we didn't even see it," Kiara corrected.

Cida squinted. "What are you two talking about?"

"The gate. The Aperture of the Void. I took him there today."

"You what!"

"Calm down. Nobody saw us. It was like we were never there."

"Well, you must have a whole lot of luck saved up. Don't think you'll be as fortunate next time."

"There won't be a next time. I get it. I'm a prisoner even in the place I escaped to."

"Come now—"

"Look, can we just drop it?" Kiara snapped. "What I was trying to say was, just think of Madressilva. We haven't ever felt the sun for more than mere moments at a time, let alone ever seen it, and we felt it's departure like losing a part of our souls. She lived with its constant presence every day and it was taken from her in the blink of an eye."

"I can't imagine . . ." Hadyn said. "And her poor sister."

Cida nodded. "Her poor sister indeed. But let's find out what she's gonna do about it."

Kiara and Cida fell quiet and waited for Hadyn to read

Day Twenty One

The talk with Salin went surprisingly well today. And I feel . . . Torn. Caught up in the middle of something I'm afraid I don't understand myself.

Don't get me wrong, the day started with the same irrational and indignant anger that have become my constant companions. Because, yes, I actually was granted a private conversation with our high king today, but not before hours of waiting around with nothing but a glass of water offered to me. Then, to my consternation, when our benevolent king finally decided he could fit me into his important schedule, he greeted me as if an old friend. He was once again the Salin I remembered from before. And he actually remembered me from the Brotherhood.

I had forgotten how young our new king is. Really not much older than me. But with his boyish smile softening his features merely at the sight of a familiar face, it made me wonder, if not understand completely, just how difficult the weight of the responsibilities would be to carry for someone his age. Especially someone with an upbringing like his, never poured into by a father, never invested in or even cared for.

After he asked me a few cordial questions about my family, I was determined to stay on track and told him my concerns about the countenance of the whole community. Apparently this very issue had also been heavy on his mind. He asked me if I had any ideas, desperate for all the help he could get.

As a baker and cook, I, of course, had my own suspicions of an improper diet.

At my suggestion, a light sparked in his eyes and he said it only made sense. With our new lack of sunshine, we needed to be eating things that we just weren't yet to compensate for the deficiency. We talked of these things excitedly as if we were two young scientists discovering something together. He said he would put his best physicians on the problem and that they would issue the diet to the public as soon as they found a sufficient outline for one.

Then he asked if I would help him.

I still don't know what to think of the way my chest tightens even as I write this.

He wanted me to work with him and his physicians. He said no one else had thought to bring this problem to him, that he appreciated my boldness.

You have to know Salin to know how I felt. He's handsome and smart with a personality that could charm a snake, not to mention he is now the king of our city, and he appreciated me.

I didn't know what to say except a definite yes, but if he appreciated my boldness so much, I decided to be bold with my second complaint, and that was the overworking and mistreatment of my sister.

Salin seemed appalled to learn of such treatment and assured me he hadn't known anything about it. Before I even decided if I believed him or not, he promised me it would be remedied at once and that she would never again have to work past a time that suited her health.

I thanked him kindly then and prepared to take my leave, but he didn't see why I had to go. He, apparently, had nothing to do until he had to meet with his top physician for dinner and thought we could talk. He said as we might have before, if time and circumstances would have allowed.

I was shocked. I didn't know he even knew I existed. But with nothing else to do myself, I didn't see why we couldn't, and to my surprise, we talked quite easily together as if we really had once been friends. Conversation flowed a little too easily perhaps and led me to ask another one of my bold questions.

Ever the one to have to stick my foot in my mouth, I am honestly perplexed as to how I muster up the courage for such impertinences. Yet I continue to do so without reform. I asked him if he truly respected or even actually believed in this so-called god that had just destroyed our world. I asked how he could worship something that deliberately stole from us and imprisoned us.

Here, expecting him to finally lose his composure he had been so effortlessly displaying, I was shocked to see him smile. He looked me directly in the eyes and said, "Maddie, what you see as destruction and robbery, is truly and most definitely mercy."

I spent some time trying to decide if I despised or appreciated his name calling. I like my name, strange as it is. My mother is from Portugal. But it is a mouthful. All the same, Maddie has, in the past, been a name reserved for my family and friends to call me only.

I still haven't decided.

Salin continued by saying it was Fleard's right all along to create a world. The inevitable destruction of Elohim's world was held off as long as it was out of the kindness of that same mercy. He told me we should feel honored to be counted among some of the ones left alive. He begged me to think on the fact that we were some of the chosen few that he wanted to keep alive, while he decimated the entirety of the earth, though we have done nothing to deserve it.

Something about his words made me feel suddenly sick, as I watched a frighteningly dark light begin growing in his eyes.

I ignored the twisting in my gut and asked what he meant by some of the ones left alive.

He answered with a question. "You don't think there are others around the world also kept safe in underground colonies?"

I said I hadn't thought about it.

He said he had and that he knew it for a fact because Fleard himself had told him, through the watchers, of course.

The dark light in his eyes sparked to a burning fire when he said that, and I knew then that his passion for this was real; not some tale he spun merely for control.

He continued by saying that, naturally, we could never get to the others. The only way to them would be through unfathomable miles of solid stone. He said that Fleard knows we would kill ourselves trying, so he has already placed the watchers to guard the unmapped tunnels beyond the city for our own protection. He called them the Forbidden Caverns.

All at once, I felt more trapped than ever before.

Then he waved a hand and said he would rather talk of lighter things, surprising me more by lowering himself even further from his lofty throne and coming back down to earth. We laughed and talked about all sorts of pointless things, the sort of conversations where time seems to stop existing.

At length, I realized just how much time I must have spent there and told him I should go and tell Cecilia the good news.

He understood and politely walked me out.

Before I left, he asked me if I would mind terribly if he called me his friend. He said he didn't have anyone he could consider a friend even when we lived in the Brotherhood, and I was the closest thing he had to one.

I said I'd like that, and with a winsome smile, he bid me farewell.

I know I was probably wrong to feel any bit of fear, but I can't make up feelings as real as those. All the same, any hard feelings faded steadily as I walked home. So excited to tell Celia, I nearly forgot about all the bad and only thought of how kind it was of Salin to listen to all my complaints and promise to do something about them immediately. I felt heard for the first time in a long time.

Celia thinks I shouldn't trust him so easily. I think she worries too much; she always has. She asked, what about Tommy?

What about Tommy? He's just a chum. And it's not as though Salin asked to court me. I'm only helping him create a diet for the city.

She was pleased enough when I told her the news, but even that smile didn't last long. I just hope she gets better soon so she can be happy like me.

"That's the end of the—"

"What?" Kiara cut him off. "That slime!"

Cida snorted and bolted upright from where she had slumped against the wall.

"Really? You're nodding off at a time like this?" Cida looked guilty, but like she didn't know what for. "I can't believe she's falling for that filth's web of lies! Does she still remind you of someone, Cida?" She huffed. "I take it back. Her sister is the smart one."

"Kiara, he manipulated her," Hadyn said.

"Exactly. And she fell for it! I just can't believe he got away with that rubbish! How easy is she?"

"Let's not forget it was your ancestor who was doing the manipulating in the first place," Hadyn shot back.

Kiara raised a brow. "We're playing that game? Cause I don't really see a worse one, the mastermind or the girl falling for the mastermind because of his good looks and charm. Anyway, with the way that this is going, I wouldn't be so sure he's not your ancestor either."

Hadyn fidgeted, cheeks flaring red all of a sudden. "You think . . . But that would mean . . ."

"Listen to you two!" Cida's eyes were wide with mortified amusement. "And you know that's not true. Imelda was the first queen of Caverna."

Hadyn frowned at her, and Kiara just smirked back.

"Doesn't change the fact that this is messed up," she said. "She should have never given that man a wink of trust."

Hadyn sighed. "Maybe it won't be forever. Maybe it will turn around to spite him. We just have to see what happens next."

"Hadyn, this isn't a story; it's real life."

His eyes blinked with deep hurt, but he didn't say anything.

"Well, whatever happens next," Cida started, a seizing yawn interrupting her mid sentence, "it will have to wait for tomorrow."

Groggily collecting herself, Cida said her good nights, but only Hadyn answered, and left them to a painful silence.

Kiara kept her face to the stone floor to avoid his eyes. "Hadyn, I'm sorry."

"It's alright. But I don't think of it as a story, Kiara. I never do. But sometimes hoping is the only thing left to do, and there's nothing wrong with that. That same hope is the only thing that's gotten me through this . . . hopeless life."

"I know," she said, finally looking at him. "And I only insult its value . . . because I envy it."

Hadyn didn't know what to say. Suddenly looking up from the closed cover of the journal, he searched her face.

She offered him a small smile and stood up. "I'll see you tomorrow, okay? Goodnight."

"Goodnight, Kiara."

The Place Always

Kiara sat up as if she had a rod in her back, gasping like a free diver coming up for air. Her arms, her legs felt rigid, paralyzed even. Her breaths came in rapid puffs, her chest much too tight to breathe normally, and she could all but see the creatures crawling out of the shadows beyond her one light. She tried to focus on the flame, only see it, and count the seconds of each exhale, but pounding footsteps echoing in through the fissure deprived her of even the simplest form of coping. Kiara pulled her blankets up to her face as her heart hammered inside her chest. Who was in the Forbiddens? How did they find her? What would they do to her?

"Kiara!" a desperate voice called, but she didn't dare answer. "Kiara, are you alright?"

Just on the other side of the fissure now, Kiara could hear the person shuffling through. Body filled to the brim with violent, trembling fear, Kiara thought she'd faint before she even saw their face.

Hadyn pushed through the crack, a lantern of his own illuminating the alarm on his face.

The sudden relief sprung a leak in Kiara's eyes, and two big tears rolled down her cheeks. Despite his visible confusion, Hadyn rushed to her side and knelt on the ground.

"Hey, it's okay. What happened?"

Lip trembling, she buried her face in her blanket to hide any more tears. "I'm sorry!" she sobbed. "I'm sorry I'm this way! It was just a dream . . . It's always dreams."

Sighing in relief, Hadyn leaned back. He sat quietly until she could lift her head again. And when she did, she seemed to have come to her senses, finally fully awake.

Wiping her eyes she asked. "What made you come?"

"I heard you. I thought you were in trouble."

Kiara closed her eyes in shame. "I'm so sorry."

"It's alright. You don't have to apologize."

Wrapping her blanket tighter around herself, Kiara gathered one gulp of air and released it in a quaking breath.

"You know," Hadyn began, "it's late enough. It's not like I would go back to sleep anyway. I could stay . . . if you want."

"Oh." She blinked. "Okay."

His eyes wandered across the floor. "Do you want to talk about it . . . Your dream?"

Kiara looked away and shivered.

"Only if it helps," he added hastily. "You don't have to."

"With this dream, it's always the same," she said. "With time, the memory of it fades, but every time I dream it again, it's as vivid as ever, and I know I've been there before. I'm in these tunnels, but not like the Forbiddens. They're cobbled . . . they're *made*."

Hadyn watched her closely, but she couldn't look him in the eye while she spoke.

"They're so dark . . . and they just go on like they have no end. If they do, I've never found it. I *can* never find it. I just feel so trapped and somehow, I feel like I'm put there, just dropped in place, cursed to wander endlessly. And then," she paused, mustering the strength, eyes widening with horror as if she saw them now, "there's these creatures. They find me. Not always, but most times, and I can never run—" Her voice broke and she could say no more.

Once the wave of terror passed though, she did feel better. For once they weren't just rattling around in her head, tormenting her until she could sufficiently distract herself. For the first time, the horrors were outside, almost set loose, and she could actually feel the free space in her mind.

Finally she looked at him. "Thank you."

"For what?"

"For listening. I've never told anyone that before."

"Anytime."

It was Hadyn's idea to get an early start on learning, so pushing the nightmares further out the door, they dived straight into the colorful world of the jungle. Kiara began with avid enthusiasm, but as the morning dragged on, she knew better than to think she was learning anything new.

"Agh! I've read these books countless times over. I'm not learning anything that I didn't already know!"

Hadyn looked up from the plant journal. "Really? Nothing?"

"Well, here and there there's something that I didn't catch before, but yeah, pretty much." She sighed. "I know your learning and I'm glad for that. And I suppose repetition won't hurt."

She tried to go back to reading and Hadyn did the same.

"But there's got to be something in here! That's why my mother gave them to me, isn't it?"

Jumping from her latest outburst, Hadyn closed his book. "Kiara, maybe we should take a break."

"Good idea." She crossed her arms and leaned over the pond to watch her fish, but couldn't see much past her reflection, her flaming hair distracting her like a bright, irritating light. She wished that there was something that would just tell her what to do and how to escape.

Hadyn watched her painfully as she looked at herself with such disdain, brow knit and quivering with countless frustrations.

She smacked the water to break the terrible picture of her reflection.

As if the splash had disturbed the slumbering of some cavern dwelling beast, a great roar erupted from absolutely nowhere and everywhere at the same time.

Kiara and Hadyn clamped their hands over their ears as the roars continued over and over again, twelve times.

Bong! Bong! the sound hammered, and, as usual, the earth ground out it's reply, pebbles and dust falling on their heads.

Only when the final toll rang through the cavern and down their spinal cords, did they even begin to lower their hands.

"Goodness!" Hadyn said. "Why in Caverna are those so loud here? I nearly choke on my own spit every time."

"Well, because . . ."

"Kiara?"

The start of a grin curled on her lips. "There's someone you should meet."

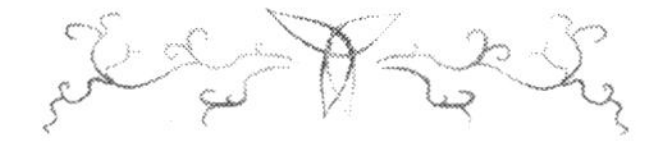

Once she managed to convince him that she had no

intentions to leave the Forbiddens, Hadyn finally mustered himself to get off the ground and follow her into the dark passage running along the back side of her hideaway.

Kiara told him a little bit about Tick on the way, but Hadyn wasn't sure if she had gone slightly mad in her time alone out here, or if he believed her and so had also gone mad himself.

As they approached the door to Tick's clock room, the sound of raging shouts were muffled from the other side. Kiara snuffed the lantern and put her ear to the door.

"Tick, you ludicrous interloper! Mind your business and stop trying to meddle in things that do not pertain to you!"

Heavy foot falls stomped through the room, and Kiara and Hadyn ran farther down the tunnel to hide themselves. But the door never swung open, though they did hear a timber-splitting slam from inside the room.

"And so departs His Majesty," Kiara whispered. "Now you know what I mean when I talk of his temper. Come on, let's go see if Tick's alright."

"But he never came out."

She shrugged. "There must be another way to Caverna in there."

Kiara stopped at the thick door guided by the faint line of light on the ground, and listened to make sure she heard no more voices. She did hear one voice— Tick's, and he was talking to himself, telling himself a story about three bats that wanted to catch a glimpse of the sun for once instead of sleeping all day. She wondered if he even understood what he was talking about.

Shaking her head, she knocked twice and waited. Tick opened the door and looked at her with a puzzled expression, his eyes constantly shifting back to Hadyn as she began to talk. Kiara thought of calling herself Betsie again but she didn't want to lie to him anymore, and he wouldn't remember anyway.

"Hello there. I'm Kiara. We've met before." She watched him expectantly. "Do you . . . Do you remember me?"

His expression melted from confusion, to thoughtful, to utter surprise that he did, in fact, remember something!

"Now that you say that . . . Yes! I do remember your bright eyes. And if I recall correctly, you are not a spirit?"

Kiara laughed. "Yes."

He looked at Hadyn again, his eyes lingering this time.

"This is my friend," she introduced with a smile, "Hadyn."

Tick didn't remove his gaze, but narrowed it more intensely. Hadyn nervously shifted his weight from one foot to the other.

"Have we met before?" Tick asked. "It's strange for me to remember so much, but I do feel like I've seen you before, later in time, but yet in the past, when you were older, but yet younger."

Perturbed, Hadyn brushed him off. "No, we've never met. And trust me, I would remember."

Kiara snuck a look at him sideways, raising a questioning, copper brow.

Tick turned his gawking back to Kiara. "Why *are* you here?"

Kiara shrugged. "We came to see you."

"Me?" His eyes wandered like this was some strange, new thing he had no idea what to do with. "Ah, where are my manners? Please, come in," he said, stepping aside.

"Thank you." Kiara smiled. "What did the king want?"

"The king?"

"Yes. Why was he here?"

Tick's eyes grew wide. "The king was here?"

"Why, just a moment ago—" Kiara huffed. It didn't matter. "How does he get here anyway?" she grumbled more to herself than anyone.

"Well, he always comes up just through that door."

"What?" Kiara followed Tick's pointing finger to a trapdoor in the far corner of the room. "A secret tunnel bypassing the Forbiddens . . . Interesting."

"Now that I think about it, no one ever comes through the door you used. At least I don't think so . . . Where does it lead?"

"Well, it leads out."

"To the sun?" he asked with childlike excitement. "To the sea?"

"No. To more tunnels. To a city that's never seen the sun."

Tick's shoulders drooped. "Oh."

"You're really not missing all that much," Hadyn spoke for the first time since stepping in, though he still looked like he wanted to bolt, so much so Kiara felt the urge to hold onto his arm just so he wouldn't. But then she couldn't stop staring at the trap door.

"It's just like the tunnels into the Styx. Don't you think?" she said quietly to Hadyn. "Do you think they could be connected in some way?"

Hadyn shrugged. "I'm not sure. I assume this one leads to

the palace."

While they talked, Tick stood off a ways and began a soft chant under his breath, mainly consisting of lefts and rights with no discernible pattern.

"Left, right, left, left, right, straight . . ."

"You don't think it could lead to multiple locations?" Kiara asked.

"No. I don't think anything. It's a trapdoor. It's entire existence is a question mark. Speaking of question marks, what is he doing?"

Kiara turned to see Tick still chanting sing-song like. "Right, right, left, straight, straight . . ."

Kiara waved a hand at him. "Um . . . Tick?"

"Hmm?" he said lucidly.

"Oh, nothing." She decided to let it go, not expecting any straight answers anyway. "I was wondering though, last we met, you talked of a place called Nowhere and a place called Always."

Tick smiled like he had just settled into the shade on a balmy afternoon. "Ah, my dreams."

"Yes. I would like to hear more of them, if you wouldn't mind telling us."

Tick looked uncertainly at Hadyn again.

"Don't worry. Hadyn wants to hear about your dreams too."

"Alright!" Tick said, delighted that he had someone to talk to besides himself. "Come. Sit down!"

Since the room had nowhere to sit but the table's one rickety chair, they sat on the ground and waited, like children ready to listen to a bard's extravagant tales.

"Oh, where do I start?" Tick said, tapping the pads of his fingers together. "Well, let's see. The King lives in the Place Always."

"The king?" Kiara asked.

"Yes, *the King*. He is the LORD of everything."

"The Creator."

Tick smiled. "Precisely! And he loves all of creation, to whatever end."

"But that's impossible. How can you love someone who doesn't love you?"

"It is not impossible. Nothing is impossible for Him. He does love all and He wants us to do the same."

Hadyn remained silent, but Kiara had more questions.

"So, even me?" she asked. "He loves me even though I don't know Him or know if I believe in Him?"

"Yes, even you."

"Tell me more," she said, and after that had no more interruptions.

"The Place Always is a perfect and beautiful land, full of peace and joy, and the times I dream of there are blessings greater than any other. There are no tears there. Not a soul can be heard weeping. Laughter and praises fill the once hollow mouths of those who go there. There is no place for fear or darkness. The King will watch over them and He shall be their light. Those who never belonged, will never feel out of place again because they received the truth that they are sons and daughters of the King!"

Kiara smiled at Hadyn, his gloomed mood seeming to have lifted the more Tick spoke.

"All creation sings with jubilant shouts," Tick continued, "for they are finally as they were created to be, perfect and free from pain.

"I have walked there in my dreams. I've known things that I've never seen. There are things there that don't exist here, wonderful things. Sometimes I forget . . . like the voice I hear there. All I can remember of it is the kindness.

"Far away in the Place Always, the balmy breeze is swept in from the sea and foamy waves gently lap the shore. There is a great city on a hill that I have only seen from a distance for it is not my time to go there yet. It gleams in the light of day, as radiant as the sun itself. I have walked through the forest on the edge of the white shore in the cool of the day and it is as pleasant to the soul as everything else in that wonderful land."

It was most difficult to imagine, full of so many things they had never seen, but their hearts ached with a joy that both satisfied and made hungry even as he spoke, replete with longing, but at same time filling them up. The words settled on Kiara's soul like a welcome salve and brought a long awaited rest to her mind.

"It sounds as though you speak of the place beyond the darkness and yet infinitely better than any I've heard," she said.

"Oh, but I do. It is far beyond the darkness, untouchable by even the most powerful shadow."

Just then Tick's face grew grave. "But I will not tell you of the place Nowhere. I do not have the heart to burden you with such things."

"That's alright. I'd rather not hear of it," Kiara said, not wanting to do anything to taint the beauty that had gathered in her mind and seemed to float in the air about them. And seeing the horror it brought upon Tick to even think of such things, she preferred not to upset him further.

Then, even before her curious mind could think of another question, Tick stood and walked toward the clockwork contraptions. Her gut twisted with dread as she feared what came next. Tick went about his work, watching the last sand grains spill into the next jar and sounded the bell once. When he turned, Kiara searched his eyes. He looked tired, but a sure clarity filled the space where she expected confusion and alarm.

"What's wrong?" he asked her.

He had not forgotten! "Nothing." She smiled. "Things are more right than they have been in a long time."

"That's nice." Then a wide yawn took hold of his face. "Though I thoroughly enjoy your company, I am very drowsy and I'm afraid I must retire with what little time I have till the next hour."

"Of course," Kiara said. "Thank you for telling us about your dreams."

Then Hadyn unexpectedly added, "Yes, thank you, Tick. It was a fine pleasure meeting you."

"Yourself also, Master Hadyn. You are both most welcome to come by anytime you like. And maybe next time I'll remember something else! Maybe even why you look so familiar."

Hadyn's eyes dropped to the ground and he sighed. "Perhaps you will."

They said their goodbyes then, Kiara's implied with a smile and a nod, but never said.

Once they were out the door, their lantern relit for the journey back, Kiara beamed in the firelight. "He remembered!" she squealed.

But Hadyn had already stomped into the dark, his pace brisk enough to make it difficult for Kiara to catch up with him.

"Hadyn? Hadyn, where are you going? What's wrong?" she cried, but he never once answered.

Kiara found him in her hideaway, staring into the dark mirror with disdain, the crack in the glass running straight across his broken expression.

"Hadyn?"

"It's my father."

"What?"

"Tick knew 'em. He knew my father . . . Look at me. I look just like him and I hate myself for it!"

Kiara stepped further into the room, taking tentative steps as she struggled to understand. But the closer she got the harder it became for her to continue to watch him. She'd seen that expression too many times before, in her own reflection.

"He killed her, Kiara," he spoke through clenched teeth. "He's what killed my mother."

"What are you talking about?"

"She just couldn't take it anymore, and when my sister got sick and didn't have the strength to fight it, she couldn't hold on any longer. People said, she followed her daughter, that the sickness took them both, but she didn't have the fever like Viviana. She just died, Kiara. I didn't know till then that people could just go like that. But I never lied to myself. Even as a boy, I always knew what killed her."

Kiara didn't know what to say. Her face flushed hot with held back sorrow. "And you think because you look like him . . . that somehow makes you like him? Hadyn, you're his son; not him."

"That's not the point," he snapped, then sighed. "He would always say, he wasn't about to do anything else, that gambling made him enough money. My mother would always try to encourage him, tell him he could do so much with the talents he had and make some honest money, but his answer was the same every time— she couldn't make him. So he'd stumble off to the taverns every night, get so drunk, he could hardly walk . . . And yet . . . *he* knew him. Tick. I just know he did."

Finally, it all made sense, but now Kiara *truly* didn't know what to say, fearing if she told him, she'd only upset him further. Yet, he deserved to know.

"Hadyn . . . your father, he worked for the king."

Hadyn's head fell and his fists clenched. "How do you know that?"

"Your father was Alister Stone?" He nodded, so she continued, "Alister, he would speak with the king sometimes and get orders from him."

Hadyn wouldn't turn around. "But why? Why would he lie about it?"

Kiara bit her lip. "I don't know. Maybe he was one of the Nameless, sworn to secrecy."

His shoulders slumped further and he let out a sighing sob. She felt his pain like her own. She knew exactly how deeply it cut to be lied to by one's own family. She walked over to him and went to put a hand on his shoulder, but it hovered there, as she fought uncertainties of how he would react. What if he pushed her away?

She pulled her hand back and said instead, "I'm so sorry, Hadyn."

Finally, he looked at her, tears pooling in his blue eyes. "It's not your fault. We have to find these things out at some point . . . Both of us."

"You're right."

He gave her half a grin. "And we'll be alright."

"You know," Kiara said, trying to make the darkness go away. "You don't have his eyes. Your eyes are different."

"Yeah, I suppose they are."

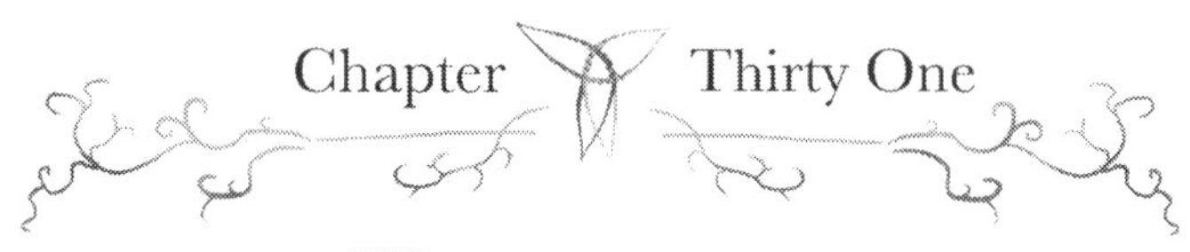

Chapter Thirty One

PACTS

Day Thirty Two

I don't know what I'm supposed to feel. Strangely enough, I only feel stupid. There's no one to be angry with but myself.

For the first few days I made excuses for him, excuses that only add to my bitter regret. We were making so much progress on the diet. And he made it so easy to do so . . . So easy to be around. Then he grew distant. Our work was coming to a close. He said I had it more than handled, that I didn't need his help as much anymore. But did that mean we couldn't talk either?

Then there is still the question of Cecelia's work hours.

I thought, he is very busy, and with all things considered, he could have pushed back the complaint of one girl working in the livestock sector. But now, nearly two weeks have passed with not a single hour taken from Cecilia's schedule. And I haven't heard from Salin in four days.

I won't lie to myself anymore. He manipulated me. And with the diet finished, he doesn't need me anymore. He tricked me into believing he valued my opinions. He used me.

I think I get it now. The youngest of seven sons, he had the same probability of rising to power that a mouse has at growing into a lion. He never cared about us, just the satisfaction of ruling his own people.

Celia warned me, but I didn't listen. My own sister, and I believed a mad man over her.

I'm so sorry, Celia . . .

"Well, it's about time you came to your senses!" Kiara threw her hands up in the air.

"Kiara!" Cida chided, a blanket wrapped around her shoulders and a steaming mug of tea cupped near her face. She spat out a snotty sneeze and switched out the mug for a handkerchief.

"She's right." Hadyn sat up on his bunk he had put together

with his back against the wall and the journal in his lap. "I wouldn't be so quick to judge."

Kiara reared her head back in offense.

"And anyway, can we just read the journal without the outbursts for once. And I mean that for all of us," he said, but Kiara knew full well he meant it for only and exclusively her. "Oh, and bless you."

Cida smiled at him with a stuffy sniff.

Kiara just crossed her arms. "Very well . . . Proceed."

Hadyn cleared his throat.

Day Thirty Three

Another meeting was called today. As everyone gathered in the newly built town circle, I debated on staying home. I didn't want to go, didn't want to see him, but I went for Celia, because she couldn't. I dragged my feet on the way, dreading seeing his smug face. Little did I know, I wouldn't have to.

After only a short moment of waiting in the crowd, a little man, I didn't recognize, with a nervous face and constant wringing hands came out to speak to us.

I couldn't help but roll my eyes. Salin had grown to be even above speaking to his own people and now had dogs to command and do his dirty work.

The man said his name was Alto. He explained the reasons for the depression and fatigue and finally issued the new diet everyone needed to conform to if they wished to feel better. To my shock and perhaps horror, he actually mentioned me by name as the lead researcher to thank.

Of course, I didn't get any stares or anything. No one knows Madressilva James by name. But I did not expect the credit, all the same.

He dismissed us by saying there is nothing more to report and I guess I feel the same.

Day Thirty Seven

The diet has already begun to help. I swear, I felt its effects almost overnight. It's not the most pleasant thing. The raw liver of any animal isn't the easiest thing to get down your throat. And I never have liked fish—

Hadyn stopped cold and looked up from the book, face twisting and eyes widening in shocked horror.

Kiara knew the question hovering on his lips before he even asked it.

"They eat their livers out!"

Cida couldn't seem to bring herself to swallow her mouthful of tea, but she refused to spew it. They all sat, locked in a three way stare down.

"Well they must have found out a way so they wouldn't have to forever," Kiara reasoned. "Because, clearly we don't participate in such savagery anymore. We only eat mash and meal. It's not as though white meal is really fish . . ." She shook the thought. "Anyway," she smirked, "I wouldn't be so quick to judge, or interrupt with an 'outburst.' "

Hadyn's twisted face melted into a frown. "Very funny." Sighing, he drew the book closer and continued the entry.

Also, how and where are they keeping fish? Where in the world did they get them from? I guess those are questions to ask Cece.

Speaking of Cecilia, the diet has improved her health immensely, but she's still extremely run down. She doesn't seem to have the energy for anything anymore. Mom and Dad are worried about her and, frankly, so am I.

Hadyn paused before moving on to the next entry, a sad sort of heaviness pulling down on his shoulders.

Day Forty

Cecilia confided in me with a disconcerting bit of information tonight, when she got home. I could tell from the look in her eyes that she was agonizing over whether she should even say anything. She said she could get in a huge amount of trouble if she told anyone, but she just couldn't keep it to herself any longer. After making me promise I wouldn't speak a word of it, she told me she was beginning to worry about the health of the livestock. Some of the animals, especially the cows, have started showing signs of illness. She doesn't work with the agricultural side at all, but she has made some acquaintances who do, and they have voiced similar concerns about the plants not growing well in the firelight.

Celia said it could be nothing, but told me she wouldn't have been able to live with herself if something happened and she hadn't said a word.

I noticed how light hearted she appeared despite the fear inciting news, and asked her what could be credited for this welcome change. She told me of a friend that has been keeping her entertained by regaling her with stories of his time growing up on his family's farm, an older gentleman, named Elijah. She told me that hearing about things of the past made her feel connected to, what she called, home again.

I had not liked that she called the Brotherhood home, but I think I realize now that she simply meant earth as we knew it once before.

I was happy for her that she had found a kind heart in this dark time, that is, until I learned that he is one of what the Brotherhood used to disdainfully call, the Pure Ones. Christians. Stubborn remnants of the Brotherhood's former self. Believe it or not, the society used to be zealous believers of the Christian God, but certain men, namely Salin's forefathers, joined and helped them throw off such childish hindrances, only to entrap them in more rubbish beliefs.

Most of the Brotherhood's accusations against them always seemed unfair to me, but that does not mean I sympathize with them. I don't believe we need to be subject to or controlled by anyone, divine or mortal. I told Cecilia I didn't want to hear about it and desperately advised her to stay far away from that man.

Kiara drew a breath, held it a moment while she stared sadly at the floor, and puffed it out in a huff. Hadyn waited, knowing she had something to say.

"You two were right," she said, raising her eyes to them each in turn. "She is angry. I knew it before, I just didn't want to say it because . . . I'm just the same. And you know what? I'm worse, because I've given up on hope *and* I'm angry. It's that anger that drives her to do stupid things, even to hurt the people she loves."

Cida butted in, "Kiara, you can't—"

"Please," Kiara continued. "I'm asking you to help me, to stop me when you know I'm going to do something I'll regret, to tell me when I'm believing lies." She looked at them both, earnest gravity in her eyes. "Will you help me?"

Hadyn found it hard to look directly at her, but he nodded anyway. Still, it wasn't enough. She needed both of them. Kiara looked to Cida who pressed her lips tightly together and shrugged before she said, "Of course."

"Madressilva didn't listen to the cautions of her sister and look at what happened." Kiara shifted her gaze between them. "We need to listen to each other. We *have* to trust each other. Or else we'll stay in just the same place as her. Deceived . . . and trapped. Tell me . . . promise me I can trust you."

"You can," Cida said, evenly, but Hadyn just fixed her with a gaze as intense and uncertain as a cold wind.

"Kiara, where is this coming from?" he asked.

"Please." She closed her eyes. "Just promise me."

"You can." He nodded. "I promise."

Kiara sighed like the long awaited end of something was

finally over. "And I promise both of you. We'll get through this, but only if we hold on to each other."

Before they all headed to find sleep or wait for it to find them, they decided to read one last entry, so Hadyn found the place where they left off.

Day Forty Four

My sister has taken ill today. We don't know what it is yet. Celia thinks it could have something to do with the ever weakening state of the livestock. She said, it's not just the cattle anymore, but the sheep are growing weaker as well. I knew this would happen to her. They ran her into the ground with all that work. And now I'm really worried for her. It shouldn't be this way. I should be the sick one. I'm the one who can't keep my mouth shut. Who falls for lies. Who is more likely to get people hurt with my rash decisions. Celia is too good . . .

I won't be alright again until I know she's fine. But selfishly, part of me can't help but be a little happy. Because it means she gets to stay home no matter what Salin does about it, and I get to see my big sister more. 'Course, I can't see her until after I get home, but my shifts at the bakery aren't nearly as long as hers were.

Tommy stopped by today. He listened to all I had in me to vomit out, and encouraged me to make it right with Cece, said our relationship as sisters is much too important to let one fight ruin.

Maybe Celia's right, I don't deserve him. I know she is only teasing, but maybe she's right. She always is.

I hadn't talked to her much since I yelled at her about the friend she had found in the Pure One, and now, with Tommy's kind counsel, I've finally had the time to apologize and make up for my harsh words.

"Poor, Cecilia. I think I can understand a little of how she feels." Cida blew her nose on the handkerchief. "I fear these late nights are wearing me thin."

"You're right." Kiara looked at her worriedly. "Maybe we should take a break. We don't have to read tomorrow night."

"And who would bring you your meals? I'll be quite alright, once I shake this. Don't you worry yourself about me, Missy. You do enough fretting the way it is."

"Well, alright, but you've got to promise you'll try to get some real rest tonight."

Touching a hand to Kiara's cheek, she smiled at her. "I shall try."

Before Cida left that night, they made an official pact. Kiara promised to no longer despair, from now on she would use her time wisely, squeezing out all the knowledge she could from her mother's books and teaching Hadyn all she knew. Cida would be their eyes on the inside, and continue to come every night to talk with them and bring them anything they needed. They swore with all their hearts to protect one another and to watch each other's backs. And most of all they promised to come back.

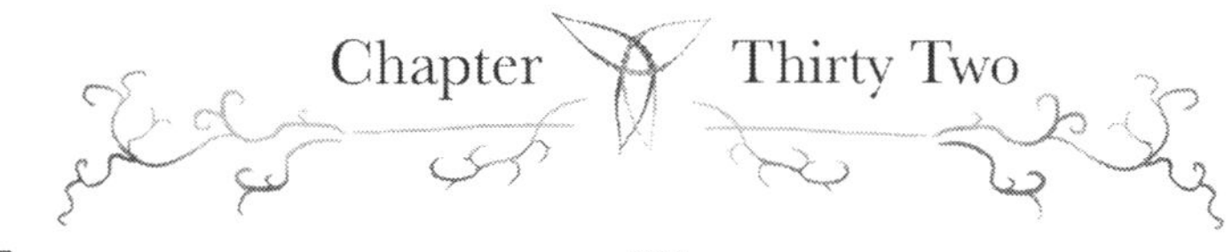

Chapter Thirty Two

Amara Lacrimis

They spent the next day gleaning all they could from the books, trying to get ready for something that with all the knowledge in the world, they could never prepare themselves for. They visited Tick (who had a natural knack for making Kiara laugh) more than once, the three of them already fast friends, and talked of many things from Tick's wonderful dreams to their pets— Kiara's fish and Tick's two mice friends, Herbert and Aubrey. At times, a familiar fog would creep into the blue of his eyes and they'd grow restless, mostly when he talked of things that troubled him, but always they'd steady again. Like a fresh breeze sweeping through the chaotic hills of his mind, the mist would clear.

That night they met with Cida in their regular rendezvous spot just beyond the entrance of the Forbiddens. Having become an almost inseparable team, their time with Cida, when not reading the journal, was usually filled with laughter and good, wholesome conversations, making partings bittersweet indeed. But that night, the night after they made their official pact, the atmosphere of their meeting took a turn into the dark as Cida arrived with some acrimonious news. She plastered a smile on her tired face, still trying to figure out how she would tell her, but the news showed in her eyes and Kiara knew her friend too well to be fooled by a painted grin.

"What's wrong?" Kiara asked. "I haven't seen you like this for some time." Though Kiara, with a churning in her gut, knew what the look was about. Cida's pain was not for herself. Her father had found Kiara out and it was only a matter of time before he found his wayward daughter and locked her away forever. Or once again some hapless soul was in harm's way because of her reckless actions.

"Let us sit down first," Cida said. "Bad news can always wait another minute."

Reluctantly, Kiara complied and Hadyn watched them both with concern as he followed.

Once they had settled down and Cida was sure that Kiara's head was a safe distance from the ground, she tried to begin, but the words jumbled up in her throat, and she feared she'd need a map to find the right ones. Cida sniffed, but Kiara couldn't tell if it was because of her cold or held back tears.

Kiara grabbed up her hand. "Speak plainly! For this torture must be worse than anything you could have to tell me. What has happened?"

"Something terrible. Something that I . . ." She bit her lip. "I hate to be the one to tell." Cida bravely fought her tears, trying to be strong for her. "Your father . . . he has announced his engagement to Lady Cunningtin and will adopt her eldest son, George as his heir."

Kiara sat back, shocked. That was it? Part of her was relieved, but it settled in soon enough. She thought she had run every worst case scenario through her mind, but not this. Once it faded, once she realized there was no reason to fret over those things, the relief dried up like a fish stuck on land, and she smelt the stench. It seized her throat and burned her eyes until she wanted to gag. If he found her out, she could be afraid. If he hurt someone else, she could be angry. But this . . . this pulled her under, into a drowning sea of sorrow.

The words stung like nothing she had ever felt before, but it was the things in her head and the titles that now gripped her like a chain around her neck that made her heart ache, that made the tears fall. It was as if she was there again, standing before his cold gaze, waiting for him to seal her fate like she could do nothing else, listening to him breathe in hate those same awful things.

You are nothing.

You are replaceable.

Kiara stared at Cida, not even seeing her as she fell into blackness. She puffed out a sigh, her shoulders crumbling under the wait of her grief.

"I'm so sorry, Kiara. I'm so sorry." Cida said as she began to cry for her.

She pulled her into her arms and Kiara's head collapsed on her shoulder. Hadyn stood close, pain wrecking his expression. He never knew what to do or say when someone was in tears. But he tried to give as much comfort as possible by just being there.

Kiara saw him through the curtain of tears in her eyes and she reached for his hand. He blinked at the gesture, but after only a moment's hesitation, took her hand in his and gripped it tightly. Kiara clung to her two friends, knowing for certain if she let go, she would be lost in the dark and she wouldn't make it out again.

Cida stroked her wild curls. "I know this is awful. It makes me sick with sadness . . . but you can't give up now. You—"

"I won't, Cida. I won't."

They listened to her cry long, sorrowful sobs and wept with her as good friends would.

When Kiara finally spoke, her voice was wracked with confusion and frustration. "Why does it hurt like this?" she said through her tears. "I swear I hate him. With all my heart I hate him! So why do I care?"

"Because it makes you feel replaceable." Hadyn said. "It makes you feel like there is nothing special or good about you that would make someone sad that you're gone."

She looked up at him, wondering how he knew the things that were yet only blurry pictures in her head.

He matched her gaze and didn't let go. "But, Kiara, those are lies," he said, his words as unyielding as adamant. "Nothing and no one could ever replace you, and you have done nothing to deserve this."

Kiara smiled at him, the corners of her mouth quivering with feeble strength.

"Hadyn's right," Cida said, giving her shoulder a squeeze. "And I believe, deep down, he's only trying to fill the hole left there when you . . . freed yourself. But no matter how hard he tries, he will never be able to replace you. Because there isn't anyone in this world quite like *you*, my dear."

Kiara hugged her. "Thank you, Cida. Both of you. What would I do without you? You help me fight off the monsters in my head so much better than I ever did on my own."

Hadyn grinned at her word choice. "That's because we have them too, remember?"

"Of course." Then wiping her eyes and nose with as much decorum as she could muster, she attempted to pull herself together. She gave a cold, breathy laugh and looked as though she might say something more, but then shook her head. "Well, Cida came all this way," she said, "so I think we should still read."

"Are you sure?" Hadyn asked.

"Yes. Let's not pay him any more thought than he deserves."

"If you say so. But we can do something else."

"It's fine, Hadyn. I shouldn't care anyway."

Cida looked at her sadly, but gave in and nodded for Hadyn to get the journal.

When Hadyn settled back down and scanned the last page they had read, his eyes grew wide.

"What is it?" Kiara asked.

"This is a really long entry!"

"Must be important," she said, evenly.

He studied her a short moment before quietly sighing and returning his eyes to the journal.

Day Forty Eight

Yet another meeting was held in the Town Circle today. Cece was home for once, but she didn't feel up for going out. Mom stayed back with her, even though Cecilia insisted she go, and Father came with me.

The town circle was different this time. Instead of its quiet uncertainty, the whole crowd buzzed with commotion. Everyone seemed to know something we didn't.

I still can't put into words my feelings for the ridiculous things that took place there tonight, but I'm getting ahead of myself. I will try to recount the events in order as best I can.

As I listened to the crowds, I caught a few key words that made my blood run cold~ livestock, resources, starvation, sickness and worst of all, plague.

My father shot me a sharp look and asked if Cece or I had said anything. I gave him a quick and definite shake of my head. Then my gut gave a twist. Tommy!

Just then his highness himself stepped onto the stage that had been recently built for this one use, and tried his best at quieting the crowd.

I was honestly surprised to see him. What was so different about now that he didn't just send the man called Alto in his stead. So fired up just at the sight of him, I had half the mind to join the crowd with a disruptive shout of my own. But the word plague shot another arrow of fear to my heart, and I wondered with a shiver what could be so serious that Salin came out to say it himself.

He managed to quiet the boiling crowd to a low simmer and wasted no time. "My friends," he said, "I regret to say this, and I can't believe it has come to this, but . . . the rumors are true. A sickness has spread through the livestock and the crops will not grow by firelight alone."

My stomach felt like it had dropped to my feet, as the crowd upheaved in another wave of outrage. This was no way to die. My mind pictured the end all too well, each of us clamoring over each other for breath and the last of whatever's left, sealed in here like it's our tomb.

Salin raised a hand and continued, "We have no evidence that this illness can affect humans, but if nothing is done soon . . . we will starve."

The crowd did not cry out again. It was silent as a graveyard, every individual utterly devastated. I felt it like a terminal diagnosis to my own health.

"But, my friends, do not despair just yet," he said, with feeble hope. "There is yet an option, drastic as it may be. And that is bringing our plight to Fleard himself. As you know, he is our new ruler, and though distant and at times calculating, he is not devoid of mercy and kindness. I am prepared to brave the realm of the watchers and take our humble request to them, so long as you all support me."

The crowd gazed at him stupidly, most likely shocked, just as I, at how ridiculous he sounded. Then, starting with the shout of one man, the whole crowd began to voice their agreements.

Salin looked over the people with a doleful, sort of noble regret in his eyes as if he wished he didn't have to do this, but would never turn his back on his people.

It made me sick.

"Very well," he said and began his journey to the Forbidden Caverns, the crowds following behind.

I pushed my way to the front of the crowd, partly for reasons I didn't even understand, but mostly because I wanted to make sure he didn't play any games.

Once at the entrance of those unmapped caverns, Salin stared into the dark, his back turned to us. With a misty-eyed look, he turned slowly and gave us all a sober smile.

"If I can not appease or convince the watchers with our humble query," he began, his voice breaking just barely, "I am grateful to have made it this far and will be honored to die among all of you. If I don't come back, I leave in charge my friend and the smartest person I know." His eyes found me. "Madressilva James."

I know my eyes must have grown to the size unnatural for human eyes to do, because as he gave me a smile both sorrowful and dutiful, I didn't even have time to process my shock, for he turned without another word and disappeared into the dark.

Father found me at this time, and he had Tommy with him. Tommy gave me a questioning look I had no answer for. I asked him if he had said anything about the livestock, but he said he hadn't told a soul. Then we waited in silence with the rest of the crowd for what felt like an hour. Then, with everyone's boredom reaching a peak, a horrible cry of pain ripped up the tunnel banging on the walls, the echoes causing it to meet our ears far too many times than we could have ever dared to bear. Suddenly a split second flash of bright light lit up the entrance to the tunnel, the only sound to be heard like the crashing and shattering of a large stone echoing up the passageway.

The crowd gasped and voiced its collective and morbid amazement.

Another flash, two in rapid succession this time, and then nothing. We all waited, holding our breath together. Then, almost when we feared he would not return, Salin came stumbling out of the tunnel. The people gave a few cheers of joy, but I gasped with horror. He held a hand against a bleeding wound on his face and appeared altogether exhausted.

Tommy gave me a look of concern, but returned to watching the scene with intense scrutiny.

The man called Alto suddenly produced a small stool from nowhere at all and brought it to Salin. He took it gratefully and patted the small man on the back.

The crowd waited, once again holding their breath, this time for news of their fate, not just Salin's.

Salin took his time to catch his breath, building an unnecessary amount of suspense. "Fleard has . . ." he tried to begin. "Fleard has agreed to help us."

The great shouts and cries of joy raised in that place, carried to the stone ceiling and bounced back, doubling the gratitude and relief felt throughout the people. I felt my own spirits lift in spite of myself.

But though Salin smiled, he did not look so unmitigatedly happy as the rest and everyone quieted down as they realized this.

"I regret to say there are conditions," he began to explain. "Fleard has agreed to supply our every need and only our needs. There will be a ceremony held on the first day of every month to gather our resources from a sacred cavern. Now Fleard has not been so unmerciful to not allow us things we are familiar with, but we are never again to see them in their unprocessed forms. Though devastating, it is only natural, seeing they are the creation of Elohim, the very things Fleard means to put an end to.

From this day forward, flora for delight, fauna for companionship, music for the ear, colors for eye, and light from the heavens, will become the Five Forbidden Gifts of Elohim."

With those words, I felt the life drain from my blood. Everything good, everything I loved, now gone? I felt robbed of my very heart. Father slipped his hand into mine. The people around us whispered to themselves, all feeling the loss like one of their own limbs.

"I know, it is a grievous loss," Salin said, "but it is the way now."

I felt a burning fire ignite in me at that moment and suddenly I could *not stay quiet. "And what if we don't?" I said, bold and clear. "What if we don't obey these . . . restrictions?"*

Father tried to silence me. But Tommy agreed backed me up.

Salin looked surprised, but his eyes drooped with heavy fatigue once again. "They thought there would be those who questioned. That is why they gave me this." For the first time, Salin dropped the hand that covered the side of his face, revealing a bloody gash running down his cheek.

The crowd gasped and winced.

"A mere taste of what they will do to those who resist, for those who deem it worth rebelling. Is that answer sufficient enough for you, Ms. James?"

I didn't reply. I couldn't take my eyes off the jagged wound.

"I suggest you all go home. Today has left us with much to process."

When the crowd began to disperse, without any more questions. I couldn't believe my eyes. I realized my feet couldn't move. Tommy had to pull me out of it, calling my name over and over. Thankfully, he did before I was too far gone. Father began to lead me by the hand through the throngs and suddenly I was just a little girl again, afraid and lost, clinging to my father as if I would fade away if only I let go. I threw one last look over my shoulder and caught a glimpse, through the churning bodies, of Salin still sitting on his stool. Our eyes met. He looked extremely sad, but his eyes still held something else, something that I would never again let myself ignore the feeling of sickness it caused.

Hadyn, Kiara, and Cida, stared at the floor, unable to ignore their own sort of sickening feeling churning in their stomachs. Kiara's passed the fastest though and, soon enough, she was finished dwelling on gut feelings; already scheming.

A light flicked on behind her eyes. "That's it."

Cida cocked her head. "What's it?"

"That has to be a lie," she said, "about the resources. I'm sure they started dying off, but I'm certain they found a new means to keep Caverna supplied. We sneak into the ritual room," she paused for effect, "we find out just what that means is." Then she mumbled to herself, "But I just don't see how he did that with the lights and crashes. It's like the watchers actually attacked him."

Hadyn closed the journal. "I don't think it's that simple."

"Why not?"

"The people behind this, including your father," Kiara rolled her eyes, "are not the type to be so careless as to allow loopholes like that. And how would you get there, let alone get in?"

A grin curled on her lips.

Hadyn gathered a measured breath. "You know, I've

actually begun to fear that look?"

She chortled and pulled something from her pocket. "This will get me in." She twirled a silver ring in her fingers, the king's signet plain to see.

Hadyn's brow bunched like he didn't fully understand what he was looking at. "How did you get that?"

"Cida got it for me when we planned your prison break. You think you could get another for Hadyn, Cida?"

Lucida's eyes grew wide, as she realized she was being dragged into the very thing she was politely sitting in a corner avoiding. "Oh-I . . . Well, I don't think it should be too difficult. But, Kiara . . ."

"Yes?"

"I'm not sure if I think you should go," she finally spit out, and the silence that followed hung her words in the air like dead men.

"Then I'll do it with neither of your help." She glared at them both. "I'll go by myself. You both said you wanted to help me search for an escape. And now, when I'm doing that very thing, you want me to stop?"

"And you said you wanted us to help you when you're going to do something you will regret!" Cida chimed back.

"But this is about escaping. Don't you want to get out!"

Cida sighed. "Not like this. It doesn't feel right, almost like I can feel there's no escape that way."

"Oh, you can feel it, can you? Well, you want to know what I can feel? I feel the weight of this cursed prison crushing down on me, suffocating me, stealing little pieces of my soul everyday. I feel a chill that I can't shake, no matter what I do. And a pull so great, I might tear down the middle if I don't reach this place, I just know, was meant for me, for all of us." A tear slipped down her cheek and she softened. "My own father . . . has moved on, Cida, in little more than a week. There is nothing left for me here *but* the hope of escape."

Silence separated them, isolating them to the separate rooms inside their minds.

"I'll go with you."

Kiara turned to Hadyn, saw the resolution set in his eyes, and nodded. "Thank you." Then turning back to Cida, she said, "I know you worry, but we have to chase every chance we get. And if you don't know that, maybe you need to figure out where your loyalties lie."

With that, she turned and scampered off to her hideaway without so much as a goodnight.

Hadyn watched her go and turned back to Cida, his expression one of a torn heart. "Just let her cool off," he said. "She'll come around and realize."

Lucida chuckled and smiled knowingly. "You don't have to tell me. I've known Kiara since she was yet a wee lass. Even as a child, the princess always knew what she wanted and not much could stop her, or turn her away. It's best you learn that now."

Hadyn raised his eyebrows with a nod, but he had nothing to add.

Cida grinned like he was hopeless and cocked her head towards the tunnel leading to her hideaway. "Go ahead. Go make sure she's alright. She's had a rough night, all things considered."

"I'll try to talk to her."

Cida bent to gather up her things. "Good luck."

Hadyn gave a laugh, but Cida reinforced her satire with a turn down of her mouth and a raise of her brows, and he wondered if he would be right to be afraid. His wonderings had taken him so deep, he nearly forgot Cida still stood there.

"I'll see you both tomorrow," Cida said, attempting to snap him out of it.

"Right. Goodnight, Lucida."

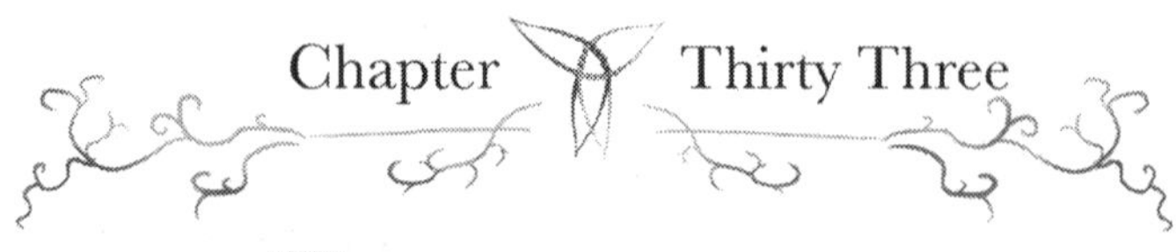

Chapter Thirty Three

Cloak...

Hadyn found Kiara sitting at the edge of her little pond, one hand propping up her face and the other trailing lazily on the water's surface. An unopened naturalist journal sat at her side.

"She's angry with me, isn't she?" she spoke without turning around.

He walked further into the room. "Oh, absolutely furious. I barely said a word to her before she flew into a rage and stormed off back to the palace." He plopped down next to her and she lifted her head off her hand to look at him, questions in her eyes.

He smiled.

"That's not funny."

"Well, does that sound anything like Lucida to you?"

"No." Kiara turned her face back to the pond. "And I'm all the worse for it."

"What? Why?"

"She's not mad at me. I know she's not."

"Yeah. Because she's your friend, and she knows you're just upset. How is that worse?"

"Because . . . if she's not angry with me, I have to be angry with myself."

Hadyn closed his eyes and shook his head. "What in Caverna would make you think that?"

She turned to him. "Because if she's angry at me, I can be angry with her . . . and I'm safe from the pain, from the sadness. It protects me. But what am I supposed to do when that anger is turned on me? What's there to protect me then?" She fought it fiercely, but her nose grew red and her eyes welled with tears, all the same.

Hadyn searched her face carefully. "This isn't just about Cida."

Her lip quivered and she managed to barely shake her head before the tears rolled off her cheeks. They fell into the water of the pool and sent delicate ripples across its surface. And even insignificant as they were, they carried all the way to the ends and the very edges.

Hadyn didn't put an arm around her, unsure if he even knew how to get his arm to move in that manner. They sat a foot apart in a silence dictated by sorrow.

"I wish I could take back what I said to Cida. I didn't mean to be so harsh. I hate myself for treating her like that. I hate myself for believing there could be anything good in . . . him, for ever believing he could change, for being surprised when he moved on." Twin tears rolled over her cheeks. "I miss her . . . so much." A moment of silence passed as more tears fell from her eyes. "I've missed her for four years. And now that I know she's out there, but torturously unreachable, I fear it's almost worse." She drew in a breath. "That's why I have to do this, why I have not changed my mind."

"I didn't expect you to."

"I have to see, with my own eyes, what really goes on there."

"I agree."

"And there's nothing you can do to—"

Hadyn just looked at her, a soft but serious smile on his face.

"What?"

"You have to do what you have to do. And it's my choice to follow you. I haven't changed my mind either."

Kiara sighed, the tension slipping off her shoulders almost visible. "I have to find a way out of here, if it's the very last thing I do."

"And that's just what we'll do. Rest today, then when tomorrow comes," Hadyn continued, "we'll be more than ready to make another charge against the darkness."

Kiara's eyes wandered contemplatively, "Rest today, so you can fight even harder tomorrow. That's what my mom used to say."

Hadyn cracked a crooked smile, "Smart mom."

The smile lighting her face dissolved like a puff of dust. "I can't rest . . . not when I fear closing my eyes."

Hadyn's face fell and he thought a moment, but only for a moment and then stood up. "Then rest we won't. And instead of rest up, we'll read up." Grabbing her hands, he pulled her to her feet and began pushing her over to her pile of blankets while she craned her neck at him with mild alarm and confusion. He sat her down and placed the journal she'd planned to read in her hands and a blanket over her legs. Then he moved over to where he usually read by the fish with a journal of his own. Kiara stared with her mouth open as if she might make some sort of protest, but Hadyn just smiled and looked down at his book, so she shut her mouth.

For Hadyn's sake, she tried her very hardest to read and keep her mind on things of learning and not of problems, but even her heart was distracted, and though the hurt in it had ebbed, it still throbbed dully with a pain that she feared, would never fully go away. And to attempt to read with a heart in turmoil, is a fool's errand entirely. If you've ever tried, you would know.

Though she managed to stuff a few words into her already cramped mind, the next morning she would struggle to remember even which journal she had read, to no avail.

Just when Kiara's mind started to drift the furthest yet into treacherous waters, Hadyn looked up from his book. "Kiara?" he asked. "What makes the sky cry?"

She almost laughed, partly because of his serious tone of voice, but also because she had asked herself the very same question many times before.

She smiled sadly. "I don't know. I've often wondered what the sky has to be sad about? Up there above the world, above everything, free from pain and heartache. It has no one to lose or miss. It has no rules to fall under. I imagine the air must be so sweet up there . . . So why do the books say water falls from its face as if it weeps?" She shrugged. "I don't know. Perhaps we'll never know."

Kiara yawned and Hadyn went back to reading. Her eyes felt so dry and hot from all the tears. The lids, stiff and scratchy, took that much more effort to open after every blink. Not a minute later Hadyn looked up again, another question on his tongue.

"Kiara," he said, but Kiara was sound asleep. Somehow, despite the night's bitter happenings, she actually looked peaceful. An expression, Hadyn realized, he had not seen on her face once since he met her. He smiled and went to take the book off her lap. He doused all the lights but one, just how she liked it.

"Goodnight, Kiara," he said as he left.

When Lucida returned the next night, Kiara and Hadyn had their cloaks ready, though Hadyn had made her swear on her most favorite forbidden treasure that if Lucida didn't bring them a second signet, she wouldn't go. Whether she would have kept that promise or not, we may never know.

While they waited for her to arrive, they sat quietly in their meeting spot, which Hadyn had now decorated with *his* forbidden treasures, as it was also where he had been staying.

Hadyn sat on his bunk, attempting to read from the avian journal while Kiara sat on the ground, drumming her fingers on her lap so fast they nearly blurred together in one fluttering mass, among other types of fidgeting.

Hadyn gripped the sides of the book tighter and sighed through his nose. "Something on your mind?"

Kiara smacked her hand flat against her leg. "What if she doesn't come? What if she *is* angry?"

"Kiara, she'll come," he said, closing the book. "And I told you, she wasn't even upset when she left. Don't worry." He hopped off the ledge and offered her a hand up.

Kiara ignored the gesture. "Maybe she just didn't have the time to contemplate it yet."

"Didn't have the time to contemplate what exactly?"

At the sound of the voice, Kiara shot up and shoved past Hadyn. "Cida!" she cried. "You're here!"

Holding a lantern in one hand, Cida placed her free hand on her hip. "And where else would I be, Missy?"

Kiara placed both her hands on Cida's shoulders. "Cida, I'm sorry for how I talked to you. I should've never said those things."

Cida wore a warm smile both in her eyes and on her lips. "Oh, enough of that. If I'm not mistaken, we have a whole world to find."

Cida slipped her hand into Kiara's view, pinching a silver ring between her fingers.

Kiara covered her mouth with a gasp. "You did it!"

Behind her, Hadyn shook his head in amusement, and Cida passed him a knowing smile.

"Do you really think that low of me that you'd expect me to slack on my part just because I'm," Cida sniffed "sick." Fluttering her eyes, she added. "I feel inclined to take offense."

Kiara laughed. They both knew that was never the reason for doubting her coming. Then growing rather serious, she said,

"Thank you."

"Of course. Now, let's get you two prepared. I can't believe you're not ready yet. You know, it's almost time? So, the ritual sanctuary is—"

"On the void side of town," Kiara interrupted. "Yes, I know."

Cida frowned, miffed by the rude interruption, but only for a brief moment. "And the ritual starts at—"

"Midnight. Yep, mhmm."

Cida huffed, but continued, determined to add a piece of new information. "But—"

"But all participants arrive early out of holy respect," Kiara finished. "I know it may not look like it, but I did live in the Palace once."

Sighing, she said, "Yes, of course. Well, Missy, if you know so much, why don't you two have your cloaks on already?"

Kiara smirked and went to grab hers.

They both put on their cloaks and signet rings, certainly not perfect disguises, while Kiara's dragged on the ground, Hadyn's didn't quite cover his feet, but they would do the job.

"Ugh," Hadyn sighed. "If I never wear a black cloak again, it will be too soon."

"Oh, come on," Kiara said, her eyes shining beneath her hood. "This could be . . . fun."

"Your confidence is inspiring."

Kiara elbowed him and tried her best to frown, while Cida watched with a grin on her face. Realizing, all at once, just how close the two of them had become, she felt her heart swell with a conflicted sort of twinge and she wondered if it was any bit like how a mother might feel.

Walking up to her to steal her attention one last time before they left, Cida fiddled with her hood as if she could make it hide her face better. "Just," she sighed, "be careful."

"We will." Kiara smiled. "We'll be back before you know it."

"And I don't doubt it. The participants will be coming from their homes all over the city, so just walk calmly and naturally, and no one should give you any trouble.

"Understood," Kiara said. "We'll see you soon."

Cida watched her slip away, but before it was too late, she caught Hadyn by the sleeve. "Stick together," she said, fixing him with a stare that could pierce through a stone wall. "Whatever you do, don't let her out of your sight."

"I won't," Hadyn said, and he meant it.

Cida managed a smile as she let him go and nodded for him to catch up with Kiara. Hadyn promised himself that he would keep Cida's wishes, but when he finally found Kiara well on her way out of the Forbiddens, he remembered how much easier that could be to say than do.

"Kiara!" he hissed. "Kiara, wait up!"

"Oh, there you are!" She spun around. "Isn't it great to get out of the Forbiddens again?"

"Well, sure, but this isn't exactly a leisurely excursion to the market."

"No. But it's something. We're finally doing something! Sitting around reading that journal does me no good."

"But we're learning."

"Not enough. Come on. We don't have much time."

They walked at a pace just short of painful for Kiara, doing their best to match the placid float, step for step, of those they saw on their way, if they were even stepping under those gliding cloaks.

"You know," Kiara whispered. "If you weren't here, I'd be walking much faster."

Hadyn decided not to answer her for so many reasons, it was a reason of its own.

"I mean . . . it's a good thing. I meant it in a good way."

"Oh."

More figures slithered out of the shadows and forced a premature end to their conversation. Though they were cloaked just the same as them, Kiara and Hadyn couldn't have felt more out of place, as they became surrounded by the ghostly pilgrims. These specters knew the way well, never placing their feet where they hadn't already planned ten steps ago. They walked in even, confident strides, as smoothly as water might flow.

As the two strangers in the midst simply worked on looking like they belonged, they came to what seemed like a path of sorts, lit with torches specially for that night. At the path of lights, rather than continuing to advance from every direction, the figures began to fall in a line.

Kiara looked to Hadyn and he just nodded his head as if to say, *Go ahead. I'll be right behind you.* Kiara thought she'd rather hide behind him, but there was no time to argue. They fell in line with the procession. With the drudging pace, one might think they were dead men walking to their own graves. They walked in silence under the light of the torches, the odd flap of a cloak and the whisper of the flames when they strode past them making the only sounds they heard the whole way. Even their feet landed noiselessly. For Kiara this was a simple enough task, but she heard Hadyn clomp down a little too heavily a few times, and in the silence, it was deafening.

The light of the torches shut them in and the world around them out, the brightness not only illuminating, but contrasting, building up a tunnel of black space around them and making it impossible to see anything beyond. Kiara and Hadyn looked left and right sometimes in an attempt to understand just where in Caverna they were, but the soundless marchers fixed their gazes straight ahead, deviating their attention for nothing, so Kiara thought it better than to risk a full turn of her head, even if only to steal a comforting look at Hadyn. Just knowing he was there would have to be enough.

While the cloaked specters maintained their beam-like focus on their destination, it was all Kiara could do to keep her feet from shuffling and her mouth from yawning. Her mind wandered. She wondered just how many cloaked figures there were, but she could only see the few three in front of her without leaning too overtly to the side. She wondered, if they pulled down their hoods, if she would recognize any of them. She wondered if she could find this path of light during day hours when all of the city's lights were lit. She wondered so much and about so many things, she didn't even notice when the line finally began to slow and then halt altogether, continuing on until she would have marched straight into the marcher only a few feet in front of her.

She felt a hand grab the back of her cloak and tried not to gasp as Hadyn risked breaking character to save her hide.

Kiara held her breath and felt a bead of sweat drip down from her temple.

Espionage is a quiet, slow, and painful game for those unprepared to endure its difficulties. And Kiara (belatedly or not) began to realize with each second of that held breath, just how unprepared she was.

At length, Hadyn released his grip on her cloak, nothing but stillness and silence ensuing after the slip. Kiara could only send out a mental thanks to him for saving her life yet again. Then with the adrenaline melting into shakes, Kiara began to wonder with some impatience, why everyone had stopped, standing there in silence proving itself even worse than marching in silence. She was forced to stand there without speaking and without moving, not even able to glance back at her only source of comfort in this painful situation. One thing consoled her though, and that was her near to complete surety that it couldn't get any worse. That's when they started, quiet at first, but as more took up the call, they spoke in one voice, somehow loud though each one barely spoke above a whisper.

"Decem . . . Novem . . . Octo . . ." they chanted, sending immaterial spiders crawling down Kiara's spine.

She may have picked sign language as her second language in school, but she didn't need to sit through hours of skull-numbing lectures to know the hooded specters were speaking Latin, she just couldn't understand it. Wherever she heard it, whether in the echoey halls of their dark stone temples or even in the streets when one of the high ministers passed by, praying under his breath for all those lesser than him, it was always spoken in a chilling whisper and always sent shivers throughout her body. Now was no exception.

As they continued, not a single word was the same or even slightly understandable, but knowing she couldn't discern it, she focused in on other things like the pulsing rhythm of every word. The reliable pauses and stops were familiar somehow, and soon enough she had it figured out. They were counting! But for what?

"Quattuor . . . Tres . . . Duo . . . Unus," the voices said. Then they hushed, and for one frozen moment there was complete silence. Such sudden silence, Kiara's ears range with their own noise just to fill it.

The specters waited, and not knowing what countless people around her were waiting for, terrified her, tightening her muscles like springs ready to explode.

The silence only reigned for little more than a second, but that second felt like a minute, that might as well have been an hour. And finally it was shattered, utterly decimated, as a roaring bang clanged through the cavern and set Kiara's springs loose. She jumped clean off the ground. Then, before she even hit the ground, the next bang was let loose and everything started to fall into place.

Midnight. They were counting down to midnight.

The whole line listened in silence as the rest of the twelve ominous tolls rang out. Kiara thought of Tick, sitting in his little room with his homemade earmuffs pressed tightly to his head. A comforting smile tainted with dangerous determination twitched on her lips.

This is for Tick, she thought, *and Cida, and everyone else who never deserved this imprisonment.*

When the twelfth clang sounded and the procession resumed their march, Kiara could go forward without another question, because whatever they were going to find at the end of this line, she would meet it boldly for the hope of escape, if anything at all.

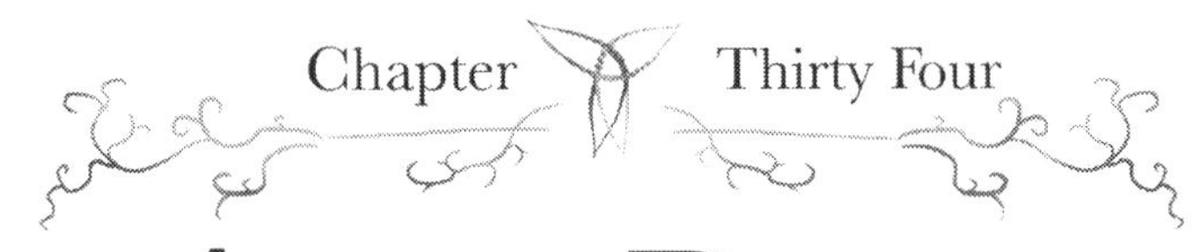

Chapter Thirty Four

...And Dagger

The line moved along at a brain-numbing, stop and go pulse, but Kiara refused to let her attention slip away for another instant, keeping her eyes fixed on the feet of the person in front of her. Whenever they stopped, she stopped, and when they walked again, she followed, focusing solely on the mission ahead. Then the walls closed in. She felt them constrict around her and looked up to find they had entered a short tunnel, the wooden double doors of the entrance swung wide open, so the line marched straight in. More torches lined the walls of the narrow tunnel, scarcely wide enough for Kiara to stretch her arms to the sides. At the far end, two guards stood at another pair of open doors, regulating the entries of what could only be the ritual sanctuary.

Kiara felt her heartbeat quicken as they drew closer, but less out of fear and more of a violent fluttering of anticipation. This could be it, the very thing she had waited for, looked for, longed for her entire life. It was so close, she could taste its freedom on the tip of her tongue. She could feel it pulling her forward, so much so, she nearly followed straight after the figure in front of her without stopping at the guards. The guards were dressed just the same as all the rest here tonight, black cloaks with heavy draping hoods to conceal their faces, except these two carried long spear shafts, tipped with wickedly sharp, and toothed, metal heads, forked like the tongue of a snake, and they lowered these fearsome weapons of correction in front of her. Like bars on a cage, they clanged with resounding rejection as they crossed each other.

Kiara blinked at the glinting steel just inches from severing the tip of her nose, but before suspicions could raise to alarm, she remembered her role and what she had to do to play along. With a flick of her right wrist, she flung the sleeve of her heavy cloak off her hand. Like she had done it many times before, she hung her arm in the air limply, so the guards could see plainly the signet ring on her index finger.

The concealed faces of the guards gave no hint to their decision. They simply stared, faceless and expressionless until, finally, the metal of their spears grated across one another as they pulled them back to their sides. Kiara didn't wait for any further permission. Stepping forward, she left the guards and the narrow tunnel behind her, letting her sleeve fall back over her hand just as an attack of uncontrollable trembling took over both her palms.

Kiara stepped into the ritual sanctuary, a perfectly round room with cobbled walls and a high ceiling. Torches, circling the room on the curving wall, along with a crude looking, black metal chandelier illuminated the space with an eerie, dim flicker and cast dark shadows about the room. Kiara waited for her eyes to adjust, but even after they did, there wasn't much to see. The room, it seemed, was just a round room, and besides the dark mass in the middle, it was empty too.

Kiara forced her feet to keep moving as she fought to understand what she was seeing. She didn't look behind her. She knew Hadyn would follow. She could see a circle forming around the room, so Kiara followed the last hooded figure to the left side and took her place in the growing chain. There had to be at least forty of them altogether and not everyone had even arrived inside yet.

Finding where she should stand next to the stranger, Kiara looked to her right to see Hadyn just walking up, but he was busy taking in everything else. While the rest of the hooded ones filed into the circle, Kiara attempted to take another guess at the cumbersome mass in the middle of the room. She followed it up its obscure and irregular sides all the way to where it tapered at the top. There, nearer to the light of the chandelier, she could make out a little more than the mere silhouettes at the bottom. The candles' glow shown on what looked like different sized crates and barrels. There were raw wood planks and coils of thick rope and smaller things yet indiscernible in the low light. But Kiara didn't need to discern them. The gears had done away with their cobwebs and were turning again. This wasn't one mass, but a whole pile of many things, stacked nearly to the ceiling, the one reason everyone was here.

"It's the resources," she whispered, leaning ever so slightly towards Hadyn.

"What?" he whispered back, leaning ever so slightly towards her.

"The resources," she repeated. "Caverna's resources. They're already here . . ."

"How did they get here?"

Kiara tried in vain to steady her breathing as her eyes darted about the room. "I don't know."

The walls wrapped around and enveloped them in solid cobblestone. As far as she could tell there was only one way in and out of this room, and even that way was temporary.

"Hadyn . . . I—" she tried to voice her concerns, but a loud bang cut her short and made her jump.

The final black pilgrim had at last taken their place and completed the circle. The spear wielding guards then shut them in, slamming the doors behind them, the echoes rapping off the walls.

No one moved. No one made a sound, at least none that Kiara could hear over her own deafening heartbeat in her ears, and exploding thoughts in her head. How did it all get here? Seeing it here, just simply existing, it made her dizzy. This was their life, the very substance of their survival. Without it, no one would be living in this underworld of hell. To believe it was dropped here as a gift from the gods, or in this case, a god, was madness unthinkable to Kiara. But to think it had gotten here by any other means whatsoever, was nearly just as impossible.

Her breaths came and went shorter and shorter, like someone had a rope around her neck and just kept tightening the knot.

She had been so caught up in proving her theory right, in proving her father and all of Caverna to be a liar, that she never once considered what she would do if it wasn't a trick . . . if it was real.

How can this be real? she thought, but her mind answered her with silence.

Totally unprepared for such a blow, Kiara found everything, every surety she once held onto, every suspicion she ever had of the dark, on trial in her mind, and nothing could hold up against the accusations. Tears welled in her eyes as she fought to understand.

Without warning, the stranger on her left grabbed her hand. Kiara flinched, but with a quick look around the room, she realized the whole circle had linked themselves together by the hand. She left her hand because she had to and held tightly to Hadyn at her other side. Then, all around the room, the black pilgrims began to speak, chanting in that same breathy whisper, words that frightened her but told her nothing.

Again she wondered, with all the hooded strangers holding hands, if she knew any of them or if her father was among them. Then an intruding thought entered her mind that she wished desperately to unthink. She wondered if her *father* was the person on her left. Suddenly she felt very sick. Everything they went through tonight was for nothing. Their own search for escape had somehow done the one thing she thought impossible, and left her feeling more confined than ever.

Every sense began to numb. The chanting voices were drowned out by a static in her ears and a radiating heat pulsed up her back into her head.

Hadyn saw her sway ever so slightly and feared she might faint. Kiara feared it too, her mounting terror only inviting more black into her vision. She had never passed out before and didn't know what it would even be like, but she had succumbed to the fact that she was about to find out just when she felt a reassuring squeeze on her right hand. Like a brave beacon of blinding light, the simple gesture pushed back at the growing darkness, and with something tangible to hold tight to, Kiara felt herself coming back. She turned her head towards him, mouth suddenly so dry, and could see the whites of his worried eyes illuminated by the torch light. He nodded his head and rubbed the back of her hand with his thumb, while Kiara imagined all the things he would be saying if he could. He would tell her to hold on, that they'd get through this and he'd be right there the whole time. To just hold on.

As if she had heard him, she nodded back, maybe not in the comforting way he had, but still it did bring him relief to know she would try to hold on. As the monotone chants droned on, Kiara gripped his hand like her last hold on a ledge as she hung over an abyss, all the while touching the stranger's to her left as little as she could. She closed her eyes and tried to focus on holding on, not on the disappointments, not on the uncertainties, but simply on holding on. Though she would be deprived of even that as her concentration was ripped from her with a sudden tug to her arm. Kiara looked to her left to see the figures marching again, and if she didn't follow, she'd soon be dragged. She went to tug Hadyn along, but he needed no prompting, the stranger on the other side of him all but ready to trample him if he didn't get moving. Everyone knew it was time, everyone but the two of them. Drawing a shaky breath, Kiara mimicked the rest of the figures, each playing follow the leader with the next. As usual, she realized all too late just how wrong it was for them to be here.

It was all wrong, standing with the rest of these, acting like they believed, following along in worship. Her skin crawled with a thousand skittering legs as the voices hissed in her ears. Despite her attempts to hold on, her grip alone was simply not enough to keep her from falling. She felt herself diminish inside and her light go out. Because sometimes when you hope for something so greatly and that something doesn't happen, it is then that the greatest amount of hope is destroyed.

So she slipped away, cowering into some place in her mind where she could hide, and after much circling, hand holding, and bowing, the black tide of pilgrims, at last, began another journey and receded.

Still, Kiara did not come out of her mind. She didn't have to, her only task, to follow without question the person four steps ahead of her. She followed and she followed, out of the ritual sanctuary, passed the guards with the toothed spears, through the narrow tunnel, and out into the path of torches. And even when the world grew dimmer and the walking shadows began to disperse on the edges of her vision, still she followed.

A tug on her hand pulled her out of line. He made her look at him and she raised her gaze to his, but her eyes didn't see him. She looked straight through him. Hadyn searched her face. Her cold expression worried him. She didn't know what to believe, and if he was honest, neither did he.

"Come on," he said, his voice hoarse with held back emotions. "We need to get back to Cida."

Besides a tear slipping from her shining eyes, she didn't change, she didn't move. Prepared to guide her the whole way back, Hadyn began to tug her along, but she wouldn't budge. Kiara wrenched her hand from his and started the long dark walk back to the Forbiddens.

Chapter Thirty Five

THE PURE ONE

Without another word passed between them, they arrived back just before the bell struck one lonely toll. One after the other, they walked into their meeting room where Cida sat anxiously by the light of a single lantern. Despite the sleep pulling on her lids, when she heard their footsteps, she popped straight to her feet.

"You're back! Oh, thank goodness, you're safe."

Neither returned the greeting. The first thing Hadyn did was peel the heavy cloak off his back, ball it up and hurl it behind a toothy row of stalagmites. Kiara pushed straight past Cida and all the questions in her eyes and hurled herself into a corner and pulled her hood lower over her face, leaving Cida to spin around, hands palms up at her sides.

"Yes, good to see you both too." When Kiara didn't move, she flopped her hands to her sides. "Won't you at least tell me what happened? Hadyn?"

Trying his best not to take Kiara's treatment towards him personally, Hadyn sat on the edge of his bunk and gave a sad shrug. "You were right, Cida."

Lucida sighed and her shoulders slumped with heavy resign. Kneeling down in front of Kiara, she watched her own fidgeting hands and asked, "Would it make you feel any better if I told you, I didn't want to be?" Kiara hugged her knees and stared out from under her hood at nothing. "That actually I was hoping against even things certain that I was wrong?" She questioned her gently with a raise of her eyebrows, placing a hand on her knee, but Kiara might as well have been part of the stone wall of the cavern for all the reaction she gave her.

Lucida sighed. She had tried the loving approach, treating her like the fragile piece of glass she seemed like sometimes, and had come up dry, so she decided to switch tactics and offer her some tough love . . . even if it was the wrong decision.

"Well, it's true and I won't have none of," she waved a hand in front of her blank stare, "this. 'Cause what's more? You're not the only one stuck here, Missy. You're not the only one that this affects."

Kiara's eyes flared with offense, shocked that she could actually think that was the reason for her silence, then she cooked her a remorselessly sour glare.

"Oh, you're looking at me now?"

"You actually think that's how I feel?" Kiara asked.

Cida looked down. "No. But your pouting like this isn't going to make things better."

Deliberately frowning, Kiara turned and resumed her blank stare.

"Oh, come on, those were words. You actually said some things. Don't retreat now."

Kiara shot to her feet, leaving Cida to crane her neck to look up at her. "You think I don't know those things? I know it doesn't just affect me. I know, maybe better than anyone, that this affects everyone!" Her eyes softened and she looked at both her companions in turn. "But most of all, this affects both of you, because I told you to hope, and I let you down. You followed *me* . . . and I failed you." Her gaze grew distant and hopeless and she fell back against the cave wall. "It's all my fault."

Cida stood and put her hands on Kiara's arms. "No, it's not. And what fault? No harm was done here tonight. Maybe you didn't find an escape, but at least you tried. So what if I was right? If you listened to me every time I was afraid of something, we would never get out of here. Hadyn and I, we were completely free to say no to you, but we made the choice to help you. We wanted to. We may not have found our key to freedom yet, but you know what you do have the freedom to do?"

Kiara turned her eyes up to her without raising her head.

Cida smiled softly and slid the back side of her finger down Kiara's nose to the tip where a tear had collected. "Fail. You have the freedom to fail."

Kiara's eyes narrowed in astonishment.

"And I'll do it with you." Hadyn hopped to the ground to join them. "I'd rather fail and fail again with you than sit another day in this musty dungeon simply rotting little by little. So what've you got in mind? Give me those crazy, dangerous ideas from the deepest vaults of your boundless curiosity. Because whatever we do, I'm with *you*."

Hadyn didn't know if he had said all the right things or even if he should have spoken at all, but when it managed to pull a smile and then even a soft laugh from her lips, all uncertainty evaporated as fast as a puff of smoke. Cida's approving smile didn't hurt either.

"And so am I," Cida seconded.

Kiara smiled at them both. She didn't have to say anything. The gratitude shined in her eyes. But then her smile faded and she looked down. "But I don't have any ideas in some deep vault. That was it. I really thought that would be it . . ."

"Well, maybe we just need to *learn* some more before we can go and do." Hadyn grinned at her.

She shook her head and bounced with a chuckle. "Alright. You win. Tomorrow night we'll read the whole time Cida's here."

"Why tomorrow?" Cida asked.

Kiara sighed. "Because you need to rest so you get better."

"Rubbish! Rest is for infants and the elderly, not to mention the dead. Do I look like any of the three?" Kiara just grinned at her. "After a night like tonight, no one will be sleeping anytime soon anyway, trust me."

Kiara shook her head. "Urgh! Where is that blasted journal?"

In accordance with their routine, Hadyn sat up on his bunk and read to them while Kiara pondered the words with the intensity of a meat mallet in the hands of an angry butcher, and Cida fought sleep off as persistently as a sloth.

Day Fifty Two

I can not forget the dreadful turn of events, still a fresh and open wound of the recent past, but I will not deny my sheer happiness just to have my sister back. Celia is still unwell, but that does not stop us from enjoying each other as a family and creating our very own little light of joy. The James will not be so easily snuffed. And not all has been dismal darkness. Just the other day we found out we share our residence with a little family of mice. I have taken to sharing scraps of our bread and cheese with them and already they will eat right from the palm of my hand. I consider them wonderful companions. A small act of defiance, I'll admit, but it's enough to keep me sane for now.

We gather around Celia's bed each night, Mr. Mouse and family included, and listen to father tell us stories, some that he has kept locked in his memory from when his parents told them to him as a boy, and some he spins just for our own delight. I still hear Mother humming softly from time to time. I just fear the day it will all have to end.

When Hadyn finished the entry all Kiara could do was sigh. He watched her carefully, but she didn't meet his eyes.

"Please keep reading."

At her wish Hadyn turned his attention back to the book.

Day Fifty Three

A grey haired man came to our house today, asking if Cecilia James lived here. He had kind eyes and a contagious smile. I assumed he must be Elijah, the man Celia had told me about. The Pure One . . . My first thought was to be rude and turn him away, but it's not too often that I see a face as kind as his anymore and the very thought that he remembered Celia and wondered about her disappearance, warmed my heart. I introduced myself and brought him to Celia's room.

She was so happy to see him, I instantly felt awful for even thinking about sending him away.

He said he came to see her because he couldn't imagine how she was getting by without his unrivaled stories.

This got a laugh out of Celia and I liked him from that moment on.

He told us a few very entertaining stories, or maybe they only appeared so because of how badly all three of us longed to see our home again.

Celia said as much. "I miss the sunshine and soft green grass under my toes."

"I miss the river behind our house and the way the birds always used to sing in the branches just over the water," I added.

"Aye," Elijah agreed. "I miss a lot of things. Most of my family stayed behind with the Brotherhood."

My heart broke for him and suddenly I felt like I couldn't complain after that.

"But I trust my God will get me through," he countered.

That's where he lost me. I told him I didn't understand. Wondered how he still trusted the god that just destroyed our whole planet? "

Elijah shook his head slowly, eyes closed in peace. "No. I believe the world still exists up there because I trust my God."

Now he had my attention.

"Let me tell you a story."

I almost laughed, but then I looked at Cece's pleading eyes and sat down on the edge of her bed.

Elijah told me a story I've heard before, the story of Noah and the Ark. He said there was one time and one time alone that God sent a catastrophe so great it destroyed the face of the earth, leaving only one man and his family alive.

This meant nothing to me. In my opinion, He did it once, nothing's stopping him from doing it again. It doesn't matter how much time has passed in between. But then Elijah said something I'll never forget.

God promised not too.

He said, He made a covenant with Noah and promised to never do it again. Elijah, then produced a small book from a pocket. The little thing was plain and ripped, but suddenly, beyond my own reckoning, I felt I was in the presence of something undeniably holy.

Elijah found the place quickly as if he had come to it many times of late, and read. I asked him if I could write down the words.

This is what it said,

Then the LORD said in His heart, "I will never again curse the ground for man's sake, although the imagination of man's heart is evil from his youth; nor will I again destroy every living thing as I have done. While the earth remains, seedtime and harvest, cold and heat, winter and summer, and day and night shall not cease."

Genesis 8:21-22

Hadyn froze, staring awestricken at the book in his lap.

Kiara cocked her head. "What is it?"

"It's just those words . . . they're different somehow."

"You mean the handwriting?"

"No." He shook his head. "It's still Maddie's patient handwriting, but the words aren't hers."

"Well, of course they're not. They were copied down from a different book."

"But it's not just that . . ." He looked at her, a quiet reverence sparking some kind of unworldly wonder in his eyes. "It's like they're more important. More important than anything I've ever read before."

Kiara wouldn't have said it herself, but deep inside she could feel it. The same thing glowing in Hadyn's eyes, had ignited in her heart as he read the words. She just wanted to ignore it.

"Well, I suppose you're right," she said.

"That's because they were spoken by the Creator," Cida

spoke up for the first time since they started reading.

Kiara puffed a deriding breath as she turned to her. "I thought you were asleep."

Cida rolled her eyes. "Kiara, this is the God your mother believed in."

"*Believes*," Kiara spat. "She's still out there, Cida."

"I'm sorry. That is not what I meant. It just slipped out that way."

"It's fine," she said, but it didn't sound fine.

"Wait, the queen believed in a Creator other than Fleard?" Hadyn asked.

"Yes. The same one I hear rumors of from the servants and in the market," Cida answered.

"I guess I know what you're talking about. I never gave it much thought because, like you said, it's always in rumors, always a secret. But my mother, whenever she grew especially fed up and braver about the consequences, would talk of something similar, sometimes mentioning a secret group of people who believe in that which is forbidden."

Kiara looked at him in astonishment. "Unbelievable! Of course you two know another thing I don't. Blast my ignorance! People believe this? There are others? Why have you never spoken of this before?"

"Well, like I said," Hadyn began, "it was always just a whole lot of rumors."

"And that's changed how?"

"This!" He slammed the back of his hand into the journal, more out of excitement than anger. "This changes everything! Kiara, this is the same Creator! He was here at the beginning and he's still here now."

"So?"

"How do you not see this? Why do you think Caverna has fought so hard to keep this a secret, to snuff this out? You think it's because it's a bunch of foolish, useless talk? And in spite of all their attempts at eradication, this is the Creator who has survived through generations of secrecy, in reverent whispers and hidden places just like this one here!"

Feeling like it was all she had, Kiara remained defiant, squashing the bright smiles in his eyes. "And what of it? Why do you care if He's real or not?"

"Because this Creator is directly connected to the outside

world."

That got her to stop. She had no words to add.

"Hadyn's right." Cida scooted closer on her hands. "There's a reason why it's secret. Why would someone go to great lengths to cover up something that's just another made up, meaningless fake."

"They wouldn't," Kiara said. "No one would." Though the realization only made her feel more sad. Because the more real He looked, the more punished she felt.

"Can we just keep reading?"

Hadyn sighed and found his place after the part copied out of Elijah's book.

Elijah said God created the rainbow for a symbol of His promise.

For the rest of the time Elijah stayed and talked, I couldn't help but long to see a rainbow one last time just to look at it in this new light.

"What's a rainbow?" Hadyn asked.

Kiara smiled in spite of herself. "I don't know. From what I've gathered, they're in the sky, but they hide away most of the time, only coming out after it rains. They're like a bow of every color you can imagine." Her smile faded. "Really just another thing said to be given to us from the Creator that we can't even see."

Hadyn sighed.

"I'm sorry. Go ahead and read on."

Day Fifty Four

Celia and I talked a lot about what Elijah said after he left, and still, today, we can't stop thinking about it. It's like I have hope for the first time, maybe even in my life. Hope for a better life, hope for true freedom. When I rationalize within myself, I think I have no reason to trust this God over any of the others I've been told to believe in, except that I've never felt this way before.

Speaking of never feeling this way before, I don't think I've ever hated someone more than I hate the man that showed up at our door today unannounced.

When I answered the door and saw Salin, I thought of slamming it right on his smug face, but I am a reasonable person, so I thought it might be wise to maybe use words first, if not the most minced.

"What are you doing here?" I asked him tersely, only barely acknowledging the stranger accompanying him.

"I heard that your sister is yet unwell. This calls for some concern," he said. The scar on his face was scabbed over, but still appeared very gruesome and

painful.

I didn't care what he cared about and asked him politely to go away, but he insisted. Said he brought his best physician, the top researcher on the town's new diet, the diet that he couldn't have created without me.

Yes, I suppose I did recognize the doctor. But I caught it this time, his trying to manipulate me. Before I could be charmed, I made the distinction. I would not be so easily deceived ever again.

He ended by saying so genuinely, "Maddie, I want to help."

"Don't call me that," I said fiercely and crossed my arms, but realized quickly enough, this behavior would most likely not be tolerated for much longer as our high king became ever more comfortable with his position of lordship. With a sigh, I lead them to Celia's room.

My sister was not happy about this in the slightest, but after the doctor looked her over he seemed to have an idea of what could be wrong and gave her some medicine that could help.

Before they left, Salin made sure to tell me that he had meant what he said just before he had entered the realm of the watchers. He looked as though he wanted to say something more, ever continuing to perplex me, but I thanked them both politely and sent them on their way, not saying another word to him.

Glad to be rid of him.

With the end of the entry and the sudden silence that followed, Cida snorted to life, her chin falling out of the palm of her hand.

Kiara rolled her eyes.

"Huh? What did I miss?"

"See. This is what I didn't want to happen."

"I'm sorry. I've been awake for most of it, really."

Kiara stood up and waved her hands down at her. "No, it's fine. You didn't miss a single thing. I'm sure of it. Just more useless information. This whole thing has been an incredible waste of our time." She sighed. "I'm going to bed. And you would too, Cida, if you know what's good for you."

As she stomped off, Hadyn's gaze met Cida's. They exchanged thoughtful glances for a short moment, then Hadyn turned to follow after her.

"I would leave her be this time, if I were you. There's not much helping her when the person she's angry with is herself."

Hadyn looked at her painfully. "But I have to try."

"In the morning. Let her sleep on it. It's been another long night. You should rest yourself. Then you can try."

With that, Cida sauntered out of the cavern, the stone walls catching her soft coughs and delivering them to him long after she was gone.

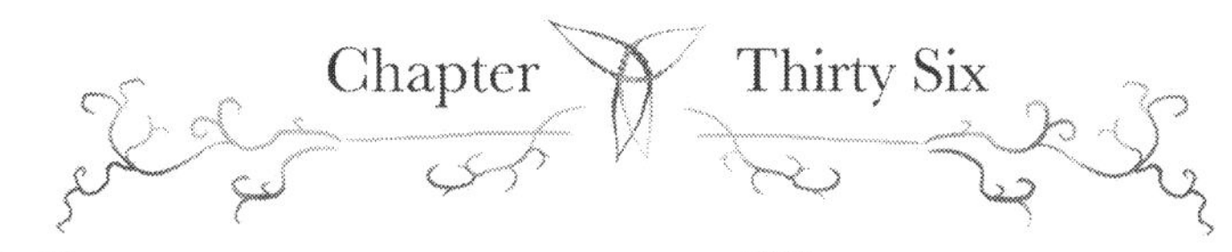

What are Promises if not to be Kept?

Kiara awoke to the sound of soft shuffling and clinking. Prying open her eyes, the flickering light of a lantern seeped into her squinted lids, and not just from the one she tried to keep lit all night. A dark shadow loomed across the wash of the light and Kiara sat bolt upright, heart racing in her chest. Her flight inciting fears melted to sheer confusion however, when she saw Hadyn at the far side of the room, now kneeling down under a low hanging lantern and fiddling with something laid out on the ground.

Kiara narrowed her eyes and realized he wasn't aware she was awake. She cleared her throat expectantly.

At the sound, Hadyn jumped like he had been caught doing something terribly wrong and clanked his head smartly into the metal lantern hanging so dangerously above him. Kiara stifled her snickers into a snort and got up to see just what in the world he was up to.

"Oh! Kiara, you're awake."

"Yes . . ." Kiara took hold of the lantern he had sent swaying to still it. "And wondering with some concern just what you're doing here."

Hadyn rubbed the back of his head. "Sorry. I wanted to leave before you woke up. But I wasn't finished yet."

"Finished with what?"

He gave her that bashful smile of his and a red glow crept into his cheeks. "This."

Kiara moved to where he gestured for her to stand, all confusion and amusement dissolving from her face. There, laid out on the stone floor, was a work of art. Hundreds of gemstones shimmered in the light, arranged in the form of an arc. Hadyn had used every color, though they weren't uniform like the real thing, for he had only his imagination for a guide. The colors flowed into each other in a liquid, fluid way. Sometimes clumping in larger groups of yellow or greens, but then melding into a blue or orange, and other times mingling altogether in areas of no rules at all.

Kiara's eyes flicked to the empty chest against the wall, lid propped open, then back to the masterpiece. It must have taken him hours to put together.

"What's this?" Was all she could manage to say, her eyes roving over it in astonishment.

Hadyn shrugged. "I thought it might help. That the promise might mean more to you, if you could see it."

Kiara turned to him, sadness in her eyes and a fragile smile on her lips. Her heart swelled with a warmth, quickly spreading into her cheeks and such a foreign feeling of unfathomable gratitude. So unaccustomed to its wonderful embrace, she didn't even know what to do with it. She wanted to cherish it, store it up for when she needed it most, but something in her held her back. She felt a wall go up. Unlike the warmth, the wall was very familiar and she knew it was meant to protect her. For whatever reason, she felt she needed it, to keep her safe. And so it rose, just as the tears started to well in her eyes, and she regained some distance.

"Thank you," she said with more control, almost like a royal receiving a mandatory gift, and the amount of light that faded from his eyes nearly killed her. "It's beautiful."

Hadyn smiled bravely.

"And it does help, very much," she said.

Hadyn blinked. "Oh. Well, you're welcome."

"How could I ever repay you?"

His smile fell completely. "You don't. You don't have to do anything. Kiara, I did this for you; not for me."

"Yes, but something that kind doesn't deserve to go unappreciated."

"But you did appreciate it . . ."

"Oh, come on." She cocked her head. "I'll think of something. But let's eat breakfast first."

Reluctantly, Hadyn followed and they ate their meal with a side of nearly unbroken silence. Despite the awkward breakfast however, the rest of the day went fairly normal as they read and played Backlobash and tried to come up with new rules for the game, because they were both tiring of it.

As much as they had learned and taught themselves ways on how to make the days go by, on how to cope with the boredom, it was an ever intensifying boredom and an increasingly difficult job to accomplish. Kiara didn't know what she would do without Hadyn, even with him, by the end of the day she couldn't ignore the growing urge to rip her hair out one fistful at a time. And the day only got better because when Cida dropped by that night, to Kiara's great "joy," they continued her most favorite pastime, resuming their usual activity of nightly journal readings. Little did she or any of them know, it would be their very last time participating in the aforementioned routine.

Day Fifty Seven

Celia seems on the road to recovery. She has more energy and a little bit more fire, I might add. Things look promising for a full recovery. I am extremely grateful, I just hate to have to owe my gratitude to Salin.

It does leave me to wonder though, what sector of work they will place her in, now that there is no livestock.

Hadyn gave a small smile at the rare, fortunate turn of events and with nothing to add, continued on to the next entry.

Day Sixty

"What!" Hadyn stopped himself before he even began and stared at the page, horror twisting his face.

"What? What is it?" Kiara shot up reflexively, but walked towards him slowly as if any sudden moves could trigger a terrible catastrophe.

"She's gone . . ." he read. Then he met her gaze, a terrible sadness pulling at his eyes. "My sister is gone."

"What?" Kiara lost her strength to stand up straight. "But she just said she was on the mend. She was getting better! They gave her the medicine. This can't be right!"

Kiara looked to Cida, but she looked just as confused and heartbroken as the two of them.

"This can't be right . . ." she whispered again, and collapsed back to the ground.

The harsh reality sank further, like a nail sinking into the flesh of her heel only to find bone, as Hadyn bravely continued to read, though she could tell it was painful for him too from the disjointed and choked sentences.

This doesn't feel like reality. I feel trapped in a glass world where every little thing could shatter with the lightest tap. My heart, if I even have one anymore, hurts so bad. I feel so alone.

I don't even understand. She was doing so well, only getting better, and then . . . gone.

I didn't even get to say goodbye. They took her body before I got home, because of some ridiculous reason about contagion?

The people have been talking . . . spreading rumors of a group above even Salin in command. They call them the Buried, because of the way they work beneath the surface. They have no names. They have no faces. It's as if they don't exist.

I don't know what I think. But if not them, I know Salin himself had something to do with this.

I'm so sick of all the lies. I want answers! I want justice. I will not be satisfied until I see, with my own eyes, Salin's wicked head on a spike.

Mother and father said she went peacefully . . . They were with her.

I just wished I could've said goodbye.

Hadyn held the book limply in his lap with a broken stare as if his heart had just been chucked into a void. Cida bowed her head, seemingly in respect, but also to hide her tears. But Kiara didn't feel sad. She felt the licks of the flames first, just the pricks of the sparks, but it didn't take long to fane and feed the hate. That burning seething hate. She knew its dangers, she knew its risks, but she needed its fire. What else could burn away this cold sorrow, this robbing numbness?

She hoped Salin got what he deserved in his time. Like Maddie, she would have given anything to see his wicked head on a spike. But a certain feeling told her he didn't. Because those are the kind of things that happened in this twisted life. Terrible men roam free to do more terrible things and good people, loved ones . . . are taken. They are cut short.

I wished I could have said goodbye . . . The last words of the entry drifted through her mind like tragic, restless ghosts, seeking peace never to find it. She should have been able to, but Cecelia had vanished. They took her before she even had a chance. Just like Kiara's mother and anyone else she had ever loved.

She shivered at the thought of the Buried. She would have dismissed it as a mere travesty concocted to distract gullible people from the true villains, if not for the fact that she had heard with her own ears the cold voice that seemed to command the very King of Caverna.

And to think of the ongoing abuse, the destruction of lives, and the deceptions used to cover up and do away with those blatant crimes. Yes, she already knew it well from her own life, but here it was at the very beginning. These people, these monsters, had been reeking hell with no consequences since the creation of this damned prison.

For some time she didn't see anything but the raging red of her own thoughts, and in the quiet of the sorrow fumigating the room, her thoughts sounded like a scream. Her hands balled into fists and they shook with violent tremors. The red, however, ebbed to the edges of her vision as she noticed movement in the room. Cida had recovered almost completely and had gotten up to walk across the room. Kiara watched her close the distance between herself and Hadyn and place a hand on his shoulder. Trying to make sense of the action, Kiara shifted her gaze to Hadyn and what she saw tilted her hastily wrought rage on an axis. A single tear dripped from his eye and slipped down his cheek. She hadn't expected him to cry. Why be sad about it when he could be angry? But something about the sight stole some of that rage and she realized with some concern that she couldn't get it back.

Cida, still resting a warm hand on his shoulder, turned her face to Kiara and offered her free hand. But Kiara remained sitting and averted her eyes from the gesture. She didn't need to be consoled or comforted because she wasn't sad. When she looked back, Cida had returned all her attention to Hadyn who was scanning the passage again, eyes still pleading it wasn't so.

Kiara sighed and her hands unclenched. "Hadyn, you don't have to read anymore. We can be done for the night."

"No." He nodded his head decidedly. "I want to."

With a nod of her own Cida retreated back to her spot. Kiara wouldn't have said it, but she didn't know if *she* wanted him to read anymore. Alas, he was braver than her and with a huff he began again.

I've lost count in these humdrum, mundane days. I only know it has been close to a year since my last entry, since . . . my sister's death.

Everything was changing so quickly before, but now life has come to a halting stop. Tommy Stone came for a visit today. I haven't seen him much since we lost her. I guess I pushed him away. I can't blame him for not coming around.

And no matter the distance between us, it was nice to see him.

There is not much else to report, except that I fall deeper into despair each day.

But before I go about my day, I've been thinking a lot about this and I thought I might just write it down before I forget. Half is the truth of the other half's lies. The first words will give you the necessary key.

Hadyn scrunched up his face. "What's that supposed to mean?"

Kiara shrugged. "Sounds like gibberish."

Cida looked more confused than both of them combined.

"Well," Hadyn's face scrunched further, "that's it for that day."

"Curious . . ." Kiara said

"Wait a minute." Hadyn's eyes roved over the page like a hound sniffing out something amiss. "This next part looks different. Her handwriting has always been patient, but this looks flawless. It seems to still be hers, but it's almost as if she took painstaking care that this entry remain legible."

"What does it say?" Kiara pressed, leaning forward where she sat.

Hadyn wrapped his fingers tighter around the journal and read slowly.

Day Seventy of the Second Year.

Never thought I'd say this, but I'm actually getting used to life here. Younger me would still be complaining. Younger me would have been ungrateful.

Haydn reared his head back, and muttered under his breath, "Since when?"

Kiara's brow bunched, her simmering anger creeping back up to a boil, and Cida looked absolutely lost.

Collecting himself, Hadyn took a deep breath and forced himself to continue.

Vanity has worked its evil on me, but I will be a slave to its devices no more. From now on, I will be content with what I have and be a great good to my community. Never again will I challenge authority. Younger me is gone. Verily I say, I will serve my king and respect the throne.

Remember

Hadyn stopped mid sentence, with a strange noise escaping his throat.

"What?" Kiara asked. "What is it?"

"That's it." He turned the page over with a frantic jerk. "There's nothing more. It looks like she didn't even finish."

Kiara shot to her feet and looked over his shoulder at the page. There, after the last word was an unintelligible scribble, as if she was made to stop in a panic. It seemed like it could have started with a *w*, but that's all that could be discovered. Hadyn grabbed up the rest of the pages and flew his fingers over them, flipping through each one, desperately hoping to find some clue or explanation for such a sudden and wild change in her posture and voice, but every scan came up blank and empty.

"Do you think they found out about the journal?" Hadyn's voice was choked with pain.

"They had to have at some point," Kiara said. "Why else would its key have been in the secret library? But who cares about that? What's all that rubbish about her coming to terms with her life?"

"Who cares?" Hadyn countered. "Kiara, they could have killed her!"

"They didn't kill her," she said dryly. "She had kids, didn't she? Married that Tommy Stone by the looks of it. Otherwise you wouldn't be here." Hadyn realized he couldn't argue with that logic and relaxed a fraction. "But what's more," Kiara continued, her voice rising with tension, "there's no reason to kill someone who's given in. Who's given up."

"I don't know," Cida chimed in. "It doesn't sound like her at all. It might be some sort of pledge."

"You think someone made her write it?" Hadyn asked.

"Perhaps."

"By whose volition it was, is not the point," Kiara said. "Pressured or not, she still wrote it."

"Kiara . . . put yourself in her shoes." Cida took on a parental tone in attempt to defuse the mounting tension. It did nothing to defuse, in fact, it did the exact opposite.

Kiara jabbed a finger into her own chest and spoke with a sharp stop after each word. "I am in her shoes." She threw the hand out to encompass them. "We all are!" She searched their faces, wondering how they didn't see what was right before their eyes. "Maddie refused to believe it was all over. We refuse to believe this is all there is. What's the difference?" She held up a finger and though her voice had lowered to a desperate whisper, she spoke clearly to make certain they understood. "One year. That's all it took. How long do you think it will take before we give up too?"

Her hands balled into fists at her sides once more and Hadyn noticed with a flicker of a glance.

"Her sister died," Hadyn tried to say. "It stole her hope."

"*Your* sister died. Hadyn, your mother died of a shattered soul. This place crushed her. You say your father killed her. And maybe he did. But do you think she would have given up, if she was free to leave, to get away and start a new life with the child she still had?"

Hadyn's jaw clenched and he looked away. Maybe it wasn't her place. He had told her those things in confidence, but she didn't know how else to make him realize what she so clearly saw.

"They broke her. A person who had seen the far reaches of the world, who had lived a free life and they broke her. You don't think the last entry sounds like her; that's because she went mad. This place drove her to the very edge of insanity until she believed the same lies she was trying to fight. Don't you see? Even if there is a world out there, there is no way to get to it. We can never get out!"

Hadyn's lips went tight in a twisted frown and he shook his head. "No. You don't believe that."

A dark shadow passed across her expression and she cocked her head defiantly. "Don't I?"

He held her gaze, pleading with his eyes while she remained cold. Kiara broke the stare first, in her heart, not giving up, but moving on. Standing up, she began to walk away.

"Stop!" Cida spoke with an authority as rare for her as the alexandrite stone Kiara had once given to a friend in hope. A hope that Cida knew she was throwing away. "Just stop!" Kiara jumped and stopped in her tracks. "You said you wouldn't give up." Cida's voice broke and the short lived fire was doused. "You promised."

Kiara turned her head half way, her silhouette shadowy in the outskirts of the lantern's glow, but she wouldn't look at either of them. "Yes, well . . . promises are broken everyday."

And with those as her parting words, Kiara left them, dissolving into the shadows of the caverns like a phantom, devoid of every tangible thing, and found her way back to her hideaway without a light for the first time. She ran a limp hand along the cold, clammy walls of the tunnel, and yet, compared to the deadness in her heart, they felt warm. No fire she had ever known could restart this forge, long cold, due only to her own neglect.

She stumbled through the dark, though she never felt lost, or at the very least didn't fear it. She had been lost her whole life. What made any difference now?

She felt her soul slipping by and she didn't even try to reach for it. A familiar feeling, when everything and nothing matter all at once, it didn't take long for her to recognize it, but after years of its unwelcome visits, never once introducing itself, she had given up on trying to identify or define it, except for the slipping, but not just of her soul; of every feeling, dream, will, and hope. Down they went, the bad with the good, into a pit where everything, abstract and concrete, is reduced to a muddled grey, vomited from the dispassionate, sour stomach of a creature born both of apathy and the despondent lie of self isolation.

A weak glow in the distance caught her gaze. There wasn't a doubt in her mind that it was her hideaway, but that didn't mean she didn't question how, feeling a dull sense of surprise to see a light left lit, when she clearly remembered dousing all the lanterns before she left. But surprise is a far cry from comfort.

As she drew nearer to the light and she could make out more shapes, the mineral and rock formations confirmed what she already knew. Everything was familiar. She knew this place well. Locating the fissure, she turned sideways and slipped inside her cavern. Then, as she made it through the narrow gap and turned to face the room, she just stared in, her gaze as hollow as ever.

One of the flames of the hanging lantern danced with a feeble flicker. She narrowed her eyes at it, unsure how it was even possible, but too tired to concoct any explanations. Finding the mysterious light nothing more than an irritating nuisance, she strode across the floor of her cavern, prepared to snuff it out. Her feet fell in heavy clomps. Stopping at the lantern, she raised a hand to open the small, glass door and froze utterly still. There on the floor, below the lantern, was a splash of color, a masterpiece in its own right. Hadyn's rainbow . . . exactly where she left it. So why was she so surprised to see it? The individual gems caught even the dimmest of glows and sparkled with a calming quality in her steadily blurring eyes. The sight cracked something in her slipping, hollow soul and she felt something. Here she was ready to give up, to despair, and muck about in the thought that the world was in a mire, told they could rise above it. With false hope, they make themselves believe they can achieve total separation from the slop, only to fall back down deeper than before, destined to fail. That's what she wanted to think, destined to fail and incapable of doing good. But she couldn't. She was robbed of even the most meager comfort of succumbing, all because this one thing, simple as it was, preventing her. Because Hadyn *had* done good.

She remembered what he had said about doing it for her and not himself.

But can people actually act outside of selfish ambition?

When she thought about it, Hadyn and Cida were a bigger reason than she would have first thought, as to why she couldn't believe those things. Two people who had been nothing but kind to her, nothing *but* good to her. Her eyes roved over the abstract rainbow. Hadyn, a boy who had done nothing but respect her, and yet his own opinion of himself was so terrible.

The tears that had filled in her eyes ran down her cheeks as she fought to understand this upside down world. She crumbled to her knees, in front of the crystal mosaic. Raising her head to the limitless black above her, the tears fell from her eyes like a steady rain.

"How can I have faith in any promises you make?" she spoke without care of her volume. "What reason do I have to trust you?"

When no answer came, she hung her head and wept into her hands.

What rainbow could be born of this storm? she thought and stood to remove herself from this wretched state.

With one hand on the lantern to keep it steady, she opened the little door with the other. Giving one last, teary glance at the art on her floor, she whispered to the nothing around her in a choked voice, "What are promises, if not to be kept?"

Then with a quick puff of breath, she blew out the light and threw herself into darkness.

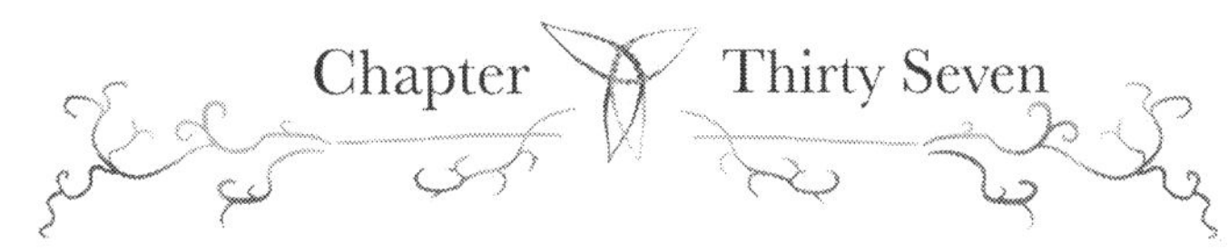

Chapter Thirty Seven

Business as Usual

That morning, when Kiara woke up, there was no shuffling or clinking of gemstones falling into place. There was only silence, emptiness, darkness, and the bile of nightmares on her tongue. For the first time in a long time she went to sleep in total darkness and awoke in darkness. It chilled her to think she hadn't cared. It frightened her to think of the things she was feeling the night before. She didn't want to think like this, but she didn't see another option.

Shaking a quivering shiver, she fumbled in the dark to light a lantern that she could carry with her about the room. She walked over to the gems Hadyn had laid out on the floor, a riot of color compared to her muddled thoughts of grey.

He would most likely leave her be to give her space, most likely heeding the motherly advice of Cida, but she didn't want to be alone. This was life now and she didn't plan on wallowing; only living normally.

As she began to go about her morning business, the bells struck ten times and she couldn't believe how long she had slept, but more importantly, she couldn't believe how long it had been since she saw Tick, and decided she would pay him a visit today. But first she would find Hadyn and see what he was up to.

As she made her way through the caverns, Kiara felt a strange lightening of her heart as if lead weights chained to its very valves had been unlocked and lifted off, and though the feeling was as preposterous as it was bathetic, she chose to simply shrug and be grateful for it. She was feeling the initial result of changing one's outlook on a poor situation into a positive one. As you've most likely experienced, you feel better . . . for a time, but if the heart doesn't change as well, it will never last. Though in some instances, I'm not convinced the heart needs to change or even should.

Kiara could make out the glow of a distant lantern now and slowed her pace as she wondered how he might act, but she shook the hindrances away, content with the fact that she could only control her own behavior.

Nearing the cavern, she rapped out an echoing percussion on the cave wall with light taps of her knuckles. “Knock, knock,” she sang, before rounding the corner.

Hadyn sat on his bunk, a book in his lap and his nose in its pages. His gaze was so intense, Kiara was surprised he didn’t burn a hole in the book, and his concentration so fixed that even when he looked up, he scarcely saw her, a short nub of a pencil sticking out from his mouth and his brow remaining scrunched as he fought to understand something disconcerting. Kiara could tell he was tired from the way his left eyelid drooped more than usual. Hadyn blinked twice and recognition dawned on his face.

He pulled the pencil from his mouth and swallowed down a build up of saliva. “Kiara?” he said, and there was no small degree of surprise in his voice.

Kiara stretched her arms to her sides with a satisfying yawn. “Mornin’.”

“Did you just wake up?”

“Pretty much. Though I can see you can’t say the same. What, did you stay up all night?”

Hadyn gave a small raise of his eyebrows as if he was annoyed, but said nothing more, and Kiara decided not to ask.

“Surprised to see me?” she said, smiling.

Words evaded him. Hadyn couldn’t tell if it was lack of sleep or something else entirely, but he was feeling especially intolerant, and it couldn’t be helped. With a tight shake of his head, he scrunched his brow and looked at her in utter confusion, disbelief, and exasperation all at once, while Kiara simply continued to smile.

“I don’t get you,” he finally said. “Last night, it was like you were a whole different person. All that talk of giving up and breaking promises? I was worried about you. So no, to answer your question, I did not expect to see you. Oh, but this morning, you stride out here like your world and the one around you has always just been a bright, cheery place, without a touch of shadow. And what is this?” He narrowed his eyes and raised his hands, palms up, towards her. “You’re smiling? I mean, wha . . .?” His breath died in his throat as if this was just too much.

She couldn’t help but chuckle at how worked up he was getting. "I hadn't had time to contemplate yet," she stated with a shrug.

"Contemplate what exactly?" he said, trying hard to sound patient.

"Life. It may sound silly to you, but if this is my life now, I refuse to do the expected and feel sorry for myself. I will move on and live my life."

"If not for freedom, what is there to live for? Kiara, do you hear yourself? You talk to two people." He raised two fingers to emphasize his point. "And one of them, you only get to see for a few short hours after a constricting curfew. You are prevented from seeing anyone else and confined to a series of inhospitable caverns that were never meant to be lived in."

"That's fine . . ." she said with an uncertain quiver. "I don't want to talk to anyone else. And that's three people. You forgot about Tick. Actually, I was on my way to see him."

"Oh, my apologies for forgetting to mention a man who forgets just about everything else. What do you think made him like that, Kiara? You used to know."

"I don't know. Maybe he was hit on the head. Or is it so hard to believe he was born like that?"

Hadyn couldn't help it any longer. He burst with laughter and he didn't care.

Kiara frowned at him. "Make fun of me all you want. I'll just add you to the list of people who refuse to take my feelings seriously."

"I'm not making fun of you," he said, still smiling, but then he grew rather serious, rather quickly. "I'm laughing because it's comical. It's comical that you would believe your own lies when you have frowned upon others who have done the same. And let me tell you, the irony is priceless." Hadyn let the dig find its mark and returned his attention to the book in his lap. But when Kiara didn't retaliate with fire like he expected her to and only stood there wordless, he squeezed his eyes shut and he sighed.

"Look . . . I'm only telling you these things because I care."

When, again, she didn't even make an attempt to defend herself or argue with him, Hadyn realized just how off she was acting. His eyes grew sad like he just didn't understand.

Kiara rolled her eyes. "Please don't look at me like that."

Unaware of his own expression or how he could fix it, Hadyn diverted his whole face back to the book. And for the first time Kiara noticed just what piece of literature had captivated so much of his attention. Maddie James' journal lay open on his lap to her very last entry. Though it wasn't the last entry anymore. On the once blank page next to it, Hadyn had scribbled away until he had filled it with hundreds of hardly legible notes and countless graphite smudges, matching those on the side of his right hand.

She moaned. "Please, tell me you did not stay up all night doing what I think you've been doing."

Hadyn avoided looking up and tapped the butt of the pencil against his other hand. "What do you think I've been doing?"

"Seriously?"

"Not all night."

"Unbelievable." She threw her hands in the air and looked as though she might walk away right that very second.

"Kiara, I really think there's something more to this ending than just a simple surrender. There's something off. It's like I can smell it, like an awful stench."

She smirked. "You can smell it?"

He closed his eyes in exasperation and his whole frame slumped. "You know what I mean. I think she could have been trying to say something here. Something that's not clear, but hidden under everything else that is."

"Do you know how crazy that sounds? You've probably read that entry over a hundred times by now. If *you* haven't seen it yet, how are you or anyone else for that matter, ever going to?"

"No, no." He raised a hand and shook his head. "You said *Maddie* had gone crazy, but I won't let you call me crazy, because I don't know anyone who would classify your behavior of late as particularly sane."

Kiara grinned, astonished. "Hadyn, I haven't lost my mind. I'm just," Her shoulders slumped and her face fell. "So tired . . . of trying . . . of failing."

"Then rest," Hadyn's reply was simple, yet carried a desperation that contradicted that simplicity twice over. "If you're too tired to win, then rest. Just like your mom used to say. How does it go?"

"Rest today, so you can fight even harder tomorrow . . ." She laughed softly, but it faded to a sigh. A pang of acute missing stabbed her heart. If the letter from her mother was authentic, and she had no real reason to believe it wasn't, could she really go through with giving up and leaving her out there?

She stared at the opposite wall with a hollow unbroken gaze, unaware of how closely Hadyn watched her.

"Did you have another nightmare?"

With a slow blink she faced him. "How'd you know?"

"Just a guess," he lied, knowing her eyes never looked that green unless she had been crying recently.

"A good guess . . . but I don't want to talk about it." With another sigh, she crossed over to where he sat and hunched to take a look over his shoulder.

She squinted at the atrocious, scratched out notes. "Can you even read any of this?"

"Yes," Hadyn said defensively. "I wasn't at the orphanage for their academic studies, you know."

Kiara pulled her lips in to stop from smiling. "Sorry. So . . . have you found *anything* out?"

"Well, I—" he scanned over the notes as if searching for something, anything. ". . . No."

"Hadyn, don't feel bad. If there's nothing there, you can't blame yourself for not finding it."

"But there is something there, Kiara! I know it."

Kiara straightened. "Fine. I know I can't make you stop. You go ahead and do what you will and I'll do what I will. And *I* am going to see Tick."

"I'm coming with you." Hadyn slapped the journal shut and jumped to the ground, his feet clad in nothing but his stockings.

Kiara made no indication that she felt either way about his coming and simply began walking.

Hadyn rushed to put on his shoes and, hopping while he pulled one on, he called, "Don't you want to eat first?"

"Already did," Kiara's words echoed back to him.

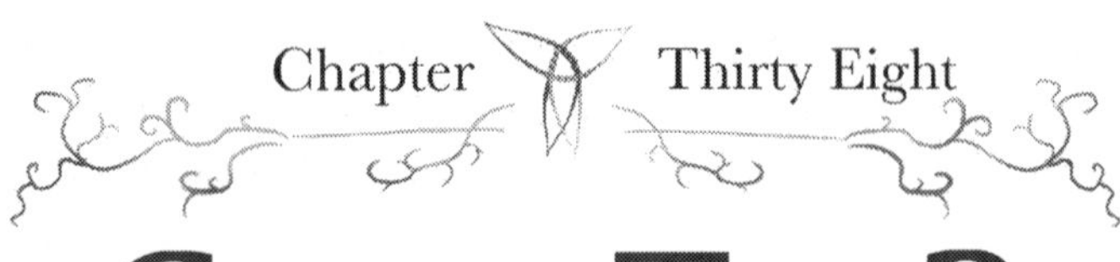

Chapter Thirty Eight

Cold Tea?

When Hadyn had finally managed to wrestle his shoes onto his feet and achieve a pace fast enough to catch up to Kiara, they walked beside each other in a companionable silence. Kiara held the lantern and lit the way while Hadyn clutched the journal close to him under his left arm.

Kiara eyed him judgmentally. "I can't believe you're bringing that thing."

At first he didn't understand, his thoughts tangled up in hidden messages. He followed her gaze to his arm. "Oh, well you better believe it. Besides, maybe Tick can help."

Just then, they came to Tick's door. Kiara knocked, turning to him and raising a copper brow. "Really? The man who forgets just about everything?" She put a hand on her chin. "Do you remember who said that?"

Hadyn felt his blood pressure rising as he opened his mouth to retort, but the words never left his throat, the thick door swinging open and washing them both in the glow of Tick's little home. Kiara turned to him with a beaming smile, but as always, Tick squinted and scrunched his brow questioningly at both of them. He rubbed the lenses of his quirky goggles as if he knew them, but something was distorting the way he saw them.

Then he gasped and an enormous grin split his face from one ear to the other. "Oh! Dear faces of dear friends. Come in! Come in!" He ushered them inside, pulling them by the hands. Closing the door behind them, he laid a hand on both of their shoulders and just let his eyes rest on their faces for a moment. "Oh, I've missed you." His eyes wandered. "It has been long enough to miss you since I last saw you, correct?"

Kiara laughed. "Yes, Tick. Perhaps too long."

"Well," he clapped his hands like a small boy, "you're here

now. To what do I owe this visit after 'too long,' Bright Eyes?"

"I just wanted to see you."

"And great is my thankfulness that you did. Though . . ." He scratched his head, adding to the mayhem of his black locks. "What should we do? What we did last time is rather hazy, I must confess."

Hadyn laughed. "You showed us how Herbert and Aubrey can collapse their ribs to fit into the most shockingly small cracks."

"Oh, that's right! Fun times. Shall we do that again?" Tick asked and began to whistle for his mice friends.

"No!" Kiara blurted. As her battle between fascination and disgust over the aforementioned activity had yet to produce a victor. "I mean . . ." she raised two crafty brows,"if they're not around, they could be sleeping, and we should let them rest."

Tick smiled warmly. "Always so thoughtful. Oh! I know! I'll make us some tea and we can just talk."

"That sounds wonderful."

Tick skipped over to his cramped kitchen and began to open and slam every one of the few cupboards he had. And when he came to the last one and still did not find what he was looking for, he proceeded to rewind and do it all over again.

Kiara stood in the middle of the room, near Tick's sand contraption. As hard as she tried to keep them contained, her eyes began to wander, the one piece of her where her curiosity could not be chained. She had always been able to keep her hands to herself and even her tongue could be bridled if such a great need arose, but her eyes remained as untamable as her wild curls. She tried to focus on the draining sand, each grain cascading into the jar below the last. She reminded herself she was now content with her life, but it was like it knew her name and called out to her in pulsing chants to find it again, each time wearing her resolve down a little more. Despite her best efforts, her roving eyes danced over the sand jar contraption and inevitably landed on it. The trap door.

So many mysteries. So many possibilities. It struck something to life in her like a spark from a hunk of flint, the part in her that wanted to seek, to find out. Suddenly she wondered if her subconscious had more reasons in mind to come here outside of seeing Tick.

Hadyn sat down at the only chair in the room and set the journal down on the table, barely big enough to support the meal of one man. He saw Kiara's sideways gazing and watched her carefully as he pried open the book. He looked back and forth between her and the object of her concentration and was unsure if he should be scared or elated.

"You alright, Kiara?"

"Oh, where is that blasted kettle . . .?" Tick muttered behind him as he continued to turn his kitchen upside down.

Kiara whipped her head around, to find Hadyn. "Of course."

"You're thinking about where it could lead."

Kiara bit her lip and crossed the room to where a black kettle, stained with white mineral drippings, sat upside down on a crate, just to the right of the cabinets. Picking it up, she turned it over and handed it to Tick.

Tick scrutinized the object like he had never seen it before in his life. Then, taking it hesitantly, recognition dawned and a triumphant smile spread across his face. "Ah, there it is!" he cheered and held the kettle up like a battle sword.

But Kiara didn't see. She hardly noticed giving it to him, her mind much too preoccupied.

"It does seem like the obvious next thought," she said to Hadyn, "with all the tunnels and trapdoors we've already been through."

Tick continued his work and poured a pitcher of water into the kettle with an expression as dignified as a knight accepting a medal, but his face fell when he realized he had also forgotten where the tea was. Thankfully a quick check under the lid of a ceramic pot ended that search.

"Yes, but have those tunnels led us anywhere helpful, even once?" Hadyn asked.

"No . . ." Kiara grumbled. "Still, it doesn't just go to the Palace. Of that I'm sure."

"And so am I. I'm sure it leads to plenty more sacrifice chambers, dungeons, and clandestine clansmen hideouts, all of which, I might add, very unhelpful."

Kiara huffed and rolled her eyes, and Hadyn buried his nose in the journal, but neither could focus on fuming or code cracking, because along with the clinking and clattering of Tick busying himself in the kitchen, came the mildly disconcerting sound of Tick beginning to talk to himself. He chanted under his breath in a singsong way and carried on as if nothing had changed. Hadyn raised his eyebrows and shifted his gaze from Kiara to Tick's back. Kiara turned around, but before she spoke, she listened.

"Left, right, left, left, right, straight . . ." Tick spoke

rhythmically.

Directions . . . Kiara realized, just like he did last time they talked about the trap door.

"Tick? What is that?" she asked.

He jumped, nearly dropping the tea cup in his hand. Slowly, he turned around and looked for who had spoken to him. "Oh, Bright Eyes! What? What is what?"

"What's that you're saying?"

"Oh, just some silly directions."

Kiara's eyes grew wide and she threw a look at Hadyn, but for whatever reason he quickly looked down at the journal and pretended to be lost in concentration. Unsure what he could be trying to do, Kiara continued without him.

She cocked her head amiably, but her gaze demanded answers. "Directions to what?"

"Sometimes the king gets lost and he has to work out where to go next. He sits in here and says over and over and over and over and over—"

"Wait? The king? Tick." She narrowed her eyes, attempting to reel him back in. "Which king?"

Tick gasped and clapped his hands over both his cheeks. "Caverna has more than one king!"

Kiara's brows scrunched down over her eyes. "What? No."

"But you just asked me . . ."

Resisting the urge to claw her own face, she said, "Oh, silly me. I must have forgotten there's just the one."

"Don't be embarrassed. I forget things all the time."

"So you've said. But, Tick, why do you repeat them?"

"Repeat what?"

Kiara bit her cheek and Hadyn fought a snicker, never looking up from the journal he pretended to give all his attention to. "The directions, Tick. The directions."

"Oh! Well, for some reason I can easily remember them. And I like to remember things," he said contentedly, and Kiara smiled despite her impatience. "I help the king," Tick continued. "*Now* when he gets lost, we work out where he needs to go and I tell him which turns to make."

"And it works? He doesn't get lost?"

Tick looked offended. "He keeps asking doesn't he?"

Kiara smiled. "Of course. How could I have ever doubted you." Then, with a sideways grin she had an idea. "Let's see if I understand this correctly, If I needed to get to, oh, let's say, the Palace, you could tell me how to get there?"

"Left, right, left, left, right, straight, "Tick said without even a nod, as if he just couldn't say it fast enough.

"Incredible!" Kiara marveled and even Hadyn couldn't keep his head down anymore.

"What about . . ." she thought for a moment, "the Styx's?"

"Right, straight, straight, left, right, straight!"

Kiara laughed. "Tick, you're amazing!"

"Really?" He beamed.

"One more!" she said, smiling, and then she dared to ask it. "What about out?"

Tick blinked at her, his mind as white as a blank slate and Kiara almost heard the splat of her heart falling out of her chest and hitting the ground.

"I'm sorry," he said. "I don't remember any places called out."

"No, no, not a place. A way out, Tick. Is there a way out down there?" His brow scrunched. "An exit? An escape?" Her voice cracked. With every guess, she felt her fragile hope sink deeper into the burning acid of her doubt.

The silence pooled about them, thick as the uncertainties they faced. Kiara turned to Hadyn and he was already staring at her, a broken expression tearing up his features.

"You're upset," Tick said finally. "I'm so sorry."

Kiara turned and smiled at him. "It's not your fault, Tick."

"Perhaps not. But I'd like to make it my fault that you cheer up."

Kiara couldn't help but giggle. "Be my guest."

"Ah ha, and what timing, for the tea is done and ready to cheer!" he said, spinning back to the kitchen and bringing her a plain mug.

Kiara didn't question how it could be done so soon. She only thanked him and took a sip. Immediately after, however, her face twisted up and she yanked the cup back from her lips. "It's *cold*!" she exclaimed around the sip she had yet to swallow.

"What?" Hadyn asked.

Tick looked crestfallen. "You don't like it?"

Kiara swallowed the cold tea down hard, but she was already grinning when she repeated. "Tick, it's cold!"

Tick just looked at her as if he didn't understand how that

was an excuse for her rude behavior, and brought Hadyn a cup.

Hadyn felt the outside of his mug and stuck a pinky in the liquid. He looked up, astonished. "It is!"

Kiara shook her head, amused. "Tick, have you never heated up tea before?"

His eyes wandered. "Heated tea . . ." Then he scrunched his brow and began to pace. "Hot tea? The king doesn't allow fires any bigger than a lantern in here. There's no chimney, he says. But hot tea? I couldn't even imagine it."

Kiara was in a fit of giggles now and it couldn't be helped.

"Is it really all that funny?" He looked to Hadyn.

"Probably not as much as she's making it out to be, but yeah," he laughed then too, "it's funny."

"I've just never tried it that way." He put his hands up.

"Well, you're going to today," Kiara said, recovering her composure.

"But how?"

"I'm sure I can rig something up for you. And you know why?" Tick just looked at her, as she grinned in adoration at her dear friend. "Because it's your 'fault' that I cheered up."

His confusion melted into a smile of his own and (as was his way) he carried on as if nothing ever happened.

"What have you got there, Master Hadyn?" he said, striding over with his hands behind his back.

Hadyn lifted his head from his hand. "Oh, this? Actually I was hoping you might be able to tell *me*."

"Oh?"

"Yeah. It's a journal entry written by someone who lived a long time ago, but I'm not convinced that's all it is." Hadyn caught Kiara's eye-roll across the room as she worked on rigging up a way to hold the tea kettle over four lit candles, and chose to ignore it.

"What else could it be?" Tick asked.

Hadyn huffed. "I think there may be a hidden message."

Tick clapped his hands together. "Ooo, exciting! . . . And you think I can help?"

Hadyn shrugged. "I don't see why not. If nothing else, you're still a fresh set of eyes."

"Alright. What have you got so far?"

Hadyn ran a hand through his curls. "Not much. But see here, how she starts each entry by emboldening the first letter?" he pointed out the bold letters with the nub end of his pencil and Tick nodded. "Seems like a quirk, right? That's what I thought until I read the last entry. Not only does she make the first letter of the first sentence bolder and larger than the rest, she darkens the first letter of *every* sentence. It's different. And see here." He slid his hand up the page. "In the entry before this, she darkened the first letter and this *B* in, *But before I go*. Coincidence?" He raised his brows, shaking his head. "Or connection? See, I think she separated the two only to throw off unwelcome eyes, but that they're actually connected! I just don't know how . . ." While he squinted at the page, running his eyes over the two passages, the hairs on the backs of his neck stood up as he noticed a presence behind him. His eyes grew wide and darted back and forth, but something in him froze, feeling like if he did anything, but ignore her, he might ruin any chance of her being interested in the cypher.

"Any thoughts, Bright Eyes?"

So much for ignoring her. Hadyn turned and blinked at her. Hands behind her back, Kiara leaned in just enough to be obviously interested in the journal. Hadyn raised his eyebrows at her, content to resort to snark.

She straightened and shifted her eyes between the journal and both of them. "What? No." She swept her nose into the air. "I'm just waiting for the water to heat up."

Hadyn shook his head and turned back to Tick. "Kiara doesn't share my suspicions. So, you think you can make anything of this?"

Tick adjusted his goggles. "Well, it seems to me that the hidden message is in this entry." He pointed to the last one. "And the previous one contains the clues on how to uncover it."

"Okay. I can agree with that."

"That considered, she tells you right here, the first words will give you the necessary key. Now in cyphers and codes the key is usually a certain word rather than an actual key."

"How do you know that?"

Tick shrugged. "So what are the first words?"

"The first sentence in the last entry."

"Correct!"

"Yes, I gathered that. It's in my notes here."

Tick looked at the notes. "Fascinating! What language is that?"

A high pitched, giggly snort burst from Kiara as she poured the tea.

Holding the notes, Hadyn's face fell. "Unbelievable," he muttered.

Without turning around, Kiara pounded her chest and cleared her throat as if the laughter could be passed off as a simple cough or sneeze.

"Bless you," Tick said, and Hadyn rolled his eyes.

"Anyway," he said, slamming the notes back down. "How can the first sentence be the key?"

Tick scratched his head. "I'm not sure. The whole sentence can't be the key . . ." Pulling off his goggles, he rested them on his forehead and rubbed his knuckles into his eyes. Then he froze, and when he popped his goggles back on, his eyes were bright with an idea. "What if, instead of a word, it is a number? The number of words in the sentence!"

Quickly, Hadyn counted the words. "Thirteen . . ." He shrugged. "Well, it's something."

Tick raised a finger. "Something indeed," he said, and when Kiara placed a steaming mug in front of him, he thanked her and took a gingerly sip as if he had never had tea any other way.

Kiara and Hadyn exchanged glances and watched him carefully.

Tick set the cup on the table, licking his lips. "My, that is a fine cup of tea. I don't remember ever having better. In fact, I don't think I ever—" He stopped, his eyes growing even wider than usual and Kiara burst with laughter. "Heavens!" he cried. "Did you *heat* the tea?"

"Yes, Tick. I told you I was going to."

"Did you?" he asked and took another, more deliberate sip of tea. "I have to say, this is rather marvelous."

"Good. Because now that I've hung the kettle up like this, you'll never have to have another cold cup of tea again."

"Thank you. I will try hard not to forget this gift."

"I know you will." Kiara's smile fell to a look of worry. "Oh, but you *have* never forgotten that fire can burn you?"

"Of course not. Well, at least not that I can remember."

After a skipped heartbeat of silence, they each broke into laughter. They had to laugh. If they didn't, they'd never leave him, too worried he'd forget so much, he wouldn't remember to breathe.

They stayed with Tick for a while longer and talked while they finished their tea, but as always Tick's eyes began to droop, and like a suddenly dying light, he grew too tired for even talking.

Kiara fell silent mid-sentence and grabbed the mug out of his hand, growing limper by the second.

"Huh?" He jolted back awake for a moment. "Did you ask me something?"

"No." Kiara smiled. "But you should get some rest. We'll come see you again soon. Hopefully before you can miss us too much."

Tick gave a heavy nod of his head and smiled drowsily as they led him to his small bed. He seemed asleep before his head even rested on his pillow, and before they closed the door behind them, they could hear him snoring softly.

As they walked back to the hideaway, Kiara swung her arms and puffed out her cheeks with a huff. "So, what should we do now? You know life could get unbearably boring extremely fast if we don't go with it and learn to entertain ourselves."

Not surprisingly, Hadyn remained silent.

"Oh! *I* know!" Kiara grinned. "We could find new caverns to explore! Maybe even find more alexandrite. Or we could sneak into the Palace," her lips twisted mischievously, "play a trick on Shrike! Now that everyone believes I'm dead, he'd be so shocked, he might just drop dead himself!"

Hadyn's face twisted in mortification. "Kiara, we're not going to do that."

She shrugged with mock remorse, like she didn't see the problem. "Well, what then? We have to do *something*."

"Yeah, we do. Keep searching for a way out." He shook his head. "You know, you can drop the talk. You may have given up on this." He raised the journal and shook his head again. "But you haven't given up. No. Otherwise you wouldn't have been asking Tick about those strange directions he mumbles out."

"They're not just strange mumblings. There's something to them. It's like I can just feel it."

Arriving at the fissure to her hideaway, Hadyn held up a finger and smiled knowingly behind it, before slipping inside. "Exactly."

Kiara opened her mouth to reply, but no words came out.

"Face it, Kiara," his words echoed out of the cavern, "it's not in your nature."

Kiara went in after him, huffing as she shoved her way through. "Even if we stumbled upon something and miraculously, out of nothing, we got a new lead, they're too good. Like shadows, they work in the darkness and never come out of it. Besides Nnyric, it's as if they don't even exist. How can we fight something we can't see? They stop at nothing to silence those that threaten their secrets. Do you really think Cecilia just died? She knew too much. Just like my mother. Just like my grandfather."

"Yes, but they can't very well kill us, if we're already dead, now can they?"

Kiara shook her head, a dangerous smile on her lips. "You know I used to be able to win these things?"

"Hmm. Maybe I'm just getting good at arguing. Or maybe you don't have anything to honestly argue about."

Kiara sucked a breath through her teeth, aggravated enough for her words to be lethal if she let them. "I'm still not going to help you with that ridiculous journal."

He shrugged. "Suit yourself."

Kiara took a measured breath through her nose, closed her eyes, and spoke slowly. "I'm going for a walk. And don't you say, suit yourself," she said as she slipped back through the crack.

"I was going to say be careful!" Hadyn called and cringed when the only reply he heard was a metal crash as she ran into something with her lantern.

Chapter Thirty Nine

Cyphers and Stubbed Toes

Kiara kicked at loose and brittle stones as she walked, swinging her lantern recklessly at her side. The cavern walls flashed with her shadows and echoed her angry mutterings.

"Stupid!" she seethed under her breath. "Stupid journal. Stupid riddles! Blast it. Blast it all! Blast Hadyn in all his superiority. *Maybe you don't have anything to honestly argue about,*" she mocked. "Oooo! Blast how he knows how to make my blood boil!"

She gave a growl of a huff and stopped in her tracks. Shining her light about, she looked around for familiar rock formations, and soon realized she had already come quite far from her hideaway, without even a destination in mind, except to go. That's how it always was, just running, running until she found something . . . except she never found anything, and she never stopped running.

Kiara's lungs filled with air in a way that looked almost painful and she let it out in a heavy, heavy sigh. Suddenly she just felt so tired. She wished she had somewhere to go. Somewhere to sit and just be quiet. Somewhere where she could feel her soul fill up for once instead of drain. Her hideaway, she realized, had sufficed for a time, but it would take more than her own secret cavern to fill this hole, to meet this inherent longing for rest.

No longer angry, she lowered herself to the damp floor. Hadyn was right. She didn't have it in her to give up. Not like this. No matter how tired she was. No matter how scared she was to go on, it altogether terrified her to stay stuck. She just didn't see how the journal was their answer. They had what they needed, but they were hidden in the questions, in the unexplainables. She had contented herself to avoid these things, because their very definitions frightened her and because to think of them, meant thinking of things that pained her, like disappearances and sudden deaths. But like a sleeping monster, something inside her woke up in that moment, and through the lack of energy and rest deprivation, it ran on the adrenaline of necessity.

Picking herself up, she forced herself to crack those questions back open and dig deeper than she ever had. Kiara turned back to her hideaway, nearly shaking with fear, but most certainly finished with giving up.

Slipping back in through the crack, one look at Hadyn (though she knew it without having to look at him) told her he hadn't moved once since she left.

"Ugh! I Can't believe you're still agonizing over that petty journal."

Hadyn held up a finger. "It's not petty and I'm not agonizing. I think I'm finally onto something."

She flopped down a few feet in front of him. "Yep, and then you'll run into another dead end, and then a locked tight door, then another, and another, because that's just the way life is."

Hadyn ignored her and turned back to his notes.

Kiara sighed. "Look, while I was walking, I did some thinking."

"Oh, really?" he said, shuffling through the many scribbled up pages. "Cause I didn't make that connection."

"And I thought," she continued, "you'd be interested to hear my conclusion. But, no matter. I see you're much too busy."

Slowly lifting his eyes as if it was drudgery, he dropped the papers down.

Kiara smiled and then let out a pent breath. "You were right."

Hadyn's impatient expression softened with somber, cheerless surprise.

"You were right all along. I can't give up. I know that now. I think part of me always did." Kiara wished he would gloat, crack a joke, or say anything at all, so she wouldn't have to confess a word more, but he just listened and stared as if he knew she had more to say.

"I only say those things about dead ends and shut doors because . . . they terrify me. I'm afraid of being let down, of being stopped, told no, and turned away. How can anyone have faith that things will one day be different, when they never have been before? How do you do it?"

He shrugged. "Do what?"

"Hope."

"Well, because . . . I guess it's because, for me, I don't see it as a chore. To me, it's a gift."

"A *gift*?" she said the word as if she never had before.

"Yeah." He brightened. "A really useful one."

Kiara wanted to smile, but her face remained contemplative. Then she got up only to sit back down by the heap of all the loose rocks she had piled together from whenever they fell from the quivering ceiling. She picked a few up and began chucking them absentmindedly into a dark corner on the far side of the room.

"You know, when I was out walking, I got to thinking and not just about giving up." She threw another rock and its collision echoed about the cavern in overlapping clacks. "There are things, *a lot of things*, that happen here that don't have a logical explanation. No, they don't have any explanation at all." Another rock, a little bit larger, a little bit louder. "No matter how hard you think! It's like my brain just woke up or something." She bounced her next pick in her hand. "Take Cida's cold for instance. If we've really been isolated with nothing but a void around us for hundreds of years, how is it that people still get sick, that people die because they're so sick? I'm no doctor, but if we've gone through times where disease is gone, shouldn't that mean it has run its course and is now eradicated? How does any of it come back?"

She chucked the stone and Hadyn nodded, only half listening as he tried to continue his work on the cypher. After all, he wasn't just spitting words just to say them when he mentioned maybe being on to something. But that arresting lilt of hers he had come to rather enjoy was riding on her excitement and new found energy, changing her words and begging him to listen more closely.

"And then there's—" Kiara cut herself short when she lobbed another stone. The dark corner responsible for eating up all her throws flashed with a split second of brilliant light.

She reared her head back. "Did you just see that?"

Hadyn didn't look up from the journal. "See what?"

She slumped and rolled her eyes before she shot to her feet. "Come here! Help me look!"

Carrying a lantern to the shadowed corner, she scanned the ground peppered with chipped and halved stones.

Hadyn arched a brow. "What are we looking for?"

"Something."

He searched the ground, but like Kiara, saw nothing but

grey and cracked stones.

"It doesn't make any sense . . ." she mused. "They're all the same. But when I was throwing them, something happened."

"What kind of some—"

"There!" she exclaimed, spotting a rough, white stone with a jagged side. "This must have been it!" She snatched it up and scrunched her brow. "Quartz? . . . Interesting."

"Kiara, what—"

Kiara slammed the stone on the ground before he could finish, and like a flash of lightning, they were blinded in an instant.

The echoes of the crash melted into their silence.

"Light," Kiara whispered.

"What did you just do?"

"Nothing. It's the quartz."

She picked the stone back up and slammed it down again, unable to stop watching, the stone breaking into smaller and smaller pieces and the flashes dwindling to a fraction of each previous show.

It filled her with such unmeasurable delight, and not just because it was beautiful.

"That's how he did it!" she cried.

"How who did what?" Hadyn asked, already heading back to his journal.

"Salin!" she squealed, beginning to pace the room. "That's how he fooled the city. It wasn't otherworldly powers, but simply a fantastic phenomenon of our perfect gems! Just like everyone else with something to hide, he had knowledge of Caverna's gems. Ya' ken?"

Hadyn's gaze wandered to the side. "Sorry?"

"Oi! You follow me?" She revised.

He nodded unconvincingly. "Sure."

"Which reminds me . . ." she mused. "Of my questions, the Styx being number one." She raised her eyebrows at the overwhelming enigma and walked faster as her passion rose, heedless of where she even placed her feet anymore. "The Clansmen would spill blood for gems. I mean, what's the deal with that?" She threw her hands in the air. "In a world where gems are forbidden everywhere but the Styx, where's the demand?"

Now that was interesting, Hadyn thought and looked up just in time to see Kiara heading for a jagged irregularity in the stone floor, a ledge that had often caused many a throbbing toe in the past.

Though today it would make its greatest conquest yet.

"Kiara! Watch out!" he called, but he was too late.

The toe of Kiara's shoe caught on the sharp lip and sent her sailing forward. Pain shocked up from her knees and hands as she managed to soften her fall before collapsing on her side.

Hadyn ran to her to help her up. "Are you alright?"

She raised a hand and growled. "I'm fine."

Knowing there was nothing he could do when she got like this, Hadyn shook his head and reburied himself in his notes. Though, something was different this time. Like some invisible wall had at last crumbled, his eyes felt fresher and the pages seemed to have more information to offer. As his heart began to race, he stared at the most recently scribbled page for a whole five seconds before his eyes rounded to the size of saucers.

"I've got it!"

Kiara scoffed. "Yeah, and I didn't just fall on my face."

"No, Kiara, I think I really figured it out!"

"How?"

"Look!" he said, nearly exploding with excitement and Kiara shuffled over to sit near him. "Tick figured out that the key is the number of words in the first sentence. Of course, that number is thirteen, and, Kiara, I've tried everything. I've taken out every thirteenth word, then every thirteenth word from a bold letter. I've rearranged them, I've even shuffled them around apart from the rest of the text. Everything I do only makes the entry make even less sense." He raised a finger. "Until now. Hopefully."

"Hadyn," she moaned impatiently.

"Please . . . just listen," he begged and Kiara shut her mouth. "Thank you. Now," he continued, "through all my attempts and guesses, I have failed to acknowledge one crucial piece of information and that's what Maddie said here." He pointed with his pencil and read out loud. "*Half is the truth to the other half's lies.*" He looked up and grinned at her. "What is thirteen half of?"

Kiara didn't understand. "Twenty six?"

"And that's the number of?"

Her brow scrunched as she thought so hard she grazed right over the obvious, that is, until she didn't.

Kiara gasped. "The alphabet! Thirteen is half of the alphabet!"

Clapping his hands together, Hadyn threw his head back in laughter. "Exactly!"

"But that's incredible! How in Caverna did you think of that?"

"I don't know. It just kind of came to me when I sat back down."

"What do we have left to do?"

He raised his eyebrows. "We?"

"Oh, come on, Hadyn. You can't seriously hold that against me."

"But, you didn't believe in me?"

"No. I didn't believe in the journal. I didn't believe in Maddie. I'm not like you. I couldn't keep hoping in things I had no reason to. But," she paused and looked him in the eyes. "I never doubted you. So, please, can you forgive me?"

He smiled. "Of course. And to answer your question, I believe all that's left to do is what Maddie said, and switch the letters in the last entry out with the correct letter on the other half of the alphabet."

"And how do we do that?"

"Like this," Hadyn said, and on a fresh piece of paper he drew a line. He wrote out the first half of the alphabet above the line and the second half below. "There. Now this way we can clearly see that A is actually N and the other way around, and likewise all the way down the line."

Kiara squinted at what was supposed to be the English alphabet. "Clever. But maybe I should do the writing."

Hadyn sighed and handed her the paper. "Whatever." Then, turning back to the journal he said, "Okay, the first word is never."

"Got it. And like you said, according to the chart N is actually A." Kiara wrote the first letter in the message down and felt her heartbeat kick up a knot. She licked her lips and squinted at Hadyn's poorly written alphabet. "Okay, next letter is E. That's . . . R."

While she continued to decode the first word, Hadyn tried to finish it in his head and guess what it could be, but even after she had switched the last letter, the very best they could do was cock their heads, hoping if they looked at it a different way it would make more sense.

"*A-rire*?" Kiara tried to pronounce, though it sounded more like she was trying to talk around a mouthful of food. "Is that even a word?"

Hadyn didn't do well to hide his frustration. "Let's just keep going."

"Fine. What's the next word?"

"Thought."

After Kiara switched the letters, she had to laugh as she said, "*Gub-H-G?* What in Caverna?"

If she was honest, Kiara was ready to give up at arire, but for Hadyn's benefit, she proceeded to switch the lone I for a V. Though her patience ran out when she switched the word "would" out for something completely composed of consonants.

"Hadyn, this is not helping us."

He sighed. "I know. But what if it's a different language?"

With a cringe she answered, "That's still useless to us."

"I'm sorry," he said, his shoulders slumping further with defeat.

"Sorry for what?"

"Leading you into false hope."

"Hey." She made sure he looked her in the eyes before continuing. "Just because we haven't figured it out yet doesn't mean it's over. This is definitely some kind of cypher, I'm sure of that now. We just haven't cracked it yet."

Hadyn smiled softly.

Kiara smiled back and continued troubleshooting. "Now, what about these bold letters? What's the deal with them?"

"I'm not sure . . . Sometime when I started working on this, I lined them up here," he said, referring to a note sheet. "But, as usual, they don't make any sense."

Kiara took the paper. "But look, together they're already gibberish!"

"Yes?"

"Don't you see? When we tried before, the words turned into nonsense. Maybe if we try the alphabet switch on these letters, it will have the opposite effect!"

The smile grew slowly on Hadyn's face. "It's certainly worth a try."

Kiara swapped the first three letters until she had the word all. "Hey!" she beamed, "an actual word."

"Keep going."

Kiara wrote two more letters. "*Allis*?" She cocked her head. "Could be someone's name."

"Why would she want to encrypt someone's name?"

Kiara shrugged.

"Well, we haven't used all the letters yet."

She nodded and continued to switch out the last four letters, but even with Kiara's neat handwriting, they could not make sense of it.

"*Allisalie*," Hadyn pronounced for the first time. "What could that mean?"

Kiara shrugged. "Could still be someone's name."

"No," he said harshly, shooting to his feet. "If it's someone's name, that person is long gone and is no help to us. That can't be it!"

Kiara moaned and leaned her head back against the stone wall.

"Allisalie . . . Allisalie . . ." Hadyn scratched his head and muttered the word over and over, each time saying it slower and slower, until finally he straightened. He looked straight through everything around him, his eyes bright with a discovery.

"What?" Kiara asked. "What is it?"

"All is a lie . . ." Hadyn breathed.

"What?"

"All is a lie!" he said again louder and grinned, completely astonished. "Here, I'll show you."

Rushing back to the notes, he snatched up the one Kiara had written allisalie on, pressed the paper against the cave wall, and wrote it out again underneath, except this time he added four distinct spaces. Kiara stood to see better.

Pointing to each word, Hadyn read them out loud. "All. Is. A. Lie."

She stared in shock. "Incredible! Then she didn't give up!"

But Hadyn's smile melted faster than it came. "But wait a minute . . . that's it? This can't be right. It doesn't tell us anything we don't already know."

"Or does it?"

"What?"

"Hadyn, think about it. She wrote, *all* is a lie. I think that means more than just her behavior. It's Caverna. It's how it came to exist. It's every king that ever ruled, every lie that was ever said."

"Again, how is this new information?"

Kiara's eyes sharpened with intensity and she bit her lip. "Maybe she's not telling us how much of Caverna is a lie, but asking us to pay more attention to it?" Kiara could see Hadyn starting to think. "What if we've been so focused on the truth that we've failed to see what some of the lies are covering up?"

"That's genius," Hadyn said. "Okay, so what about the Forbiddens?"

Kiara puffed out her cheeks. "Where to start? They placed the lie of the watchers in the Forbiddens to keep people out."

"Which keeps people from exploring on their own," he finished, "and from finding Tick and the trapdoor tunnel in his room."

"Right. And that reminds me, with that trapdoor connecting the Palace with the Styx, it proves my suspicions about the king knowing the Stygian market exists."

"The king knows about the Styx . . ." Hadyn took a moment to process that.

"Of this I'm certain," Kiara said.

He squinted. "Why would he lead over half the populous to believe they don't exist?"

"Why indeed? Maybe this is one of the lies Maddie wanted us to pay attention to."

"You think the Styx were already around then?"

She shrugged. "I don't see why not."

"Nnyric wants to keep the Styx's hidden?" Hadyn was confused. "But that's too much like protecting."

"Unless there's something there that he wants to stay in existence, something of his, something he's in control of."

Hadyn's face washed white. "The gem operation."

Kiara sucked in a breath to speak, but ended up just staring at him.

"I always thought the clansmen mined because that's how the Styx worked and they wanted to own its streets," he continued. "But you're right. How is there ever a demand unless you have something someone else doesn't? Here in Caverna, if you know enough, it's not difficult to procure a few stones for yourself. But with the daily flow of gems that goes through the Styx, with the amount that goes to the Clansmen and never comes back, they have to be going somewhere." Hadyn spoke slowly. "Somewhere where people don't have them. And who better would know of a people with such a lack than King Nnyric himself?"

Kiara didn't know what to feel. She *thought* she should feel elated. They were actually getting somewhere, but in reality, she only felt sick. She placed a hand against the wall to steady herself.

"You're telling me, the king has been trading . . ." she tried to keep breathing deeply, "with the outside . . . all this time?"

"Kiara, this is big. This could lead us to the outside, if we follow it carefully enough. Doesn't that make you happy?"

"Sorry. It's just," she slid down the wall as her face drained of color, "it all makes so much sense. This is how he does it. He could trade for resources. He could trade for services." Kiara laughed. "With the amount of arums he could trade for, he could buy this whole, cursed city into secrecy! It even explains how people still get sick. Because with the amount of regular contact with the outside, who knows what kind of illnesses are brought back in!" She fixed Hadyn with a look. "But what about you? You were a part of it. What else do you know?"

"Nothing," he said defensively, surprised she would even ask. "Do you really think they would tell me anything? Their Blackcoal?"

"I suppose not."

His offense melted quickly enough, and he settled to the ground close to her. "We do need someone who knows more. Someone on the inside."

Kiara gave him a funny look. "Maybe we do . . ."

The look in his eyes said he wasn't following.

"Though it will have to wait until even after Cida comes tonight."

Hadyn wanted to ask more, but was stopped by the subtle tears filling in her eyes.

"What is it?" he asked.

She turned to him and through the tears there was a light burning brighter than fire in her eyes. "Hadyn . . . we could get out."

The reality hit him and he suddenly felt the need to catch his breath. He put a steadying hand down at his side and blinked as the thought of it made him dizzy. When he looked again at Kiara, the beaming smile glowed bright on her face.

"We *will* get out."

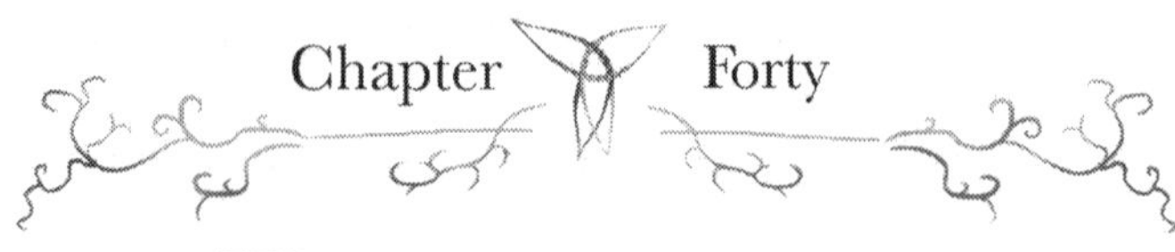

Branded

For the rest of the day, they counted down the hours until Cida was to arrive. Kiara told Hadyn about a particularly strong hunch she had about someone in town, but they wouldn't be able to follow that hunch until after curfew anyway, so they would tell Cida first.

It was agonizing, waiting around for her with all their excitement pent up inside, but as time dragged on and stretched so lingeringly that it could no longer be defined as mere hours, Kiara actually began to dread her coming, not wanting to leave her friend. Never had she parted from her not knowing how long it would be before she saw her again. And when Cida finally arrived that night, Kiara was torn.

After the call for lights rang through town, Kiara and Hadyn waited at the entrance to the Forbiddens. They didn't say much to each other. Hadyn had put the pieces of Kiara's somber mood together and knew that though this was good news, not all good news is easy to share.

But not wholly incapable of excitement, they both wore ridiculous grins when they spotted Cida walking up through the darkness, and ran to her sides. Blurting their greetings, they rushed her inside.

"What is the occasion? What is all the excitement and the hurry for?" Cida asked, smiling.

"Cida," Kiara grabbed her shoulders and looked her dead in the eyes, "we think we have found a possible way out."

"Oh my . . ." One of Cida's hands went to her heart. "Are you sure?"

"Yes." Kiara laughed.

"But last night . . . you were devastated."

"I was wrong." Kiara said. "Listen. There's not enough time

to explain everything, but Hadyn cracked a cypher in Maddie's journal."

Cida turned to him with her wide eyes, but he couldn't tell if it was from shock or amazement. Though at this point they were basically the same thing.

"Well, Kiara and Tick helped," Hadyn said modestly.

"What did it say?"

"All is a lie."

Cida just stared and swallowed hard, but Kiara regained her attention. "It got me thinking, a whole lot of thoughts, and soon enough we realized there's much more going on with the Styx's gem operation than meets the eye."

"The gem operation . . ." she muttered, yet trying to even begin processing.

"I know this is a lot, but there's a man in town and if Hadyn and I can find him, I think he may be able to help us. But we'll have to leave very soon."

"Will it be dangerous?"

Never one to mince words, Kiara replied, "Most likely."

"This is just too good," Cida said. "Too good to even believe my ears! Not that it's dangerous, but," she smiled at her, "you could finally leave!"

Kiara looked down and said with a forlorn sigh, "Yeah."

"Oh, Kiara, don't be sad for me. This will be a joyous parting. You can't be torn." She raised her chin with a loose fist. "This is what you were born to do," she whispered. "Your red hair and green eyes were only a presage of how you will shake the very existence of this city. You will go and find your mother, and with her, you can come back and expose the lies of Caverna to the light I know you'll find out there."

"Oh, what am I going to do without you, Cida? You've always known how to make me feel better."

"Hey, you have this one." She reached up and messed Hadyn's already messy curls around. "And from what I've seen, he's better than good."

Hadyn blushed and smiled shyly, feeling unworthy of the compliment.

Kiara smiled. "Yes. I don't think I could go if I didn't, but I will miss you tremendously, all the same."

"And I, you, dear friend."

Kiara gathered herself before she could cry. "But it's not

goodbye yet. We'll be back before you know. Hopefully with a plan."

"Yes. I'm sure of it."

Not lighting their lanterns yet, they set out using only the meager light that the night guards had put out. They clung to the shadows purely out of a desperate necessity for concealment, hopping from one void of darkness to the next, longing to stay in the light, but fearing being found.

When at last they arrived, the same two guards stood at the entrance of the prison, talking in hushed tones, subtle hints of laughter betraying the volume they tried to maintain. They talked and told each other stories as they tried to make the long night hours go by easier.

Kiara and Hadyn sat invisible in the shadows, just beyond the light.

"Those two won't give us any trouble," Kiara whispered. "They're the same guards as before, and last time they didn't see me until I stood right in front of them." She watched the entrance with fierce focus. "If the shifts have remained the same, he should be coming just now."

Hadyn nodded, though she couldn't see in the darkness and minutes later footsteps echoed up the stairs. A hulking form, silhouetted by the torches of the tunnel, appeared and grew taller with each step. When the giant at last stopped growing, he came out into the light.

"What's got you tied up in knots, Smash?" the braver guard asked.

Hamish Clungston loomed in the lantern light, if possible, looking uglier and angrier than ever. He gave the guard who had dared to speak to him a murderous scowl, his barrel chest puffing laboriously, but gave no answer, before looking ahead and walking away. Kiara felt her heart skip a beat as he began walking straight towards them, getting closer with every step. Kiara and Hadyn couldn't help but think he was glaring right at them, that his burning need for revenge had given him the ability to see in the darkness.

Kiara's legs were springs ready to explode. Hadyn reached for her hand, ready to pull her to safety. But Smash walked right past them, lumbering like a ghostly ship into the night. He did not carry a lantern; he liked the dark the way it was.

When they couldn't hear his footsteps anymore, they both let out their held breaths.

"Oi, what was that?" The guard with considerably less brazen guts asked.

"What? There's nothing. Don't tell me that cloaked fella has still got you all jumpy. Really, Newton, that was weeks ago."

Kiara grinned mischievously despite what was at stake.

Just then, a much smaller, more slight figure than before walked up the steps and out of the tunnel. This time it was Stegler and, unlike his predecessor, he clenched a lamp in his boney fist.

"Evening, Stegs. What did you do to the old fist to get him boiling today?"

"Absolutely nothing," Stegler said and he sounded sick of the subject before it even began. "He was in one of his moods today and I knew better than to tease him."

"Probably just hates your guts and merely looking at you sends him into a fit of rage." The guard slapped his knee, bouncing with laughter.

Stegler slumped his shoulders and began to walk away.

"I'm just playing you, Stegs. We all know how Hamish gets. But don't ever call him that or he *will* want to kill you just when lookin' at ya."

"Yeah, Winzor has witnessed his hate for that name first hand," the one called Newton said.

Stegler sighed. "See you tomorrow," he said as he walked away.

Kiara and Hadyn popped to their feet. This was it.

They slunk after him, following a safe distance behind. Stegler's lantern guided them through the dark of Caverna like a beacon.

Kiara felt such a great sense of trepidation as they followed him across town, electricity tingling down into every nerve ending as the adrenalin pumped through her veins with every quickened heartbeat, like they were doing something terribly wrong and at any moment they might be caught for their crimes. But an exciting kind of wrong.

Unwittingly, Stegler led them into Terminal Avenue, never showing any sign that he knew somebody followed him. Because of the dark, the stench caught Kiara off guard, even though she had smelt it before. She could feel her eyes begin to water as Stegler turned down a foreboding alley that she didn't even know existed. Somehow the darkness was thicker in here, seemingly eating away at Stegler's light. Random noises to their left and right made her jump. Apparently, around here, curfew wasn't as commonly observed.

Kiara tried to control her breathing, but it was already loud enough for her to hear. Hadyn found her hand in the darkness and gripped it tightly, partly to remind her that she wasn't alone, but mostly because he wasn't about to lose her in the pitch alley.

Up ahead, Stegler stopped in a doorway and instinctively looked over his shoulder before quickly slipping in the door.

The two found the door, just barely in the thick darkness, and as they stood there, all but trembling, any courage that Kiara might have had drained away. Neither knew what to do, and with who knows what lurking around in the dubious alley, neither wanted to say a word.

At length, with no other option to think of, Hadyn slowly raised a fist and rapped out a steady rhythm on the door. They held their breath in the silence until they heard footsteps from inside, followed by a series of clicks, all at different pitches, like a great deal of locks unbolting. The door cracked open just enough to see out and then a little more as a trembling hand holding a lantern stuck out, the flame inside quivering fearfully. Stegler's squinted face peered out from behind the light.

"Who be calling on me at this late hour? Don't you know, it's much after curfew?"

"We're aware," Hadyn said, "and we're sorry to disturb you, but we need your help."

Since he wouldn't tell him his name, Stegler gave him a closer look. He recognized the cloak first and his eyes widened with fear. He looked on Hadyn's face in horror.

"You!" he pointed a trembling finger with his free hand. "But they said you were dead!"

Stegler retreated in and slammed the door shut. Barely thinking, Hadyn stuck his foot between the frame and the door. He winced and swallowed a cry of pain as Stegler smashed the door on his foot, suddenly wishing he would have given the action a little more thought. Stegler abandoned the door, leaving it to creak open as if by a ghostly hand, and ran for a hiding place.

"We mean you know harm!" Kiara called as she stepped inside. "You don't have to be afraid!"

Hadyn grabbed her arm before she could go any further. "Kiara, be careful."

"I'm not afraid. He's the one who's scared. What can he do to us?"

He let her go, though he knew first hand how dangerous fear can make a person, not just from the pain Stegler's terror enhanced arms had inflicted on his foot.

"We don't want to hurt you!" Kiara resumed pleading. "Stegler, we need your help."

Hearing the youth and desperation in her voice, Stegler paused his mad dash and stopped by the fire in his sitting room. He thought he recognized her voice, but didn't know to what face it belonged. The flame's warmth spread up his back and the amber glow of the room seemed like the safest refuge for now. Grabbing an iron from the fire, he stood his ground.

"How do you know my name?" he called back to her.

Kiara exchanged a glance with Hadyn as they advanced towards the voice. "Because we've met once before."

Stegler pointed the fire iron in the direction of her voice. "And I'm supposed to believe I just don't remember?"

"Perhaps."

"And what, by chance, would a dead man and a young girl I don't remember want with me?"

His words led them to him, until they could see the dim glow of the fire. They crept forward until they stood just outside the room, not wanting to scare him anymore than they already had.

"As I said before," Kiara formed her answer slowly, "only your help."

As she raised her hands to remove her hood, Hadyn eyed the tip of the iron burning red hot in Stegler's white knuckle grasp.

"But . . ." Stegler stared at Kiara and the iron clattered to the ground where it sizzled and left a charred mark in the wood. "He killed you!" he cried and backed up until he bumped the mantle, knocking trinkets and portraits to the floor.

"Please!" Kiara reached a hand out. "You don't have to be afraid."

"We are both clearly alive," Hadyn said. "Don't you trust your own eyes?"

"Of course. And I did not believe in ghosts until now. And you," he looked at Kiara again. "He must have charmed you in death, so that even when he died, your soul would not be free of him. You are chained to him and you both walk as specters in the living world."

Kiara smiled at him. "You have a great imagination." Her words were warm and disarming. Unwittingly, Stegler relaxed a bit. "But I will assure you," Kiara continued, "I came here of my own volition. Hadyn did not murder me, nor is he dead. We are both very much alive and in need of your help."

"But none of this makes sense. Help me to understand a few things. Tell me what the princess could need my help with, and maybe I'll consider. Why did you fake your own death?"

Kiara stepped a bit closer to him. "I needed to. I'm not the princess anymore. I left that life behind. And as for Hadyn being a murderer, the king made that up all on his own. I never meant for him to get caught up in this. There's so much you need to know, that everyone needs to know, but so little I can tell you without putting your safety at risk."

"What does that mean? Words can't kill you."

"It's not so much the words," Hadyn said, "but the knowledge. If your tongue slipped up, if they knew that you knew, they would kill you."

Stegler gulped. "*Who* are *they*?"

"Shadows of people, whispers of nameless faces. You can't find them. They make sure of that." Hadyn said.

Even being so close to the fire, Stegler shivered with a chill. And yet, they wouldn't have said he looked surprised. For it really wasn't news to him at all. Hadyn's words echoed around in his mind just like the rumors that bounced off the cavern walls of Terminal Avenue every so often. There was an idea, murmurs of things just like what he said. Though it wasn't certain anybody knew anything, as only vague pieces of the story floated around, never quite fitting together, like the information you accumulate by listening to only one side of a conversation that doesn't want to be heard.

"The only thing I can tell you," Kiara said, "is that Caverna is not what the king says it is. He's been lying to us about what's beyond the caves and we are on a search to find a way out."

Stegler looked at her gravely. "But what do you want with me?"

"Kiara says you were once a clansman," Hadyn said. "Is that true?"

Stegler gaped at both of them, suddenly looking like a snake ready to strike. "Where did you hear that! Mereaze?" Then he thought he understood. "Oh, I see. You don't need my help. He sent you, didn't he? His Blackcoal, to do his dirty work. He couldn't just leave me alone."

"No! That's not it at all!" Kiara cried. "I heard you. I heard you talking to Clungston."

"You were a part of the Whitefang, weren't you?" Hadyn asked. "Mereaze's clan."

"I don't know what you're talking about or where you got your information, but you've come to the wrong house." He looked at them dangerously. "And you need to leave."

Kiara searched his eyes in disbelief. She didn't understand.

Hadyn hadn't given up yet. "I think you know more than you say."

Stegler scoffed and began placing things back up on his mantle. "And why's that?"

"Because only people associated with clansmen call me Blackcoal."

Stegler set up a crude wooden carving only to knock it back down again with the slip of a hand. He sighed, his shoulders collapsing as they stared at his back. "What do you want?"

Kiara tried to speak as gently as she could. "Only answers to our questions."

Beginning to chuckle, he turned around. "What questions? What could I possibly know? I barely made it out of there with my skin intact. I'm done with that life."

Kiara looked to Hadyn and he nodded. "We have reason to believe," she began, "that the clansmen have been secretly supplying the king with gems, so that he can trade them with the world beyond the cave. And we want to hear what you know about it."

Silence fell over the three of them and for a moment Stegler almost looked caught. Then he sputtered, breaking into a grin. He chuckled and kept going until he was roaring with laughter.

Kiara felt her heart skitter like feet across ice. Staring in disbelief she hissed, "Shhhh! Curfew was called hours ago! You said it yourself."

"Oh, but it's hilarious," he said flatly, not looking as amused as his words might suggest. "Here I was, terrified that with one wrong move, I could be pulled back into that living nightmare, and you come out blubbering about something that doesn't even exist!" He finished with another chortle.

The tips of Kiara's ears burned red as he laughed in the face of their plight. "You don't believe that."

"Think what you want, but why ask me anyway? You have your own certified clansman right there."

"I'm not one of them," Hadyn snapped. "I never was. I was just a kid when Mereaze made me start mining, but even as I got older, they never told me anything."

"And what makes you think they treated me any differently?"

"Because you *were* one of them. You were on the inside."

"And now I'm out."

"And you're free," Kiara said. "Aren't you grateful for that?"

"Oh, more than you know, Lass. I don't know if you've been listening, but it's *because* of that very freedom that I will not go back."

"We're not asking you too. But doesn't your freedom make you want to free others?"

"Not if it means mine will be taken away."

"So, that's how it is. You live in constant fear that they'll come back for you and take it from you, because why? You don't believe it's real? That you don't deserve it anyway?" Stegler's face registered that she had hit her mark somewhere. "Well, this is your chance to prove you do. To do something right."

"I chose to break Hadyn out of prison before I knew it was him, simply because I could not remain free knowing someone else was caged for my actions."

Stegler's eyes flickered as he realized she was there that night, masquerading as the second cloaked figure, the stranger that saved his life.

"And I want to free as many others as I can," Kiara continued. "I want to free myself. If we can escape, I can't tell you how, but we will be able to do just that." Her eyes took on a fiery glow, reflecting the light of the hearth. "So if the clansmen are hiding something for the king for their own personal gain, you better believe I'm going to find it." She paused for a breath. "So, if you know something . . . about the clansmen—"

"Even *if* I knew something . . ." Stegler cut her off, his patience barreling to an end. "If you really think I would help you with *anything* that has to do with the man who gave me this for a parting gift . . ." Stegler jerked down his shirt collar to reveal the beastly mark of the Whitefang clan permanently emblazoned into his skin, not neatly like a brand might do, but jagged and gruesome as if done by a blunt, rusty knife. Stegler shook his head. "You're wrong."

Kiara's face twisted in horror and Stegler pulled the shirt back to hide the awful mark, but though Hadyn grimaced, he didn't look surprised.

"Now, please, if you'd be so kind as to excuse me so I can clean up this mess before I go to sleep . . ." Stegler didn't wait for a reply; he simply turned his back to them and resumed picking up fallen objects and placing them back where they belonged.

Hadyn glared at his back with both shame and pity for the coward he saw so clearly. "Come on, Kiara, we'll find another way. Though," he turned back to Stegler once more, "you should know, you're not the only one with scars." Putting an arm around Kiara, he guided her out of the room.

From the scattered keepsakes on the floor, Stegler plucked up a small cap, only big enough to fit a child. Stiff and dust coated from years of disuse, Stegler held it in the worn places that welcomed his fingers. Unshed tears stung his eyes. So much loss. He had thought it'd be easier if he never cared for anyone else. If he only cared for himself, he would never have to feel that pain again, but here he was and the pain was as fresh as the day he lost them all.

He thought of Kiara and how she had helped him even though she didn't even know him. Long had the kindness of the second hooded figure haunted his dreams and plagued his nighttime thoughts, and now he knew her name.

"Just," he took in a heavy breath, "one more thing, lass."

Kiara turned around, expecting to see a scowl on his face as he delivered one last warning, instead she saw sincerity, the most his eyes had held yet.

"I never got to thank you," he said, "for what you did."

When Kiara understood, she blinked and looked down. "Oh, I—"

"I might not be alive if it wasn't for you."

"Well, the keys wouldn't have been taken if it wasn't for me either."

"Yes, but . . . you didn't have to give them back."

Kiara set her face with certainty as she locked her gaze on his. "Yes. I did."

Something had broken, Kiara could see it in his eyes, a wall had come down, one layer of a fortress he had spent years of work building in vain. But when all he did was stare, Kiara turned first this time and Hadyn followed her out of the room.

Stegler watched as they faded into the dark of the house. His features twisted and scrunched as he battled his own fears and selfish needs. He could not recall a day when he woke up without self-preservation as his soul ambition. With no one else to care about, life was simpler, but he had realized over time, not easier. For as long as he could remember, fear had ruled his life and ordered his days. With his stagnantly same life, he had managed to ignore this sorry excuse for living, but now faced with these two brave souls, just kids compared to him, with their ambitions set deep in something so much bigger than themselves, he was forced to ask himself, if his freedom was so fragile that he had to fight and hide to keep it, was it really freedom at all?

This is your chance to do something right . . . the young princess' words drifted through his mind. Long had he waited for a day to come along and hand him a chance to change his worth. And how greatly would he regret it if, now that it came, he threw it away as dross.

Stegler clenched his fists around the sides of the little cap and closed his eyes with a sigh. He could kick himself for even allowing his mind to begin those thoughts, but the damage was done. And as if a great fire had burned his selfishness down to ash, there was no going back.

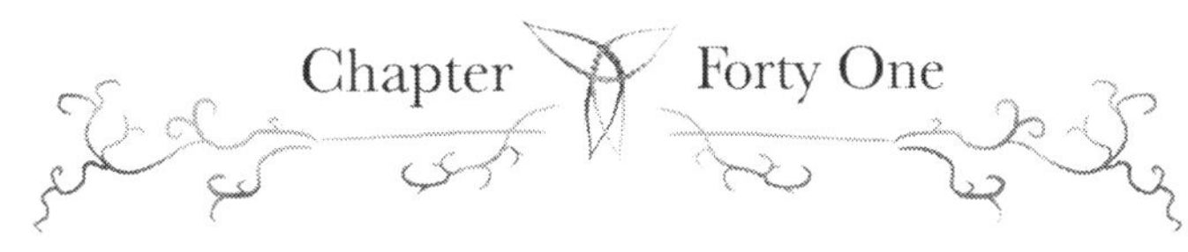

The Imperium Act

Kiara tried to hold in her tears, tried to be brave as yet another proverbial door slammed on her face, all but breaking and bloodying her nose with it's force.

Hadyn walked silently beside her, fearing what another disappointment would do to her and feeling the sting of it himself.

"Kiara, we'll find another way. We don't need him. We can do this on our own."

"But I don't want to do it alone. Hadyn, I'm tired and I just . . ." Her chin quivered and her eyes filled with tears. "I just want some-one to tell me what I'm supposed to do."

He hated to acknowledge it, but she spoke his thoughts out loud. "I know," he said.

"What . . ." She struggled to even say it. "What do we do now? Hadyn I—"

One tear slipped from her eyes and she shuffled a step closer to him. But it was a hesitant move, as if she didn't know what she wanted from it. If she was honest, she just wanted to fall down, crumple up, and not move for a very long time. She choked back a sob and stumbled into him, finished with standing on her own. After only a moment's hesitation, he put his arms around her and held her in a gentle hug. He let her cry, let her mourn the loss. But never a full storm of tears and more a weak leakage of what little was left in her, Kiara began to pull herself together.

"Come on," he said softly. "Lets go break the news to Cida."

With a hand on her shoulder, he tried hard to find her eyes in the dim light, encouraging her to take another step.

She nodded.

"Wait!" a voice called up the street, strained between secrecy and urgency. "Wait! Please, wait!"

Unsure if she was hearing things in her desperation, Kiara

turned around, too befuddled to expect anything. But there was Stegler, running up the filthy street towards them, his bare feet slapping on the cold stone.

At last, he caught up to them, leaning over with hands on his knees, sputtering to catch his breath. "Thank you . . ."

Still uncertain of his actions, Kiara and Hadyn watched him carefully until he recovered.

Stegler swallowed hard. "I don't know how much I can help you . . . and I know I don't deserve it, but if you give me another chance, I'll tell you everything I know." When they continued to only stare at him, he held up the wee cap. "For my brother."

Kiara gazed at the hat with doleful round eyes, while Hadyn fixed him with a thoughtful look. "What can you tell us?"

Stegler's face flickered with a smile, but it faded to graveness. "Not here. We can not talk here."

Once again back in the steady warmth of Stegler's hearth, this time Kiara and Hadyn sat in his chairs as guests rather than intruders.

"It's called the Imperium Act." Stegler stood near the fire and as he stirred the coals, the embers flashing red on his profile.

Kiara shivered. "What is?"

"What you're looking for, lass." He leaned the fire iron against the brick of the hearth and turned to face them. "Only Whitefang clansmen know of it. Every week, hundreds of gems are sent out of the city."

Kiara's face held no expression as she fell back and sunk into the backrest of her chair. Finally, she had certainty. For the first time one of her conspiracies was verified by mouth.

Hadyn's feelings weren't as simple. "And you never wondered where you sent them?"

"Look, I feel terrible for the things I did as a clansman. Haven't you been listening to me? I never want to go back to that life. I suppose we all couldn't have cared less if we knew where or why they were going, so long as we got paid, and stayed on Mereaze's good side. Don't tell me you never longed to defy him, but were too terrified, too beat into submission to do anything about it."

Hadyn looked away in defeat and humiliation.

"Hey, I'm not trying to come down on you, kid," Stegler said, donning a gentler tone. "It was rough. I wouldn't wish it on anyone. And I know you understand that."

"So how does it work?" Kiara piped in. "You say you send them out of the city, but how? Why? When will it happen again?"

"Whoa!" Stegler grinned at her enthusiasm. "One thing at a time. Our orders . . . *their* orders come from Mereaze, who gets his directly from?" He paused for effect and Kiara's eyes fluttered closed, knowing the rest all too well. "You guessed it. The king." He gave a quick raise of his brows. "But that's not so surprising, and the rest is simple really. The king promises to turn a blind eye to the rest of the clansmen's business, pays them handsomely, and they send the gems down the river in barrels, no questions asked."

"River?" Kiara narrowed her eyes. "What river?"

"The one that runs beneath the city." He shrugged as if she should know.

Kiara's face washed white and her breath caught, not from horror or fear, but from the sheer weight of the knowledge.

Hadyn's eyes flicked across her face. "Kiara, are you alright?"

"That's it!" she cried and shot to her feet, unable to sit any longer with such excitement bubbling inside her.

"What's it?" Stegler asked.

"Don't you get it? That's how the gems get to the outside!" she said breathlessly, looking as though she could burst into both tears or laughter at any moment. "If we find a way to get shipped down the river with the gems, we could finally get out of here! So," she grinned at him, "how do we get there?"

"Well, that's the thing, lass. You can't."

Kiara's shoulders slumped as she shook her head. "What? But you've been there."

"Yes, and believe me when I say I would help you if I could, but the only way to the loading dock is through an elaborate series of tunnels, tunnels we were always blindfolded in. Even Mereaze doesn't know the way. There were other men, men who never so much as told us their names. They would guide us through the tunnels, but not one of them knows every way. There is only one person who knows where all of those dark tunnels lead."

"The king," Kiara said.

"Correct. And without those nameless strangers, you'll be lost, of which I don't advise seeking out. You think the *clansmen* are dangerous? Those men slit clansmen's throats for simply speaking to them."

"Then we'll find our own way," Kiara said definitively. "How hard can it be?"

"Hard?" He chuckled. "Try impossible. It's a labyrinth down there. A maze! It was designed to get you lost. If you go down there as you are now, you may not come back again. And that's not even saying anything about the king's mutants."

Kiara blinked and raised her brows in mock shock.

Stegler's eyes wandered with the conspiracy. "Rumor has it that the king has a disconcerting hobby in breeding monsters, and casts his unwanted defects into his labyrinth to keep out unwelcome guests . . ." He let his words hang in the air, but Kiara and Hadyn made no sign that they bought it. "Oh, come on, what's it going to take to make you two stubborn kids understand the dangers?"

"With her?" Hadyn asked. "More than that."

He sighed. "Even if you got down there without a single scrape with danger, I don't know how, but they'd know, and they'd find you."

"What do you mean?"

"It's just that people talk . . . but it's not only that, because when information conveniently turns up for them, it's hard not to think they have eyes even in places where they don't."

Hadyn shook his head. "You're not making any sense."

"That's because it doesn't!" Stegler replied. "Look, all I know is what I hear. People call them the Buried."

He waited for them to gasp, wet themselves, or simply shiver, but Kiara just cocked her head. "Still?" she asked, exchanging a wide-eyed look with Hadyn.

"What do you mean, still?"

"It doesn't matter. So what if these things are real? If they're living in the shadows, or inside people . . ." the shiver caught up to her now, thinking of her father, "or whatever they do. Don't you see how this only makes it more urgent for us to go down the river with the gems?"

"But I'm telling you, to get anywhere down there you'd need—"

"A map," Kiara said. Her smile still had a few details to work out, but it was wily all the same.

"Well, I was going to say that, yes." Stegler blinked. "But there was never any created for reasons I'm sure you can assume easily enough."

An impish look crept into her eyes and lips. "Maybe not intentionally."

Hadyn eyed her sideways. He hadn't seen a look like that on her face since the plan to crash the resource ritual room, and had mixed feelings about its return. "You don't think . . ."

She nodded, her smile growing like a bonfire in a brittle field. "Yes, I do!"

Stegler looked back and forth between the two of them and waved a hand. "I'm sorry, did I miss something? I don't see how I've helped you at all."

"You've helped us more than you know." Kiara crossed the room to him. Tears pooled up from the bottom of her heart and into her eyes, but he remained nonplussed. "Thank you," she said and to his great surprise, pulled him into a tight embrace.

If Kiara would have let him go right away, he might have fallen over from shock. Stegler huffed as he remembered to continue to breathe. He looked to Hadyn with wide eyes, but he only smiled and watched.

"Just one more question," Kiara said as she released him. "When will the next load of gems be sent out?"

Stegler averted his eyes and fidgeted, she waited expectantly. With a huffed grumble, he said. "Today . . . before curfew breaks."

"Well then," she turned her smirk on Hadyn, "sounds like we have a ride to freedom to catch."

"But, wait!" Stegler cried.

"Thank you again for all you've done," Kiara said to him, "but, please, don't try to stop us."

"No, I mean to say . . . I'm coming with you." He nodded and solidified his resolve, though his eyes looked terribly unsure, like he might just might faint. "Yes. I'm coming with you."

"No," Hadyn said. "We couldn't ask that of you."

"And you didn't."

"But, why?" Kiara asked. "Why would you help us?"

"Because where you're going, you could use all the help you can get. Because, when you could have left me for dead, you saved me." He let out a heavy breath. "Because when all is said and done, I would be honored to be counted as half as brave as the two of you are. And besides, how often do a pair of ghosts knock on your door in the middle of the night and ask for your help?" He winked.

Kiara beamed at Hadyn and he managed to work up half of a conflicted smile.

"And we would be honored to have you help us," she said.

Stegler eyed them both and his gaze lingered on Hadyn. "You're sure?"

Kiara nodded and turned to Hadyn again. After a brief pause, he gave a fleeting smile. "Welcome to the team."

Stegler grinned and rubbed his hands together. "The team," he said gleefully. "So, what's the plan?"

"First," Kiara grinned. "We have to pay a friend a visit."

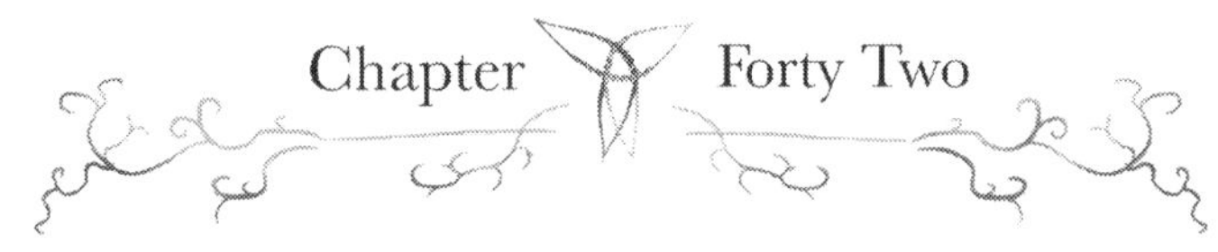

Until Next we Meet

Kiara and Hadyn led Stegler across town and to the pitch, wide entrance of the Forbiddens. Stegler gaped up at the yawning jaws of the tunnel as if the stone fangs would come crashing down on them at any moment.

He swallowed down a lump in his throat. "So . . . this is where you've been hiding out all this time."

Hadyn eyed him warily. "Yeah, and if this doesn't work out, we would appreciate it if it wasn't ratted out."

"Hadyn." Kiara shot him a scowl, but he just shrugged.

Once Stegler had processed the dig, he peeled his eyes off the dagger tip sharp stalactites. "Oh, I assure you, my lips are sealed," he said, whipping a finger to his lips.

"See," Kiara said. "And more importantly, this is *going* to work out. There's nothing else for it."

He shifted his eyes from Stegler to Kiara's steady gaze and softened. She was good, using his own words back on him. "You're right."

"Now, back on track with the lot of you rats!" a deep voice called out of nowhere, echoing about the cave. "Or I'll have your heads on spikes!" Even with the irregular squeak at the end, Hadyn just about jumped out of his skin at the unmistakable voice of his former master. And even though she'd only met him the one time, Kiara too recognized the voice immediately and whipped her head about for the brutish rogue in the tattered, brimmed hat, heart suddenly racing.

Stegler broke into a wheezy laugh. "Whooo! I knew my Mereaze was good, but I really had you there!"

Hadyn glared at him. "What kind of low life, spends his time practicing his impression of one of the worst men alive?"

Stegler answered by repeating exactly what Hadyn said in a

voice not so different from his own. Kiara gaped.

"Don't have to practice," Stegler said. "Ever since I was a wee lad, I've just had the knack."

Hadyn's expression didn't shift an inch. "And what a lovely talent it is."

Kiara smirked and started walking again. "Come on. Cida's waiting."

"Who, who's Cida?" Stegler stuttered as he stumbled across the city limit after them. "Is she the friend with the map?"

"No, we'll see him after." Kiara talked without stopping or turning around.

"How many people live in here?" he muttered.

Neither of them answered as they arrived back at where Cida waited for them.

"Kiara? Hadyn? Is that you?" her voice echoed out of the cavern.

"Yes, Cida. We're back," Kiara called, and when they rounded the corner, Cida rushed her with a hug.

"Oh, thank goodness! You said it could be dangerous and then you were gone so long— But tell me," she cut herself off. "Did you find what you were looking for? Did you get the information?"

"Yes." Kiara nodded again and again. "Yes, we did."

Cida covered her mouth. She looked like she might squeal with joy, but then her eyes detected the stranger in the room, the stranger that had not stopped gawking since they arrived at the Forbiddens, except now he stared in dazzlement more than fear. "Who's this?" she asked.

"This," Kiara turned to him, "is Stegler. He's the one who told us what we needed to know about the gems. And he offered to come with us."

"Oh. Well, hello! I'm Lucida."

Stegler's mouth flubbed open and shut like a fish, but no words came out. Before it was too painful, though, he snapped himself out of it. "Pleased to meet you, Miss. James Stegler, at your service." He finished with an awkward bow.

Kiara stifled a snicker, but Lucida silenced her with a look. "Please, there is no need to bow. Kiara is the only one here even remotely royal. I do believe you're the one to be thanked and honored."

Stegler blushed. "It is nothing of the sort."

"Well, thank you for your help, all the same."

He gave a silly grin and stepped back to hide behind Kiara and Hadyn.

"Oh, I almost forgot!" Cida said. "While you were gone, I went back to the Palace to pack you these." She grunted as she heaved up two packs filled to bursting with provisions for their undertaking. She handed them off and turned to Stegler. "I'm sorry. If I would have known you were coming, I would have packed a third."

"Aw, don't worry about me."

"No need to." Kiara fumbled, trying to get a grip on the unwieldy pack. "Think you packed us enough food, Cida?" she teased.

"Well, you never know how long you'll be wandering in the dark."

Kiara and Hadyn laughed as they donned their packs over their cloaks, and Cida joined with her own short-lived mirth, but it ended in a bittersweet sigh.

"So this is it then? It's finally time," Cida said.

Suddenly feeling more and more like an intruder, Stegler shuffled his way out of the cavern, mumbling something about waiting around the corner.

"I suppose it is," Kiara's brave smile crumbled mid sentence, "and like sitting with you on a school morning, I find myself not wanting to go."

"No, Kiara, you do, you're just scared and don't want to leave behind an old friend. But this old friend is going to be fine and I will be waiting for your return. As for being afraid, Kiara, don't forget about the Creator. Just because you don't trust it or refuse to think about it, doesn't change the fact that He's there for you."

Kiara chuckled. "Couldn't let me leave without a nugget of wisdom, huh?"

"Never." Cida reached out and stroked her soft cheek. She could feel her own strength waning and the tears coming. "Go," she whispered. "Find your mother. Go find the world that you deserve to know."

The flood walls broke and the friendship that the three had cultivated in their hearts over the recent past overflowed in the form of tears.

"You take care of her, Hadyn." Cida said and to his surprise, pulled him into a warm embrace.

Cida then hugged Kiara and they cried on each other's

shoulders.

"We'll be back before you know it," Kiara sobbed.

"No . . . No, my Dear, I'm afraid you won't. Not this time."

Kiara searched her face, almost for a way out. "I don't want to say goodbye."

"Then you don't have to. I will see you again, Missy," she said and gave her nose a light tap.

"Then, until next we meet," Kiara revised.

Cida smiled. "Much better."

Then, knowing the longer she stayed, the harder it would be to go, she let her eyes rest on them both in turn and took her leave.

As Kiara wiped her eyes, she felt a warm hand on her shoulder. She turned to him and smiled.

"We can do this," he said.

"Together," she added. "I'm glad you're with me."

He returned her smile with that sweet, bashful one, the first thing she liked about him when they met, and together they left the room they had spent every night in, just the two of them and Cida, sharing laughter and tears, fears and fragile hopes . . .

And they didn't look back.

They found Stegler where he had decided to plant himself around the corner.

He brightened when he saw them. "Are you ready?"

Kiara gave a solemn nod.

"Good. Because we don't have much time. If we want to make it through the Labyrinth and down the river before shipping time, we must be quick."

Picking up the pace, they swept through the tunnels and caverns they knew so well from their daily treks to and from Kiara's hideaway and Tick's home. But when they came to the fissure, Kiara stopped in her tracks. It was really just a crack, most people would pass it as just another crevasse leading to more cramped darkness, but she knew it as more. No light shone from the opening. It was dark inside, just like every night she had come to escape the nightmares, before she stepped inside and set it aglow to burn the shadows out of her mind. Her safety. Her hideaway.

A seizing fear tightened a grip around her throat as she stared at the jagged, wickedly black angles of the secret entrance, afraid she'd never find another safe place if she left the only one she ever had, and turning away from it felt too much like abandonment.

"Princess? Is something wrong?"

Kiara hardly noticed Stegler's question, having not responded to the title for so long. "Kiara?" Hadyn stepped into her line of vision. "Are you alright?"

She shook herself from her thoughts. "Yes, I'm fine."

He cast a look to the entrance of her hideaway and then turned back to her. "You sure?"

"Of course." She forced herself to smile. "Let's go see Tick."

At Tick's door, Kiara knocked on the wood with fast, merry taps, nearly bursting at the seams to tell her dear friend the good news, while Stegler just stared at the door in the middle of the Forbiddens, as if it were a man with four heads.

When Tick opened the door, Kiara rushed inside.

"Bright Eyes! Master Hadyn! What a joy to see you both again so soon! Why, it feels like just earlier today that I saw you."

Hadyn chuckled. "That's because it was."

"Oh. How about that? To what do I owe—"

"Tick!" Kiara interrupted, grabbing a hold of his shoulders. "We found a way to the outside world! We just need you to tell us the directions to go in the tunnel under the trap door and then we'll be out. We'll be free!"

"But that's wonderful!" Tick exclaimed. "That's the best news I've heard in a long time! Though I can't recall having heard any news for quite some time."

Kiara giggled. "I want you to come with us, Tick. Come and escape the darkness with us."

Tick sighed heavily. "Dear Kiara . . . I so wish I could. But," he raised his hands and shrugged sadly, "I can't."

Kiara's face fell, not understanding in the slightest. "But why?" she cried.

"I can't leave, because I will not have another hapless soul take my place. I won't let someone else be shut up in this room to lose their memories and identity, while I run free." He nodded. "No, it is better this way."

Kiara fought within herself, trying to understand how this could be fair, yet nothing could change the fact that he was right. He was strong enough to do the good thing, the brave thing. Still, the unknown reason why he had to be the one to make that choice, raked at her skin like jagged knives.

Kiara looked down to hide the tears filling her eyes. "I understand. But, my noble friend, I will come back and get everyone out. I will not forget about you."

"I know you won't, Bright Eyes," he said, gently raising her head. "You're too good to ever do that." He smiled at them both. "Oh, I will miss you both so very dearly. You're the most best of friends I've ever had. Or . . . that I can ever remember having." He scratched his head and got them both laughing.

"We're going to miss you too, Tick," Kiara said.

"No matter how long we're gone," Hadyn finished.

Kiara turned to Stegler, laughing and wiping her eyes. But he hadn't even fully stepped inside and had yet to cease staring at the entire room with any look but unmitigated bewilderment.

"Sorry, Stegler," she said, grabbing his attention. "I'd introduce you, but . . ."

"I will most certainly forget," Tick finished, nodding along. "Maybe even before you leave."

Stegler smiled hesitantly. "I see. What, may I ask, is this place?"

"It's the town bell." Tick shrugged as if it was obvious.

"Right . . ."

Knowing there was no time to explain the strange reasons of the place or lack thereof, let alone the way the room even worked, Kiara elected to leave it to his confusion and continue the plan with Tick.

"So, do you think you could draw us a map, Tick?"

"Depends on where you need to get to."

Stegler sputtered with a stifled laugh. "Wait. This is your plan? You think this man can help you get to the Imperium Docks?"

Kiara shot him a look as sharp as razor blades, but Tick had heard all that he needed.

"Right, straight, left, left, straight, right, straight, right, left, straight, left, right, left, straight." Tick gasped, out of breath, and blinked at Kiara. "Will that do?"

Stegler couldn't get his jaw to stay shut.

Kiara smiled at Tick. "It's perfect. Do you think you could write that down for us?"

"For you, Bright Eyes? Anything."

With paper they brought him, Tick leaned over his unreasonably small table and wrote out the turns they would need to take, mumbling them under his breath as he went. Kiara's hands shook as she took the finished note. They had directions and for once, all they had to do was follow them.

A smile glowed on her face as she wrapped her arms around him. "Thank you, Tick!"

"But, it was nothing."

She squeezed him tighter. "It's everything." Taking a step back, she wanted to say more, but she realized the things she wanted to say required sitting and talking over unhurried cups of tea as they might have done every of their lives and not gotten sick of it, times when nothing forced them to say goodbye, but Tick's own sleep deprived eyes.

"Tick, I . . ." The words died in her throat. Nothing she could say could change the difficulty of what they had to do.

Tick's eyes drooped dolefully. "It's alright. You have to go. And I wouldn't dream of keeping you a moment longer, for so great is the journey ahead of you!" He smiled, and guided them to the trap door. "Come on. I am honored to see you off."

Tick opened the hatch and Stegler was the first to climb inside, but before he disappeared completely, he looked up at Tick and said. "Thank you. I've been in those tunnels many times. Without your help, we might be lost forever."

Tick smiled and Stegler resumed his descent.

"Well, this is it." Kiara shrugged, bravely trying to fight the sadness. "But it is not goodbye. I could not bear it to be. We will see each other again and we will sit and talk as we did before and tell you of our adventures." Tears pooled in her eyes. "So this is . . . till next we meet."

"I like that," Tick said as his own eyes, behind his glossy goggles, grew even shinier. He hugged them both.

"Don't forget about us now, Tick," Hadyn said.

"Oh, I won't. How could I?" He chuckled, but then locked him in an unyielding gaze. "You keep her safe now, Master Hadyn."

"I will," Hadyn said.

"And if I know anything about you, Bright Eyes," he turned to Kiara with a soft smile, "you will be watching out for him too, right?"

Kiara smiled back. "Right."

"Until next we meet?"

"Until next we meet," Kiara and Hadyn both said back to him and Hadyn followed after Stegler through the trap door. Once he was far enough down, Kiara climbed in and looked up at Tick. Kneeling beside her, he held the hatch open. Not another word passed between them, but Kiara couldn't look away. Tick fought it bravely, but she knew on the inside he was hurting. She wanted to believe he was too different, that it wouldn't affect him the same way it would a normal person, but Tick knew what it meant to miss, he knew the pain of loneliness, no matter how much he remembered of the time that passed.

She didn't see how this wasn't the right thing to do, and yet it tore her heart like something terribly wrong, too much like the first time she left him in the fog of his own faulty memory.

Then Tick reached out a hand, and grazing her face with a gentle touch of his fingers, he nodded for her to go. Kiara shut her eyes in resolve, if he could be that brave, so could she. And when Kiara lowered herself far enough down, Tick shut them in the dark.

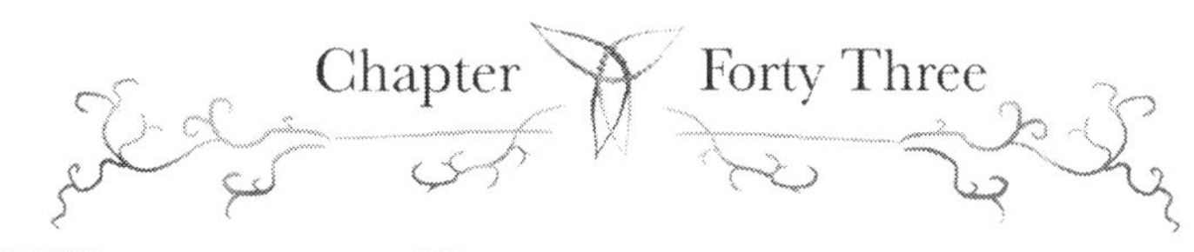

The Labyrinth

"Now, if we stay close and keep to ourselves, we should have no problem getting to the docks," Stegler explained.

All three stood in a cramped, boxy space at the bottom of the ladder, with only their lantern light for illumination.

The flames lit up Kiara's frown from below. "Should," she repeated. "I love the way that fills me with certainty."

"Well, lying to you won't do no good either."

Hadyn scowled at him. "Can we just get out of here?"

"Of course." Stegler struggled to shuffle around and turn to the door opposite the ladder.

Hadyn turned to Kiara as she wiped her cheeks and then her wet hand on the skirt of her dress. "You alright?"

She gave a tight nod just as the whining creak of hinges crawled into their ears. Stegler peered out the door, but the profound emptiness they all soon found in the hall must have been enough to put his fears at ease. After only a brief moment's pause, he swung the door wide and stepped out of the suffocating room.

Kiara crept out. As soon as she entered the hall, a chill froze her blood and iced her feet to the floor. It was empty all right, but unseen phantoms traced eerie memories at the back of her mind and sent skitters up her spine. Dark, cobbled walls stretched into the black for unspoken lengths to both the left and right, cobbled walls that brought both a familiar comfort and dread.

Just like in her dreams, she felt she had been here before, though with no idea why or when, except this time she was wide awake and knew for certain, she had never been here in her life. The feeling twisted her gut until she wanted to wretch. She placed a hand against the cold, clammy wall and immediately recoiled.

"Kiara?" Hadyn stepped towards her with his arms outstretched as if he feared she might faint.

Kiara looked in horror from him to Stegler. “What is this place? Where are we right now?”

Stegler didn’t understand. “Under the city. Well, under your friend’s home right now, but most of the tunnels traverse under the city.

Kiara huffed, out of breath even though she hadn’t moved.

“Kiara, what is it?”

She shook her head. “You won’t believe me.”

“Yeah, you’re probably right,” Stegler said.

Hadyn ignored him completely. “Why would you think that? I can tell by the look on your face, it’s serious.” He held her gaze until she gave in.

“I just have this feeling . . . I feel like I’ve been here before.”

His face registered the exact opposite of what she expected: understanding. “Your dreams.”

She blinked. “Yes.”

“Well, you always said, you never dreamed long enough to find out where the tunnels lead. Maybe now you finally can.”

At the suggestion, Kiara felt a chunk of the panic melt off her shoulders. “You’re right.” She released a dreadfully shaky breath and fished the note Tick had written for them out of her pocket. The page trembled and shivered in her grasp and she scrunched her face in an attempt to concentrate. Seeing her struggle, Hadyn grabbed a corner of the page with a steady hand. Kiara released the note and dropped her gaze, defeated.

“The first direction is a right,” Hadyn said, straightening the paper.

“Right, off we go then.” Relative to the door they came out of, Stegler turned right and led the way down the passage.

Hadyn waited for Kiara to go in front of him and then took up the rear, expecting to have to announce the next direction soon, but to all except Stegler’s surprise, the tunnel ran straight with no turns, doors, or deviations, for some lengths. Every step Stegler took, pushed back the darkness and revealed only more smooth, cobbled walls, one patch at a time. Until at last something changed. The right wall remained featureless and straight ahead led into more unmapped darkness, but on the left wall an imposing, wood door loomed into view.

Kiara cocked her head as they came up on the door. An ominous face of sorts was carved into its middle, neither fully man nor beast. It had two curved horns sharp enough to impale the thickest hides, hollow pits for eyes, and a boxy bovine nose.[1] Strangely enough, she didn't recognize it in the slightest, and she was positive she would've remembered if she had ever dreamed about it. And yet . . . the chill it gave her was just the same as everything else–familiar. It stabbed her with such a great dread, as if something dangerously powerful resided on the other side of the door. The same kind of power she had once seen control the king himself. It made her wonder, but the trouble with that was, once she started, she didn't quite know how to stop. What secret mysteries hid down here that allowed a place she'd never seen to crawl into her dreams and make itself a home?

What secrets indeed . . . she wondered, and before she knew it, her own hand began to reach out towards the door.

"Careful there, lass," Stegler's warning made her flinch. "Down here, curiosity won't get you anything but killed."

"Do you think this door counts as a turn?" Hadyn asked as he consulted the note's directions again. "Is continuing forward what Tick marked as straight."

"I should think so," Stegler answered and then cocked an eyebrow at Kiara. "Are you ready to follow the directions, Princess?"

She hesitated and Hadyn eyed her suspiciously, shifting his gaze between her and the door.

Finally, she nodded. "Yes," she said, and with one last look at the strange door, she left it behind.

They walked another stretch of featureless tunnel, nearly as long as the last, before the way properly split into four directions.

Unlike before, with the muffled, empty silence, here they could hear vague things, almost as if a barrier had been abruptly lifted. And underneath the indiscernible noises was a sound like a raging furnace, but much too far away to know for sure.

Stegler stopped at the intersection. "We're here."

"Where? We haven't even followed half the directions yet." Hadyn waved the note at him.

"The Labyrinth."

"You're telling me, up until now we weren't even in it yet?"

"Not truly," Stegler said darkly. "Keep your wits about you.

---

1. Though no true evidence has ever been scrounged from Caverna's underworld to make it anything more than pure fiction, some are determined to preserve the rumor of the breading of beasts underneath the city. Why or when the talk surfaced is also unknown.

They say, the tunnels can play dangerous tricks on the mind."

"Of course they do," Hadyn said. "The next two turns are lefts, so that way it is." He pointed down the left tunnel.

"Read that list carefully," Stegler said. "If we take one wrong turn, we may never get out of here." With that he turned down the tunnel, forcing them to follow or fall behind.

Kiara walked alongside Hadyn this time, not caring for the single file thing, and shook off a shiver. Stegler's words only watered the seed of fear her dreams had planted in her heart. Never once had her dreams involved escaping the tunnels; only wandering, forever wandering.

The turns and intersections came closer together now, and the fear put down its roots when the strange noises they were hearing only increased. Sometimes it sounded like shouting or scuffling, and sometimes she heard the odd clink like chains or some other metal object on stone, and always the vague roaring like a great fire, barely even there, but constant nonetheless. But hard as she tried, with the echoing, interconnecting nature of the maze, she couldn't find a single source for the noises, let alone a direction they seemed to come from. They just . . . buzzed in the air, numbing her to their presence until she couldn't be certain anything tangible was even responsible for them, as if the labyrinth had come alive with a network of its own voices.

For some reason, she hadn't thought to mention the sounds, but as time went on and neither Hadyn nor Stegler did either, she grew ever more concerned. She might have thought they were all in her head if it weren't for how agitated her companions looked. Hadyn's hands stayed ever clenched in tight fists and his usually calm gaze shifted constantly around the tunnel, never finding rest. Stegler walked ahead of them with a stiff gate, his knuckles long gone white over the handle of the lantern he kept stretched before him.

They didn't say as much, yet she could tell the sounds were getting to them. But now when she thought to ask, an unquenchable fear rose up out of nowhere and clamped her mouth shut.

With their next direction as straight, they came up on another four passage crossroad and prepared to pass it by without stopping. But as they came to the middle, the passages to the left and right opened up to an especially threatening darkness, and a prickling on her left arm made Kiara turn and look down the tunnel. As she stared down its throat, she felt like it could swallow her whole or that someone or something was there, staring at them, waiting for the dark to pull her in. Something very real, but untouchable and invisible, like evil lurked and guarded that very passageway. A shiver ran through her whole body and her hands began to tremble. She wrenched her face away, but that's when the screaming started. Not from the passage. No, from everywhere and nowhere at the same time. Countless, nameless, and faceless voices, screaming out in pain and misery. Distant by volume, but somehow so close, they seemed nowhere but inside her own head. The sound tore her heart and filled it with an ache she wasn't prepared for. Unexpected tears filled her eyes.

She turned to Hadyn, longing with every bit of her being for a reasonable answer, but he didn't see her, his ears pricked as he whipped his head about, his protective gaze demanding a direction to follow to the sound. Only Stegler seemed unfazed, yet not unaffected. It didn't surprise him, but his shoulders still slumped as he heaved a heavy sigh.

"You heard it too," she said. "Both of you."

"Depends on to what you're referring." Stegler turned to look at them. "The cries of a small boy?"

"Small boy?" Hadyn asked. "That was clearly a woman crying in pain. We have to help her!"

Kiara narrowed her eyes at both of them. "Wait. Are you telling me, you both only heard one voice?"

Hadyn turned to her in horror, but Stegler remained unfazed. He watched as both their faces drained of color.

"It's not real . . ." Hadyn said, "is it?"

Stegler shrugged. "Some say the Labyrinth harbors openings to the Void, and the cries are the sounds of its sucking winds whenever the doors open. Some say–" He stopped, lacking the heart to say much more, all his snark and cynicism dried up like a desert stream. "Other things . . ."

The screams sounded again and they all winced.

"What other things?" Kiara trembled as she asked, like she didn't fully want to know.

Stegler sighed. "Some say they are the voices of those we failed to save, crying out from where they are lost in the Void."[1]

---

1. Much like the rest of the rumors surrounding this enigmatic maze, it is unclear whether the voices are simply the wind and one's own imagination or if there truly is some stronghold of shrouded and buried power down there.

Hadyn couldn't be sure, but Kiara's tremors seemed to become even more violent after Stegler's answer, and he couldn't put out a rising anger at him for making her afraid.

"I don't know if there's any truth to it," Stegler continued, "but ever since I first came here, I've always heard the same boy. And he sounds just like my brother did on the day I lost him." His eyes grew terribly sad. " . . . The day I was too weak to save him," he spat the words as if even his own voice was distasteful enough to fill him with shame.

Kiara wanted to cry for him, but her own fear towered over and choked out every other emotion, demanding it be the only thing she could think about. "And the other rumors? The ones about the king's monsters? I don't suppose you made those up just to deter us from coming here?"

Once again, he seemed to fill to the brim with an overwhelming shame, as if it was his fault she was so terrified. "I wish I had, lass."

Kiara's mouth went dry. Hadyn eyed Stegler dangerously, more than ready to make her fear his fault. Then the screams raked over all their minds again, and he squeezed his eyes shut and balled his hands into fists.

"You're telling me you don't hear that woman?"

"Hadyn . . . I hear lots of voices." Kiara squeaked.

He didn't seem to hear her answer. "And it sounds like a little girl is with her too. They sound so scared. Real or not, I don't know about you, but I'm not leaving here with even a chance of someone being in trouble."

"Even if there is someone making the screaming," Stegler said, sighing the words pathetically, "what's the point? We're probably much too late to save them."

"What's the point?" Hadyn echoed. "Grow a spine! I'd rather die attempting to save them than get out of here without even trying." Hadyn got so close, Stegler had to back up, cowering before him. "But of course you'd rather just leave. You're nothing but a coward." He jabbed a finger into his chest. "And you don't care about anyone but yourself!"

Stegler didn't have anywhere else to go but against the tunnel wall.

Kiara gaped at them, like she watched two wild animals ripping into each other's flesh, the vague sound of flames roaring ever louder along with her mounting fears. "Stop it!" she cried, but she wouldn't dare get closer to them. "It's not real! You said it yourself. There's no one to save, so why are you fighting?"

Hadyn turned to her, saw the fear in her eyes, and immediately he felt a ripping need to destroy whatever was frightening her. But when all she did was keep those fear widened eyes trained on him, he realized the only thing she was afraid of . . . was him. When he turned back to Stegler and saw how close he had gotten to him, his face washed in horror. Stumbling backwards, he felt unsteady on his own legs.

"You're right," he said, suddenly struggling for his next breaths. "I don't know what got into me."

The woman's scream ripped up the tunnels again, at least in *his* head, and tore through his nerves. Another flare of burning rage washed through him. It pulled on every string of his emotions and demanded he find a way to protect her. But while he tried to fight this rising anger, Kiara's face twisted in pain and terror. She looked paralyzed by fear, ready to curl up into a ball inside herself and never come back out again, and it was that moment that Hadyn realized how much worse what she heard must be.

"We have to get out of here," he said definitively.

Kiara's eyes grew even wider. "But what's even the next direction?!"

Hadyn wrenched the note out of his pocket. "It was straight. I remember. We have to go that way." He pointed down the tunnel.

"But we've been standing here so long." Stegler's face drooped with hopelessness. "You could have lost track on where you were in reading the directions." His shoulders collapsed as he slid down the tunnel wall until he sat slumped on the ground.

Hadyn couldn't believe his eyes. "What are you doing!"

"He's giving up!" Kiara said in a panic. Then, whispering under her breath, she added, "We can't give up. We'll be stuck here forever!"

"Would you get up!" Hadyn barked at him. "Can't you see you're upsetting her?"

"Seems I've upset more than just the princess . . ." Stegler said, detached with his eyes fixed on the ground. "But who cares? We're stuck here anyway, and it's all my fault. We should have never come down here, but I wasn't strong enough to make you understand that. I'm never strong enough . . ."

"What are you talking about?" Hadyn shouted, his grip loosening on his temper.

"We're stuck?" Kiara shivered.

Hadyn looked into her terrified gaze and felt himself clawing back to some form of sanity. "No. No, we're not," he said gently and turned back to Stegler. "Look, this isn't us. You're the one who said it. I don't know how, but the Labyrinth is messing with our minds. And we're not stuck because I remember every turn we took since we climbed down that ladder and the order in which we took them."

Stegler stopped his moping long enough to look surprised. "You do?"

"Yes. Now, maybe what you said is true. Maybe you've never been strong a day in your life. I don't really care. 'Cause it doesn't mean you can't choose to change that right now. But you better get up, because we're getting out of here with or without you."

Kiara didn't share his exact feelings, but she was trembling too violently to say much of anything right now.

Hadyn turned to her, his face softening with much more patience. "Kiara, I know you feel scared, but there's no reason for it. It's just a feeling and you have to fight it. Do you think you can do that?" She gave him a shaky nod. "Good. Now let's get out of here before these halls decide to start screaming again."

Hadyn turned around expecting to see Stegler yet on the ground, slumped in his feebleness, but he stood at the ready, somehow, against the odds, looking like he had a bit of strength back. He nodded bravely.

Hadyn stopped himself from rolling his eyes, still fighting the urge to be angry with him and walked past him, claiming the lead.

Once they put the four way passage behind them, things got a little easier to bear, and the further they walked, the less they noticed its effects. Though the more they let their guards down, the easier it was for them to fall into its snares, so they had to stay constantly vigilant if they wanted to hold on to any shred of sanity.

Finally, after more directions and turns with not a word passed between them except from Hadyn to guide them, they came to the end of the list and to the very head of where three tunnels made a perfect T. They had four choices they could make: go back, turn right, turn left, or head straight for the door nestled in the wall of the tunnel. With no more directions left, Kiara bolted for the door and wrested the handle with both hands. Twisting the knob, she gave it a yank, but soon began shaking it violently in its frame.

"No, no, no." She jumped back with a twisted expression. "It's locked!"

Stegler's shoulders slumped. "Figures . . ."

Hadyn eyed him. "Oh no, don't you start that again."

"What? I can't say I'm surprised, but I'm not saying we can't still wait for someone else to come along and unlock it."

"What if that someone isn't friendly?" Kiara piped in.

"We could sneak in behind them," Stegler suggested.

"No, no . . ." Hadyn waved a disregarding hand and focused his attention on the door. "This door looks vaguely familiar."

"Excellent, so you've dreamt of this cursed maze too. Haven't we already established that doesn't do us any good?"

"No, not from a dream," he snapped and then sighed. "Just . . . let me try something."

Appraising the door as though it was a dangerous foe he had long forgotten about, Hadyn stepped towards it. He didn't bother with the knob, but simply pushed on the door with the pads of his fingers. With a meek whine, it swung open without resistance.

Kiara sniffed and stiffened. "How did you do that? It was locked! I know it was."

"It's a trick handle," Hadyn said and demonstrated. "You turn the knob and it slides the lock bolt into the catch. You leave it be and it opens as if you had done the previous. It's so you don't have to use a key, but it still keeps people who don't know about it out."

Listlessly, he turned the handle back and forth, sliding the bolt in and out of the door. Kiara stared at him quizzically, waiting for him to answer the questions she actually had on her tongue.

"My father . . ." Hadyn started to explain, "made one for our house. My mother always lost her key." He smiled. "He made her a trick handle so she wouldn't have to worry about it. He taught me how to make one too. One of those rare times when he was sober and not a half bad father." Hadyn laughed. "My mother used to tell him that if he could make things like that, then he would have no trouble making a fine living out of crafting. He never did listen though." Hadyn looked at the door. "I've actually never seen anyone else make anything like it."

She gave him a sad smile. "Makes you wonder, huh?"

"Yeah . . ." Hadyn said and then he held the lantern closer and examined the side of the door that met the frame when closed.

There, just above the handle were two letters etched into the wood. The initials *A.S.*

"Alister Stone," he said, his eye lingering painfully on the letters. "You were right, Kiara. You know, I think I liked it better when he was just a belligerent, gambling drunk. Now he's a liar and who knows what else."

"Hadyn, I'm so sorry."

"Don't be." He brushed her off, but she could hear the pain and most of all the anger in his voice. "He's gone and none of it matters anymore."

"But it does." Kiara said. "Hadyn, your pain, it's real. Don't try to diminish it. It'll only hurt more."

He smiled weakly. "I suppose you're right."

"You know," Stegler's voice came baited with sarcasm, "this is all very touching, but if I may ask, could we perhaps hurry up and go through the door that is now, so conveniently, no longer impeding our progress?"

Hadyn shook his head with playful annoyance at Kiara, but if he was honest, his patience for Stegler's attitude was wearing thin. "Wouldn't waste another moment," he said and turned to the door.

"You there!" a voice bellowed and bounced around the tunnels, freezing them in place. "Cloaks aren't allowed in the Labyrinth! Not after the prison break." A man dressed in all black marched up the left tunnel to meet them. "King's Order."

Chapter Forty Four

The Imperium Docks

"My apologies, sir," Stegler said, to the approaching stranger. "We must have missed that order."

"Impossible!" the man sputtered as he stopped in front of them, and Kiara recognized his hooked nose immediately. "The king made sure that everyone relevant was aware weeks ago."

"And I'll say again," Stegler tried to smooth talk, "I do apologize for being so inconveniently misinformed. But I can assure you we have nothing to hide."

Shrike grunted. "Well? Then you will have no problem removing your hoods in my presence."

Stegler turned to Hadyn and Kiara. "Boys, you heard the man. Hoods aren't allowed in the Labyrinth."

Hadyn's eyes flared with distrust as if to scream, *Are you mad?*

Stegler replied with the slightest tilt of his head and raise of his eyebrows as if to say, *Just do it!*

Narrowing his eyes, Hadyn slowly lifted his hands to the edges of his hood, and Kiara, with butterflies swarming a flurry in her stomach, did the same. While Shrike focused his attention on who the identity of the hooded two could be, Stegler grabbed the back of his head and sent him a hard right hook to the face. Kiara failed to stifle the scream that jumped out of her throat, but as Shrike began seeing stars, Kiara thought she'd play one last prank for old times sake, perhaps her best yet. Instead of dropping her arms, she went ahead and removed her hood and stepped into the sight of his drooping eyes. A satisfied smile curled on her lips as she waved to him. "Good night, Shriky."

Sheer bewilderment twisted his face and he struggled to raise a weak finger, just as his eyes fell shut and Stegler clumsily lowered him to the ground.

"Good luck getting anyone to believe what you saw in the Labyrinth, my friend."

Stegler narrowed his eyes. "You know him?"

She snickered. "We go way back . . . Will he be alright?"

"Don't worry. The worst he'll sustain is a headache." He frowned at the limp body. "And possibly a broken nose. But he'll wake up, so come on. Let's scoot before he does."

Hadyn watched his every movement as he pushed the trick rigged door open and walked through, trusting him less with every step he took. Kiara threw Shrike's limp body one last grin, before following them in.

Behind the door, lay another boxy room much like the one they entered the Labyrinth through, with a ladder at the other side, leading up to a trap door.

"Perfect." Stegler rubbed his hands together, and reaching for the first rung, he said, "Now, I'll go up first to make sure it's safe."

"Sure you will." Before Stegler could even begin his climb, Hadyn grabbed him by the back of the collar, made him face him, and pinned him against the wall. "What do you think you're doing? Do you take us for that big of fools? I won't let you sell us out."

Stegler's chest huffed in and out with fear as he struggled. "What are you talking about?"

"Quiet!" Hadyn pushed his forearm into his neck.

"Hadyn, what are you doing?!" Kiara screamed.

"I'm sorry that I can't bring myself to fully trust a Whitefang clansman. Retired or not."

"He just took care of Shrike for us! Probably saved our lives!"

"Yeah, with deception and brute force too, exactly how a clansman would do it."

"You were once a clansman. Would you prefer I treat you with the same distrust?" she asked.

"It was different for me. I didn't have a choice!" Hadyn shoved his arm harder into his neck. "He did."

"Please! Please!" Stegler choked, and Hadyn relented. Gasping, Stegler tried to speak.

"Yes . . . I did have a choice. I know that now. But there are times when things in life are so backwards, so wrong, those choices aren't so easy to see. I despise them and shutter at the thought of the man I used to be. Please, allow me to prove that to you." His eyes pleaded with him.

Hadyn let him go with a shove. "Why should I trust you?"

Stegler shrugged. "I can't give you a reason."

Hadyn huffed, ready to give up on him.

"Only my word," he continued, "that I want to help. That I want to do good. Because I believe what you said." He waited till he looked him in the eyes. "It's not too late for me to change. Please, tell me you still do too."

Hadyn blew a measured breath through his nose. "Of course."

Stegler sighed. "Thank you."

"But, there's no reason why I can't be the one to check if it's safe up there."

Stegler nodded. "If that's what you want."

"Kiara, start coming up right after me." She gave a tight nod, eyes still wide from the fight and Hadyn began his climb up the ladder.

After he had climbed well above their heads Kiara mounted the ladder and Stegler followed soon after, the lantern clenched between his teeth.

As they rose, each rung of the ladder another handhold to take them up and out of the pit of the Labyrinth, Kiara clearly noticed the growing quiet. The continuous noise of the riotous flames had become nothing more than static in her ears, but now as its volume died away, she could suddenly hear it again, not so much as outside sounds, but as something living in her own thoughts. And the feelings she would have thought were hers, looked as different from her own as black from white now. They tried to stay, clinging like sticky hands at the back of her mind, but were forced to fall away the higher she climbed. All at once, she didn't even know who she had been in the last— how long had it been? Hours? She felt like a stranger, like she had been torn out of herself, the parts of her that yet possessed the ability to think straight, thrown away without a second thought, and the terrible parts, multiplied and stuffed back in. And now that those things fell away, her gut twisted with the rude awakening.

Hadyn paused on the ladder above her to peer out the trap door at the top, and when he resumed his climb, she crawled out of the tunnel herself to find him sitting on the ground, head hung and brows knit in some kind of awful turmoil. He felt it too, and when Stegler popped his head out of the tunnel, his eyes said he was no exception. Before climbing out he regarded them each in turn with a grave expression and breathed a heavy sigh.

Though they had made it through the mind tunnels of the Labyrinth, all three couldn't shake an overwhelming and unavoidable sense that they had lost a battle or failed in some way.

Hadyn was the last one remaining on the ground. With some sort of unspoken agreement, they all decided not to talk about what they knew each other was feeling. Hadyn stared at the stone floor, his hands limp in his lap.

"Hadyn." Kiara huffed. "Hadyn!" but he wouldn't respond. She grabbed him underneath the arm, though she could do little to lift him. "Come on. We don't know how much time we have left, or if we have any at all."

The sound of foaming rapids rushed into his ears and his eyes cleared. "You're right," he said and stood almost wholly without her help, though when he looked at Stegler, he felt as though he could use a hand to stay steady.

"Don't worry, lad," Stegler said. "It's a game down in those tunnels . . . one that none of us were prepared to play."

Hadyn made no reply, but only turned to Kiara and nodded for them to keep moving.

Leaving the trap door behind, they walked down a rounded hallway, where the rumoring echoes of rapids tumbled together into a great rushing voice. Before they could fully round the corner, Stegler pulled them to a stop, gestured for them to wait and peered out.

His shoulders relaxed. "No one's here," he raised a wary brow, "*yet.* We'll have to move fast."

They filed out of the hallway into a long room with a ceiling almost too low for Hadyn to stand up straight. Merely a rift in the stone, a place where the earth split and never came back together. Towards the opposite end of the room, the rift steadily widened, the ceiling pulling further and further away from the ground. And there at the widest spot, running the length of the cavern, the subterranean river rushed with a violent flow right beneath the city. The water a roiling riot of foamy white and inky black, the river gurgled and bucked with a ceaseless spray, making wet hollow noises as the water slapped the stone walls where it entered the room.

Towering stacks of barrels awaited shipment against the walls, tied together by thick rope. Wooden riggings at the stone shore had been constructed to make the shipping of barrels more convenient and less strenuous.

"I can't believe we made it in time!" Kiara cried, fighting to keep her voice just above the rush of the rapids.

"Well, don't start your rejoicing just yet," Stegler crabbed. "We still've got to find some barrels that are yet empty."

They waited as he scanned the length of the room with searching eyes.

"See those under the docks?" Stegler pointed to a line of barrels in a shadowed space where the saturated boards of the docks dripped down into. They nodded.

"Them are spares. For last minute hauls. They're our best bet at some free barrels. If we can get them up on the docks, they should be tossed in first thing as the boys arrive."

"Should . . ." Kiara grumbled. "There's that word again." Eyeing the barrels across the expanse of the room, she gritted her teeth. "Well, what are we waiting for?"

Stegler swept a hand. "After you, Princess." And together, the three of them stepped out of hiding and scampered across to the docks.

In the dank shadow of the docks, bitter, musty smelling water dripped on their heads and off their noses, and made the stone slick beneath their feet.

"Quickly now." Stegler handed Hadyn his lantern and wrapped an arm around one of the barrels, which all stood at about half Kiara's height. Jamming his fingers into a gap at the top, he pried the lid open with a grunt.

A smell just like the dock drippings, but twice as potent wafted out when the lid popped free. Stegler dropped the lid where it hung at the barrel's side, attached by a short rope. Taking the lantern back, he leaned his face inside the barrel.

"Empty as a stomach on Terminal Avenue," came his muffled voice. He yanked his head back out. "Perfect!"

Kiara grimaced at his metaphor, but couldn't complain. After checking two more barrels, Stegler slapped back on their lids and lowered the three onto their sides. Then, stepping behind one, he rolled it out from underneath the docks, while Kiara and Hadyn watched.

He glanced over his shoulder. "Well, come on! We don't have all night."

They looked at each other, shrugged, and each began rolling a barrel after Stegler. They walked them up the ramp of the docks,

Kiara struggling at the back. Even empty, the barrels seemed to weigh a ton. She huffed and grunted and even turned backward to try to force it up the ramp with her back to the barrel, but it was an uphill battle and she was losing. With her strength waning and her muscles screaming out, she feared she'd be flattened at any moment. But instead of overcoming her, the weight was lifted off. So relieved, she wasn't even sure of what happened.

"I got you," she heard Hadyn say, and turned to him, a little more than embarrassed that she couldn't do it on her own.

"Thanks. That could have been a disaster."

He gave her a lopsided grin. "What are companions for?"

While they rolled the barrel up the ramp, Stegler worked on setting his and Hadyn's back upright. They rocked back and forth with hollow, drumming sounds, as he set them on the edge of the dock. Lining it up with the rest, Kiara helped Hadyn set the last one up with a huff. She looked over the edge, where the dock dropped off straight into the raging river, the spray coating her face and hair.

"Well, that was easier than I thought!" she shouted above the rapids.

"Was it, lass?" Stegler grinned. "Thought the commandeering of a few barrels would be a wee bit harder, did ya'?"

Kiara squinted and blinked. "Well, yes. But when you put it that way . . ."

He laughed. "You best get inside."

Cupping his hand, he gave her a leg up into the barrel, and Hadyn crawled into his barrel easily enough on his own. Standing up, the rims of the barrels came to their waists and Hadyn was already dreading the thought of having to compact himself down into the bottom of the tight space.

"Alright," Kiara turned to Stegler. "You next."

Stegler's face twisted with a brave kind of pain, resolved to some unspoken fate, and took a step back.

"Stegler," Kiara said, and Hadyn eyed him warily. "Come on." She forced a smile. "Get in your barrel."

He shook his head. "No. Someone has to stay back to get your barrels in the water and make sure you get down the river."

"But your barrel . . . you brought it up here."

"Only because you'd never get inside, if I told you the truth."

"No." She swallowed a lump of emotions down. "There has

to be another way." Kiara tried to clamber out, but she couldn't on her own without making the barrel wobble dangerously.

"Stop. You'll only hurt yourself. This was always the plan."

"Not for me!" she cried. "What if they catch you on your way back? What if they recognize you?"

"I've made up my mind."

"Stop! I won't let you, not after everything you've already done for us."

"But it's you that has done something so much greater for me. Before tonight, I didn't believe I could be brave," he shrugged, "let alone good." He searched their faces each in turn before adding, "Thank you. *Both* of you. For proving me wrong."

"I'm sorry—" Hadyn faltered, but when he found the strength to raise his eyes, he continued, "I'm sorry I doubted you."

"Don't be. I would've doubted me too." Stegler said. "I'm just glad you gave me enough of a chance to defy both of our expectations."

"And you have," Kiara said, smiling to hold back her tears. "Not only have you proven your courage, but your goodness too. Truly."

He turned to her with a warm smile. "I wish you all the luck in Caverna."

"Thank you, but I'm not sure that's very much."

"Then all that's out there too . . . wherever you're off to."

Kiara opened her mouth to reply, but an echoing of boisterous voices took her words. A flickering glow began to brighten down the hallway to the right and shadows of a great company of men marched nearer.

"Change of plans," Stegler said. "I'm going to buy you some time. Get situated as fast as you can and don't make another sound until you're well on your way down the river. You hear me?"

Kiara bit her lip. "But—"

"I said, do you hear me?"

Gathering a shaky breath, Kiara nodded. A wily smile curled on Stegler's lips, and as he turned away, he ran down the dock riggings, crying, "For the Princess!"

A shout of protest ripped at Kiara's throat to get out, but she knew that would only give them away and get Stegler caught, so she watched the distance between them grow with muzzled lips.

She felt a hand on her shoulder and heard Hadyn's gentle prompting in her ear. "Come on, they'll see us."

Sucking in a breath, Kiara resigned herself to leave yet another person who didn't deserve to be left. She began to lower herself into the barrel, but something stuck and she could hardly bend her knees without something restricting her.

"Our packs!" she hissed, grappling at the cumbersome protrusion on her back. "They won't fit with us!"

Hadyn tossed a glance at the ever nearing shipment men, then at the raging rapids. "Throw them in the river."

"But the food! It will be ruined!"

"It's the only way to get rid of them and not leave any evidence that we were here."

Kiara felt like worry hadn't left her face since they set out to find Stegler that night and the lines only deepened now.

"Fine." Slipping her arms out of the straps, with a cringe, she chucked her pack over the edge of the docks.

Because of the ruckus the rapids already caused, the two splashes barely made a sound. The same could not be said for the thundering volley of booms that came next. Kiara jumped and her jaw dropped as she watched one of the towers of barrels tumble over, collapsing on itself and onto the ground in front of the hallway where the men approached. But she saw soon enough, as Stegler fled the cascade of barrels and darted for cover, that this was no structural failure of the ropes or knots, but a deliberate sabotage to stall the men.

"Come on," Hadyn said. "That won't distract them for long."

Gathering up the lid, Kiara forced herself to crunch down into the barrel and sealed herself in the dark. Her breaths came in shallow, amplified gasps as every other noise became muffled and the bitter must of the barrel envelope her. Her lips silently trembled as she pleaded for Stegler's safety to whoever would listen. With her legs tucked against her chest, her knees and spine were pressed hard against the walls of the barrel and her arms didn't know where to rest. As cramped as she already felt, it pained her to think of how Hadyn was fairing.

Of course, it can not be ignored that how Hadyn fared was indeed painful as he tried desperately to arrange his longer limbs in a way that wouldn't render him permanently disfigured if he ever managed to get out.

Comfortable or not, they both ceased any squirming as they caught the muffled, yet very enraged shouts of some of the shipment men as they demanded an explanation for the barrel disaster.

"What is the meaning of this!" A voice screamed. "Who's in charge of knot tying? I'll have your head for this!"

"Sir, it appears the ropes were cut." Another said.

"Cut, ay? You sure one of those barrels didn't knock you over the head, Martin?"

"No, sir. See for yourself."

There was a sigh and stomping footsteps, but they stopped sooner than they began. "Oi!" The boss's voice rang. "What are those barrels doin on the docks?" Kiara bit her lip and held her breath as the question hung in the air. "You lazy slackers!" The boss exploded. "You have one job! Can't you finish right? Those barrels should've been sent down the river in last week's shipment."

"But we didn't leave any barrels last week."

"Ah, Will, thank you for volunteering to help Martin ship the tardy barrels. The rest of you! Take care of this disaster!"

The rest of the men grumbled to themselves as the boards creaked and groaned under the weight of the two coming up the ramp. Kiara heard them grunt as they heaved Hadyn's barrel up, but with a booming drum, they dropped it back down. Kiara cringed at the sound.

"Ay!" One of them said. "This barrel doesn't feel full."

"Are you complaining about a light shipment?" The boss said incredulously.

"And this one here is bloomin' empty!"

"Empty you say?" At last, the boss had run out of words.

The boards creaked again, as the third set of feet tracked up the ramp.

"What in the . . ." His words died away. "And you say these here are too light?"

"Yes, sir. Less than half a load, I'd say."

"Well, open 'em up. Have a look."

Kiara dug her fingernails into her hands and squeezed her eyes shut, just as a hand began to yank at the lid and the first crack of light cut into the barrel.

Chapter Forty Five

A Barreling Escape

Even with her eyes closed, Kiara could sense the light entering the dark of the barrel, and she dared not open them now. Maybe, just maybe, if she squeezed her eyes tight enough, she'd sink into the soggy bottom of this last prison and simply cease to exist, becoming nothing more than a soppy little puddle. As morbid as a fate as it is, to her, it seemed better than getting found.

"Nelson! Will! Martin!" A voice bellowed from seemingly everywhere, and the lid jammed back down with a slam.

At last she opened her eyes, but Kiara did not stop trembling, because getting found just got that much more unpleasant. She had only heard that voice once in her life, yet she would have recognized it even if it had been a hundred years ago, not when it turned her blood to ice the very same way it did before. The merciless leader of the Whitefangs had come to check in on his pack.

"You lazy louts!" Mereaze bellowed. "How often do you think I'll let you fall behind schedule, before I start whipping the flesh from your idle backs? Do you need to be whipped?"

"N-no, sir."

"Then work as though you already were!" he roared. "And get your hands off that barrel, Martin, before I sever them from your arms!"

"But, sir! The barrels! Their weight—"

"Did I ask to hear your gripings about how heavy they are? Because I can and will put you in so much pain, you'll beg to be a barrel hauler instead." His next words slipped out as calm as a trickle of water. "Is that what you want?" There was no audible reply before he roared again, twice as loud as the river rapids, "Then what are you waiting for! Toss 'em in the river!"

Hadyn's heart pounded in his chest to hear the voice that had haunted both his dreams and waking hours every day most his young life. But his ears perked up at that last sentence. Without it he might've never known the difference, he was just that good. But despite his contemptible occupation, Mereaze spoke like a nobleman, yet that last slang slipping into the order and the just barely discernible squeak at the height of the paroxysm, gave it all away.

Hadyn shook his head as much as he could in the tight space. *You're rash, Stegler . . .* he thought. *Maybe just rash enough . . .*

Kiara listened to the men grumbling, as if they had options to weigh, but in the end fear almost inevitably won. She thought she heard a splash and her heart raced at the thought of being stuck here without Hadyn. Curled up in a ball with nothing to do but wait, she hoped they couldn't hear her breathing, but the harder she tried to quiet it, the louder it got. Then she felt herself rise off the ground. In one fluid motion they swung her back and then forward and when they let her go, all natural laws of gravity forsook their reason for something that made her head spin and her stomach drop. She swallowed the scream rising in her throat just as her head hit the lid somehow, and then as the barrel crashed into the buckling rapids, she came back down hard on the bottom. The river bucked and jostled her around inside until she thought she was going to be sick, but she managed to keep silent for a minute longer to make sure they were far enough down the river. Satisfied with the distance, she pushed on the lid of the barrel, but it wouldn't budge, stuck in place by the hammering fist of the man who had jammed it back on.

"No! Come on!" she growled through clenched teeth and pounded on it until her palms throbbed. She took in measured breaths, but the already reduced oxygen levels in the barrel made her dizzy. In her mind she could feel the walls constricting in with every labored breath. She had no idea up from down any more. She spun round and round and rode up and down wherever the wicked river pleased to take her.

She could hear Hadyn calling for her. "Kiara! Kiara! Where are you?"

"Hadyn!" she screamed, but the wooden walls and raging waters ate up her voice, so he just kept calling.

No. She would not be stuck in here. She had to get out. She twisted and wriggled her right leg, screaming at the pain it caused, but finally managed to get her foot above her head. With all the strength she had left she forced her foot into the lid. It didn't break free, but it groaned with a small budge and the hope it gave her surged into her next kick. She reared her leg back, smashing her knee into her face and let it fly with a scream for good measure. The lid flung loose and immediately her face was soaked from the rapid's spray.

"Kiara!" Hadyn called, his cries turning desperate.

"I'm here!" she wailed. "I'm here!"

The frigid water bit through her clothes and the light cast from the docks shone like a lighthouse, calling them back, and warning them to go no further in the treacherous water. With the little light left, Kiara could just barely see dark, slick walls rising up on either side of the river and the turmoil of flashing white foam all about her, but there was no sign of Hadyn.

"Hadyn! Where are you?"

"Here!"

She tried to follow his voice, but the echoes came from all around. She squinted in the dark, wiping water from her eyes. There! Just down the river, she could see a dark shape bobbing up and down with the waves.

"I see you!" she shouted, but it was no use. She could go nowhere except for where the rapids pleased to toss her like a mistreated pancake.

Then, to her surprise, she started moving towards him, somehow getting caught in a faster flow of rapids.

Nearly there now, she shouted out to him, "Hadyn, reach out your hand!"

But she couldn't grab him, not because he didn't listen, but because the current, roiling with all its vicious energy, didn't let her get near him. She swept straight past him and slammed into the rough walls of the cave. Pain stabbed her skull and little lights flashed on and off in her vision.

"Kiara!" she heard Hadyn shout and shook the dizziness away as she felt the current pulling her back towards him.

"Reeeaaach!" he cried and Kiara stretched her arm until it hurt.

She could hardly see a wink anymore, but when her fingers brushed his hand, she grappled at the inky air until finally she had him. But the grip was weak and their hands much too slippery to keep it.

"No, no, no!" Kiara pleaded as the current began ripping them apart again.

Then, just holding on by the tips of her fingers, she felt another hand higher on her wrist, one that wasn't about to let go.

"I got you!" Hadyn said. "I got you."

Pulling together, they held onto the rims of each other's barrels so they'd at least be tossed like pancakes together. Though after about a minute of riding out those incorrigible rapids, Kiara's fingers ached from holding tight to the slippery rim and she honestly wondered if it would be easier to just let go. But as she lost vision entirely in the pitch darkness, she realized quickly enough how grateful she was to have something other than herself to hold onto.

And as hard as it is to believe, the charging river did start to slow, as all rapids must at some point in their reckless journey.

"Hey," Hadyn said. For the first time in a while he didn't have to yell to be heard. "Listen . . . The rapids are calming."

"I feel it too," Kiara said.

As they had whirled down the river, clinging to each other and fighting for their very lives, there, in the total darkness, the roar of the white waters had lessened to a whisper without them hardly noticing and quieted still, until they could only hear the gentle ripple here and there and the occasional drip as fat drops of mineral dredged water fell from the weepy ceiling.

Wholly bereft of sight, Kiara scanned the darkness for something her eyes could hold onto to no avail. But it wasn't all that bad. Nothing was after them, the waters had calmed, and at the moment she had no reason to doubt all they had to do now was wait.

Sighing, she loosened her grip on the rim of the barrel. Finally out of danger, her mind had the time to wander, and with a tightening in her chest and a twisting of her gut, it wandered into places just as dark as the air around them faster than she could have expected.

Her father's face flashed in her mind. He looked terribly sad. A part of her wanted nothing else than to have been able to say goodbye, not like before, but like with Cida and Tick, to pull him in her arms and tell him she'd be back soon. But when she knew he most certainly wouldn't have cared, a familiar pain cracked in her heart. The blind dark made it all too easy for all his words and lies to rush to her thoughts, all but beckoning them to plague her with swarming pain. It was an awful thing to think about, somehow stealing her excitement to escape, twisting her passion and making her afraid of even her own hope.

"Kiara?" Hadyn whispered even though they were alone, and it hissed off the water and slick walls around them, his hushed voice pulling her out of her thoughts and even cracking a grin on her face.

"Yeah?" she whispered back, just for his sake.

"About those fears . . . the ones you had in the Labyrinth." He paused and she waited in silence for him to continue. "I hope you know those weren't real. That was the tunnels . . . not you."

"But it was. Those feelings, those fears, they're inside me. I just couldn't control them. Why else do you think we didn't notice what was happening until we climbed out? It wasn't as if some new and strange thing had befallen us."

She was answered by only darkness and a drip from the ceiling.

"Is that such a terrible thing?"

Still he didn't answer.

"Look, I wasn't in your head, but from where I stood, I saw someone with the potential to harbor a dangerous amount of anger yet . . . for as long as I've known him, he's never once acted on it. I see that as strength; not weakness."

She could hear his breaths shallow and constricted, but he kept his silence.

"Oh, come on. You know I can't see your face. What are you thinking?"

He sighed. "I guess I—" his breath caught in his throat. "What in the . . ."

"What?" Kiara asked. "What is it?"

"Are my eyes playing tricks on me or . . ."

"No, wait," she breathed. "I see it too."

And without another word they floated steadily towards the faintest of glows.

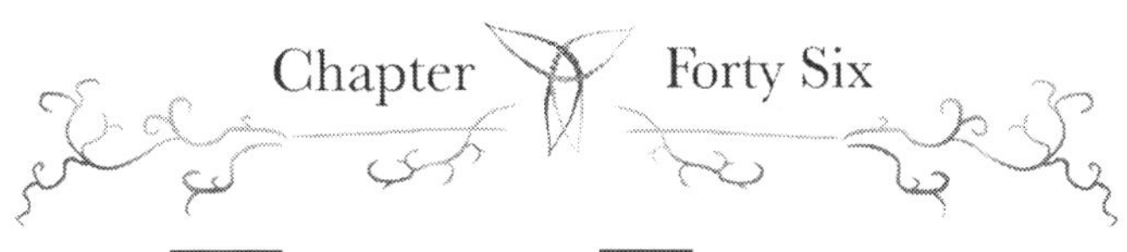

THE FALL

As they drifted nearer, eyes already sensitive to the weakest of lights, drippy, slate walls rose out of black water, rippling with gentle energy. And soon they could just barely see one another and the widened whites of each other's eyes as they stared in uncertain shock. But before they could even begin to believe their eyes, another extraordinary discovery shook the very ground of everything they once thought they knew.

The stone walls peeled away, trading their sooty rags for ivory sleeves. It was a slow fade, at first only jutting from the stone here and there, but up ahead, just further up the tunnel, the color grey became nearly nonexistent, the passage walls completely cluttered in pearly, semi-translucent crystals. They seemed to radiate their own faint light. The softest, most pure, white glow shone from them like the lanterns of angels.[1]

Since plunging into darkness, the tunnel had narrowed a considerable amount. And since they could no longer drift very far, Kiara felt safe to let go of Hadyn's barrel and reached out a hand to run her fingers along one of the smooth edges of a nearby crystal.

"It's beautiful!" she gasped, a smile of wonder on her face. "But . . . is it even possible?"

"Not that I would have ever thought in a million years of living in Caverna," Hadyn said, also lost in a soft reverie.

The passage became less like a tunnel and more like a maze, forking and splitting in random directions, but they continued to let the current take them wherever it flowed strongest and stuck together.

---

1. A true sight indeed, Kiara and Hadyn might have been the only two blessed enough to have ever seen the natural wonder of the gypsum caves. For many have searched to no avail to find any trace of these caverns that seemed to have made their own light. I fear they may have since collapsed.

Sometimes the way opened up wide and other times they had to squeeze, single file through the tunnel, ducking down into their barrels in places where even the ceiling closed in, the crystals growing some eight feet long and criss-crossing each other in a prism jam of angles and edges. But Kiara wasn't afraid. The whole thing wound about like a giant, crystal playground and seeing without the aid of firelight was such a strange and new thing, it kindled a warm and steady peace in their hearts.

Presently in the lead, Kiara ducked into her barrel, intent on not getting impaled by a sharp, intruding crystal. Then, without foretelling, the passage debouched into a whole cavernous gallery of crystals, and when she straightened, emerging from the mouth of the barrel, the sight defied her beliefs.

The rare beauty that now entered her gaze took her breath away. Ducking from the same crystal, Hadyn came up beside her and together they floated along spellbound, staring at the vast expanse before them. Everything glittered in this ballroom of gypsum. The river spilled out and flooded the whole area, creating the dance floor, still as glass. Abstract formations precariously hung from the ceiling like grand chandeliers, while figures stretching out of the water stood like formless statues, frosted with the most delicate of crystals. Some towered at a height of ten feet tall while others stood a mere foot above the surface.

Using their barrel lids to paddle and navigate the nearly nonexistent current of the room, they fought to take it all in.

"It's like something out of a dream," Kiara gasped, blinking at the dazzling roof. "Though I've never had one quite so splendid."

Hadyn paddled up close to examine one of the taller figures. "Who could have imagined Caverna was hiding such beauty?"

"But we're not in Caverna anymore, are we?" Kiara asked.

For she knew in her heart, in a way, they had already escaped. She could feel the difference. Troubles seemed far away in this quiet place. Any bit of weariness from the night's lack of sleep washed away, her eyes refreshed by the pure beauty.

Kiara stood on her tiptoes in her barrel and reached out to meet the abstract and bent arm of one of the crystal figures. A blissful smile stretched her face as her fingers were almost there to greet the delicate touch. Her stomach dropped as she felt herself tipping forward. Her screech glided across the still water and she fell back into her barrel with a great ruckusy splash. But before Hadyn could ask her if she was okay, her giggles were bouncing off the walls. He grinned and shook his head at her, and soon they both laughed as they went, feeling for the first time that danger wasn't around the next corner, fear wasn't breathing down their necks and holding their minds hostage. With every paddle, Kiara felt the distance from Caverna grow and the great gloom diminish.

Flat, little creatures[1] which appeared at home in both the water and the land of the stoney shores slipped under the surface without a trace whenever they came near, but under the water they felt safer, swishing tails and using their tiny legs to scuttled around placidly just under their barrels. With beady, undeveloped eyes and a wide, smiling mouth, they had ruffled, frilly gills of a salmon color protruding just behind the head and the thin membrane of their pale skin seemed to glow with a mint, phosphorescent light.

Kiara was glad they lived here, safely away from Caverna, knowing a creature so incredible would have certainly been deemed forbidden and destroyed if ever spotted.

Neither could wipe the smiles from their faces as they explored the magnificent cavern, their eyes never ceasing to admire as they floated in an awestruck waltz through the crystal dancers.

At the far end of the gallery, the room visibly tapered again, and upon arriving, they found the water lumbering into another wide tunnel. Inside the tunnel, the ground dropped away beneath them to depths unfathomable. And with the perfectly clear, still water, they felt like they were drifting through open air.

Kiara leaned over the lip of her barrel and looked at her unbroken reflection and then down into the deep. The water itself (though it's true depths were lost in an inky darkness) seemed to have an ambient light of sorts that shone from beneath and reflected its glow off the domed ceilings. The crystals here, worn smoothly into one another, shimmered with a pearly light.

Throughout the passage, dotting the water like a patch of giant mushrooms, stood strange mineral platforms, with only a few inches of their tops above the surface. The minerals, a pale shade of peach, seemed planed by a master craftsmen, their tops also mysteriously worn smooth while beneath, their jagged foundations

---

1. An extremely rare sub-species of axolotl, so far only known to be endemic to this one cave. They seem to use a phosphorescence (opposed to bioluminescence) for their luminance that appears directly connected to the otherworldly glow of the gypsum.

See the brown book for more information

tapered and disappeared into the abyss below.

Kiara danced her fingers through the cold water and swished her hand through the current, while she rested her chin on her other arm, completely content to stare up at the iridescent display of refraction on the walls and ceiling for hours. Wholly at peace, she didn't see how danger could have a single foot hold in this perfect place.

And because of how rare these moments were for her, I'm extremely sorry to tell you, she saw wrong.

A quiet ripple broke the surface of the water and silently lapped against the stone walls of the tunnel. Something swam, unseen and unnoticed, and returned back to the depths only to resurface. It stocked, testing and listening to the vibrations of an absently swishing hand and to the voices of the two alien creatures as they carried through the water. It poked its huge, milky eyes above the surface, seeing nothing, and then slipped back down into the dark once more.

"You love it, don't you?"

Kiara turned to see Hadyn looking at her rather intently, an expression of sweet joy in his eyes.

"Well, of course," she replied. "What's not to love? And what's that silly face for?"

"It's just that smile . . . I don't get to see it all that often."

Kiara jerked her head back. "I smile!"

"Not like that," he said, his eyes remaining soft and steady.

Kiara turned her mouth down to hide the creeping grin, but it grew too powerful too fast. And just as it burst forth on her face, she swept her hand down into the water and sent him a soaking spray.

Hadyn looked genuinely shocked for a short moment, but flicking his wet curls out of his eyes, he recovered as quick as lightning and drenched her in the cold water. The tunnel exploded with their splashing and filled with Kiara's squeals and both their laughter.

Kiara dunked her hand in for another splash when something slimy slid against her hand, something very much alive, but as cold and clammy as death. She screeched and jerked away, but whatever it was, it had absconded without so much as a splash, her thrashing having scared it away.

"You alright?" Hadyn asked. "What is it?"

"Something is in the water!" she cried.

"Like a fish?"

"I don't know! . . . Maybe."

They leaned over the edges of their barrels scanning into the water's depths.

"Well, whatever it was, it's gone now," he said, but Kiara didn't stop searching.

She bit her cheek. She had a gnawing feeling in the very bottom of her gut that it was unequivocally not gone, and could come back at any moment. She set her eyes to scouring every inch of the trench, but again, her search came up with nothing but water deep enough to make your stomach twist and all the towers with their wicked edges like inverted mounted peaks. She sighed and almost gave up her search when a faint glow drew her gaze.

"Hadyn . . . look."

There, in the depths, a blue light bloomed and strengthened by the seconds. Hadyn squinted his eyes as if it could be a trick. But as they stared, from around the jagged bases of one of the mineral platforms, a sizable creature glided into view, fish-like in every way, but bigger than any man[1]. They could see it leagues below through the dark water and could actually watch it's glow intensify. Luciferin lit up its lateral line like a lightning bolt of electric blue. Every silvery scale, leaked light in between each chink as if the beast glowed from the inside out. Strings of pale blue light ran through its ghostly green fins like the essence of souls, and from the dorsal and pectorals, orbs of seemingly pure luminance trailed behind by delicate navy threads. With one swish of its thin caudal tail, it turned and propelled itself both placidly and gracefully through the water.

"It's..." Kiara blinked. "Beautiful."

As if it heard her, the creature seemed to look up and then, working its tail more consistently now, it began to ascend the water column.

"Where did it come from?" she asked, as they both stared utterly transfixed by its glow. "I mean, this trench is so empty, almost abandoned and yet, here it is."

---

1. While this creature does in fact seem heinously unnatural, it is not wholly evident that it is in any way associated with the "monster breeding" allegedly done in the Labyrinth, its origin and/or purpose remaining a question mark to even the most astute ichthyologists and speleologists.
More on that in the brown book.

It drew closer, ever climbing higher in the water, almost beating its tale in some kind of haste.

Hadyn broke from the spell first. "Ahh . . ." he said nervously, "it's not stopping."

"No," Kiara dismissed. "It's just curious."

Closer and closer it came, and still it showed not a single sign of slowing. In fact, it seemed to only get faster, thrashing its tail ever more rapidly. Finally, her smile fell, her expression twisting from one of wonder, to that of horror as the beast drew nearer, enough to reveal the gory details of a carnivorous mouth. Filled with rows of hundreds of needle sharp teeth, some a whole foot long, the mouth widened in the ravenous grin of a year long hunger.

The sight froze her insides solid, and her thoughts stopped making sense, its misty, white eyes rushing ever closer. The head thrashed violently back and forth as it wriggled its whole body to pick up maximum speed. And in an explosion of water and light it breached the surface, mouth open and ready to take off her head. Kiara screamed, squeezing her eyes shut. A concussive smack cut through the chaos just before the monster could bring its jaws down on her neck. Another cold splash to her face got her mind working again.

Kiara wiped the water out of her eyes. The creature was nowhere to be seen and Hadyn held the two broken halves of the lid of his barrel in both hands just where he had brought it down on the beast's head.

Kiara panted, eyes wide with fear and no small degree of shock. "Did you . . .? You just . . ."

"Come on," Hadyn said. "We need to get out of here. That thing will be back, and I'm certain its second visit will be even less friendly.

Jamming the lids of the barrels into the icy water (Hadyn making due with the broken parts) they propelled themselves as fast as they could through the tunnel. Without any end in sight, they made their mad dash to an indefinite finish line, propelled solely by the yet lingering and fragile hope of sunlight they had left, clinging to it by worn finger bones.

Kiara didn't have to look behind her to know the monster was on its way back for another charge, the ceiling and walls around them beginning to glow blue with its ominous light, burning ever brighter like a bellows blown forge.

"It's coming back!" she cried.

"I know!" Hadyn shouted back. "Just keep paddling!"

But Kiara knew, as the light did nothing but steadily grow, if they didn't turn around and do something fast, they'd be nothing but a mouthful in a matter of moments. The beast could ram them from beneath, ejecting them from their barrels, and then they really would be fish food.

Her mind raced with a million thoughts and fears. *What made it swim away before? A smack to the head?* With the armor like plates of its scales, she highly doubted that. *Or the sound?*

"That's it!" she cried and stopped paddling cold.

Just like her fish in her hideaway, the beast must have been blind, yet it was able to pinpoint her exact location on the slightest of sounds, louder sounds consequently scaring it away.

Hadyn whipped his head around to see her stopped in the middle of the tunnel. "What's it?" he screamed. "Why are you stopping!"

"It hunts by sound!" she said, beginning to smack the lid of her barrel on the surface.

"So, you're ringing the dinner bell?"

Kiara didn't stop. "If we can manage to sound bigger than it, it might not think of us as a meal anymore."

Terrified as he was, Hadyn could see the logic in her thinking and took up his lid pieces to do the same.

Breaking the surface now, the monster charged through the water towards them, sending a continuous razor blade spray of water over it's back.

"It's not stopping!" Hadyn shouted, splashing up a ruckus of water.

Kiara bit her cheek, gnawing until it bled, her eyes fixed on the approaching catastrophe. With the thundering of its great tail and the pounds of water it riled into the air, their barrel lids sounded like pebbles dropping into a rapids.

"It's not loud enough . . ." she whispered, barely able to do much else. But they could do nothing more. They had dropped their packs and had nothing other than the clothes on their backs. Then it hit her, energizing her limbs to act like a jolt of electricity.

Slipping her arms out of the sleeves, Kiara peeled off her cloak, already drenched and heavy thanks to the rapids, and without much of a second thought, she swung it over her head with all her might. The drenched threads smacked down with a crack that shook the surface of the water and reverberated up the tunnel walls like a thunderclap.

Taken by shock, the beast reared back, leaving its wave of energy to ram into their barrels without it. It thrashed about and turned a violent circle, but recovered quicker than she hoped. The gaping mouth drew closer. She could see the point of each curved tooth.

She turned to Hadyn. "A little hel—" she started to shout, but Hadyn had already removed his cloak and was working on swinging it over his head. She swallowed down her words and threw her cloak over her shoulder to get the most out of the next swing. They smacked the water again and again. Kiara's arms burned from the weight of the water-logged cloak. But though their efforts slowed the monster's progress, it had grown much too bold for even the loudest noises. Kiara slouched. She felt her shoulders and biceps liquefying to useless jello. There was no way they could stop it now.

Then with one swish of its fanning tale, it turned and all went dark. Not completely. In their panic, they hadn't even noticed leaving the gypsum caves. Only a few crystals remained to emboss the stone walls here. And strangely enough, with their absence, the light seemed to leave too. But ambient light from back up the tunnel still bathed their surroundings in a grey glow.

The current flowed a bit swifter here and they could see the glowing beast getting further in the distance, now just a steadily dimming ball of light.

Kiara threw her fists above her head. "Yeah! We showed him!"

Hadyn wasn't as convinced. He watched the blue light diminish, concern darkening his gaze. "But it doesn't make any sense. The splashes stopped working. Why did it just go away?"

"You're joking, right?" Kiara snorted, but his face remained unamused. "It *left*. I don't think 'why' really matters."

"It just doesn't feel right."

"Well, I don't think it's coming back if that's what you're afraid of."

"No, it's not that."

"What then?" she asked, but as he remained silent, eyes shifting about as they drifted down the tunnel, she said, "Look, I get it if you're paranoid. That was . . . insanity. But I think you can relax now—"

"Shhhh!" He held up a finger, ears pricked. "You hear that?"

"Hear what?"

"Shhh!"

Kiara clamped her mouth shut and reluctantly listened. She could hear just the faintest noise. She narrowed her eyes and shivered. The sound roared and whispered at the same time, reminding her of the raging fire she heard in the Labyrinth, but different and just *more*, like it was heavier somehow.

They squinted into the inky space up the tunnel as the noise grew steadily louder, and they could barely make out, just before a blind bend in the passage, the hissing fit of a white line of spray.

Kiara's stomach twisted. "More rapids?"

Hadyn kept his eyes fixed ahead. "Not sure. But we better hold on tight."

When he looked, Kiara's knuckles had already gone white on the rim of the barrel. Crossing his arms over hers, he fastened his grip onto the side of her barrel and they braced themselves for the danger-harboring bend.

The water sloshed at the sides of the tunnel and buckled in the middle, making them bob up and down like pieces of inanimate driftwood.

Hadyn couldn't be certain and didn't know how it was possible, but he thought these rapids sounded even louder than the last. He might have said as much if they weren't, in fact, so deafeningly loud. And an uneasy feeling made him wonder if passively waiting to find out was the smartest thing they could do.

Too late to second guess their choice now, the current carried them far enough to see around the bend. They were losing the light too fast to make any real observations, but the dark up ahead did look somehow deeper and the water seemed to just stop. Still, the riot of spray made it hard to tell.

Kiara didn't know what she saw, she just knew it terrified her. "What is it?" she screamed. "Bigger rapids?"

Hadyn shook his head. Water doesn't just end while raging like a violent storm. And if not rapids, it could be only one thing. Finally, it made it sense.

"Not rapids!" he cried. "It's a waterfall! Turn around! Get away from it!"

Pulling apart, they dug their makeshift paddles into the turbulent waters, tossing spray after frantic spray behind them. But as hard as they tried, they only drifted closer to the edge of the falls. Nothing helped, as if the drop, the very fall itself, had a hold on them and dragged them ever closer to the fate it had prepared for them.

Kiara's arms cried out for her to give in to the current and let it take her, but her life pleaded for her to keep it with a voice just a little louder. Her muscles burned with the struggle until a scream escaped her throat. But it was all for nothing. Fight to preserve her life or not, she could not keep from going over, and the thought took the last strength from her arms.

One moment they were up top, warring against the current and the next they were tossed over, falling as just another piece of the river to an uncertain demise.

Over the edge, Hadyn could see just how far this drop fell, and if by some ridiculous chance they managed to survive this, all he could picture was how badly it was going to hurt. He felt his stomach drop to his feet as the open air whipped past his ears and water droplets stung his face, forcing him to shut his eyes, which only made his head spin even more. But he held on and managed to stay inside his barrel. Then, when the inevitable crash finally came, pain jolted every inch of him like his legs had shot up and straight out his shoulders. He groaned, but then, feeling his arms, shoulders, and legs, he realized everything was in the right place and relatively unharmed. He didn't have much time to revel in relief though, as his mind shot to Kiara, hoping to anyone listening that she had made it down just as safe.

"Kiara!" he called out, but could hear only the thundering of the falls and could see little more, the light from above almost squelched in the darkness. "Kiara!" He refused to believe the falls had taken her.

He squinted, straining to see anything in the churning black tempest. His eyes caught sight of a dark mass bobbing in the water. A barrel!

"Kiara!" His voice brightened, but there was still no answer and on further inspection, he saw the barrel was empty.

"No . . ." he barely whispered, water dripping into his agape mouth. "Kiara!" His voice turned desperate as the current carried him mercilessly onward, pushing him towards the deepening dark and away from any light left from above, knowing if he didn't find her while he still had some sight, he never would.

He thought of jumping in right there to search the water for her, but knew he could see better from where he was, not that he could see much besides the tumultuous waters and furious foam.

Tears filled his eyes and he clenched the rim of the barrel until the bones in his hands hurt.

"Come on, Kiara," he pleaded under his breath.

Not relenting for a second, his pulse quickened when, finally, he saw it, a shock of color in the storm of slate and ink shadows! He couldn't believe his eyes. If her hair was any other color, he didn't know if he would have seen her. But there she floated face down, completely at the mercy of the rapids, her red locks burning like an sos beacon.

Without another thought, he filled his lungs with the musty air and plunged into the frigid waters. Cutting through the outrage of the rapids, he swam as fast and straight as the current would allow, hardly looking up until he rammed right into her. Flicking the water and hair from his eyes, he grabbed her up and forced her face out of the water, pleading once again with anyone who cared that she still had it in her to begin breathing again.

"Kiara!" he called to her. "Come on Kiara! Wake up!"

He struggled to keep them both afloat with only his legs and soon his shouts dwindled to soft sobbing. "You have to wake up."

The waves threatened to overtake them, but even as he began to sink beneath the surface, water pouring into his lungs, he continued to hold her head up without fail.

Chapter Forty Seven

A Light at the End Of the Tunnel

Kiara's arms jolted to life. She sputtered and gasped a whooping breath. The dark surrounded her like a smothering cloth and her lungs burned from lack of oxygen, but she wasn't alone. Strong arms supported her in the now calming rapids. Hadyn wouldn't let go. And as soon as the current allowed, he came up in a hacking fit, attempting to expel the water burning like acid through his lungs and sinuses.

In the smidgen of remaining light, he spotted one of their barrels close enough to swim to and, holding Kiara with just one arm now he made his way to it.

"I can swim," Kiara finally sputtered. Her brain felt like a locked tight box, or at least some of her thoughts did as she tried to sort out what exactly had just happened, a thick fog keeping her in the dark.

"You can?" Hadyn asked.

"Apparently not very well . . . but yes."

"Oh." He let her go and retrieved the barrel by himself. "Here, I'll help you up."

Kiara didn't argue and sloshed into the water collected in the bottom of the barrel just as even the weakest lights seemed to simply go out. Plunged back into total darkness, Kiara immediately began to shiver.

"Hadyn?" she whispered.

Hadyn shifted where he held onto the rim of the barrel, accidentally touched her hand, and quickly moved them again. "I'm here." He sounded hoarse.

As her mind finally began to clear of the dank fog that choked out all coherent thoughts, the recent events came flooding back to her, raging fear and all. Falling… Falling for so long and then falling some more into uncertain darkness. Then waking, sputtering back to life . . . safe and held.

She found his hand, deliberately this time, and let hers rest there. "You–" Her words caught for a moment. "You saved my life."

"Don't mention it," he said through clenched teeth, a laugh in his voice. "We'll just add it to your friendship debt."

Kiara couldn't imagine how cold he must've been floating in the water like that, but the strain in his voice gave her a pretty good idea. "Where did the other barrel go?"

"I don't know. And I'm not about to risk letting go to search for it."

"Then we can take turns with this one. You must be absolutely freezing!"

"No, you sit tight there. And don't worry about me. It's not all that bad."

They fell quiet for some time. The walls echoed their snotty sniffing and the occasional swishing of Hadyn's feet in the water, but for what felt like hours of sightless drifting Kiara heard nothing else, until she heard even less. Sometime, long after she had lost track, it had grown even quieter. The gentle swishing had stopped and she realized she heard only one set of sniffing and it came from her own drippy nose.

Panic shot through every nerve and she felt for his hands. When she found them, she breathed a sigh, but they were ice cold and he merely held on with a feeble grip.

"Hadyn?"

"Yeah . . ." he slurred. The rasp was gone from his voice, but now he sounded much too sleepy for her liking.

She dunked her hand in the water and it bit like a harsh north wind. Not the kind of temperature one would find relaxing to float in for hours. And she didn't have to be an expert in bodily functions to know he was suffering, fading even. All because he had to save her.

"Hey!" she said brightly, taking care to steady the quiver of fear in her voice and grabbed up his hands to make sure he didn't let go. "Maybe if we talked, the time would pass faster."

"Go ahead . . . I'll listen to you."

"No." She tried to smile and let it be heard in her voice. "It will only work if we both talk."

"About what?"

"Well, what do you think it's going to be like? You know,

out there and all?"

He gave a lazy snicker. "Warmer probably."

She laughed. "Okay. What do you think it will smell like? Air without restrictions and walls to make it grow stale? Goodness! If freedom ever had a scent, it must smell just like that! Don't you think?"

"Whatever you say, Ara . . ."

Kiara couldn't tell if the nickname was deliberate or just another slur. "What are you looking forward to finally getting to see the most?"

"Sunlight . . ." He shivered. "To be warmed and surrounded by light and see that sk-sky you're always talking about."

"Me too," she said quietly, silently hoping they'd both live to see that dream come true.

"I'd like to bask in that light right about now," he added. "Like we did at the gate . . . sipping some hot tea. We should have some right now."

"I'm afraid we don't have any. But I'll tell you what." She rubbed his icy hands. "As soon as we get out of here, I'll make you a fresh cup, first thing. But you have to stay awake for it. Wouldn't want you to miss it."

Kiara waited for a reply and after several seconds it came, just a whisper. "Sure thing."

She felt his grip weaken, and squeezed his hands tighter. "No. Hadyn! You said you'd stay awake."

"I'm . . . I am awake."

Her heart beat double time as she could only imagine his slowing down. This wasn't fair. She should be the one freezing to death. If anyone deserved to escape the darkness, it should be the one who had never doubted they would. The one who, if their roles were reversed, wouldn't have even begun to despair. She thought to switch with him, but didn't think she'd be able to lift him into the barrel.

The worst part was, she'd be fine, and keep floating on until she found some kind of end or way out. And for the first time, she didn't know if she wanted to escape, if she had to do it without him.

"If You're out there," the words poured from her mouth into the darkness as unthought as an exhale. "Do one thing for me. Please, save his life."

Kiara felt his grip loosen another notch.

"Come on, Hadyn!" she whimpered, gently slapping his

face. “Wake up.”

“I never . . . fell asleep.”

Kiara hoped that was true. “Good. Just keep your eyes open. Look at me.”

His face looked as pale as the gypsum crystals they had passed and his lips were so blue, it appeared painful, but his eyes, however droopy, were open and he tried bravely to keep his gaze locked on hers.

“That’s it.” She smiled, but her brow scrunched. How was it she could even see him?

In the very height of her fear, she hadn’t even noticed the subtle and gentle lifting of the darkness. Not so much as to be considered bright, but still she could see and a fallow glow dusted the side of his face, which was much closer than she would have known in the darkness. Pulling back she turned towards the source of the glow.

Up ahead a bright light shone at the end of the tunnel, strong enough to reach down through the stretch of drippy, dank darkness, and flood her eyes. The sight filled her up. It cracked her heart in two only to overflow the rend with aching hope and brilliance.

“Hadyn, look . . .” Her eyes brimmed with tears. “A light.”

She beamed at him and when he lolled his head back to see, a sleepy smile turned up the corners of his mouth.

“We’re going to get out,” she whispered. “Together.”

A hollow bumping at the left side of the tunnel caught her attention. There, the other lost barrel floated aimlessly into the stone wall. Her heart leapt in her chest. Holding Hadyn with one hand she used her free hand and the barrel lid to paddle over to it.

“Hadyn! You don’t have to be cold anymore!”

With the golden light streaming in at them, he seemed to wake up a bit and with what strength he had left and Kiara’s help, he lumbered into the free barrel as lethargic as a sloth. Then, fully spent, he slumped down inside, his eyes drooping dangerously.

“Don’t worry,” Kiara whispered, keeping a hand on his shoulder. “We’re almost there.”

Water dripped off the stalactites and caught the light in twinkling crystal drops, like tree branches after heavy storms. The surface of the river reflected the radiance like a glittering path they simply had to follow to reach the light. Kiara tried to make sense of the glow, but to her shadow trained eyes, it looked like nothing more than a wall of pure light, untainted in every way. The closer she got, the harder it became for her to even glance at its splendor without closing her eyes from the sting. She had never seen something so brilliant!

Just yards away, she gritted her teeth to behold it, so she turned away and focused on Hadyn. Practically unconscious, she made sure to keep him close every inch of the way.

A sound met her ears, like the thundering falls, but if the previous one shouted, this one laughed, with a silvery giggle, as pure and bright as the brilliance that now enveloped her so completely. She squeezed her eyes shut and grabbed up Hadyn's hand, frightened of what might become of them, of what it would do to them. Then huddled and shaking with fear, the unexpected happened.

Nothing.

The gentle falls continued to chatter and laugh somewhere off to the left and the barrel beneath her feet remained floating the same gentle way. She felt warmth seep into her cheeks and issue its thawing into every inch of her clammy skin. And she knew the word before she ever saw its light. Slowly raising her head, her eyes fluttered. Burning, white light knifed in and robbed her of sight, but she forced her lids to stay open. Squinting and shielding her eyes with a hand, shapes began to form. Her eyes burned and watered, but she couldn't have cared less if the tears rusted on her face. And when her eyes, at long last, began to adjust to the absolute splendor, she thought if she could make a wish to never have to close her eyes again, she would, in a heartbeat she would.

She gasped, realizing all at once that she had been holding her breath. And, oh! How the air had never tasted so sweet!

Green filled her vision and sent her senses reeling. They had emerged from shadowy darkness straight into an emerald wilderness, lush and thick with leaves and life. The rushing sound of the youthful falls begged her attention. It poured into the creek from a separate, above ground tributary. Shallow and a friend to the sun, the stream brought a flush of warm, tropical water to the frigid subterranean creek.

Kiara swished a hand in the water to test the temperature and with a grin swept a splash onto Hadyn's sleeping face.

He sputtered, eyes fluttering as the warm water brought some life back to his cold bones. He jolted awake to Kiara's beaming face and a blinding halo of light around her.

She laughed at his befuddled expression and moved aside.

The light cut like daggers to the back of his mind, so instinctively, he shielded his eyes.

"No. Keep 'em open," he heard her say. "You're gonna want to see this!"

Still in shock from how he woke up, when his eyes finally saw more than blinding white, he fought to remember how to breathe.

"I knew it . . . I'm dead." Hadyn flicked his wet curls out of his eyes and just stared in silent disbelief, while Kiara blinked frantically and rubbed her eyes again and again to make sure it wasn't all a trick.

A bracing wind picked off the water and hit them both in the face. Although the air was thick and close, to a couple of cave dwellers who had never felt a breeze in their lives, it felt like a wild gust, full of freedom and promise, as though it were the winds that beat against and berate the cliffs of the northern Pacific. The breeze stirred a group of blue butterflies from their hiding spot in the tall grass and they took flight all about them.

Kiara laughed, and she didn't know if she had ever heard such an unfettered noise grace her tongue. She couldn't breathe deep enough. Every single smell was new and wonderful. She gulped in deep breaths, drinking in the free air, trying to support her brain with the oxygen needed to think all these thoughts that whirled through her mind in a blur.

Hadyn stood spellbound, but completely and undoubtedly awake, locked in some kind of extreme wonder. He thought to call it something, but even he didn't have a name for this feeling that he just had to make room for in his heart.

They turned to each other, child-like grins on both their faces and exchanged identical glances of such wide-eyed and wild hope. At last free, they had finally found themselves, indeed, enveloped in a vibrantly verdant forest.

Kiara threw her fists over her head, and screamed at the top of her lungs, "WE MADE IT!" her voice echoing throughout the quiet forest. But it didn't come back the way it always did in Caverna. Her cry steadily fading, she felt like she had thrown a part of herself out there into that vast unknown. "Yeah!" she yelled again just to hear her voice leave her once more.

At a time like this, one might try to explain how one felt, but the words ecstatic, euphoric, nor blithesome could stand in for the feelings of Kiara and Hadyn at this moment. Nor could they say, they were overwhelmed. Bliss or jubilation did not express the thoughts of their minds.

For the sake of not seeming redundant and going on in telling you what they *didn't* feel, I will settle on the word joy. As simple as it is, joy is the only word that could come remotely close to what they felt in that moment of their liberation, when they walked out of the darkness and into the light.

When Kiara, hands still raised triumphantly in the air, crashed her fists back down into the warm water and covered them both in the splash, it didn't take long for the actions to manifest into an all out rematch of the splash war of the gypsum caves. Kiara jumped out of her barrel and dove head first into the crystal clear pool.

The tropical water seemed to wash her clean from the inside out, flushing the lies out of her deep cuts, soothing the places where the chains had worn raw on the wrists of her mind. She did think of her father once more, but this time it was for the joy to be rid of him, to have found, at long last, all the things he had tried so desperately to keep her from.

Surfacing, she flicked the water from her eyes, a bright smile on her face. "Come on!" she beckoned. "The water's warm this time."

Hadyn smirked. "I was just waiting for the best moment," he said and jumped in close enough to capsize her with the splash, and the battle continued.

They laughed and hollered with absolutely no heed to cap their volume, their joy overflowing like a bubbling spring.

Hadyn stopped first. Kiara almost took it as an opportunity to get an undefended splash in, but his expression gave her enough pause to freeze the swing of her arm. His gaze was fixed on something above their heads and he almost looked sad. Kiara was just trying to decide if it was simply water from the pool or if he actually had tears in his eyes, when, without diverting his gaze for even a second, he lifted a hand under Kiara's chin and slowly guided her face up.

Her lungs swelled with a gasp. Around them, the trees grew so close they seemed to create a leafy roof, but there, above the clear pool, a rend in the nearly impenetrable canopy opened up to a gift of pure blue sky. It stole into the forest and their hearts, gracing them with light. Only a small piece in all the enormity she only imagined was out there, she believed she could have stared into its freedom forever, if she allowed herself, and never become discontent. So long she had wished to see the sky, at a time even doubting its existence, and now here it was, bluer than any gemstone she had ever collected and deep enough to get lost in.

When they could find it in themselves to rip their eyes away, they lowered their heads and their gazes found one another. No longer a mystery, Kiara knew for certain there were tears in his eyes, because they spilled out now over his cheeks. And when she raised a hand, she realized her own face was wet with tears. Kiara tried to get a handle on at least one of her feelings, yet with so many thoughts and emotions, they trampled one another in one giant mess. One giant, beautiful mess. Though as the damages of trauma go, her fear managed to stick out above the rest, still not able to shake the dread she had felt floating in the dark while Hadyn slowly slipped away.

"Hadyn, I—" Suddenly, she didn't know what she wanted to say.

"What is it?"

She looked at his big, innocent smile. "Nothing."

Turning back up to the rent in the treetops, a laugh bubbled up out of her throat, but neither said a word, knowing that, most times, words only get in the way of moments like these. Moments like these are meant to be savored, soaked up by each sense and trying to add to them in any way is like deliberately robbing them of their natural blessings.

The skylight enabled all sorts of wild growth and untamed abundance in and around the banks of the pool. And when they turned to look around once more, it was like seeing it all for the first time all over again.

Kiara never knew such color existed and every leaf, each tree, twig, and blade of grass surpassed her wildest imaginings. They ached for all they had been missing and all they would see as a joy so high pricked their hearts, producing both a deep adoration for all they beheld and a longing for something so much bigger than all of it, the latter more felt than understood.

While Hadyn just tried his best to comprehend the new sights, Kiara had gone into an observation frenzy, examining every leaf and flower at the edges of the pool with equally abundant fascination. The trees grew up around them taller and stranger than she could have ever dreamed, the bases wide and fluted. Some of what seemed to be branches came back down like roots to the ground.

And, to Kiara's continual amazement, she could not find one in sight alike to another. All about them, they grew up so high, their tops disappearing in a thick, entangling canopy where only glimpses of sweet, golden light leaked through the ever varying shades of jade and emerald that grew like leaves, but shimmered like jewels.

Kiara spun around to better take in the scene. The spring water skipped and tripped over the moss blanketed rocks of the falls, playfully spilling into the glass-like pool. Long grasses hung over the banks, dangling their elegant fingers in the water, and small trees, near the water's edge, bowed their bushy heads along with the branches of the larger ones, all seeming to lean in close to take part in the perfection of the oasis.

Flowers speckled the area and filled the air with new and delicious smells. Little ones grew up amidst the grasses with delicate pink petals, singed dark at the edges. With a light touch of his hand, Hadyn examined a patch of blue blossoms near the water's edge, petite and modest with a splash of golden yellow bursting from the middle. Orchids grew higher in the trees, colorful epiphytes with the most incredible patterns. Some were sparse, while others hung in lazy clusters, draped over the water from their host trees, some ruffled and lacy white like a wedding gown, others variegated and star shaped, their colors and pigments changing with a kaleidoscopic pattern.

Kiara laid back and floated on the water. She closed her eyes, breathing in the clean air and just listening to the effervescent laughter of the falls. Hadyn smiled at her when he finally pulled his attention away from the flowers. He knew exactly how she felt, because he felt it too, like they could stay in this place forever. Stay by the perfectly blue water in the middle of a green paradise, and just exist, wholly at peace.

And yet . . . deep down, they knew they had to go on.

They may have escaped, but they had not succeeded in what they had set out to do. Not yet. Their journey was not over. There was more to discover. There would be more paradises to find along the way and, though true, there would be some dark places that they would not feel as keen on staying in, it was the journey that they had set out on, and one they had to see through to the end.

Kiara stood up, and opened her eyes with a sobering look of reality. Hadyn met her gaze and with a measured breath and gave her a nod.

"Do you think this is the river?" Kiara asked. "The one my mother mentioned in her letter? That we're supposed to follow?"

Hadyn shrugged. "Depends. How many rivers are in the world?"

Kiara blew out an overwhelmed breath.

"But," he continued, "for now, it's the closest thing we have to direction. I don't see what harm could come from following it."

She contemplated this, nodding her head back and forth and then finally up and down.

"And we can even keep riding the barrels," he added. "At least for now."

Clambering back in their barrels, they let the current take them. As they floated into the never ending sea of green, they felt not unlike lost boats with no headings or place to weigh anchor, only tethered to each other.

Unlike the bountiful area by the pools made lush by the skylight, the forest before them was little more than a labyrinth of trees, the dappled light that once danced gracefully with the peaceful sway of the boughs above diminishing to mere ambience on the almost eerily bare ground. A tangled mess of vines and searching epiphyte roots hung from higher branches like ship's riggings, clogging the view even further and where they could see far, everything got hazy with the blue-green of distance.

One solitary leaf fell and floated gently to the forest floor.

"It's so quiet," Kiara said just above a whisper.

The vast and continuous forest seemed to eat up the sound of her voice. She found the sight intimidating and suddenly felt so small, and somehow unwelcome in this new land.

For the first time in their lives, they were free, their chains slipping off into the restless water beneath them. But like pond minnows set loose into the ocean, the world felt like it could swallow them up in it's enormity.

"I guess I had thought it wouldn't be too far," Kiara said, "to find her. But now . . ." she looked about her, "seeing this place with my own eyes, who knows how big the world is!"

"I think it's bigger than we could fathom, even now."

Clinging to the sides of each other's barrels, Kiara turned to Hadyn, her emerald eyes sparkling with all the joy, mischief, and trepidation of a journey's start. "Into the green?" she asked.

Hadyn returned her gaze with gentle stability. “Together.”

The End

. . . though it’s really just the beginning

I have come as a light into the world, that whoever believes in me should not abide in darkness.

John 12:46

Acknowledgments

"You've left out one of the chief characters - Samwise the Brave. I want to hear more about Sam. Frodo wouldn't have got far without Sam . . ."
— J.R.R Tolkien

My Sincerest Thanks

First and foremost, to my family. For always being there for me even when I didn't think I was worth it. For never giving up on me and more importantly never letting me give up on myself. My very own chasers of the monsters in my head. Thank you. You all are the most important, most dearest thing in my life. I love you.

Particular thanks to my bro, Daniel, for always being that extra boost of encouragement and assurer on all things "cool."

And to Emilie, my sister and best friend. My only company in what would be the lonely days of actually writing these books. My role model, with her level head and sheer diligence in being the boss entrepreneur she is. Thank you for listening to my endless rambles and infinite "plot hole breakdowns."

And last but not least, to my dear mama. No one has cared for, taught, or loved me better. My books would not be what they are without you. God blessed us five unimaginably when He gave us such a strong, loving, good mom.

A whole whoppin' thanks to three very special ladies. Terri, Dani, and Stephanie, I hope you know how much you guys mean to me. You three were the first people I shared my work with outside of my immediate family, and your encouragement and constructive criticism shaped the way I look at my own writing. You guys gave me confidence and helped me believe in myself. I hope to read your finished works one day too.

To my wonderful map maker, Cora Hurst. You turned what could have been a stressful process for me into a complete joy. Thank you for making a dream I had contented to tuck up on a shelf for a while into a mind-blowing reality!

Thanks to my dear editor, Pam, who helped me feel confident on the last round of edits, catching things that my eyes, which are far too familiar with this story, couldn't catch.

And though these thanks are from the bottom of my heart, they don't begin to compare to continual and never ending thanks I have for Jesus Christ, my Savior. With joy uncontainable, I give all the glory back to my God, without whom I would have never finished. I once said, without Him, I am no more than unqualified, but with Him, I can do all things. The greatest thing being, to bring Him glory in all I create and bring His love to those with none. And I meant it.

And thank you, dear reader. Without you, a book is just a bunch of words on several hundred pages, but with you, the story comes alive again, gaining a whole host of faces and places and finding a home right in your very heart. Thank you for giving my story a home.

If you'd like to join the crew here on the S.S. Hideaway, what are you waiting for? Hop aboard! We'd love to have you, mate!

My website: elliemaureen.com

If you enjoyed this story, please consider writing a review on Amazon, Goodreads, or both! It's one of the greatest forms of support you could give me as a self-published author and it would make my day!

About the Author

Hi! I'm Ellie Maureen, a Christian, YA and MG fiction author with a voracious affinity for just about every genre. I started writing at sixteen years old and never stopped. I live in Minnesota with my family and feisty kitty cat. Besides being an avid storyteller, I'm a violinist, artist, and naturalist, at my happiest when I'm out in God's natural world, especially when that involves climbing to high elevations or getting soaked in some form of water adventure.

Find me aboard the S.S. Hideaway

elliemaureen.com

Or follow me on Instagram!

@ellie__maureen

If you liked Forbidden consider lending a huge hand of support and writing a review!

Made in the USA
Monee, IL
20 October 2021